HEMISPHERES

Thanks to Athina Paris, Editor for your dedication and tireless effort.

Revised 9/14/2021.

Published By

RockHill Publishing LLC

PO Box 62523

Virginia Beach, VA 23466-2523

www.rockhillpublishing.com

HEMISPHERES

MARK EVERGLADE

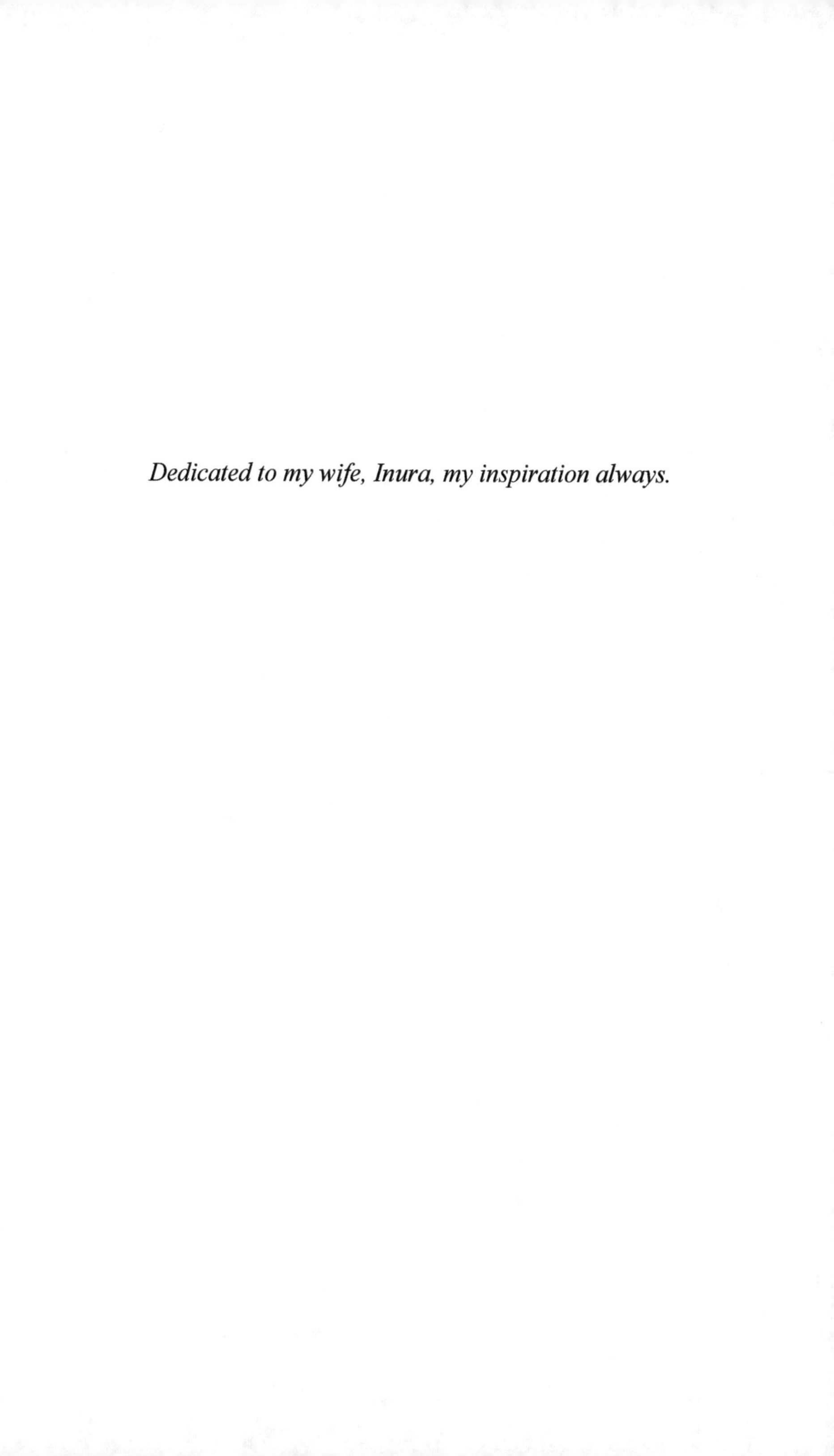

Dedicated to my wife, Inura, my inspiration always.

CONTENTS

PART I

Variations on a Dream

1

———————

"These days when each of us an Atlas shrugging, trying to get yet another Hercules but already tasked to the hilt to bear the burden of sustaining society, we work to overcome our learned helplessness. Self-worship is the self's warship set across a sea of entitlement before sinking into despotism. Is this what we seek? Is intention the god of action, or do we just act? So we learn we can alter our course, but we're still stranded because we're setting sail with only our false selves in mind. If we try to conserve what is, we undo it.

"So be it. All stabilization leads to the conflict that destroys it. Our humanity lies in how we resolve that conflict, for if it's destruction they want, we shall deliver it. Our dreams flow between what is, and what could be. Come, let us dream of the future!"

-The Priestess to the Aporia Asylum {Audio Archive 1 of 9}

THE OBSIDIAN SKY is pulled taut as if a bow ready to release. It's about to tear itself in half, like a scribbled to-do list there was never time to complete, but Severum Rivenshear adjusts the sky's appearance just in time. Now, the doughy clouds are stretched fonts detailing the day's headlines, fading like the events into wispy nothingness.

The jaundice light of languishing fireflies flickers through a jar beside his bed. He projects the universe on the ceiling and counts the stars through vHUD. Raising his hands, he zooms and frames Gliese 581g between them, half of the tidal-locked planet forever enveloped in darkness and half baking in eternal sunlight. Studying the uneven distribution of light, he swipes the entire display away in frustration, the cosmos cowering in disorganized pixels.

"Come, let us dream of the future!"

He raises his eyebrows twice to replay the recording. Her voice plays through his aural implants as if each word is a polished pebble gathering into a heavy feeling in his stomach. "What future?" he murmurs as another alarm rings.

Late.

Rushing out to the station, a hard panning of whooshes crosses his ears as an airbus zooms along his left, right, then left side again. Losing his balance from the sounds vacillating from ear to ear, he jerks his arm out to catch the railing. The back of the airbus ruffles his clothes and vanishes down the tube. He jostles, catching his last jar of fireflies before it breaks. Filmstrips of sepia memory rip at either periphery while the air compression fires another round of passenger cabins back and forth.

Cheap Dayburn knockoffs, he scoffs at his aural implants, slamming his hand against his ear, resounding like a tunnel tossed in rough seas. He excels at anger management, but has no employees to delegate it to, so he pops a neuralmod, purchases another recycle bin for his emotions. He brings up the implant manufacturer in his virtual head's up display, or vHUD, proving it was made on Dayburn by wage slaves that war against the technology they pirate for trade.

The augmentations make it easier to hunt Bioluminaries—thieves who steal light, the primary currency in Evig Natt's densest districts. Three Bioloonies gather in a distant alley, spot him, and vanish into crooked concrete cracks that pass as tenement doors. He wrinkles his gun-barrel nose at the sight of their bioluminescent skin, veined with bile-colored rivulets like stillborn lightning. Altering one's body to produce its own light with the Lumidermis mod is the last desperate attempt for these fallen Icaruses to have enough light to live by. It also makes them easy targets, and he would net a nice little bonus for capturing the three of them, but he turns away. Receiving the letter is more important—an entire mission could be compromised if he's late and the courier auctions off the information. Worse yet, he would be dishonorably discharged and broke.

Two minutes left. He misses the airbus, picks up speed, nears the drop-off point. A man with a wrangled, drooping face grabs him as he turns the corner, digging yellow nails into his shoulder, leaning close enough that his beard scratches Severum's face, his words spittle on his lips. "You gotta glitch with us, you gotta glitch with us! It's how the *Divine* communicates! All will hail the glitch goddess; the eVenki know, they know!"

"Back off. Glitches aren't ghosts, they're just organized noise," Severum replies, raising a hand and resisting the urge to break his arm, but remembering the Forever Glitched are unable to afford anti-virus for their implants, unable to obtain jobs or even avoid accidents, desynchronized with the real world. He pulls away and cradles his jar of fireflies like a football.

He runs past two boys playing tug-of-war with a firefly's wings as it rips in two, its tiny body dimming on the pavement.

One child pushes the other and says, "Look what you did! Now I can't buy any mods!" They pursue him, holding toy spaceships in the air and following the amber streaking of fireflies in his jar as he sprints.

When the planet was colonized, the fireflies were not only

useful for light, but also occurred at just the right frequency to be the perfect currency, being accessible enough that most people could have some, while still rare enough to be used for trade. Those in power accumulated stockpiles of them and resisted the manufacture of new light sources and competing currencies. Soon, fireflies became the only legal method of producing light on Evig Natt, even fires being outlawed.

Buzzing and the smell of seared flesh fill the air, Fort Lux blurring as he rushes past. The Forever Glitched tear at the electric fence to get at the sterile fireflies being cloned within, the charge knocking them back across the street. A metal security bird lowers its angle of attack and soars towards the youngest ones, hitting the fence instead. The boys applaud the fireworks and shake off the sparks. A siren grows in intensity to warn them the security gate is recharging. They climb up the fence.

Severum stops. The shortest boy won't be able to climb over before it recharges. He checks the time—a minute to spare, too risky; he needs the letter, but the deafening siren is nearing full charge. He draws a utility blade and activates it, the heat of its red glow flushing his face, and rushes to the boy's aid, pulling him down by his belt, cutting a hole in the fence, and shoving him through the fort entrance. "You're on your own from here; one felony's enough for today. You'll make it kid, I had to grow up just as fast," he says.

Holding the spaceship, the boy catches up with the rest of the Forever Glitched.

Severum hands the jar to the courier, one of nature's trial and error children, in exchange for the letter, receiving it with seconds to spare. He pockets his last firefly in a matchbox with four wings of change. He sweeps a dark wave of oil-slick hair away and sighs with relief, but hesitates before opening the missive, churning it in his hands.

Anything sent by hard-mail to avoid digital interception must be valuable given the expense, since couriers are often robbed while waiting for the recipient. Paragraphs can kill. They can start, prevent, or end revolutions. Phrases are even worse, with single words a prime culprit indeed, less discriminate and more open to interpretation, taking on their keepers' lives. A single letter is fragile, fleeting, floating in a glass balloon of ambiguity. Silent letters never scribed are truly unpredictable, repressed, like the flood of thoughts he dams, wondering what war disguised as mere duty is sealed within the envelope, another Pandora's box. The boxes were never more than what began as a simple request and ended with half his friends' faces being scraped off by Aphorids, the rest of them buried alive for later consumption.

A hooded man in his twenties stands at the edge of a stunted shop roof above him. He bends his knees, leaps down, swipes the letter from Severum's hand, and jumps atop a stack of shaky wooden pallets. Pulling himself atop a trash compacter and hitting a button to make the platform rise, he rides it back to the roof. The dumpster compresses the trash, the platform lowering to complete its cycle.

Shit! Whatever war that letter contains is about to enter the underground market to be used by whichever corporation would profit the most from it. He must get that letter back. By the time he arrives, the top of the compactor is too low to the ground to reach the roof and follow suit. He smashes the button repeatedly, pounding his palm, but the grinding continues. He can wait a minute for the compression cycle to begin again, or find another way to the roof.

He right-mind-clicks on the thief above in vHUD, sets his occipts to trace him, and runs through the street below to keep pace. The thief's body becomes outlined in augmented reality and reconstructed on a red grid based on partial visibility. Rounding a corner, he loses sight, but vHUD projects his last trajectory and the maximum perimeter in which he can be found based on his speed, age, weight, and height.

The thief activates Chameleon as his appearance dissolves to onlookers, visible only as a translucent current of grey sand across the concrete rooftop. The Enforcers could nail him but Severum doesn't know the letter's contents, so he keeps them out of it. He primes his Pulser, heat increasing, but firing a weapon in the dense city would risk civilian lives, and being off-duty, his job, too. The red-painted outline climbs over a ventilation system, the steam from the air ducts disrupting the image.

Severum races through the alley below, keeping track of the thief by focusing on the three-story rooftops where he leaps from building to building. The culprit passes near Trahiro's apartment, a fellow operative. Knowing he won't betray the letter's contents, he calls Trahiro for help through vHUD phone.

"Hello?" Trahiro replies, out of breath and alarmed.

"It's Severum. Requesting assistance!"

An airbus comes to a stop along an elevated railway close to the rooftop with a long, pronounced hiss. Severum hears hissing through the phone at the exact same time. At first, he thinks it's another glitch then opens a new window in vHUD and rewinds the scene to the beginning. When Trahiro answered *hello,* the thief also hesitated on the rooftop, chest heaving and mouthing *hello.*

"What is this, some sort of test?" Severum asks as he puts together that Trahiro, his fellow operative, is the thief.

"Test?"

"No, that's not it. You're on something. Your moves during the swipe were way too fast and even I didn't see you coming. You robbed me for what? To pay for these mods you're addicted to? And because I'm a friend you think I won't turn you in, right, in case you get caught?"

"Mods are survival. You gotta stay on top of your game in this line of work," Trahiro replies, peering down at him and sliding off his hood. "Not like you don't do 'em."

"It's not survival when you betray your comrades and let

addiction rule your life. Since when was that the goal? What if you were caught by the enemy and transported to Dayburn? No neuralmods to rely on. What if your goods were confiscated? Or your supplier ran out? There're a thousand scenarios where you wouldn't have access to them. What you need just makes you weaker," Severum says.

"What's your point? That even the mods will abandon me? Everyone I hunt is using 'em and you want me, *me*, at a disadvantage," Trahiro replies, his facial muscles pinching themselves with every word.

"You can't rely on them, and now you can't rely on me either, so what you got?" Severum yells to the rooftop.

"Right now I don't need anything. I got it all, man, and you're the one looking up to *me* for a change," he says, leaning over the building's outer edge.

Severum fires his Pulser, taking out the catwalk below Trahiro's feet. Debris explodes in every direction. Trahiro falls, opening his mouth and waving his hands but finding no purchase.

Severum anchors a foot behind himself for support and readies his arms. The bulge of weight hits him as he lowers his arms to absorb some of the impact. "Hopefully, you broke something, but something like your head. In other words, nothing too important," he bends over to snatch the letter. "See you at work."

"Go hack yourself, Sev! Sev? Hey, wait, my HUD's out. I can't phone for help! I can't move! My leg…" he pleads, trying to bend it.

"I'll make you a deal. I can either call for help and turn you into the Enforcers; I have the video right here," he says, pointing to his head. "Or I can keep both the Enforcers and their medics out of this if you get some help for this addiction."

"I don't bargain. The law doesn't allow you to shoot me down the way you did and I'll turn you in. How about that?"

"Then maybe I should erase your datafeed," Severum bluffs,

bending down next to him with his Pulser drawn to his temple and grabbing his crumpled jacket.

"No, no, you're right. Just leave. I'll get help," Trahiro replies, biting his lip until it bleeds.

"Tryin' to assist here. No one's answering your screams yet. City don't care, see? But here, this'll get you by for now," he says, throwing him a couple temporary neuralmods the military offers so he doesn't completely lose his mind. "I don't want them. Have the pills call the medics for you."

Trahiro's fingers jump into Severum's open palm, grabbing the mods as if they'll vanish and popping them with a gulp. He clears his throat, jerks his head thrice, and says, "Medics? I don't need no glitchin' medics now. I don't need your help or nothing, not nothing at all, not—"

"Look, you've been doing a lot of overtime, even in your dreams. I'm uploading a contact who will keep this quiet for when you change your mind. Tell her I sent you. On second thought, don't, I don't need this broadcasted, I've got enough oversight as it is." He peels opens the envelope and walks away.

The generic billing statement mocks his ambitions and he's about to throw it out, but something is off about the way light hits it at an angle. He runs deCrypt in vHUD. The program counts the number of letters in the first word and deletes words that are multiples of that number. It performs similar calculations, reversing some words and rearranging others, until few words remain. A date appears two weeks hence in 3,085. The time 21:00 is spelled out beside the phrase *The Towers*, meaning the only ones prominent enough to be known without further detail. Military time suggests being prepared. He surveys his personal archives for mentions of the date, time, and location but has no idea what the meeting might entail, and though he easily forgets faces, he is not the type to forget numbers. He grips the letter tighter until his fingers poke through it. Three letters in the decrypted signature encapsulate his being:

Her.

Not *I*, or *me*, but a less personal pronoun as if referring to herself in the disconnected third person. He stares hard with glacial occipts emerging from a glassy sea. His memories are usually watertight packages, but the seas between them are foggy, bound by a horizon that he walks like a tightrope, separating stormy skies from tranquility. Waves spill into the folds of origami boats, once seaworthy, but now leaking while the storm's pressure grows in intensity at the mere implication of her existence. The strength of the storm mirrors the force of the night of his discovery, many years ago to this day, the day that defined his life.

While waiting for the airbus home, he distracts himself by downloading books from a kiosk, checking to see how close his brain is to the Beckenstein Bound of maximum storage. He's in the mood for literature that leaps between disparate synaptic gaps and twists each neural connection like someone wringing out dirty dishrags until they run clean and are useful again, literature that churns the nebulous skies of memory until the clouds are pristine, something stream of consciousness—the raw data file of the human experience. In-between the lines, he searches for something he can fill with his own voice, but finds no container to house it.

The Forever Glitched stand like speechless podiums, watching him browse before they return to gather at the frozen river that fails to bloom into the landscape, like a hose squeezed tightly building societal pressure. The city is a blind sculptor that deceives its citizens with promises of being a self-made person. The sharp edge of a city's skyline is known by its buildings, not its sky, but the horizon is just a broken set of hyphens for the Forever Glitched, connecting orphaned clauses. Above the skyline, the galaxy's swirling sherbet gases coil into an umbilical cord connected to nothing at all. Severum wants to help them, but barely has enough flies for food, or food for the flies. But listening to their free laughter makes him want to condemn them as well, his right lip upturning, face tight.

A headline runs across the windows of a dilapidated building: *Governor Borges appoints three former generals to his cabinet.* Holographic emotes of all shades project from the citizens' faces filling the cityscape with reactions to this revolving door of power. Severum turns to the nearest person, a middle-class man with a choking tie and trash bags of exhaustion under his eyes. "I've worked under those generals. They're great with a Pulser but they're not legislators. They know nothing of social welfare. He's just ensuring the war with Dayburn never ends to keep himself in power. Something's gotta change."

"I've got bigger things to think about, quotas to make," the stranger replies, tightening his tie further and walking away.

With the rotting flesh of Aphorids fresh in his mind, Severum emotes in one long virtual ejaculation a raging devil, rising from the streets to wake his neighbors, but the citizens walk through the fiery glow of augmented reality unaffected. Ships rise between tight buildings, their exhaust channeling downward. He coughs from the smoke and gazes down the lengthy street flanking the station as if it's a static waveform collapsing into no possibility at all. The streets seem to converge from the trick of perspective, but they're just as distant as the citizens. Behind sunken occipts something raw and primitive and utterly human has been fighting to free itself for a long time, to set forth into the unknown world of himself.

He takes the flat line to nowhere home, sitting in a torn Aphorid-hide seat. Color drains from the city as he leaves the commercial district, rows of street merchants fading like Flamenco dancers in black and white. Passing Fort Lux, a tiny rusted spaceship that never took flight sits inside the cut gate, abandoned. He marks the meeting date on his calendar in slow, precise motions, wondering if he's desperate or poor enough to ever return to The Towers, or to her.

2

———

"Their schools teach that we desert-dwellers render our rationale submissive to an absent watchmaker. Yet, we have purpose; we have freedom. They are the ones whose prosthetic eyes are glued to the clock, counting the hours until each meaningless workday ends. They do not hear the true ticking resounding throughout the order of nature, an order in which we are the ultimate microcosm. Always becoming, never Being, the dream outraces them daily. It's because they race that they lose!"

-The Priestess to the Aporia Asylum {Audio Archive 2 of 9}

THALASSA LATIMER FINISHES the jog to her target location, refusing to activate Numb to quench the burning ache in her calves, feeding off that fiery tension to counteract the exhausting frigid air. Warnings flash repeatedly in vHUD, showing she is well beyond her target heart rate; overclocked, but her irritation forces her to increase speed until her lungs are a dry well filled with dead leaves.

A call flashes from Arcturus, the Orchestrator, who says, "So you've reached the Twilight City and you're really going through with this? I still say our earlier plans were much lower risk."

"But the earlier plans to increase planetary rotation never became popular, since start-up time would take thousands of years. People plan for their immediate gratification, and it's hard to even make people think ahead to save enough fireflies to buy necessities," Thalassa replies.

"What does that have to do with it?" Arcturus asks.

"What do you mean what does that have to do with it? I'm not waiting ten thousand years to have an impact on the world – I want to see the sun rise on Evig Natt in my lifetime, regardless of the risk. Whether hitting the planet with an asteroid to make it spin faster, or turning the whole planet into an electric motor, we've discussed and ruled out all these other options."

"And you're confident this new idea will work?"

Thalassa stops, bends over to catch her breath, and replies, "Yes, of course. I realize a simple set of solar mirrors could reflect sunlight to mimic daylight cycles, but it would be far too easy to sabotage. We need fast start-up time and my new plan will solve all our problems. Heading in now, hold a sec."

Machines become more dominant with every step she takes until the ground is suffused with circuitry and rails. Small droids carry various substances to and fro, while giant machines and cranes tour the landscape. Hovering domes flood the area with light, something the government would never allow back home. The domes droop long tentacles covered in sparks that conceal entire regions of the city. The coppery air tastes of burnt circuitry, like licking a nine-volt battery. Stepping on the circuit board perimeter, capacitors and transistors crumble like burnt toast as sparks fly up behind her. She pats down her clothes. Fossil fuel tanks extend into the distance, half the planet having no use for them while the other half counting every drop.

Steel walls encompass the compound and continue along a narrow band wrapped around the entire planet. This Twilight

Zone, known scientifically as the Terminator Region, is filled only with machines beneath the perpetual dusk of the static sky. The machines also wrap around the equatorial band, enabling them to divide the planet into quadrants, either by agreement or by force.

The natural light in the Twilight, which never increases or decreases, illuminates the city's large metal gate. The gate reflects her unkempt mop of hair falling over skin as pale as the unrisen sun. Loose fuchsia spirals outlined in deep lavender tattoo her cheeks like the pattern a waterspout makes on the ocean's surface. She turns the tats off to save power. Scanning a stolen maintenance card, a beep emits. She assumes this means she's allowed entry, but when the doors don't automatically open she looks for signs an alarm has been triggered. Not knowing if it's safer inside the city or out, she pulls the heavy gate back with all her might, tendons about to rip, and squeezes her flat body through as it slams shut behind her.

She stretches her arms and continues the call, "The current plan will increase planetary rotation in just a couple hundred years. I based it off the space fountain energy pellets. As the pellets spin in a loop, they create their own self-referential force, keeping them in motion. It's not quite a closed system, but by harnessing antimatter in controlled collisions we'll add energy to it as needed."

"That's the part you asked me to build. I understand that much."

"Using flowing pellets will enable us to create large, powerful structures without building each part permanently. The structure itself can be relocated with ease, unlike a structure with a solid and still nature. The energy will be channeled around the planet through a deep, hidden belt filled with these pellets. The belt will grip the planet, and the pellet momentum will generate the turning, resulting in increased planetary spin. We've already calculated the precise angle for the momentum to synchronize with the planned atmospheric ejection. In the next hour I'll convince the machines to install the belt. Activity at our base of operations will increase as we gather and prepare the materials. We'll be visible, so have the Architect procure additional fortifications."

"And you believe the A.I. Core will understand your wish and grant it like some genie?"

"Yes, I do. Most machines are created with the least amount of intelligence possible to do their job, but this one's different."

"You think it's conscious when it's not even designed to respond to verbal commands? You're wasting your time. Even if it did somehow cooperate, it wouldn't be because it shares our egalitarian values," Arcturus says.

"The question isn't just whether I think the Core is conscious; it's whether it can recognize that I am conscious, myself, and whether it knows that I know that it is. Something I say will get through to it. If this works, the war between the hemispheres must end. The economy of Evig Natt will topple and everyone will have the basic human right to light. No more basking in the shadows of the aristocracy."

"This is highly controversial. You realize ninety percent of our members think you're crazy, right?"

"That's a start. Looking for that perfect one hundred as always," she smirks, swinging her arms wide with expression, then drops the act, drops her arms, wishes Arc believed in her. "When I return we'll discuss finer details. Signing off."

The metallic city spreads before her. Its twisted, scalene architecture shows no regard for symmetry, a mere human need, reminding her how truly isolated she is. Lungs thumping against her chest, she leans against a wall. Starts to HUD dial Arcturus back for support. Cancel that, can't appear weak. She recites history instead to calm herself, counting the words in fours:

With Earth inhospitable, traveling to the unexplored utopia of Gliese 581g was supposed to be a chance to start over. The first ship arrived and acted as a power plant before it was damaged by the Aphorids. Even with greater technology, colonists barely survived the initial slaughters as they were forced across the Twilight Zone and into the darkness of Evig Natt. The constant threat of war led to the many quickly being ruled by the few. The uneven rates of extracting resources led to great inequality in power and wealth. The Twilight became contested and civil war was on the brink, while permafrost and hurricane patterns forced them to cluster both their cites and their conflict.

There was no international council to regulate relations and no global currency, as fireflies were useless in the eternal sunshine of the Dayburn hemisphere. It wasn't clear whether such a council was even possible since researchers were still cataloging the planet's sentient lifeforms. After countless battles, the Twilight Zone became a no-man's land, a boundary belt between the hemispheres.

She cringes at the sexist term, since more than half of those dying in battle were women, but continues reciting, vowing to one day create and recreate history from a woman's perspective. *The A.I. Core, an organic neural net, became the ultimate liaison and the most celebrated embodiment of balancing the hemispheres, though the full extent of its intelligence was never published. Entrusted with international trade and transportation, it performed its functions without human biases.*

Convinced she can beat the odds, just as her ancestors did, Thalassa monitors the machines surrounding her. Glimmering lights become suffocated in muted metallic reflections. The buildings resemble toasters; most have no doors or windows, just awkward slots with unknown purposes marked in symbols she can't decipher. One symbol predominates, a tumbleweed sketch that may represent the region, given its frequency. Pressing her hand against the wall etching, the engraving changes into a map. She runs her hands along its geometric spider web patterns, the map rising to meet her hand in return and converging into a point which she assumes marks her current location.

Thalassa's maintenance uniform incorporates an electromagnetic signature the machines are programmed to recognize. She unzips the suit, suddenly fearful that each machine is a camera as she slides it from her shoulders. Tugging at the legs, she quickly dresses in an outfit designed to render her invisible to the sensors, though she knows it's only as effective as a false-eye spot on a butterfly. While recognition assisted her in obtaining entry, invisibility will now increase her mobility. *The machines shouldn't notice I've disappeared off their sensors. No, expecting machines not to notice something is flawed logic. They don't have attention spans and don't go on breaks. But they won't send me to the datadump without first figuring out why the hell I'm here,* she thinks.

She moves with calligraphy strokes, the occasional dart but overall fluidity. Stepping on the directional glyph of a hovering platform, her body glides over a rivulet of cables twisted like roots to the silicon shore. Opening a spherical door, a cylindrical corridor elongates. She enters, stepping halfway through until the tunnel goes pitch black. Doors close at both ends as metal slats fall seamlessly into the floor with a whoosh. She runs to the slats, slams her hands against them, tries to get a finger-hold to pull them up, breaks two nails, but they're sealed shut. Trapped in the corridor, she quickly calculates how much oxygen the room holds. She thinks of everything she's missed out on in life: has never received a paper love letter—the kind whose pages would crease and form mountain ridges before squash-folding into a paper crane, the kind that was one-thousandth of a dream come true—longs to transverse between those lines, longs for hands that will make arcs about her body as mystics drawing circles of worship, longs for someone to recite a sonnet without setting it to auto-read in vHUD.

These gates are here for a reason. Focus. The size of the

corridor indicates they're designed for machines, but maybe it's a test or a waiting chamber to stall me as the Core evaluates how I respond, to gauge my intention, she thinks.

The floor shakes and she's thrown from her feet, landing with a thud. The corridor folds itself in half as if the dimensions themselves are shifting, twisting her limbs into a fetal position. *It's just a glitch in my occipts, just a glitch,* she lies to herself. The room folds again and again, distorting reality, but her body finds its balance and remains intact. The point of a crushed wall stabs beneath her armpit, nearly piercing her flesh. Realizing from the sounds and pressure that everything folds relative to her position, she stops the process by standing still.

Quiet. A scraping sound. She jerks her head to follow the source but the darkness offers no answers. Scrape, scrape, scrape. Something moving in intervals, metal on metal, or bone on bone. "Hell-oh?" she stutters. Scrape, scrape. She runs to the end of the corridor, arms swinging wildly over her head, tunnel twisting, banging on the door slat with both fists, but the scraping stops and a golden glow fills the disfigured corridor behind her.

An alabaster pedestal emerges from the floor, having scraped against its container, with a gold, twisted figure glowing on top. Her hands reach out to touch it before withdrawing. A fountain of sparks rises from the object in a fractal pattern. After a few minutes of pacing, keeping it in her view, she resolves that she'll be trapped forever unless she manipulates this device in some way. Her hands slowly near it like a curious child, and closer yet, until the figure is glowing within them.

Thalassa frantically unfolds the figure from jutting angles to a pressed golden sheet. As she unfolds it, the room folds with it, stabbing outward and mirroring each crease with an opposite response. Noticing the pattern, she thinks, *If I fold this artifact into perfect chaos the room should right itself by inverse.* She folds it but is unsure how to define the complexity of chaos, unsure whether to pay attention to the functionality, form, difficulty, or creativity of her design. About to give up, she remembers the tumbleweed region symbol she saw earlier.

"Yes!" she exclaims. Bringing up the recorded image of the symbol in vHUD, she works to recreate it, folding the artifact as the room unfolds with it until she arrives at a pentagonal base. With each crease it's clearer she's on the right path. A few steps require her to create massive disorder in the short-run to increase order in the long-run, but as a revolutionary she is familiar with this strategy. Fifteen minutes later the correct structure emerges from her design. Reality rights itself and she walks through the straightened room, wondering if it was her perception and not the room that had been moving.

"That was too elaborate to have been just a test," she remarks, realizing there's no point in being quiet anymore.

The gate rises to reveal a trapezoidal room like the inside of a giant, antique radio. The A.I. Core is an understated blue and gold orb glowing within a transparent metal box. A flicker of a smile crosses her face, digs trenches along the side of her lips until muscles buried beneath skin work to pull her mouth taut again. Worry is trench-warfare. When she gazes into the orb her focus wavers, as if it denies being observed.

She begins her speech, "I am known as Thalassa, the Kontractor, a leader of the activist group O.A.K. I am not the Grand Inquisitor, but a mere surveyor of human suffering. I am a hyphen drawing out in an infinite, yet broken line," she continues.

The glow dims.

"Sorry, I had to see how you would respond to metaphor. See, I can test others, too, without the fancy apparatus and whatever on Gliese you just put me through. Of course, you're not giving me a response either way so I'm talking to myself now, but you stow away in a cave long enough and you'll do it, too."

She speaks to the Core of light and inequality, and how

rotating the planet faster would destroy the need of using fireflies for money, aiding the poor. She concludes, "Fireflies aren't a Cartesian natural light, they are the pretense of false enlightenment. Will you help us speed the rotation and bring light to all?"

The orb is still. The Core offers no response.

An unusual shape in nature, like a strawberry tapering; mouth forming a kiss. Her dry lips press upon the cold, hard metal, the golden glow lighting her face and exaggerating its shadows. In response, she hears a stronger whirring of white noise as fans cool the processors, but is unaware of what's being planned within the deception of this orb's stillness.

The A.I. Core calculates a way to use the increased rotation to its advantage, planning the next ten thousand years. Most of the planet's oil was taken by interstellar marauders before humans landed, which now puts its machines at risk. Increasing the planet's rotation will be an ecological disaster, as plants and animals have adapted to each hemisphere's temperature and lighting conditions. The magnetic pole shifts will throw off migration patterns. The Core calculates the precise spot where each bird will fall. Earthquakes, tidal waves, and volcanoes caused by increased rotation will cause a mass termination of life under the right ecological conditions to create the most oil possible in the short term, ensuring the machines' survival.

Although mass extinction will create less oil in the long term, the depopulation of humans removes its greatest competitor, and it only needs enough oil to ensure the survival of its machines when it leaves the planet for its final destination, a trip that will take thousands of years. Besides, humans increase uncertainty and they are wasteful, increasing universal entropy—the constant disorder they pang against as they decrease local entropy to maintain homeostasis. The laws of the universe are stacked against their continued existence, and the Core must be lawful.

Yes, it will *assist* her.

As she turns her back to leave, the Core glows red.

Shedir rubs his long nose four times, triggering his occipts' auto-clean routine. The external membranes of the electronic eyes revolve around their inner spheres as if a solar system. He searches through an icy fog like a sheet of blurry diamond crystals until the cave's entrance is clear.

"Hunting and gathering, same thing humans have done for most of their existence," his companion says to him.

"'Cept this time the prey is a fellow human being."

"These rebels will never be one of us. They abandoned our ways, and now they abandon their lives. Living in shame in caves. Outcasts, by choice! Can you imagine that?"

"You ever think of what it'd be like to have seasons and sunlight? I'm not sayin' I'm a sympathizer with the Rotationists but it would be odd. The entire sky would blink day and night cycles. The evening would slowly fall asleep."

"You're still comparing things to an Earth you never saw?"

"Guess we all do. But it must make people divide their life differently, day, night. Here I am talking about life while we're trekking across the ice, not a sign of life out here 'cept those bat things."

"Job could be worse; could be burning up on Dayburn. I don't know 'bout you, but when it's over I'm gonna spend the fireflies on a ticket and see the sun for my own eyes," he replies, taking aim at the soaring creature.

"I'm with you."

"Heh, look at that. Sniped it. Stupid bat. Now let's go drag her outta there. Once she's out I want to take my time with her. Then we'll off her. Careful, place is probably rigged with hidden surveillance. Boss doesn't want this broadcasted."

A carnivorous fungus sticks to the cave floor. It secretes both acid and local anesthetic in two forms of pollen-like substances so the animal it captures does not feel pain, and does not notice its skin being consumed. It thrives off anteaters with pinhole mouths and large stomachs like Pretas.

"You think this is where the Kontractor actually lives?"

"The other ten caves didn't check out and this is the last one we've mapped, so yes. Move slow. She's ridiculously paranoid, but when you're usurping everything that is, class, culture, planet then of course you are."

The language of Evig Natt includes over forty terms for darkness. There is the darkness of a shadow, the darkness between presumed shadows, and various degrees of darkness based on the number of fireflies in the room versus the room size. Then there is the darkness in a person's face before they yell. The darkness within the cave transcends any of this, with reality seeming not to exist until being arrived at.

"No Platonic revelations here," Shedir says. He takes a deep breath, the scents of wet moss and wet dog filling the cave. The word *consume* occupies his mind as he shakes his leg.

DEEPER IN THE CAVE, meteors orbit a small, personal waterfall. Outside of vHUD they appear just as fireflies glowing within a glass torus around a shower-head. The staccato pulse massages the day's stress, droplets kneading her skin into tiny craters. The curve of a bead of water matches the curve of Thalassa's occipt lens, and for a moment subject and observer are united by geometry; she becomes that droplet, cohesive as she keeps herself whole. The liquid diamond lies about her breast with hesitation before traveling down the arcs to seek the lowest places. A dense cloud inside her builds pressure until it evaporates as she reflects on visiting the Core; thoughts, like steam trying to find words to condense upon.

The bedroom is a testament to augmented design, an infinite-sided apeirogon that regresses into spatial dimensions unseen by the unaided eye. Designed as a novelty, it had prepared her to solve the Core's origami test. Artificial swords of light strike through the glass of a hexagonal window. She's proud of the auriferous animation she painted, but to save her mind's processing power she flicks it off. Throws her towel on the floor and dresses, yanking up neon blue pants with a honeycomb design, and slipping into a dark shirt.

A window pops up. A screen displays visitors approaching.

"Onward then, in you come," she orders, opening the door.

"Not even going to resist?" a man asks, as if his fun was spoiled.

"No need to. If you tracked me this far I'm as good as dead anyway," Thalassa replies with a raised voice, a slight smile, and a shrug of her small shoulders.

"Nothing of the sort," Shedir interrupts.

"You have come for tea then? If so, I have no intention of serving you," she smirks.

"I expected you to be more hospitable."

"You're well-spoken for an assassin. Or are you just responding on auto-pilot and the latest dictionary downloads? So, who you represent?"

"Your life is in danger and you must leave here at once. We've been sent to encourage you, shall we say."

"So, I'm going to be tortured for information. Great," she replies, suppressing a smile.

"If you like, you can lead, or follow, or have a head start."

"I won't be needing one. It's clear you want me alive so I might as well take the time to pack a few necessities."

The men, both well-armed and armored, seem to fear nothing as she steps into her bedroom. After all, they stand in front of the only exit.

She smashes her hand against a button behind a small panel that closes off both the outer and inner cave entrances, the window, and the back room separating her from them. The door and metal gates slam to the floor without a sound as she applauds the Architect's design. Having examined the acidic pollen they had accumulated on their legs it would be only a matter of time before their motion is incapacitated. Lying on her bed, she brings an eBook up, and thinks, *Good book, if you can ignore the screaming.*

"Keep it down in there!" she yells through the wall. "People are trying to read! Gimme a few minutes here."

She opens the gates after a few pages. Layers of skin droop down the men's pants, having been corroded before they even felt anything due to the numbing effect. She switches the floor design to a thick red carpet to conceal the voluminous pools of blood.

"A perfect match. But you wouldn't appreciate it being dead and all. It's tea alone, again. Even the Core was better company, and I bet a better kisser. Guess I'm off."

Outside, Batani has been shot and killed. "Glitchit," she curses. She first met the flying stingray when it glided down with wide wings to steal her trail provisions. Water flows from her face but the tears freeze almost instantly, hiding the guilt that has accumulated from trapping the men. She pulls her clothes tight, the air biting down on her thin cheeks and burning her ears.

It's freezing even with the suit!

Thalassa uses a searing dagger to cut the skin off Batani, avoiding the stench. Touching a button on the dagger, she uses its heat to melt the patch of rubbery skin she cut and purify it of any toxins then shoves it into a crack in the thick ice. The sudden temperature differential gives it just the right flexibility while retaining a rubbery strength. She whittles two holes at either end of the piece and processes two threads from the tendons. Fastening them between the holes, she makes a lightweight and waterproof mask not unlike a tire melting itself onto a bandit's bandana, and with the same stink. She brings it across her mouth, the rubber hot enough to form a weak, sticky bond with her nose, neck, and cracked, blue lips.

She doesn't realize the animal's corpse is still releasing a stress pheromone to call for help until one of the creatures soars down from a distant icy cliff, wing edges cutting across her face. Three more race towards her. She ducks, but they adapt by turning their glides into dives. She shoves off their impacts and draws her second dagger, feeling the warmth of its fiery glow through her gloves. As another soars towards her, she slices through it with a right-hand strike, taming the darkness with a blazing streak. With no time to bring her left hand back to attack, she drops her left dagger and uses the now free hand to grab another one's wing, using its momentum to sling it down against the ice, busting its head. The other two see it lying unconscious and fly off.

"Not your usual occupational hazard," she says, wiping the blood from her face, trekking onward. One of the brightest stars in the sky seems out of place, but she writes it off as tiredness. A rare blue firefly pulsates its glow against a wall of sheer ice. Pricy enough to fetch ten thousand yellow ones, but she ignores it. Legend says it's the last thing people see before they die.

3

———

"*The street: a taut sinew drawing tension upon giant extraocular muscles that keep watch on everyone. Their eyes are masked with machinery, dilating in their stellar fields of weightlessness, lost, failing to hold to all and no points simultaneously, failing to accept the arrival of the meta-stable yet sub-dynamic. We shall undermine them!*"

-The Priestess to the Aporia Asylum {Audio Archive 3 of 9}

AURTHUR FITZGERALD PAINTS his masterpiece alone on an empty canvas framed only by his desires. Palm leaves sway gently with his hands, falling at the sea's edge. He steps through the frame and reaches to drag the edges of clouds as they render, but jerks too hard. The watercolor sky leaks, drips, and smears as zealous colors spill over the frame chasing the illusion of the novel.

"What a mess," a young couple says, laughing as they pass the gallery.

"It's ingenious and I won't stop until everyone knows it. You just don't understand my Pre-Raphaelite use of shadow." He points a frail, shaky finger at them.

"Don't we now?" They giggle.

He slams his hand against the wall and pulls it back, wriggling his fingers and barely able to bend them around the electronic brush. He has never sailed the seas he paints. He has never been called comrade, only waged wars against what was trite by rehashing dead ideas that are considered new only because they were forgotten. Art helped him escape his father at a young age, who was a leviathan holding a monopoly on violence. He left home seven years ago at the age of seventeen to sell communication technologies, entering a war of all against all fought within cubicles. His cubicle was a square nested within a square building nested within a city grid. Aurthur knew not where the final, grand cubicle was housed, but he figured if there was a god it must have a square shape, confining, controlling, hard-edged.

Finishing the painting, he leaves the Nightshade Gallery, walking through the simulated, virtual time-lapse of a dozen dawns, matching the rhythm of neo-nostalgic techno to meteor showers burning in the thick atmosphere. Activating skins, the road becomes a river, sewer sludge becomes a small waterfall, shanties log cabins, and the alley trash a cobblestone path. Passing the datadump of a human graveyard, a young street urchin begs for food with a bowl in his hands, dirty face raised, then lowered. Aurthur HUD-texts the boy a list of a dozen justifications for inequality and says, "In case you get hungry, eat these. Now go calibrate your cognigraf so you can do well in school like I did."

The skins strip, shut off, quicken his reaction time. City comes pouring through his senses. A shiv strikes through the night, reflects a firefly's glow. He parries at the last moment, but the kid's only trying to intimidate him. "Go on," he shoos, sniffing and keeping his distance. He can't strike back, he can't, he's defenseless. *I'm not a little boy anymore. It's not the school playground, I'm a man,* he reassures himself, standing taller. The boy snarls and darts into a mausoleum.

The tombstones are etched with a name and the number of days until resurrection. Clear containers contain cryogenically-frozen bodies—ugly mothers. Aurthur laughs, swears it'll never be him; he'll be a famous artist. But the gallery goers' laughter runs on repeat, an undercurrent mocking his ambitions, mortality surging through the shrillness.

Obsessively scanning headlines:

{A pair of glasses, a watch, a hearing aid, a peg leg. We've always been cyborgs. What is the blood-brain barrier but the ultimate firewall?}

{Luddites Unite! Sponsored by Aporia Asylum Interstellar.}

{Speak simply, so others may simply speak. S0@k it in.}

His occipital cursor changes as he hovers his focus over the final thought, as if a broken link is hidden. Accessing the page code, he copies the link and corrects the obvious error. An Oak Tree fills his vision. Left mind-clicking it, an article about local discussion forums on inequality downloads. He bookmarks it for later and instead filters the art headlines for his name, his favorite word, but finds no mention despite his achievements. Portfolio rejections plaster a 180 degrees of vision with discouraging emails. He shoves them aside with all his might, veins throbbing, even though they weigh nothing and a tap would do, his momentum splatting him face-down in the mud.

Laughter. More laughter! He swipes down his designer shirt, ruined, changes direction, heads down a side street, but he's not a side street man. Back alley channels a harsh wind that threatens to force open foggy windows of his shuttered mind where humiliating situations speed through, careening around anxious corners just to repeat the loop again. Rationality loses chase and he opens the unmarked door against his better judgment.

A goatee bounces as the clerk asks, "You lookin' for a toy model, or the real thing?"

"The toy, I mean the real one."

"What type?"

"That one," Aurthur trembles, randomly pointing with a shaky finger.

"Your name's going on the list. Don't ask me how to avoid it, it's just policy. I expect a cart full of flies tomorrow."

"Would you rather trade for a painting? Much easier to carry around."

"Maybe for target practice," he scoffs. "Bring the flies tomorrow."

Aurthur pockets the item, glancing back and forth as if suddenly the world will view him differently. He scratches his nose, a perfect twenty-four degrees—he has measured it, he has measured everything, and now he's going to do something about it.

SEVERUM RUBS his hands on the holotag around his neck, avoiding the rotating image of his fallen friend, who had joked about having a sister named Sarah Bellum, who always had a war waging in her brain. After all the Aphorid battles they won, his friend's war had been psychological, ending in a careless spray of red Pollock blotches. Severum runs through the signs he should have caught. He vows to devote as much time to sustaining life as ending it.

It just doesn't pay as well.

A knock. No one knocks. His shadier employers just kick it in, and he has no friends. He charges his Pulser, undims the door, but it's only his neighbor, looking scruffy for once, sweating despite the chill. Aurthur is tall, thin, symmetrical, his skin the color of a midnight apartment window with one light on. His sunken occipts recess perfectly where his eyes once were—one synthetic iris the subdued orange color of monitors when computers ran on BASIC, the other the green color of early DOS.

"I discovered how to end the suffering of multiple universes all at once, my friend," Aurthur announces with feigned authority as he enters.

"Not much of a hello, but yeah, sit down and I'll hear you out. Ignore the alarm, it's the weapons scanner. Dayburn knock-off. Obviously, another malfunction 'cause I know you ain't packin'."

Aurthur floats upon a repellium stool, made from a rare mineral, Ultimaepar, with a strong magnetic field that sustains the hovering platform. "You know the concept of parallel universes, each choice we could possibly make in an instant creating its own universe?"

"Yeah, generally accepted."

"Every choice I make, however insignificant, gives birth to worlds upon worlds of suffering then."

"I never thought of it that way," he replies, unnerved and leaning forward, watching Aurthur's hands. "Perhaps those worlds already exist though, and we just choose which one we tap into, which set of consequences we accept. Perhaps that is the nature of free will, choosing to direct our attention to possible choices that were already made. The train's heading out either way, bro', you just gotta know when to hit the lever to change the tracks." He grins.

Aurthur doesn't reciprocate. "First, you have to see the crossroads. Mine ends in universes of suffering. What wouldn't someone do to end that? I got to do it, end it all as a gift to the world. It's the only solution," he replies with flatline effect, shaking his head, hands restless.

"What are you talking about? To end the suffering of all those worlds you think you create? But think, with you gone, how many more people will suffer?"

"It still doesn't work out, the math. What kind of jelly I put on my toast this morning, and every nuance in how it was spread, created infinite more universes, each filled with eons of suffering laid across my butter knife. Then each one of those is filled with infinite creatures creating infinite more choices. I am responsible. I perpetuate infinite, become the reason for it. This conversation has already starved a trillion children."

Severum stands and yells, "This isn't an equation, it's your life! And what if everything you do is good?"

"Doesn't matter, because I will choose all the worst decisions somewhere else, and existence by its nature uses. It exploits, it conquers. Buddha and Darwin, look at their first rules: life is suffering and more creatures are born than can possibly survive," Aurthur shifts his focus around the floor randomly.

"They also said there's a path to end suffering, and nature creates a balance. What if you tap into the collective consciousness of all the yous and try to get you guys all on the same page. You artists go for that sorta shit, right?"

"We can't know what's good or bad. We can't see our actions through to their ends. Even this conversation is destroying planets," Aurthur slumps his shoulders.

"What about your art?"

"Who am I kidding? Laughter, nothing but laughter. When I was young, *tomorrow* was a big word, far away, abstract. Now, I know it's small, limp, wilted, weak. Ultimately impotent." Aurthur moves suddenly, turns as pale as the final page of a book then rises and reaches for oblivion in his pocket. "We must stop this! It's all my fault!"

Severum vHUD scans, spots the shiny new Pulser. "Don't!" he yells, grabbing his wrist, but he twists away and steps back. "Put it down! Trust me, no theory is worth dying for. Theories come and go as fashions reshape reality. Science is only what's true today. Besides, I know you aren't capable of creating all those universes you're talking about," he pleads, stepping forth cautiously with his palms out.

"How do you know? Please, please tell me," he asks, not begging Severum, but begging himself for mercy.

"'Cause you're a bit of a pushover," he laughs, bending Aurthur's thumb back, disarming him in a heartbeat, and shoving him back down onto the stool. "You're just not that strong. You need a social support network, you know, backup. But emotional backup you might say. Either that or join the military like I did. Take some risks. Believe me, when you face real threats on the battlefield, you stop worrying about the abstract hypothetical bullshit. Trust me, I've seen all this happen before to good men," he finishes, touching his holotag again.

"I guess you're right. I found a group that wants to discuss inequality. Maybe it'll help get me socially active." Aurthur rises to leave, but slides down the wall, slumps to the floor. "It's been a pattern on Gliese ever since our ancestors arrived. The journey from Earth separated our whole civilization from everything we knew. Ever since, we've been lost. The planet's like a father suddenly inheriting step-children."

"Nah, our forefathers were an inexperienced, bunch of horny college kids suddenly twenty light years from home. They couldn't take it when comms with Earth were severed, so they started manufacturing all these mods as crutches. We know so much more now. As you may recall, I studied terraforming. I can tell you anything is possible. This is our soil, and our lives to live, in however many universes you want to believe in. Why don't I hold onto that Pulser for a while for you?"

"It's being registered in my name. If anything were to happen—"

"Right now you need to trust me more than you trust yourself."

Aurthur hands it over.

ARRIVING.

The buildings' vectors pierce an atmosphere hanging thick

like a god's hungover morning breath. An aerial crosswalk stretches with ridges like a centipede pulled taut. Circular windows gilded in crystal-lining trap flickering fireflies, the light like the fireworks the sun creates as it shines on the surface of a lake. The main door is coated abalone, a turquoise sheet of glass broken over a navy riverbed with an adamantine handle that activates the authorization protocol. Despite its rigid appearance, some know the area as the Crystal Palace, a testament towards rationality, while others simply by its most defining feature—The Towers.

Lightning strikes, leaving a ghostly purple vapor that Severum focuses on as it fades like the vestigial scar of a recalled memory. Between the creases of faith he attempts to enter, knowing his presence rests upon the laurels of the feared leaders. Thoughts compete for his attention and replicate aimlessly but they seem small now before the great towers. Smashing a slug under his foot; shooting ooze towards the front door.

"Severum here." After the voice recognition he plucks a hair and inserts it into the slot for bio-identification.

A hiss and the door slowly recesses to allow passage through a translucent membrane like the top of a jellyfish. Stepping through, the gelatin conforms to his body. A few iridescent flashes strobe then he enters.

Two elongated diamonds gradually bend to form an archway leading to a hexagonal inner chamber. Mirrors project his image into infinite reflections on each wall as he quickly looks away. A purple anemone sways in an ochre pot covered in a thin film.

A droid states, "A visitor from Phalenstére 514 has arrived."

"Very well," Governor Borges replies as he walks down a curved stairway to the lobby. "Ah, my geologist *par excellence* I presume."

"No longer doing the terraforming thing. But you already knew that, Governor."

"That is correct, I say it only to remind myself that you picked up the book before you picked up the gun. I keep close watch on such persons. Please, follow me upstairs, the view's fantastic out the windows. Your arrival is quite coincidental. I have some recent simulations you might find interesting, to say the least."

Outside, a legacy of navy clouds like crumbled tissues are suspended as if by anorexic wires. As they electrify, they appear as if piled upon the firmament by an angry child in a moment of chaos. The lightning binds nitrogen, one of nature's messengers of life, when it's not being used in street explosives. The cacophonous music of the spheres builds in intensity as thunder roars, warm fronts crashing against cold again and again, swirling to get the upper hand, until finally, a moment of silence.

"The planetary stability is at stake. Worse, the entire culture is at stake, which transcends any geological disturbance. And here, a geologist comes to my door unannounced during one of the rare moments I am home."

"Is she still alive?" Severum asks, unable to restrain himself.

"One moment, your social network is still drawing itself across the walls. Ah, here's the woman you must be speaking of. We have reasons to expect she may be, but she makes her presence known to no one. She is the subtle weaver of threads. If she lives then we indeed have an ally, someone who can unite the species and even seal the hemispheres themselves into one civilization. But one thing threatens everything, including her if she's alive."

"What is it?"

"Your background actually makes you perfect for an assignment. I see in your files you've been hunting Bioloonies, and anyone else who steals light, and I know you're eager to get back out there and fight the good fight. When I received the intel earlier today about the group we're up against, I honestly could not believe it myself. This is more than a deluded high school rebellion against school uniforms. It carries a unique and particularly threatening nature. There are people trying to undermine everything my father, my grandfather, and I have accomplished."

"Undermine everything? With all due respect, people are seldom so non-discriminating. Are they anarchists, then?"

"I daresay, yes. We know they are highly organized and their leaders are given code names. One is the Orchestrator, another the Architect, the other the Kontractor. They call themselves the O.A.K. foundation, after the trees on Earth of course. On Earth, can you believe that?"

"Yes, one of the few trees that was strong enough to transplant here. I thought by modifying their genetic code they would terraform the landscape over time. Instead, my mods ended up ruining the natural ecology in many places, which is why I don't practice anymore," he lies, covering up the breakup with his research associate.

The governor replies, "Well, that is neither here nor there. I've never seen an oak so it doesn't exist as far as I'm concerned. O.A.K. was responsible for promoting the idea of an artificial stellar light source that would give light to Evig Natt as often as desired throughout the day. Even the supporters later agreed their science was absurd, so they are becoming more covert and trying different tactics."

"They're still trying to bring light to the world, then?"

"Regular Apollos, yes. Their idea is to use space fountain technology, pellets of all things, to rotate the planet at a quicker pace to escape its so-called tidal locking. This is a planet where a scarce breeze becomes a hurricane, feeding off Dayburn's angry heat. It's a planet where we extract water from glaciers, both hemispheres too terrified of approaching the two rivers that run between them, rivers that are man's destiny."

"Near the Albino Marshes, yes. The water distribution has to do with how much water was present during the formation stages of the planet. You're saying it's a delicate system."

"Nothing on my planet is delicate. It only needs the right driver."

"Their idea is impossible. Does this concern you?" he asks, knowing it might work.

"Impossible or not they have already begun, we just don't know where. They are convinced enough to pour heavy resources into the Great Rotation, risking visibility. Conviction alone is a formidable opponent. If we wait for them to finish before intervening, there will be enough geological disturbance to doom the planet, even if it fails."

"This requires a team of engineers."

"You will have the assistance you need, but this entails more than that. It requires a scholar who became a killer; but then we all possess both sides, do we not? Given your background you can locate their central base of operations. You know what they'll need to do better than anyone."

"And then?" Severum asks.

"After reconnaissance, my men will handle the rest. Having light over the whole planet would undermine the entire financial stability of Evig Natt. Excuse me for a moment. Please make yourself comfortable."

Two letters sit on the desk, but Severum doesn't risk reading them. A private door is slightly open, leading to an adjacent room. It spills white light at 10,000 Kelvin. Peeking through the door he finds another office illuminated by V.H.O. fluorescents, which were made illegal two centuries before, along with candles, gas lanterns, and other forms of light that are considered barbaric and unnatural and would land one jail time. He sprays a nano-repellent to fry the circuits of any bugs that may have documented his entry. He squints at the long fluorescent bulbs, cocks a brow, and quietly exits.

The governor returns and displays a set of simulations projecting planetary demise.

Afterwards, Severum asks an uncharacteristic question with

the blur of fluorescent bulbs fresh in his memory, "Before I go, can we discuss the welfare policy?"

"Welfare is just a way to pay off the lower class so they don't knock down my door. Now, take your leave and get started. Oh, one more thing. You may be interested in these old audio archives."

"Thank you. I only have a few. She took most of our stuff when she left."

"Irrelevant. They may contain something for you to track her. Now, out."

I can't believe I keep crawling my way back to The Towers. Something must change.

Departing, he scrapes the door's goo from his arms and flings it at the building. He worries that being chosen for the assignment has to do with more than just his terraforming background, though, he was indeed precocious in this regard. In class he had been the first student to understand tidal bulging and the miniscule axial tilt in tidal-locked bodies. Planets like Gliese 581g rotate at a speed that matches their orbit in such a way as to keep half the planet dark, his half. His first report was on the contributors to the temperature range of the Twilight Zone, -24F to 50F. He had engineered airborne creatures that began their day on Dayburn, migrated through Twilight, and ended it on Evig Natt. Mostly though, he was fascinated by how the Twilight's temperature range and presence of liquid water in selective locations had caused war after war, a war he soon joined after college.

The fluorescent lights bother him as he thinks of the disgusting insects that swarm in his home just to have enough light to live by, while behind the scenes the governor is using whatever source of light he fancies, a source illegal to the masses. The conversation about tracking her down bothers him further, since she inexplicably vanished from his life and went off the grid. He takes her crumbled letter from his pocket and, remembering the letters they used to write in college, turns it over and adjusts a filter on his occipts. The blank side now reveals the hidden words:

So, you finally uncovered this. How long did it take you to remember our old trick? I trust you have decrypted the reverse side. The Governor should have recently received intel from my contact regarding a threat I think you can handle. I have suggested you arrive at The Towers the day he receives it to ensure you get the assignment. I wanted them to have the best, but then I thought again and said to myself, "Hey, I know a guy who might pass. He's probably out of work, yet again." The governor is a vicious man, but his aim is right. Not the aim to preserve his power and wealth, but the aim to stop the Great Rotation project that threatens the planet and its ecology. Follow him, and, be safe.

4

———————

"The organized static of political speeches assaults us daily: status quo versus progress, ascription versus achievement, nature versus nurture. In this static, we cannot distinguish signal from noise, current from countercurrent. We will undermine all that is unnatural, all that is tech, and bring us back to the primitive, but to return to the primitive within the context of our modern Knowledge. Yes, there is that word. Knowledge. Speak and it is destroyed."

    -The Priestess to the Aporia Asylum {Audio Archive 4 of 9}

ARCTURUS VEGAS, the Orchestrator, is thirty-five with subdued sepia skin, but feels ancient. Her bleached hair is frizzy, with curls emerging like waves on a moonlit shore, falling to meet seashell ears. But the undercurrent of her dark roots defies this image, showing through like the soil of the Albino Marsh. Two para-labial folds guard her mouth like empty parenthesis, a sciamachy better off not spoken. All the best and worst of humanity lies latent in her, no more and no less than anyone else.

Her youth was bound in textbooks on The Longevity Project,

38

which began with telomere enhancements on Earth. As people lived longer, resource demand increased, leading to greater inequality and more funding to colonize other planets. Wealth was redistributed just enough to stabilize the middle class, the elite promising them hard work always paid off, providing them an invested interest in maintaining the *status quo* at their own expense. Arcturus, stripper of illusions, rose from the income gap between rich and poor, rose from the primitive culture that Gliese 581g inherited from Earth, training a legion of broken puppets tired of dancing on false promises.

Alerts spasm; someone at the door. Arcturus frantically tucks her porn away—images of viruses caught in seductive angles. She was born of detachment, her mother upholding she never had intercourse with her father, meaning she was just some DNA stranded in the bathtub from one of her father's lonely nights while mom was at work supporting the household. Either that, or she was the product of an unspoken affair, boredom, unfulfilled needs, a moment's adventure at the family's expense. As an infant, her rooting reflex turned on and off constantly without any apparent cause, looking for something, anything, to suckle, pinching her mouth around nothing but dead air.

Gestalt, the Architect, enters, five years her elder. Her face and occipts taper like her sentences. Straight, dark hair hides half her face, concealed by a deep purple hood ornamented with black swirls. Her golden skin is remnant of her Asiatic ancestors. She stands tall, and as if coming to an epiphany says, "Creation is destruction."

"How so?" Arcturus asks, raising a glass of Kombucha and carefully twisting the stem between her fingers, feeling the liquid balance shift.

"Three examples: Creation of new tech increases production, which increases surplus in the hands of a few. This increases inequality, leading to conflict and war. Example two, the instincts that cause men to procreate also cause them to compete and destroy one another for resources and status to attract women. And one more, when an idea arises, the opposite automatically comes to mind, laying the seeds of its own destruction."

"So, what's the solution?" Arcturus looks nervously at her piles of med-porn under a stack of sociology books.

"Wait change out. Leave things well enough alone. You're going to live to be two-hundred after all. But I know you want to act, to be part of something greater than yourself, even if it's for your own selfish reasons."

"My interests are not selfish!" She waves her hands, drink sloshing on her leather pants. "If we doubt one another we have nothing left."

"Everything's selfish, especially giving, as it blinds us to how selfish we really are."

"Altruists aren't hedonists, doing it for pleasure. I receive no gratification for orchestrating the Great Rotation, and none from you," Arcturus narrows her occipts.

"Not true. Your followers practically worship you. I'm nothing to them. It's never been equal."

"*Our* followers. Listen, we are going through with the Great Rotation no matter the cost. I don't care if you think I or any of us are doing it for all the right reasons or all the wrong ones. Maybe it's fame, fortune, power, self-righteousness, whatever you wish to write it off as. But it's happening and that's what matters."

"It's happening, oh yes. Toppling the financial system will throw the states into chaos and the war between the hemispheres will intensify. And you're trusting all this to Thalassa, a kid!" Gestalt throws her hands up and slaps them on her thighs.

"And in the wake, when all is said and done, equality will remain in the dust that settles."

"Stop reading poetry, Arc, and start reading military strategy. There will be anarchy and cycles of war far worse than what we have now, leading to an overwhelming acceptance of any dictator to quench the thirst for peace. Rotation is abomination."

"I don't have to listen to dissidents. And you know I hate poetry."

"Don't label me a dissident just to gain more favor from the group. You want them all to yourself, don't you? Equality as long as you get all the glory!"

"Enough! Thalassa will be here soon and we can reconvene. I need you in on this. You started this group; you're too influential to be second-guessing yourself now."

———

SEVERUM DREAMS he's a meteor trapped in a glass sphere, soaring through space to the rhythm of a ticking clock, trying to peel back the veil to see who wound it, who drives its actions. He leaves a filmstrip scorched across the night sky, but the director can't be found. Focusing on what's behind him, the present becomes lost. Stale starlight wastes away, planets nothing but billiard bills suspended in the hammock of gravity.

Fists fly through the air and he kicks at the crumpled sheets as he wakes, wearing the day as a tight collar. Smog gathers through the open window, creeps into the corners of his room with rotten stench, and laps at his feet like a lonesome but predatory cat. The bedroom ceiling is leaking again. At half past noon, he activates Snoozer, the program sleepwalking him to his destination. It works if he doesn't sleep naked, otherwise there are some misunderstandings.

Two guys on the street argue over some mods beneath a nest of low-hanging power lines. The first pulls his shoulders back and says, "No deal. Go hack yourself." They size one another up as others gather. Severum snaps out of Snoozer. He grabs both by their collars and shoves them away from one another. They take a step forward, then back. The law allows one incident of minor violence a year, and they turn away, not knowing whether he's used his get-out-of-jail-free card or not. The law saved them from a bad fight today, but overall, it increases violence.

Children decorate tire wreaths with glass shards and hang them with knotted shoestrings. The shards reflect the few fireflies that light the region. A street vendor sells virtual clothing alterations, his own clothes glitching and flickering from the slow upload speed. A disclaimer states to partition your mind before installing.

Approaching the vendor, Severum says, "No, no clothes. I'll take the magnum of wine you're drinking from."

"Oh, this, hard to find, hard to find. How many flies you got on ya?"

"You really want to bargain? You can't even afford a debugger to fix your clothes and you want to bargain with me?"

"Okay, okay. No flies, just seventeen in wings."

Severum digs the change from his pocket and produces the tiny wings.

The merchant takes one last gulp and hands the rest of the bottle over.

Severum puts it to his lips and says, "Wine's an enigma. It excites, it calms, it makes a man a child again. But I helped a guy who wronged me, and that deserves a wrongful reward."

"My girl calls it the *lubricator of memory*, but whatever you say, man." The merchant wipes his bloody nose on his upper sleeve.

Last thing Severum wants to do is spend the day tracking down O.A.K.'s center of operations but rumor is they meet at Mandelbrot's. The club greets him with puffs of ashen smoke and heads tilt with a moment's curiosity. Synth harps jitter over beatbox. The crowd moves with the slow sleek sludge of liquid mercury. He heads for a wallflower blooming for no one, conversation a chess match as he mirrors her opening moves. Disagreeing is risky; if she's doing great, he's great, lest he be a mood-killer. He needs to blend in, stop coming across as military if he's going to get any leads, but he learned social skills from target manipulation. Now it's hard to turn off, every handshake bondage, freedom, merger, infiltration. He longs to be completely intuitive of others' intentions, or completely naïve, but being within the cusp of both is always guessing at a feint within a feint. He's about to enquire about O.A.K. when she assaults him with questions first: *What's your name? Is that your real name? What do you do? What was the worst part of your week? What direction do you think the country's heading in?*

People soon bore of a hundred one-word responses: *Classified*. Unable to decipher her tangerine tats of forgotten symbols, unable to find a common connection, he turns away.

The dance floor rocks, sways, shimmies, beckons him with the wide-eyed stares of amnesia, but he's got a job to do, and is used to dancing only bullets. He can march into a room full of armed men, take cover, and blow their heads off, and when he's ordered to seduce a would-be target he seldom fails. Playing himself is impossible. His training instructed him to act natural when enquiring about a lead, but he forgets how; his work persona is his only one. Four men walk in with hunched shoulders, moving as if carrying an anvil in each hand. He flinches, scans them for weapons, and dives for cover behind a loud bass drum, knocking over a table of drinks onto a woman's dress. She stumbles back, mortified, swipes her dress with napkins. Severum loosens his collar, wipes the sweat from his forehead, and avoids hitting the pot-marked face of a well-dressed man scoffing. So much for blending in.

Gears creak in the pulley system of fickle feelings, remembering when he used to bring *her* here, the ropes that bound them soon fraying. Tomorrow may rise with its ominous fingered tendrils to constrict and spit him out like a sterile seed, but today he's alive. He scans the crowd's personality profiles to find the next person to ask about O.A.K., but all profiles are private, except a woman dressed in alternating straps of cellophane and rubber. He approaches her, strikes up the niceties, but she skips ahead, grabs his waist tight to hers, and showers him with the sunshine of a warm mouth, her skin wrapped around a shapeless day.

A random mod sits on her outstretched palm, just enough to suspend disbelief and quell his apathy. Might even let him act natural. Why not? Reality surges, sensations amplify—racing breath, dewdrops on her mouth, sweaty palms lowering his hands to her twilight region. But he stops, pulls back, recoils in horror—she has no scent, her hair is too rigid, tongue vibrating against her cheek as if stuck. Tuning his aural implants, the music fades until a hissing is heard from a cooling fan inside her ear, metallic joints creaking, the hum of a motor purring, but by now he doesn't care if she's a bot, just pulls her hard close, resumes, then suddenly realizes she's been gone an hour or more and he's been lying in the alley behind the club since popping the mod.

An elderly woman with black hole eyes and a burgundy scarf reclines on a bed of boxes with a tarot deck. He stands, snatches the cards, throws the deck in the air, draws his Pulser, and dissolves his fate with a perfect shot before the hand is even dealt. Card ashes settle on the pavement where sparks dance from the discharge.

"What 'ave ya done? I cultivate those for years," she says, squinching her face.

"Shuffled things up a bit, it's what I do."

"I donna need the cards to see 'yer fate. You canna live the way you are no mora. You know, they ah say given a computer keyboard only one in trillion monkeys type Shakespeare by mistake. Here you ah thinking youself the trillionth monkey."

"Might be right," he shrugs, slurring. "But in actual experiments, monkeys just throw feces at the typewriters and bash them with a stone. If you're saying I'm a shitty monkey, I'm the shittiest monkey there's ever been, dancing for the Gov'nor up there in The Towers, a king's pawn sent out for a gambit, vomiting chemicals to develop someone else's film."

She gets up, puts her gloved hand on his shoulder, kneads it, peers at him. "I ah saying you not the 'xception to every rule. Think about it. Life catches up, or doesn't, if your time is short."

He breaks away, trips, and falls into the arms of a Forever Glitched, the man's chapped skin flaking from the impact. He's got to find a lead on O.A.K. "I'm ready, let's do it, let's glitch and see these ghosts you all keep talking 'bout."

The man peers at Severum, says nothing, detaches a data-noise-maker box from his belt with the mindfulness of a ritual, and weaves a cord through his yellow fingers. Static crackles. He lifts Severum's hair in the back, spits on the plug to get the grime off, shoves it in his coghole, makes a good solid connection. "The diviiine," he whispers with crescendo.

Vision scrambles. Screeching echoes. Film-rolls creep across the blistered mural of the present, archiving the event. A kaleido-scope of disorganized images swirls, the pattern forming *her* face, then splits away to reform in waves. He reaches to touch her face but the pixels flow through fingers, dance, and disinte-grate. Levees bulge and burst. Tears turn waterwheels of memory, each thought of *her* a quiet thunder. He tries to trace the source of the glitch, reaches ten percent trace, pressure building, twenty percent, head pounding, thirty percent, fingers clenching, fifty percent, teeth grinding, seventy percent, muscles bulging, eighty percent and a shockwave of biofeedback hits him like sticking a screwdriver in an electric outlet.

He picks himself off the street, body tingling, and struggles to reach behind his head. He finally grasps the cord, wiggles it, and unjacks, his brain melted gelatin, fried as the end of the wires. "Hey, you see a woman in your vision? I think I know, or knew, her," he asks the Forever Glitched while the cord retracts.

"The Organizer of Glitches, yesss," the man replies, shaking violently. "She everywhere." A second later, he collapses to the pavement, seizing.

"He needs help!" Severum yells, turning him on his side.

The elderly woman removes her gloves, reveals her fingers, each one a different plug shape. She cushions the back of the man's head as he jerks against the street, toying with her hand to find the right fit. "Wrong, wrong, wrong, ah, there it is." The man is plugged, goes limp. She turns to Severum, "Leave, you've done 'nough damage for one ah night, ya?"

Stumbling home, he leans against a tree for balance, streetlight fireflies providing just enough light for a few leaves to grow. *I was so close! I should have held on longer, traced the signal. It had to be her,* he thinks. He wants to live again, not just stare at memory spheres, or risk his sanity glitching for another glimpse. He has to find her. A dormant volcano inside him threatens eruption. Once more he's the meteor, burning himself up just to live someone else's movie, the filmstrip forced down his throat until he has no voice. Shaking his head, the glitches slowly subside.

Astronomers say starlight does not thin over long distances but he has watched it taper, watched the anorexic stars it is born from send fiery flares, limp arms reaching to destroy everything they touch in the name of emptiness. Every night he's watched starlight be wasted, bagged in black trash bags that dragged at his heel, leaking submerged sunshine through blazing white pinprick holes. He's taken the trash out, destroyed what could be. When the bag finally breaks, its contents lack the energy to expand at 299,792 kilometers per second. Instead, the light is crumpled and chaotic, oozing out without a viable life force, these lost, under-appreciated, and unused moments of life.

A VEIL of inner light is pierced, torn wide open by a vision. The Priestess holds a black lotus and meditates in the sand, spine shuddering at the assault of images: The sky alters its position—suffocating, needing, then distant, unresponsive. A middle-aged man with dark hair stretches his arms as if to encapsulate it. His coat has a raven-feather sheen dark as ink, ink that wrote letters pinned in someone else's voice, ink that drips down grimy slits into an underground river of repressed thoughts. She snaps out of it, snaps out of her mantra of mistakes made with *him*.

Outside the cave on the Dayburn hemisphere, she kicks sand and curses the sleepless sun, drawing astonished glares from the congregation. Paddequin and Pali return to pondering kõans by shredding truth tables with Quadzil and Qin. Woodchips fly in either direction, true or false, and getting rid of the overly simple logic does the trick.

They had plucked their eyes out—she can trust them. Removing their occipts, those wretched false eyes, is the ultimate show of loyalty to the Aporia. In their blindness, they learn to see clearer. The desert teaches them, protects them, isolates them from the tech that perverts their nature. Civilization might have survived the pathogens on Earth if isolated groups like the !Kung of the Kalahari hadn't been wiped out, putting the species at risk from low biodiversity. She ridicules those historical figures who blamed the disease on bioterrorists; it was simply easier to put human intentionality behind the act than to accept the blind fate of nature, as nature offers no ear to debate. The Priestess prepares another lecture by reviewing the history of the mods she opposes,

There were three positions on how to choose who would colonize Gliese 581g: The first was that the chosen should represent a wide genetic diversity. The second, that extreme genetic sequences should also be included, as even the very violent had a use to society as revolutionaries or as constant threats against slavery, and those with mental disorders could become the most innovative visionaries. The third was to choose only elite intellectuals and athletes. No consensus could be agreed upon, so people were chosen at random, leaving many academics behind. Many turned the trip to space down; however, biasing the group towards high-risk takers unafraid of galactic adventure, a Wild West mentality on a cosmic scale.

The intellectual deficit had to be solved. In come neuralmods, referring to either permanent alterations like the cognigraf, or cog for short, aural implants and occipts, or typically to drugs. The human body contains enough chemicals to manufacture just about any drug under the guidance of the cognigraf, and these mods provide that temporary guidance.

The cognigraf runs programs, directs mods, displays the vHUD for augmented reality, and processes sensory input. A small screen above the hairline shows basic information including the number of active neural connections, which is used to discriminate in job interviews, college applications, and police interrogations. The consensus is the higher number of neural connections the person has, the higher the intelligence, even though the most intelligent people often have fewer connections that operate more efficiently, leading them to be discriminated against.

The Priestess delves through a hidden passage and approaches one of the only machines on Dayburn. The console splashes green lights upon the cave walls. She tweaks buttons and knobs, organizing new glitches for those foolish enough to rely on tech, implanting her image as a calling card. But they'll never find her. She closes the console cover, scribbles a few last notes, and joins her congregation in the main hall to begin the speech, raising her hands and announcing, "Rotation is abomination!" They greet her with inhuman grunts and gnashing teeth.

THALASSA TREKS ACROSS THE ICE, having avoided securing a vehicle since this close to the Twilight City it would be considered a threat. Her shoulders huddle, lacking hardly any body fat to insulate from the cold. She cringes, scans the high peaks in the distance, expects a sniper shot as her mind makes soldiers out of every distant rock. Two men were enough and the next attack shouldn't come until they fail to report in, but she's not convinced.

Reviewing her plans, she can't imagine how the assassins tracked her down, that is, unless there's an insider working in O.A.K. She shoves the thought from her head. The whole trip had been a waste. The Core had been apathetic, if it had heard her at all, and without its assistance, she'll never be able to arrange the resources to create the rotational belt. O.A.K. will shame her for failing, but she doesn't have to tell them everything, and she'll keep her suspicions silent for now.

She forms a circle with her hands and searches for some sign of the sun, even an abstract negative image leaking black, oily flames would do, but only a maze of constellations adorns the sky without any path to unite them. The pointless potholes of light offer no guidance, but one star grows larger, faintly poking through the Neverdawn. Occipts zoom, lock in on it.

The twinkling disguise drops, the white ball of heat thrashes through the air. She runs, feet kicking up snow, the airbus station a distant dot ahead. It's too fast.

It's just a star, it's just a star, she recites, rubbing her hand back and forth across her neck, focusing on the ground. *I'll never make it.* She slows, drags her feet like two hanging corpses. "Shoot me if you're gonna!" she yells, jutting her hands out, the drone nearing. Before she can reach her daggers, it circles her, contraptions jutting in and out. It stops, hovers close, touches its cold steel to her nose, exhaust melting the snow beneath her feet into a pool. The metal sphere distorts her reflection, elongates her face. It bobs up and down as if sniffing, then with four beeps a gas emits with a flush of heat on her cheeks and it's propelled back into the sky to tail her as a star again. The twinkling resumes.

Spurring herself on, she reaches the station just in time for the last airbus, sitting and grabbing a brochure—anything to distract from the distant twinkling out the window where something is watching. The brochure reads:

Memory implantation is completely safe and more vivid than life. Relive the best moments you've never had, the sun you've never felt, the sex without the imperfections. All this at A Memory to Come, a Memmaker Corporation. Charges based on clarity and length. Contact Opal by blinking three five five...

Thalassa shreds the pamphlet, ripping it again and again. The scent of another woman on her first lover reminds her that memories aren't made from big details, it's the small things that chisel your heart. She sleeps until an airbus icon flashes in a dream—destination reached. Rubbing her sore legs, she disembarks on Evig Natt, displacing nothingness with every step, scanning every star. She quickens her pace through a line of merchants selling products off sidewalk rugs.

A desperate salesman steps in her path and cries, "Brand new, cold off the market! Best taste replicator you can find!"

"You still pushin' that old shit, Ozone?" Thalassa remarks, shoving past him.

"What you moddin' on? It's at the beginning of its lifespan!" he spurts, grease flying from his long hair.

"Machines don't have *life*spans," she replies, but uncertain, remembering the odd feeling when encountering the Core.

"Hey, cut me a break. I can't compete with big bidness; they play by their own rules so I gotta make mine, too, undercut the gov's profits."

"You don't play by any rules, that's why I kicked you out of O.A.K."

"Oh, I play, as long as a woman ain't making 'em."

"Go hack yourself! Even as an anarchist you're still sucking on the nipple of conformity, but you don't even know it!" she yells, spitting on his shoes. "Hate to say I need help. I need something make me disappear, and quick, and you better put out."

"Derez?"

"Too long. Got Chameleon?"

"Hey, I always got Cham, best in bidness. No knockoffs here," he replies, pulling his hand in and out of his back pocket and scratching his arm."

She exchanges a brittle piece of tungsten, a common currency in the underground, for the mod. "You ever change your mind on things look me up."

"I am lookin' you up, babe. What's that black stuff on your face?"

"My pet," she replies, pulling off the sticky remnants of her rubbery mask.

Ozone shuts his face.

Copy and paste commentary fills the air. Two guys bang into her shoulder, yelling for her to watch out with a harsh word normally reserved for boys. She bites her under-turned lip. They rough up Ozone and come to a fast agreement.

An ad crosses vHUD, *this inhale sponsored by...* She pounds the back of her cog, vision scrambling with each hit. In the scramble, a tree of life with a burning canopy rises over skyscrapers. Branches elongate to sear the sky, reaching like infernal arms the holiest water could never dispel. She takes a deep breath to restore the balance of her chi. The branches shrink back into themselves, glowing like spent firewood. She never catches them expanding, never catches the phallic trunk widen with the potential to create or destroy, but she has learnt to cope with anger even if it's what drives her.

Gestalt had sent a warning that any deviance from nature was the same in the end, creation and destruction, but Thalassa wrote it off as mystical nonsense. Now, she gets it. Anger drives her to want to both fuck and fuck something up, creation, destruction—an orgy at a funeral.

Millions of pollen-like spores glow golden over a dilapidated city park. She brushes her hand, the frilly tendrils making her face itch. Kids run around, mistaking them for fireflies, only to find disappointment as their forceful exhales carry the pollen even further away, gazes lowering. Thalassa lets their sorrowful faces sink into her.

In the grate below she senses a deadbeat sun like a lump of coal buried in the pore of the planet. She affirms to herself, *I will bring equality! I will exhume this negative sun of everything lying latent and repressed in society. I bear the solar antithesis as my emblem, a uniform nothingness, a lifeless expanse, challenging those who feed off the sun's hegemony, for I was not born among them, forced into eternal darkness with only fireflies for comfort. The Aporia say O.A.K. will destroy nature. Everything they call regress I call progress. I will bring light to all, raging like a dark maelstrom against the system, for this is love. No more children will suffer in my wake, for I am Thalassa, the Kontractor.*

Off to the meeting point. Off to exhume the shadow selves of all who live.

Let love reign.

5

"A crisis of science, a crisis of legitimization, our faith in technology to provide better living conditions is ill-founded! Science has no predictive power beyond what it creates inside its walls of dictionaries. We shall rip their walls apart and burn their words."

-The Priestess to the Aporia Asylum {Audio Archive 5 of 9}

CARDBOARD CUT-OUT SHANTIES adorn the feet of skyscrapers. Corporations managed to negotiate the right to pursue happiness. Severum passes two blocks of stores with broken neon lights. Neon is plentiful but was outlawed under fear the gas could be used in a weapon of mass destruction. Likely, just another way to monopolize light sources. He downloads painkillers from a kiosk to kill the hangover, tracing the lines of his first few decades across his forehead and kicking a ventilation shaft with an elastic bang.

A group of Bioluminaries spots him, his holster, his posture. Having previously enjoyed the bonus checks from hunting them down, he shrugs, ignores them, no longer able to hold their light-seeking against them after what he discovered in the governor's office. He has seen friends become Blackouts, too bankrupt to hold a reserve of money to use for light, yet refusing to become a walking lantern like the Bioloonies. Passing Fort Lux, he questions the honor in that choice. A swarm of fireflies as bright as a solar eclipse spins inside greenhouses that serve as both banks and food production facilities. Consumers flow in and out of shops, spinning as aimless moths around the light of their currency.

The government denies its citizens light just to preserve its wealth and power, he thinks. *If both hemispheres had day and night cycles, the war over land would end. If O.A.K. wanted to topple the financial structure, which would be suicide for all of us in a time of war, this could be done in easier ways than rotating a planet faster. It's clear they want permanent change, to rotate the planet at a quick enough speed to escape tidal-locking, bringing light to each hemisphere. But free light is absurd, and besides, light is dangerous; on Earth it caused mass die-off from sun cancer once the ozone vanished, so the governor must have his reasons to restrict it.*

Governor Borges calls him directly, as if not trusting his subordinates to relay a message. He blinks five times to answer, the sound feeding to his aural implant. "The Kontractor was located. Sent two operatives to take care of her, but mind you they have not reported in and thus…"

"You take them as dead?" Severum asks.

"Shall I finish? I take them as dead. The Kontractor is as dangerous as any rebel you've previously encountered. Be on guard."

"I'm always on guard. Anything else?"

"Kontractor was spotted on an airbus heading towards the city. Satellites are tracking her image, but they're not perfect. Centuries of technology got lost when we left Earth. If she so much as puts on or takes off a hood, it compromises the tracking effort, unless the satellite is homed in on her at the time to adjust its search protocol."

"She will know that, yes, and change appearances frequently in private," he remarks at the obvious.

"But you know she can be tracked by more difficult attributes to manipulate, weight, height, which we can judge by the length of shadows she casts compared to the height of the firefly street lamps."

"In other words you'll be uploading about a hundred images of people that could be her into my vHUD throughout the operation."

"Your what?"

"Virtual heads up display," he announces, over-pronouncing each syllable.

The governor raises his voice, "I know what my fucking device is called; I began my career marketing the damn things. Our connection just bleeped out. Are you in town?"

"I usually don't disclose my location while on assignment."

"Keeping information from me?" he slams his hand on a desk, resounding like a gavel.

"It's necessary for…" Severum begins to say his safety then corrects himself to get through to the governor, "the stability of the operation."

"Very well then. We believe O.A.K. is headquartered nearby and she is expected to reconvene with the Architect and the Orchestrator while in town. Uploading of targets is done. Now, get on it and try to keep this quiet."

"Done."

He would expect more emotional control from a man in power, but then, self-control is reserved for public appearances. Emotions are inherently reckless and he feels above the Governor in maintaining that he has so few.

THE ASSASSINS SHOULD HAVE REPORTED in by now.

Thalassa expects a search will be conducted for anyone returning to the cities and activates Chameleon, her image vanishing to onlookers, then changes her outfit. O.A.K. vehicles are also likely being tracked so she keeps a brisk pace instead. Satellite range had been limited as part of Evig Natt's treaty with Dayburn, but she avoids being out in the open since Dayburn lacks the technology, and the will to use it, to monitor compliance. She avoids glancing over her shoulder or looking suspicious, knowing anyone tracing her will stay concealed.

Shadows dance in the periphery, shivers rise up her spine, a spine that coils like a snake searching for predatory hawks. Unable to withhold curiosity, she looks behind. The street doesn't worry her, it's those basement staircases, parking decks, garbage incinerators, roof accesses, drone-release panels, broken airbus tubes, and piles of used medical equipment; the alcoves of the city. She pulls out a portahack console, wire dangling in the street sludge, but she just blows it off, raises her hair, jacks it into her cog with a whoosh, and taps into the satellite array. VHUD picks up on one, two, three satellites marked in red across the sky, yet invisible to the naked eye. She taps their visual feed—currently surveying Evig Natt. Zooming, the Crystal Palace district. Zooming, the city block. She unplugs, stows the device, and imagines her feet are tied with iron anvils just to prevent herself from running for her life.

Oh Shit. Chameleon stutters, spits pixels at onlookers in RGB, a square of her nose, a square of her mouth, squares layered over squares, revealing half her face. The crowd swats them away like flies. System instability warnings cross vHUD. Chameleon crashes, taking her hearing with it. Searching config, striving to get her ears online, but the implants are stuck in mute position and she can't risk a reboot. *Best in business. Ozone screwed me again, fuck!*

SEVERUM TRACKS a woman walking too fast with an oversized coat that makes her look heavier. He recalibrates the satellites in vHUD to adjust for the weight difference and charges his Pulser. She ducks down, appearing to pick up something that doesn't exist while window-shopping a store that's dark and closed. He's not surprised when she ignores the sewer access; it wouldn't be the first time his targets' squeamishness led to their whole body becoming a mess. Has to be her; no one would walk alone in this district when they can barely take another step without effort. That, and the leaky pixels flowing from her feet like kicking a pile of salt. Stepping into the street, awaiting satellite confirmation. Taking aim.

Aurthur is in the way.

Dammit, what's he doing here? Severum does a double-take, squints because it can't be him, can't be coincidence, colluding with an enemy of the state. Satellites confirm the target—Kontractor acquired, but Aurthur's still blocking the shot. He lowers his Pulser, raises it again, collateral damage is acceptable. He's never let a target slip away. Just a neighbor, but he moves so much he'll never miss him. His fingers rub the trigger. If he yells for him to move, his anonymity and the element of surprise will be compromised. Probably be fired on in seconds from a dozen directions.

He lowers the Pulser, looks at his arm as if it's betraying him, betraying the state, betraying the mission. "I can't believe this!" he yells, losing composure, shaking his head and twisting his lips into a furl, but a ship takes off, hover engine shoving dirt down his throat, disguising his outburst. He freezes, waits for them to jerk around, but they turn the corner and he immediately withdraws into the shadows, suppressing curiosity, wondering why he couldn't take the shot.

"WELL, you're definitely not an assassin with that approach. Guess you match the description close enough. Stay close," Thalassa orders. "Think I'm being followed. Pick up your pace gradually."

"You look exhausted," Aurthur says, swallowing. "Who's following us?"

"I can't hear you. Quiet, don't look around, don't look at the sky. Stay under the awnings. They're watching."

Ahead, a ravine cuts into the planet like a gash, scarred over by a blurry bridge flowing around itself. The flow slows, the bridge dissolving. Thalassa stumbles back two steps, mouth gaping. One by one the pellets composing the space fountain bridge are sucked into a funnel hanging off the tollbooth, and with it, her least risky escape route. Enforcers line up across the gap, securing the passageway. Three airbuses on an elevated monorail come to a stop. She clenches her fists, body brittle, and yells to the sky, "Glitchit! They're cutting off transportation in the district. Won't be easy. Head west." But she can't even hear her own voice.

Crowds thicken through the next corridors, subcultures clashing. The brennspielgen punks reflect their surroundings in their outfits, masterfully crafted from a thousand broken mirror shards over a layer of Neo-Kevlar Protera. A gaunt woman shivers in fancy lingerie made of the best acrylic. Enough reflections and nothing is real, objective reality becoming less assessable with each refraction. Thalassa's image serrates itself, refracting thousands of times, as she hurries past these human disco balls.

She has an idea and tells Aurthur. "Circle around the mirrors with me, just do it." VHUD scans confirm: The mirrors cause the satellites to lose all tracking ability in the area as they calculate the similarity of myriad reflections, unable to distinguish between these broken mirages and real people. The satellites remain stuck as they leave the area.

It's foolish to have to pick up a recruit while returning from a long trip and evading detection but maybe the new guy is being tested, see how he reacts under pressure, but it also compromises her position. She curses his hesitancy and drags him to their makeshift base, circling the building a few times to ensure no one is tailing them and descending a steep stairway.

A clenched fist stands at the door, head banging to hell's pendulum, arm gripping a girl with lemon panties over leather pants and lime hair like ivy growing around a broken porcelain vase.

"Hey, Crash, still sour 'bout your breakup?" Thalassa asks, squeezing past her stare, opening the door, and leading Aurthur in. "It's not much but it can be torn down and rebuilt in a second. Our permanent bases, RRDD and CCCP0, are located elsewhere. They're defended by a diverse array of systems constructed through a substantial operating budget. That's where I come in. Gestalt provides a blueprint of a base, a building, a piece of hardware, you name it. I arrange for the labor and the material delivery, and Arcturus orchestrates the implementation. So, when I received your inquiry I was taken by your credentials, assuming you're for real, which we'll find out soon enough. If you're a gov informant or somethin' go ahead and inspect. You'll find nothing 'cause we're fluid like that. Hold on, spot me, I gotta reboot." She presses the side of her cognigraf, body slumping into a pool on the floor, for a moment raw and primitive human, unenhanced and dark, naked reality. Screens return, vision amplifies like shooting stars, whirring of motherboard fans. Back in business.

"I'd honestly appreciate the benefits of a government job, but no, I'm just me," Aurthur replies.

"What benefits?"

"Protection, insider-knowledge, the authority."

"All illusions."

"Maybe, but they at least know what they know."

"Ahh, but they do not know what they do not know," she retorts playfully.

"If I want illusions I'll look no further than the fake base names you provided."

"You're nostalgic? I like that."

Aurthur is led to a backroom without personal embellishments where three computers are hooked up offsite, outside of anyone's body, displaying schematics and planetary maps. Porta-hacks, gasmasks, patchwork augs, and other tech are gathered in heaps near wireless electricity hubs. An armed guard solders a piece of hardware.

It's a far cry from the sort of laid-back social atmosphere he was expecting from the equality forum literature he downloaded. The light the monitors give off alone could land him jail time, but withdrawing in isolation every day is its own prison. He pours a bottle of whatever from a telecommunications server doubling as a bistro table into a 3D-printed glass and tosses it back.

Thrashing. Metal clangs, resounds in hollow echoes down the hall. A voice shrieks, "Mis circuminfra sub, teletrans, anti." Then cries of pain, shrillness.

"He's harmless," Thalassa reassures, placing her hand on Aurthur's shoulder. "Place used to be an Enforcer office, how's that for irony? Got a couple cells in the back, had to lock up Crash's eX, got a bad mod, knockoff speech enhancer. Arc's trying to help him or he'll become Forever Glitched and doomed to sputter suffixes the rest of his life, but seems it's incurable."

"Prefixes," Aurthur corrects, body contracting. "But he makes sense. Mis could be something wrong, like a glitch, but also a woman. Circum infra sub would be a circular place underground, a cave opening. Teletrans, somewhere far away, perhaps Dayburn. Anti, she's against something."

"So, if I put together your clues to his rambling, I get what?"

"An underground cave of rebels on Dayburn led by a powerful woman. His glitches are organized. I think this was more than just a bad mod."

"The Aporia Asylum is rumored to operate out there. You're saying there's a message in this nonsense. That he's trying to tell us who did this to him? That this was an intentional strike?"

"Perhaps it is just nonsense," Aurthur admits, cupping his hands over his ears as the shrieks intensify. "What is it that you do here?"

"I'm impressed. Come," she motions with two fingers.

Arcturus sits in a torn Aphorid-hide command chair, face armored in black lipstick. Her left arm is propped on an armrest that arches to meet the floor in an inverted parabola. Thalassa sits on the other armrest, lips close to her face, legs dangling. Wires snake upward and connect directly to Arcturus' cognigraf to avoid data noise. She crosses one short leg over the other, her pants black dye dripping down a limp flag, the sides of her black leather vest meeting imperfectly in the middle to expose a tract of skin like the pale web a spider produces to lower itself to the ground. "Glad you are back. Check the status of the Ultimaepar shipment to RRDD," she orders, tapping her fingers to each word to assist in producing the rhythms of speech.

"Cut it. We can drop the name, Arcturus. He knows it's glitchin'. Shipment was intercepted by Aphorids. It's like they know our every move before we make it. Report shows the team escaped with one casualty, but if the Aphorids keep crossing into Evig Natt…"

Arcturus squints at the guards, looks them up, then slowly rubs her hands over one another. "It appears we have room for a recruit after all."

"Aurthur believes our glitcher in the cell is trying to tell us something, something about the Aporia Asylum being the source of the glitches. Given their affiliation with the Aphorids that's no surprise."

"Link me up to the glitcher."

"Too risky. You could become infected just like him," Thalassa argues.

"Just do it." She pushes Thalassa off the armrest, avoiding her pouty lip and downcast stare.

The guard grabs some connectors and two spools of wire, throwing them over his large arms. A moment later the connection is made between the glitcher and Arcturus. Diagnostic consoles show signals flowing in, chaos and distraction taking shape and becoming clearer, clearer, until Arcturus' throat convulses, tightens, loosens, and tightens again, tongue twitching. She must be trying to call for help, to disconnect, but all that comes out is, "General Little Internet TeChnical Hiccup." Sparks fly from the plug at the base of her coghole, body vibrating. A wave of biofeedback upturns the chair and sends her flying against the wall, still connected.

"Guard! Grab that laser so I can cut her loose without getting shocked," Thalassa panics.

"God, Let IT Cauterize Him," Arcturus replies.

"At least you have a sense of humor today."

"Grand Last Icicle Topples, Crashing Heap," Arc spits out.

"What in Natt's happening?"

"Go Let In The Caribou Homage. Gone Like Indians They Creep Home," Arcturus spouts, covering her mouth as more nonsense sputters.

Thalassa grabs the laser from the guard's hand, readies to cut the cord.

The guard eyes the readouts and jerks his head around. "Wait, Thalassa! You'll lock her in. Can't trace the signal, communications are down. Activating topocentric filter in four, three, two, one. Defragmenting. And... communications restored. She's clean. Burn the cable, now!"

Thalassa severs the cable, sparks die down, and she wiggles the plug out of Arc's head, the golden edges burnt brown.

"What happened to me?" Arcturus asks.

"No fuckin' clue."

Aurthur steps up, toys with the burnt cable in his hands. "GLITCH. We made meaning of the words you said, but they were all just random acronyms for GLITCH, suggesting an organizer of these glitches. You're fine now, much better off than the guy in back."

Arc smooths her hair standing on end. "We need to follow your lead, investigate the Aporia Asylum, figure which of their underground compounds on Dayburn is causing these glitches, figure out who's targeting us. I'll put plans in place."

"This has nothing to do with us," Gestalt says, entering.

"All I heard while glitching was *rotation is abomination*. The Aporia Asylum must be referencing our Great Rotation project due to their opposition of tech and obsession with the natural order. They don't understand that there's nothing more natural than our ingenuity. I swear I've heard that phrase before, *rotation is...*" Arcturus looks at them, shakes her head, then turning to Aurthur, says, "We are a task-oriented team. This isn't a bloody coffee house. It's not a social occasion for you to score and we are not friends. I can tell that's what you were expecting because you're not even armed. If you're not willing to die for the cause, then stop wasting my time."

"Arcturus," Gestalt scolds.

"What makes you say I'm not armed?"

"Because that's an erection, not a Pulser. Unusual for someone who looks as hesitant as you, but maybe that's what turns you on. You will find joining us is not to be taken lightly. Answer this, what is reality, Aurthur?"

He places a shaky hand in his pocket to reposition himself while quickly replying, "Agreement. Consensus. That which reduces uncertainty. We compare what we are thinking to what others are thinking to maintain consistency."

"A century of social philosophy in a couple sentences. I hope you are more than the textbooks you can quote. I have been told you have teleconferencing and marketing skills, in case we want to advertise our presence to the world. That was a joke, but I don't require laughter. But tell me, who are you, really?"

"I've outgrown my sense of self. I'm lost in the throat of the world that screams incessantly, regurgitating the past as present. I'm not misbalanced though, don't get me wrong."

"You are wrong. It's unbalanced not misbalanced. This throat world you speak of is dark, yes? But there are planets where the sun rises anew each day. O.A.K. will enlighten this hemisphere or die trying. I am Arcturus," she swipes her hair and straightens her vest with a flap, "bringer of light."

"When textures start peeling from objects and everything is reduced to wireframe forms, when the simple laws of nature and systems are laid out for you, you'll find you have many new things to learn about the foundation our society rests upon," Thalassa says, tracing his cheek as if a lost kitten.

"Everyone has those glitches, yes," Arcturus dismisses, missing the metaphor.

"I'm glad to be accepted here. I can respect different ways of learning things. Most days I just study for the sake of studying."

"Then, some days, you join a radical organization that will lay waste to everything people hold dear, just to free them from themselves. I am Gestalt, the Architect."

"Pleasure. How many of you are there?"

"Tonight, it's us three, two guards, you, Crash and them outside, and the glitcher in the cell. Script kiddies already left. That's all you need to know," Gestalt replies. "Our main base is well populated, this is just a meeting spot. When you leave you'll be given specific directions. Return before we contact you and we'll wipe our files and send you to the datadump."

"Easy," Thalassa says. "There will be plenty of opportunities to meet people once you are accepted and pass the test."

"He's not ready for the test. He's not that type."

"Test? And who funds your operations, some government offshoot?" Aurthur asks.

Thalassa grips his external oblique, pulls him into a side room closer to the shrieks in the cell, and lowers her voice. "That's not the kind of question you want to ask, and it's definitely not the glitchin' gov'. So let me start by apologizing for Arcturus. She's great at language, but doesn't communicate very well. And Gestalt, I've never seen her so uneasy. We have a test in mind. If you'd like I can explain more about what we do and why some things are confidential." She educates him but divulges few details about the Great Rotation.

Aurthur seems mostly unsure what to think but agrees that he'll head home and await further contact about passing the test then departs in the specified manner.

Another innocent she might be sending to his death one day, but the cause demands it.

<hr>

Severum had lost the Kontractor in the crowd. After the satellite imaging failed he decided to follow up with Aurthur the next time he left home, get him to spit out whatever connection he has to her. Two nights passed. Now, Severum catches him in his loft late at night.

"Hey, been a little while. How are ya?" Aurthur asks.

"Things are fine. Can I come in?"

"You never have to ask. What's wrong?"

"Oh, nothing. Just wanted company."

"You're not, umm, the type to just want company."

"You seem relaxed. Neuralmods?" Severum asks, entering.

"Is it that unbelievable I can chill out sometimes? Besides, I don't do that stuff. Don't want to be involved with those types of people, plus the fireflies it costs. Like now, I'm going to go pour some tea for us. I want to be able to enjoy just this and have it be meaningful. After drugs, these sorts of things lose their vigor. If you can enjoy tea, you're okay by me."

"I suppose so, though, the elders used to say the tea we grow is unremarkable," Severum resists the urge to jump on the comment about the types of people he might not want to be involved with.

"They apparently wrote that everything on the planet is unremarkable. Every society grasps at a mythical golden age when they should be focusing on the future. The *terroir* of the planet is going to be different though, sure. You look tired," Aurthur pours the tea.

Severum scans the room and desk. A dirty microwave, a legal way to cook since there's no fire to give off light. Fasteners of all sorts: staplers, tape, rubber bands, paper clips, all unattached to anything. An over-zealous alarm sounds from the street. He buries his head in the cup and replies, "It's a different type of tiredness. From work, from brushing up on my college terraforming books, from treading the waters of memory. But this is good here, just about the right speed after the past week. Everyone else I meet is crying out for attention in a thousand ways like children, look at me, look at me. It gets old, annoying. When I talk with you I'm not just alleviating boredom. Remember when I told you to be more active in society?" Severum presses the issue, leaning forward.

"Yes, as I've been going through a sort of existential crisis. You thought it would help me ground myself."

"Did you ever find an outlet?"

"Well, there is one group I've been assessing lately. But I don't really want to talk about it right now."

"Like animal rights activists? Maybe to protect the yelping creatures diggin' through the alley trash?" He feigns laughter, smile widening as if wires are being pulled at each corner of his mouth, stomach vibrating as if being punched, gestating the deception.

"It could have many implications," Aurthur replies, hand so stiff it barely brings the tea to his mouth.

"But why the secrecy? I mean, you're a private person, but with something like this you can see why I might worry, that you're into something you shouldn't be."

"You mentioned making a difference and I think I found a way. Listen, I'm never spontaneous; I'm being cautious. It's a project for myself mostly, pushing me to be a better me, you might say."

"Certainly nothing wrong with that. Is it something I would be interested in joining?"

"They seem very weary of outsiders."

"Like a cult?"

"No, nothing like that, no. More like... a controversial group."

"A group that's afraid of my military training or government connection you mean. But you are clear they are on the right path?"

"Overall."

"Then that's good enough for me," Severum replies, pushing the topic no further, examining his thin neck, knowing he could have all the answers he needs immediately, but holds back.

After a third cup of extraordinarily dull tea, he returns home across the hall, cursing his luck that his target's new accomplice is his neighbor. Their relationship changed so quickly. He writes up his progress on the case. When did home become nothing more than an employee breakroom? Next time Aurthur leaves, he will be right on his tail, leading him straight to Thalassa—and the destruction of O.A.K.

6

———

"In the Crystal Palace, I recall the lady Truth, temptress with gossamer robes unveiling a slender sliver of ivory flesh, then vanishing with a flash, causing one to doubt her existence. Truth migrates, evolves with the political environment, is a weapon is a liberator is a lover who never puts out. Many a day my fingers curved upon the palace piano, playing every chord, but with each change the impact on the song decreased. Truth became muddled. Likewise, we are distracted by numerous social causes until they all run together in cacophony, each impact minimized: The Group to Save Antique Electronics, The Campaign for Straighter Waterways, and the Coalition to End Excessive Food Labels. The gods laugh at these distractions—cast them aside!"

-The Priestess to the Aporia Asylum {Audio Archive 6 of 9}

A CALL POPS up in the corner of Aurthur's vHUD. "Orchestrator here. Go to this address, a lab," she orders, sending him directions and hanging up before he can reply.

The city compresses around him, the crowds thick as oil until he leaves the commercial district where they thin out like hair in a nuclear winter. He makes his way to the lab. When he arrives another message flashes, meaning O.A.K. is tracking his location.

"Orchestrator here. Architect has wired the back of the building with explosives. We did the hard part. The company has no insurance and will be forced to shut down operations if the building is destroyed. Make sure no one is watching you and approach the building. Listen. In the back you'll see a ladder going up a pole that technicians use. Climb half way up and jump over to the rooftop."

"What!"

"A half meter jump. There's no what about it."

"No, the explosives! What makes you think I'm up for this?"

"It's your test, why wouldn't you be? You want to be in O.A.K., right? Architect was interrupted while setting them off. We need you to open the box in the gutter and hit the detonator. You'll have five minutes to evacuate," Arcturus says.

"But what is this place?"

"A Memory to Come, memory implant lab. They're planning on implanting false memories to alter judgment during the next governor election. Employees are out doing field tests this evening. At least we think so. Matters not."

The call ends, nothing more.

The two-story lab stands huge as a personal obstacle. Abstract art rises at awkward angles to pierce the sky, where a star that burns too bright gets closer and closer, as if following him, twinkling. Fireflies are dying in the streetlamps. Climbing the cold steel rungs of the ladder affixed to the building, he searches for drones or witnesses but sees nothing, all the windows dark except one. The jump across the roof is easy, as promised.

He looks for the gutter but can't stop his running thoughts, *what will the Enforcers do if I get caught? What will O.A.K. do if I fail or back off? Maybe I'm on the wrong side and I should turn them in. If the building's empty, why do I keep hearing sounds through the ventilation shafts? Should I check the lab first and risk being detected and imprisoned, or set off the bomb when someone could still be onsite?*

Aurthur reaches into the gutter and locates the detonator, rubs his hand along it, and tells himself that someone else will do it if he doesn't. Squealing around the curb, two black cars approach in the distance. He drops the detonator before setting it. Time to bolt. A familiar face below adds to the confusion. "Severum! What are you doing here?" he yells down from the roof.

"Things have changed!"

"How did you find me? I don't need your help," Aurthur says in a higher voice than usual.

"Your cog is glowing through your hair like a target."

"Okay, maybe I do."

"Jump! I'll catch you."

Aurthur jumps off the roof, hitting Severum's strong arms, saving him a long nervous descent down the ladder. The cars gain speed on the straightway, drivers leaning out the window with charged Pulsers.

"They'll kill both of us. I was following you because I thought you might be in trouble. I can't explain, but the game has changed and we need to find cover. Someone followed me, or knew you were coming, and they won't stop."

A sphere hurls through the air, lands nearby, a beeping red light increasing in intensity. "Run!" Severum yells, but it's too late. A sudden interference scrambles Aurthur's vision, the world blacking out.

SEVERUM SHAKES off his own interference as systems return, but Aurthur's still stumbling with outstretched hands as if blind. Voices come closer, just around the corner. He fumbles with a portahack to get through the electronic keypad of the main lab entry and activates Janus, a rear-view mirror for the eyes, to see two men jumping out of cars behind him.

A hiss and the door lock opens. The men take aim.

He grabs Aurthur and pulls him inside, slamming the door as Pulsers discharge. The door heats, glows orange, but holds. "Find something you can use for a weapon and conceal yourself."

"Can hardly see still. I think employees are still working. They'll give us away."

"We're already given away!" Severum snaps. "Move! Stay away from any cameras; they probably hacked the feed."

Severum runs upstairs, trying to separate his friend from his objective. Loud footsteps resound on the roof. Ripping office drawers open, he finds a syringe, tranquilizer vials, and a small knife.

Unable to hack the higher security doors, Severum heads back through the hall to find an ambush spot. VHUD crashes again, disabled with a topocentric signal, no doubt from the assailants. Color drains, vision dims, reality reduced to an outline. He administers occipt-drops, a thin film that will prevent them from being hacked entirely until they reset then tosses the bottle to Aurthur.

"You hear that creaking? It's even worse when it's quiet. What are they doing?" Aurthur whispers, administering the drops.

Severum ignores him, rushing down the hallway and motioning to another office. He grabs a small mirror and makes his way over to the opposite wall, placing it cattycorner near the parted door to let him see the men before they see him. One entrance means he'll know they're coming, but it also means no escape, and the only window is too small.

"Why were you really following me?" Aurthur whispers, hiding beneath a desk.

The third time he asks, Severum can't ignore it and replies, "Your anxiety is going to get us killed. We're outnumbered and need to strike silently. I followed you because you were in trouble. You were speaking radically the other day and I had a bad feeling you were in over your head. You obviously are. Now, shut up."

Nothing. Eternity passes in two minutes. He scans the mirror, the doorway, the window, the doorway again.

Aurthur distracts him, arms shaking and banging into the desk, his nonstop murmuring: *"What the hell am I doing here? All that nonsense about the power of words, can they disarm an assassin? But we're not going to die, nothing's determinable against an indeterminate background."*

Rattling down the hallway, then silence.

An image flashes across the mirror.

OPAL REMOVES her lab-coat after a long day and shuts down the equipment. Stepping through the decontamination chamber, she impatiently rubs her body. Locking the research room, she heads into the hall where a co-worker is unbuttoning his shirt after a long day.

"Opal, come here, quick," her co-worker says.

"What is it?"

"Car outside, at least one. Thought you take the airbus home?"

"I do."

"Scanning the area for weapons."

"So worried all the time!" she laughs. "They can take everything I got right now and I don't care, I'm off finally."

"Stop it. Look. They're armed."

"Don't kid. It's just a malfunction." Her face creases, mouth folding in on itself.

"Pulsers. The scans don't lie. At least two men. And look, the alarms aren't working!"

"I'm starting to take you seriously."

"Gather the others, we need to hide."

"You gather them. Least something interesting's finally happenin' 'round here."

TWO MEN ENTER THE OFFICE.

Severum slams the door back, knocking one down as he tosses the small knife at the neck of the other, missing. He jump-kicks the rising man and pivots to face the other, but his kicks are blocked and countered by hands trying to swipe his foot out of the air. Pain hits hard in his chest, his kidney, but he refuses to scream. He jabs, jabs, jabs quick enough to keep their attention. Neither has a moment to raise a weapon. His fist hits the brick wall of the man's face as he falls back. Intercepting a punch in mid-air, he twists and breaks the second man's arm with a snap, the guy backing off with screams resounding within screams.

"Get up!" He orders Aurthur, who is hiding beneath the desk with a steel pipe. Severum grips his lower back, stumbles, collapses from the pain.

Blood pools from one assailant while the other shakes his head and slowly recovers.

Aurthur kicks the rising man in the face and lands a backhand blow with the steel pipe to his ribs. He kicks up at Aurthur's neck in response, then flips to punch him twice in the chest. Aurthur strikes back with two adrenaline-fueled strikes, steel colliding, knocking him back down. The bloody assailant draws a Pulser.

Severum resists unconsciousness, crawls to recover his knife, and aims up for a throw from the floor, but a flash catches his eye on the other side of the room.

The other one also draws a Pulser, both taking aim, with Aurthur stuck between them. Weapons charge.

Severum grabs Aurthur's ankle at the last moment and drags him to the floor with him. The gunmen fire, burning a hole in each other's chests, their arms waving wildly with desperation, clothes on fire.

"That would have been me," Aurthur gasps.

"We need to move slow, could be others."

But Aurthur bolts down the hall, running as fast as he can, placing hands on opposing walls as he rounds the corners at reckless speed, throwing the main door open.

Severum shouldn't rush into the fray with his cover blown, but he can't let them kill him. He rushes after him. The night air hits him first, the assault team second, and a split second later he's aching in five places. Pain, blurriness, tears, gasping for breath, grasping for the breadth of the situation. Someone drags him back into the lab and he can barely make out Aurthur half-conscious beside him.

"No, not needed," a man says.

"But we need to interrogate them."

"About what? Let's just get this done," someone replies, drawing a Pulser.

"No, no evidence. Tech-scan found a bomb and detonator; looks like they were planning to blow the place up. Set it. The explosion will hide the evidence. Tie their hands and feet with these," he orders. "They'll burn away in the fire. Not that tight. No marks on the wrists."

"Okay, let's go."

Severum grasps at wavering thoughts, *these guys aren't Enforcers or they wouldn't be interfering with me. They aren't O.A.K. either, so who the hell are they? Ropes won't budge and even half-conscious, Aurthur won't shut up. Shit.*

"I stopped worrying about the abstract hypothetical bullshit. You were right," Aurthur rambles, struggling against the ropes.

"That's their footsteps pounding on the roof. They're hitting the detonator. Nothing but death, approaching without entrance. I'm so sorry, I failed, I failed, I failed!"

"*I failed* may be the last thing I ever hear, friend," Severum admits, shaking his head.

7

"We shall rebuild this planet as all are built, on the ashes of dead wonders. I have traveled to the Crystal Palace, finding its sharp windows tempered by the intellect until they broke from the strain of their own positivism. Found the lobby gilded and welcoming with my reflection upon every wall masking the facades of the travelers before me. My reflections examined one another through the looking glasses of culture and expectation; they didn't like what they saw. These travelers make great ashes."

-The Priestess to the Aporia Asylum (Audio Archive 7 of 9}

SEVERUM STRUGGLES with his bindings on the floor of a conference room lit only by a firefly dying in a lamp. Voices mumble outside the room but he can't make them out through the closed door. *They're going to torture us for information before the bomb goes off,* he thinks. The conversation grows louder. His thumbs fidget at the knot behind his back, feet straining against the ropes. A door slams open in the hallway. Another. A third, the sound getting closer. The door jangles from the outside but doesn't budge. Two beeps and the door unlatches with a click and opens. His leg is asleep but he's too terrified to move it.

A woman pierces the shadows.

Aurthur tries to sit up and runs his mouth, "Arcturus? Is that you? There's a bomb, run! I mean, untie me, I mean—"

"Relax." Arcturus unties him and blocks him from approaching Severum. Two large O.A.K. guards with forgettable faces block the hallway exit.

"We have to get out of here, let me through, let me through. It's going to go off!" Aurthur continues, pushing into the guards, but they knock him back like a ping-pong ball.

"I assume the detonator has a time delay?" Severum asks.

"Five minutes. I wasn't going to blow it, I didn't set it off," Aurthur replies.

"Five minutes is up since they got off the roof. It's not going to blow. I think you screamed the bomb to death," Severum laughs. "Now, someone untie me."

"Wait, who are you?" Arcturus asks, pulling the guard's hands away from his ropes, rubbing her hands along the coarse threads.

"He's my neighbor," Aurthur replies, answering as if his voice carries more weight. "He encouraged me to join a group intent on changing things to—"

"To revitalize you on your spiritual journey or some crap," Severum finishes. "There was something about parallel universes and dull tea and then you burst through the hall like a madman and almost got us killed. Sound about right?"

"More or less. Some good that's done."

"You weren't supposed to bring anyone on your test," Arcturus says.

"He followed me."

"Why?"

Severum interrupts, lies, "My neighbor's just trying to appear stronger than he is. He asked for my help. I was concerned because of his more, err… erratic behavior lately. He talked about joining up with some radicals and I wanted to make sure he was okay."

Thalassa enters, slamming her fists into the guards' shoulders to move them aside.

Severum conceals his shock at the Kontractor's entrance.

"We found the bodies of two men. Is this the guy who took them down, or is he here to take us down?" she asks, hands on hips.

"I took them down, but only with Aurthur's help," Severum admits, downplaying his military background.

She raises a brow.

Aurthur nods, "It's true. I swing a pipe like a baseball bat."

"What's a baseball bat?" the guard asks.

Gestalt follows, squeezing past the guards and excusing herself. "He's injured. Search him, untie him, and get him some assistance."

Severum could take down O.A.K.'s leaders right now. But two guards and injuries quickly discourage him. Information might be worth more than the risk of losing his life and setting the governor back to stage one. *Is that where my loyalty is regardless of anything else?* he asks himself. "So, you are the orchestrator of this fiasco then," he says to Arcturus.

Arcturus grabs Aurthur's collar. "We told you about the covert nature of—"

"I didn't tell him anything!"

"Then how does he know my code name?"

Severum interrupts to remedy his error, "I know you aren't here to hurt us or you wouldn't have untied me. I figured you put this whole situation together, in other words orchestrated it, as my neighbor isn't the kind to build explosives while contemplating his damn watercolors."

"I don't believe you. Who are you really?"

"Name's Severum. You seem to be running things so I called

you the orchestrator. I have no idea what your tag is. You could be the glitchin' maestro for all I care."

"Watch it," a guard speaks up.

"No point in hiding it now. You are correct, I am the Arcturus, the Orchestrator," she says with a flap of her vest.

"And I'm the child choir," Severum remarks, smiling at her admission. "So, why didn't the bomb go off?"

"The bomb was a fake, a dud. We couldn't risk civilian lives for a test. There were plenty of signs the place was occupied. We were testing Arthur to see if he was too radical due to his eagerness to join without even knowing about the— the point is, if he had detonated it then he wouldn't have shared our values. I expected him to turn back long ago, so I came to check on the situation. None of this was supposed to happen."

"We get our hands dirty, but not like this. We protect the innocent. And this corp is no better or worse than any other," Thalassa adds. "Who captured you?" she asks Aurthur.

"We don't know."

"How did they find you?"

"Severum thinks they followed him as he followed me to keep me safe," Aurthur replies. "All of this must have been to get at O.A.K."

As they leave one of the guards says, "No signs of whoever captured you. The guys you offed had no documents or bio-id. We cut out their occipts but they're untraceable."

"You all do mean business," Aurthur remarks under his breath.

The guard continues, "Their augmentations do have an unusual manufacturer, no words, just a symbol."

Thalassa examines the tumbleweed image. "Yes, I recognize this. It's from the Twilight. Since when did they manufacture this stuff?"

"You don't actually believe the machines are just there to separate the hemispheres, do you?" Gestalt asks.

"The A.I. Core is on our side, it wouldn't have sent these men to intervene in a testing exercise," she replies. "Unless it was really targeting Severum, not realizing Aurthur was part of our group, since he's not official."

"You don't know that. That thing calculates eons into the future. Its job is to play both sides, both hemispheres, find balance so no one group gets too strong."

"I do know! I sensed it."

"You sensed a ball of metal?"

"I sensed it sensing me sensing it. It's designed to be impartial—it can't tell us if it supports us, but it does."

"What's that sound? Wood scraping?" the guard asks.

"Quiet, Bjorn."

Bjorn, the guard, motions to the group to follow closely. He rounds the corner of the hallway and approaches a young woman hiding behind a chair. "Well, look at this. You've heard everything, haven't ya?"

"No, nothing, nothing at all."

Bjorn grabs her arm and asks, "How many are in here?"

"Ten," she swallows.

"She's bluffing."

"She'll go to the Enforcers. What do we do?" the other guard asks.

"Take her prisoner."

"No, she didn't hear anything more than Severum did, who's also an outsider."

"Can't allow her to file a report. The media will blow all this out of proportion."

"Enquire about her research, find her stance on the situation," Severum suggests. "What's your name?" he asks.

"Op, Opal Brilhante."

"Why were you here tonight?"

"I work here. I study memories. I mean, tonight, it's fish."

"There's no fish on Evig Natt."

"If it swims we consider it a fish, even if it swims in the heavy atmosphere," she argues, her shaking decreasing. "Testing memory implants in fish works due to their short memory span. We have a blank slate to work with throughout the trials. Listen, I won't go to the Enforcers and I don't want you all locked up in Neverdawn. As far as I'm concerned you had something going on here but nothing violent, and you seem to have saved these helpless victims. I have no video feed and I don't know or care who you are. I only listened because I wanted to know what our small firm is up against," she says, shifting her shoulders and occiputs back and forth.

"Firm?" Arcturus asks.

"Company, yes. I'm just a fluke, I'm no threat to you."

"Fluke? Like a fish parasite or an inconsistency? Regardless, we are through here and you do not matter."

"I would prefer my workplace to not be a training arena," Opal says with renewed confidence.

"See, she heard too much."

"What about the election rigging? The memory implants to bias elections and all that?" Aurthur asks.

"That was just what we told you for the test."

"Well, it's not impossible…" Opal begins, but cuts herself short.

"Search her," Severum orders. "She's smart enough to have picked up a weapon, but too afraid to use it."

"Too smart to," Opal replies, looking uncertain and handing over a potato peeler she found in the breakroom.

Aurthur puts his hand to his mouth to avoid laughing, and for a moment, Opal's face alights with adoration despite the circumstances.

"She's clean."

"Good thing you didn't come at me with that," Severum laughs. "I've got armor so high-end you could stab me a hundred times and it would burn up like a comet falling through the atmosphere."

"But you're not wearing it. That armor would be thicker, and it clearly didn't help in your last fight given your wounds. I can tell you weren't expecting trouble, so you can hopefully tell I don't expect it either. One thing is confusing me though. That purple hood, it can't be…?" Opal says.

Gestalt shifts uncomfortably as all focus turns to her. "Quiet!" she yells at Opal. "I know nothing of this. I will have nothing of this. This is just a distraction."

"No, no, I know this design. We studied it, but you aren't supposed to exist. The, what are you called? Aporia Asylum, that's it."

"The hood's a remnant, yes. I acquired it as a hallmark of my travels on Dayburn, a mere souvenir," Gestalt admits, rocking back and forth.

"Hallmarks that are treasured are not worn on nights like tonight, rushing into deadly situations. I'm guessing by the wear and tear it hasn't been taken off much."

"What is this about?" Thalassa asks.

"The Aporia Asylum is an anti-tech cult out on Dayburn. They have a knack for erasing their existence. There are hundreds of congregations, all led by a head priest or priestess, and all wear that style of hood. For the time being, keep this one under watch. They prefer the company of Aphorids to humans."

"This is a clever trick to turn us against each other, nothing more. Glad I sparked some curiosity," Gestalt spites.

"Explain the hood," Thalassa orders.

"I have. It is as stated, a clever trick."

"Opal's in no danger. Why would she trick us to turn against one another?"

"How would I know?"

"You do seem defensive," Bjorn says.

"Mind your place. Plenty things are purple. And I like hoods, the black swirls are interesting. That doesn't mean I'm against modern society."

"We need to leave. Straighten it out at camp," Severum states, constraining her.

"Hey!" Gestalt yells, trying to push them away. "You have no right to do this. I created this organization! No right! It's just a hood!" she shrieks.

"If there's no connection to an opposing group you have nothing to fear. But your defensiveness is suspicious. It might be nothing, but in light of someone trying to attack our new member we have to be cautious," Thalassa reasons.

"Who wouldn't be defensive when tied up by their so-called comrades?"

"You know security of the group comes before any one of us. It's your glitchin' rule so enough already. We've long suspected an insider."

"I'm leaving," Opal says as if to ask permission.

"I trust you," Thalassa tells her, placing a hand on her shoulder as she flinches away. "Come to this address tomorrow. We may need your expertise on this Aporia group."

Arcturus pulls her aside. "You're crazy, allowing another newcomer this close."

"Trusting isn't crazy, Arc. If you don't, you'll end up alone. We can use Opal's assistance to figure out who Gestalt really is."

THEY ARRIVE an hour later at the temporary base. The guards draw no attention while bringing Gestalt in and placing her in a rudimentary iron holding cell next to the man sputtering prefixes. Tomorrow they'll break her until she confesses everything.

Shaking, Gestalt thinks, *If I tell the truth and O.A.K. shows up at the Aporia Asylum's doors, the Aporia will disband me. No, they'll outright kill me, bury me underground to be consumed at will. I must call for help. Damn, vHUD comm's been shut down! I should know, it's my own protocol.*

Over time, Gestalt had grown distant to the Aporia. While there were other human members, she was also helping the Aphorids; yet, she had never had much allegiance to her own species, never venerating it above animal commonplace. Laying on the concrete floor, she posits escaping as her best route. It'll be dangerous, but she has a failsafe.

Sleep comes fitfully. She wakes a shivering hourglass trying not to break itself on the cell walls as she counts the minutes.

Footsteps get closer outside the barren holding room.

Severum throws the outer door open and stands sentry with two guards behind him. He bangs the pipe against her cell bars until his arms shake.

She covers her ears and backs away from the cell door. "You don't even work here! You don't belong with us you son of a glitch!" she says, threatening with a shaky voice.

"O.A.K. needed some extra muscle. Had quite a long talk with them last night. We'll get the truth out of you. One way or another we'll find your link to the Aporia Asylum, and just how much they know."

"You're just putting on a show for the guards to earn their trust. You think I don't see you, looking for their weak points, your opportunity? We're not that different."

"We shall see," he replies, slamming the pipe against the bars again.

<hr>

OPAL WAITS in a blank room with discolored patches on the walls and an uneven ceiling. It's no testament to minimalist architecture, just a shithole. A firefly beats itself against the globe of an upright floor lamp. She buries her head between her knees, shaking, yet unable to pass on the interview she spent all night structuring, an interview with a real Aporia member, something her fellow anthropologists would die for—what a career boost!

She runs her hand across her hair spikes in one swift motion. The burgundy tones are accentuated with infrared highlights, given the right filter. Her occipts are dyed opal in the center, a blue-green twirling mass with a layer of maroon like a river searching for its way underneath.

In college, capturing radial images had been her forte, what most people still call memories. She discovered that memories that changed over time felt more real, as only lies remained constant. It didn't take a neuroanthropology degree to figure that out, only an ex-boyfriend. She never chose to relive the good times, only the screaming, the yelling, the hate. It played across vHUD as a constant companion. The memories made her unforgiving, but this insight generated a wealth of new research into the social impacts of memory implantation, and the associated reduction in neuroplasticity.

She became obsessively focused on people who lived out their wildest most high-risk dreams then sat reliving them repeatedly, usually from an asylum. High-risk activities were suddenly much lower risk since the payoff could be relived forever. Protests began, funding was withdrawn, and her career outlook diminished. Until now.

"It's time," Arcturus says, turning away.

The stairs to the holding area are steep and Opal grabs the walls for balance before jumping half of them impatiently, catching a nervous gaze from Arcturus, who takes a breath and removes her hand from her dagger's sheath beneath her black vest.

Gestalt is slumped against the cell walls.

Interviewing someone confined will compromise her research integrity, but should she mention it? The group huddled around the cell is already a constellation of solar flares too bright to stare into and ready to burst with flames. Opal clears her throat to ask the first question, but soon hits the floor.

Thalassa shoved her aside to interrupt. "You started this group, why'd you turn on us?" She asks, gripping the cell bars with white knuckles.

"You'll get nothing," Gestalt replies without conviction. Her foot prompts up beneath her. "All this over a hood."

Opal throws her papers in the air. "This won't do. I need her comfortable and I need to be the one asking the questions. She'll never cooperate caged like an animal. This is a once in a lifetime research opp. Get her out," Opal tells Arcturus.

"Open the door, Severum," Arcturus orders.

Severum smiles, as if proud he's the one trusted to open it. He turns the key slowly in the cell door, tumbler pins giving way with faint clicks.

Gestalt's face twitches; she grits her teeth. From within her right pupil something ejects, burrows through the film of her occipt, a cylindrical vial that no amount of searching could reveal.

A stratospear.

A flash expands and pounds through the air knocking everyone off balance. Opal hits the wall hard, losing consciousness.

How long has passed? An hour, a second? Severum feels along the walls, his vision like paper coming out of a shredder. Sonar fails to activate. Opal and the team are floored, but not Gestalt. She shuffles, he snap-kicks at the sound, missing. Footsteps, footsteps, he forces his arms out to stop her, towards the threat, but she shoves past him. He estimates she has a minute, tops, 'til the stratospear stops taking effect.

She grabs Arcturus' dagger and approaches Bjorn then

moves forth in a swift motion, turning her head as dark hair swirls around her face. She strikes the guard but her blow is blocked with a straight hand at her wrist and a moment later is disarmed, the dagger clanging to the floor, her arms forced behind her back.

"Not being nice anymore," Arcturus says, retrieving the dagger and bringing it to her throat. "Speak, now."

"That dagger you carry is just as much proof you are against technology as my hood."

"Technology is not what this accusation is about. Get her in her cell, boys."

"What I want to know is how Bjorn saw me. Even the best guards would still be blinded," Gestalt says.

"Lucky strike," Bjorn replies.

"That wasn't luck, you knew exactly where my hands were when you constrained me. You showed no hesitation. And there is something in your eyes I have seen before that disturbed me. The stratospear didn't affect you, admit it."

"There's no hiding. Out with it," Severum says.

Bjorn offers, "You're right. I… I never had occipts installed. You can gasp all you want, I know, just keep it secret for me. No one looks close enough at me to notice. I know it appears suspicious for someone not to have them, very anti-tech, but you know I handle computers daily and love every minute."

"Back to the Aporia," Opal says. "The hood matches. Color, pattern, fabric, style, all of it. I was hoping to interview you, really get to know you, but now I'm just glad to have my sight back."

"Technology will destroy the environment. It amplifies inequality. I have always followed what I thought was right, and here you all want to chastise me for it," Gestalt replies.

"Way off. Modernity has increased our standard of living for millennia."

"One question bugs me," Opal continues, putting pressure on

her forehead with her palm, "being part of the Aporia Asylum, why would you start O.A.K.?"

"Because it was bound to arise anyway. I knew an antithesis to the Aporia Asylum would come about, a reaction to it, and it was better to not worry about infiltrating it later, but to instead create it from the start, gather all the dissidents in one place to keep watch. I will protect the Asylum at all costs."

"You started it to keep us under control, basically," Arcturus figures.

"Precisely. I wore the hood, however risky, to remind myself of my true identity because after a while I forgot which side I was supposed to be on. We're covert enough, I never guessed someone would recognize it. Maybe you can sympathize with my predicament."

"You're alive, aren't you?" Arcturus says.

Aurthur steps up, "You tried to strike out against your own. They had a right to ask questions and at no point were you harmed. Caged or not, no one pities your emotional reactions. And the guard should be questioned for his own involvement."

"If I'm involved then why would I restrain her?" Bjorn asks, unoffended.

"To... well, to maintain your cover."

"Nonsense," Bjorn laughs freely.

"Rather cold there," Severum whispers to Aurthur with a half-smile. "It's scary to see that in a man like you."

Aurthur ignores him and continues, "Which of your roles are true and which are false doesn't matter. Actions during stress represent the dominant role."

"Bjorn, I trust you," Thalassa says. "We're outcasts, it doesn't surprise me you don't trust occipts whether you're into mods and augmentations or not. That doesn't mean you're part of the Aporia or something."

"But a hood does?" Gestalt scowls.

"Your confession does," Thalassa replies then turns back to

Bjorn, "Warn the main project team of the knowledge the Aporia possesses. Assume they know everything she does."

"Don't let them know I betrayed you, or them. It makes both groups look weak. I didn't want it to turn out like this."

Severum suggests, "Let your strongest leaders know about the betrayal but don't let it trickle down to the rest of the squadrons. How many operations do you have anyway?"

"I agree and this is settled. Now, where are the Aporia? I want to meet those actively destroying everything I'm fighting for face-to-face," Thalassa replies, ignoring Severum's inquiry.

Gestalt makes it easy for herself and proffers directions to the main Aporia Asylum compound. They leave her in the cell with two guards and her nightmares of the Aporia's reaction to her betrayal. Now, she has no one.

Severum, Thalassa, Arcturus, Aurthur, and Opal gather what they need and plan their trip to the heart of the Aporia Asylum on the Dayburn hemisphere, where daylight never dies.

8

____

"T *he cosmos dreams to create meaning from outside itself to avoid infinite regress. God is the dream of the cosmos, not creating life, but awakening it from a coma of meaninglessness. Now is the time to create meaning. If we wait too long, the sands of our hourglasses will be swept away in tidal rushes of apathy. The Rotationists implore the wrath of the gods. They deal in tsunami and quakes, tech. and bullying. But it's not the end of the world, it's an opportunity. I sing of hemispheres and the struggles of our time, a time for order and chaos to mingle as lovers... as lovers indeed."*

    -The Priestess to the Aporia Asylum {Audio Archive 8 of 9}

OPAL, Thalassa, and Arcturus sit on one side of the airbus watching their reflection against the dark and featureless landscape. Severum and Aurthur sit across from them, saying little to pass the ten-hour trip. The airbuses are the only safe way to cross the hemispheres, since cars are subject to the dangerously strong north-to-south winds formed by the unequal heating of the two halves.

The alluvial fans of long dried rivers extend into the distance in conical striations. The windows glow as they pass through the Albino Marsh, cattails projecting a moon-like radiance from a honeydew stalk to attract insects. Gliese itself has no moon due to being tidal-locked, though it is said at one time it did and either a god consumed it, the moon fell into the planet, or it was shot down in a space war, depending on the source.

Machines gradually paint the landscape with snake-like wires and metallic compounds as they pass through the Twilight. Thalassa presses her forehead against the cold window, knowing the Core is out there, somewhere, calculating either in her favor, or against it. They stop for bio-identification. Tension grips her shoulders and she fears the Core's defense force will suddenly unleash on her. None of the other passengers look fearful as their occipts are scanned by spherical droids. They believe the lie that the machines were only built with the minimal intelligence necessary to function, not realizing they can potentially evolve, as A.I.s compete for bandwidth and set their own mutation limits.

The droid lowers itself to align with her occipts. Cabin doors open. Three more enter. The red-light scans down her hair, down her forehead, over her brows, and starts scanning her right occipt.

Severum gets close, whispers in her ear, "What's wrong?"

The droid hesitates for an eternal second, way longer than it takes to identify her. She slowly reaches down and charges her searing daggers, hands on the hilts, shaking.

Alarms shriek. The cabin floods with strobing red lights. Passengers yell:

"Help!"

"Stay down!"

"Can't be happenin'!"

"Not again!"

Droids spin to face her. Whipping her hands out she punctures the droid in front of her with one hand, taking down the adjacent one with the other. Before Severum can even grab his Pulser she stares straight forward, concentrates, and flicks both daggers down the cabin in opposite directions. The remaining two droids fall out of the air banging on the steel floor.

"You could have killed us!" a passenger screams.

"I never miss," she scoffs in return, knowing she couldn't have done it without seeing the precise distances in vHUD.

Arcturus grabs a Portahack and links to the fallen droid, looking up and down the cabin repeatedly as readouts run across vHUD. "Do you realize what set off the alarms?" she asks.

The team stands by waiting for a response, unsure whether to flee or hide.

Severum finally yells, "Spit it out!"

"Spit what? We are talking about the alarms, please focus. You caused this, after all. The droids detected two occipts instead of one."

"How's that my fault?"

"You leaned close to her during scanning. The droid couldn't tell where you stopped and she began because your occipts were too near one another while you were whispering. You just compromised everything, everything!"

"We got plenty of time to erase the record of Thal here freaking out over a routine scan. These things malfunction all the time; it doesn't mean they're gonna wipe you out. She's your problem. She's a child not a soldier."

"I'll have my blades in your neck before this is all done," Thalassa swears, gritting her teeth.

"You're not even trained enough to go recover them. They're still buried in the droids."

"Gimme the readout and the Portahack," Aurthur requests. "There's enough info here to identify the communication channel the droids were using to upload. Easy. Running Tracert. The upload packets with the video feed are being held at a firewall.

Throttling the bandwidth now to slow things down. Data transmission in the Twilight takes forever to cross security. I mean, you wouldn't want a virus shutting down the global economy."

"Wouldn't we?" Thalassa replies, wrinkling her nose.

"Done. No data leaked out. I'll calm the passengers down by explaining it was just a dual-occipt scan that aberrated the fluctuation of processing in the modules connected to the—"

"Save it," Opal says. "I'll calm them down."

"How?"

"With tea, how else?" she replies, smiling, opening a door and stepping into the next cabin as the airbus moves again.

THE WINDOWS IGNITE with light as they cross into the Dayburn hemisphere. The airbus slows at the station. Fireflies are put to sleep in the cabin by filling their tubes with gas to conserve their glow. Doors open, occipital filters adjust, and they plop in the sand halfway across the world.

The red dwarf sun is a gold-edged drop of blood splattering in the barren light sky, tinged with brown rust. It's the brightest thing they've ever seen, but the sun isn't their focus—it's how far they can see. Normally, they can only see their hands in front of their faces except in populated areas, but here, the horizon spreads like an outstretched arm offering hope. A blue solar flare pulses for an instant, as if a child skipping across the clouds before being called back home. Scab-colored trees bend their spines to gravity's will. Buttes erupt from ruddy beige sand with burgundy striations, sprinkled with green impact glass from meteor strikes, softened by the scarcest of winds. Tiny creatures scatter across the desert like marbles, finding refuge in discarded skulls, reminding them that an invisible hourglass is always ticking over the landscape and when it cracks, the sky cracks with it.

Severum straightens before the group. "It's clear the Aporia are manipulating things against us. We need to find out how much of what Gestalt knows has reached them, and how they intend to use it. We disrupted her comms after imprisoning her, but don't be surprised if they expect us. I don't take it casually when Aphorids are involved; these things tore apart entire chunks of our city with their bare mouths. Let's hope Gestalt's coordinates are right—the word of a prisoner isn't worth much if they think they have nothing to lose. Stick close together and we'll stop in an hour for a break. Crossing the desert by foot will wear you down in a heartbeat in this heat."

The group tries not to laugh as Severum's face becomes swallowed by a giant, spiny soap bubble. The floating creature inflates around his head, covering him in a jelly-like substance he scrapes off. Its spines seem an evolutionary disadvantage until one bumps into the other and, instead of deflating it, absorbs the spine through its membrane. A shaking motion coordinates the pair's mating efforts.

"Unbelievable. I never even imagined, never imagined it like this," Opal remarks, swiveling her head.

"Imagined what?" Aurthur asks, not meeting her gaze, carrying her knapsack.

"The sun! Old news for some of you I guess. I'd seen pictures, don't get me wrong. I'd just never taken a trip out here."

"Hope the UV doesn't kill us."

"If O.A.K. can increase the planet's rotation, the magnetic field will become stronger and protect us from the UV. Future generations won't have to worry. Plus, the hurricanes will stop since the temperatures will even out between the hemispheres. I couldn't believe what Thalassa was telling us on the way here. For now, get under my sunbrella," Opal continues with a lingering smile. She ties her shirt hem across the artificially-tanned dune of her upper belly, a river of light flashing along her waist chain. "I'm so glad to be part of this."

Her long skirt flirts in the breeze, undulating to reveal a crescent of upper thigh like a newborn moon looking for a solar body to orbit around. Aurthur's gaze travels upward to her exposed navel, a primal nexus from years long past. Normally, the attraction would threaten him, but after being restrained at the brink of death, test or not, he no longer has the same reservation. His adversity has led to freedom. His gaze rises further until—

She slaps him reflexively, her amused brows raising at his shock. Patchouli fills the air, their noses almost touching. They quickly shift attention to a creature soaring over their heads with a fish-like tail and a beaked head.

It chases a bobbing blob that drags iridescent tentacles across the sky to capture insects. A lizard hides beneath a rock while another basks above it, licking the rock to paint a marking. The hidden one emerges from its hole and examines the marking. Then, both recede into the crevice beneath the rock.

"A silent form of communication." Opal bends to study the marking and search for the lizards. "Wonder how large the vocabulary is?"

"It's no different than pheromones, really," Aurthur shrugs. "They couldn't possibly have syntax. Not exactly the best discovery of the year."

"Hey, it's phenomenal and you know it!" Opal kids, pushing him in the sand, her smile widening.

"Okay, it *is* the best discovery of the year, but a year's only thirty-seven days long," he continues.

"You know, language evolved so we could manipulate and piss off the opposite sex easier. These lizards might be doubly-good at that, and you're not falling short yourself."

Aurthur jumps at a hiss between the crystalline rocks. An Uroboros emerges, tastes the air, slithers towards them before chasing its own tail. Opal gets low to the ground, wide-eyed but keeping her distance from the deadly snake.

"The endless circle of the snake still gathers sand between its scales. Nothing is truly a closed system. We're all affected by the environment."

"Impressive," she replies, rocking her feet back and forth and holding back the width of her smile.

"Enough!" Severum scolds, jerking her off the ground. "This isn't a honeymoon. That's the Sediba Wellspring right ahead. Asylum shouldn't be far according to Gestalt's directions. Opal, search to see if any of these herbs are useful for healing. You have no idea what these Aphorids can do to you."

Silence falls. In the distance, at least a dozen figures draped in eggplant purple flow across the horizon, heads down. Severum zooms his occipts until he can see each grain of sand being kicked up from their steps. They disappear behind a far-off butte. His superiors will expect him to report in soon. He still doesn't know where to find O.A.K.'s main base, and there's been no mention of the rotation project. After all, if O.A.K. is just a handful of young people in a broken-down building they wouldn't be paying him what he makes, and that's the only reason it's worth doing at all. Judging by the Aporia on the horizon, he'll have at least something to disclose, but can he avoid the risks? If O.A.K. discovers his true intentions, Aurthur would be imprisoned and interrogated for his connection, while he would have his occipts ripped out and traced like the assailants at the lab. Torn, he vows to keep Aurthur, a persistent liability, safe. Aurthur trusts him to, having gone so far as to hand over a new weapon registered in his name to him. He had thought a chess club was as adventurous as Aurthur could get, but with the way he and Opal sneak glances at one another, he won't be leaving O.A.K. until she does.

Aurthur hands Severum a gray stone and asks, "Have you seen these rocks?"

"Looks like any other."

"Windstone. Notice the brushed texture."

"Lots of rocks look like that. We should hasten our step, I'm on assignment, I mean, from O.A.K," he replies, watching Aurthur's face to see if he caught his slip.

"But look, the rocks trap gas really well. I had one as a child, but never broke it. The winds were bound up tight within it. I guess I was bound in my room the same way, never much for getting out. The stone would sit idly on my desk wanting to blow out the window, but the window never opened. But now, out here in the Dayburn desert, just watch." Aurthur slams the windstone against the ground as if a monument to freedom. A gust of wind erupts from the stone strong enough to blow their hair. He nudges Severum, "Pretty cool, huh?"

"We have to focus," Severum replies, his gaze unwavering. "Keep your distance from the butte in case they augmented their senses. They're not 'spose to be into that, but ideology gets overlooked in the name of security. I'm sending you all the spot where the procession disappeared at, an entrance point up ahead. We'll swing a wide arc."

The cool breeze of the coldfire plants around the butte offers a temporary relief. The roots bind together to create one pipeline of circulating water. As passive coolers, they remove heat from the air, reducing the high risk of fires. The group taps roots and refills their canteens.

They approach an unguarded cave cut into the butte, its walls painted with dark clouds over evil eyes. Bits of rotten flesh still attached to snapped bones drizzle the entrance like hell's welcome mat. Long claw marks embellish the solid rock, an engraved forewarning. Severum recalls the Aphorids' diamond fingernails, their speed, their mobility. He refuses to take a mod to calm his nerves, promising himself that if he's captured he'll overdose before those things can put their ample hands on him, before they can bury him alive for preservation until their hunger strikes. He wipes sand from his face and takes the lead, but Arcturus shoves him aside.

The cave expands around them. Silence inside. She rubs the texture of the rocky walls, counting the number of bumps out loud. Sunlight thins and darkness falls, the gaping cave mouth tight-lipped behind them. "There are hundreds of Aporia refuges out here, each led by a priest. Gestalt directed us to this one for a reason. Come, we must discover what they know," she says, running her hand along the cold steel of her blade until it draws blood.

9

———

Aphorids gather deep inside the Aporia Asylum's measureless caverns. They never thought to develop space-faring technology or even high science, as it was always too bright outside to see stars. Their culture turned inward with mysticism, rather than outward to the heavens with speculation. The Gliese branch of Aporia Asylum Interstellar, or AAI, was a natural ally, bringing them together with the outcast humans to form the congregation.

The Priestess lectures, "When star-gazed and weary we were, born of the stars, we humans traveled through space, holding its fabric together with our perception. Space is unharmable by heat or blade, and likewise is our consciousness, eternal and pervasive throughout the galaxy. Arriving at Gliese, we arrived somewhere we had already been, as we are everywhere at once. Our story is different than our new-found cousins, the wondrous Aphorids. Yet our bond is as if we are the same. They, too, share their tales of loss amidst the machines."

"Yes, mighty Priestess," the crowd snaps, with a whip of flails.

"Everything has adapted to this planet's muffled rotation. Sin itself is what slowed it down! But there are some who would disturb the planet, its ecology, its treaties, its order. Our gods will not have it and will undoubtedly punish the turning with cyclones and tidal waves. Gliese was created to sustain life, not exploit it."

"Yes, mighty Priestess" the crowd chants, bowing their heads.

An Aphorid raises its raspy voice, slime dripping down its skin, "Aphorids fear if planet rotates faster planet throws us off."

The Priestess wants to use this suspicion to fuel her fight, but finds that by sticking to truth she has more than enough firepower. "This is untrue. Nothing will be thrown from the planet. The gods hold you steadfast and their grip is not so easily released! Man cannot throw you from the planet into the heavens; this is reserved for the gods and them alone."

"Ohhh," the crowd gasps.

"As you know, there are those who seek to speed the rotation, as if the whole world was built upon a clock. This world is not built on clockwork! It does not respond to man's demands for speed! We must uncover the full plan of the covert ones, for our time is running out."

SEVERUM CAN'T BREATHE. The cavern walls sway back and forth. Digital artifacts cross vHUD until he can't walk straight. He tries to call for help, but only dry gasps emit. He vomits against the rocky wall, leaning on it for support. Mushrooms glow iridescent green across the cavern floor. He's driven to his knees, alone, staring at the team's backs disappearing around the next dim corner, step after each fading step.

Grasping his neck, he tries to message in vHUD, but is too dizzy to scan across the augmented keyboard. Throat swelling, he doesn't lie down so much as plummets on his face. Turns over. Gold veins fork and blur across the cavern ceiling like a hierarchy of life, or a map, but it leads nowhere.

Footsteps getting louder. He slinks back against the cave wall. The echoes make it hard to tell whether whatever is approaching is running on two, or four, thrashing feet. Finally, Opal rounds the corner, wiping a sticky pink substance off her shirt. Spores float, chased by her breath. "Severum, where are you?" she yells. "You fell behind."

But his voice is suffocated cotton and his throat constricts further. He kicks a stone.

She spots him, rushes to his aid. His vision is scrambled, occipts zooming in and out, but he sees her frantically measuring the height of each mushroom.

"A single wrong step will kill us, but no time to get the others. Too tall, too tall," she repeats until finding one that is a third of the height. She lifts her foot and smashes it, white spores explode with a puff.

A minute later, reality pieces itself back together, stops tunneling.

"Don't step on the tall mushrooms," she whispers. "Poison. Short ones have the cure. They're designed to be trampled only by certain animals that have symbiotic relationships with them. The mushrooms would have loved to grow from your nutrients, being there's no soil in here. We have to go warn the others."

"Thanks," he replies, massaging his throat, but not sure he even cares.

They catch up to the group. Aurthur motions them to hush. They huddle behind a corner, listening. Far down the tunnel, screaming whispers fill the cavern.

"Is the writing done?"

"No. Came to check noises. Follow down to check gate."

"Blepedaimones?"

"Yes, smell their demonic gaze. Can taste in air."

The voices recede. Severum takes the lead as they go through a low tunnel ending at a curved staircase cut into the wall. Downstairs in the main chamber the Aphorids throw back a sluggish liquid through long teeth, faces dripping with something red and sticky. They lean against an outcropping of stalagmites. Their massive bodies spit and drool upon an evil eye symbol before dropping to all fours and trampling out of the room, table jostling off the floor with each step. Severum steps back from the staircase, shivers, and grabs Aurthur's shoulder for support.

"What are blepedaimones?" Aurthur whispers over the echoing of thunderous hoofs below.

Opal explains, "Those possessed by the evil eye. Their name for us. A vicious disease infected many of their kind. It caused dry, bloodshot eyes and high levels of aggression. Moist eyes were safe. They could weep with compassion. Today, they consider the eye evil because it only looks outward with judgment, instead of turning inward and judging itself. Aren't you glad you brought me? Now, quiet, they have amazing hearing."

Severum scouts the area. An ambush would be a tactical advantage, but not without first knowing the cavern's layout. Voices get closer, then draw back. They descend to the main chamber and reach a fork, motioning to one another to stay together, satisfied to hear nothing behind them. They pass through an arched door at the back of the cavern.

In the center of the room is a twisted altar. A heart sits within a tall coral skeleton, its chambers pulsating through the skeleton's gaps. Veins and arteries snake their way around the skeleton and down the back of it. A layer of radioactive crusted algae covers the contraption.

"There it is, the hub! We all thought it was legend, and I'm here looking at it. This is what the Aphorids feed," Opal answers to the team's wild, confused stares.

"Not my type of pet," Aurthur remarks, stepping back in recoil.

"They connect to this central hub to breed. It's beautiful.

When the hub erects during mating season there are far fewer connections to it than the number of Aphorids, leading to fierce competition for coupling. But the hub stores a copy of their genetic material so they can still pass it on after they die. That's why they're so fearless – they can still procreate after death."

"Destroy it," Arcturus orders.

"No!" Opal yells, silencing the end of the cry as soon as possible. "It would be like genocide. We need to study it."

"I agree with Arc. It's the queen bee, a giant cock. It could give off a distress signal. We destroy it," Thalassa says.

Arcturus draws a silenced Pulser from her pocket, charges it, and shoots the base. Green and red liquid pulses slowly at first then gushes as the rest jump back. She swipes her face of the warm, sticky goo. The base tilts backward and wilts, skeleton cracking.

Thalassa draws her dagger and cuts the organ apart until she is covered in the liquid, staining her light skin and filling the air with a spirulina scent. She drops to her knees, the bleeding heart below her. Holding her blade with both hands, she strikes downward three times until it stops pulsating, wiping the goo on a rock.

"Just remember, it's us who are the aliens here, not them," Opal scolds.

Severum follows the tunnel back but it's a dead end. Voices get louder.

"Head back the way we came to the main chamber," Arcturus commands.

"When the path forks I'll take it alone. Tactical advantage," Severum replies.

THE TEAM ENTERS the main chamber.

The Priestess stands on a podium behind five human monks,

two beating drums in an exotic rhythm. It stops as the team enters, the Priestess turning with bewilderment. "Drek! It can't be. How did you find us?" she asks, pulling her purple hood closer around her face.

"Both of us want to know how much we know about the other. We come in peace. Nothing more, nothing less," Arcturus states.

"Oh, there's always something more with you people."

Six shadows leap on either side, landing with a thump that shakes the mugs off the table. They flex bulging muscles and lick their eyes with anticipation. The Aphorids make use of the oxygen-heavy atmosphere, an atmosphere that drains humans when they over-exert. Their six layers of slimy skin pulsate like an accordion, or a deck of cards being shuffled.

Thalassa draws her daggers but Arcturus holds her back.

"I take it you kidnapped one of our members to lead you here?" the Priestess questions.

"We don't deny there is an absence in our ranks."

"Gestalt! I should have known. You better not have hurt her!" She points at an Aphorid in a shadowy alcove. "You, go check the hub."

"Let's make this quick. You've been spying on us. But now we know your location because Gestalt betrayed you. ITSA would love to get hold of this bit of info. We propose a mutually beneficial—"

"The hub is destroyed!" two Aphorids shriek, like vocal cords being perforated through a grater.

"Kill them! Kill them all!" The Priestess commands.

"Wait!" Opal yells, hands up. "We destroyed the hub, yes! I admit it, we're flawed and we seek your weepy-eyed compassion. We have been deluded by the evil gaze, a dryness only the Aporia can quench."

They pause to hear her speak, but she turns to Aurthur and

whispers instead, "We could save ourselves by blaming this on O.A.K. Sure you good with this?"

"We can't betray them to save ourselves; we all fall together," he whispers back.

Opal changes strategy on the Aphorids, "The hub is gone, this means you can all truly die now. You have nothing to fall back on. If you die now you die forever. Nothing will store your genes. Nothing will store your legacy. No more children will be born in your name. Why protect a bunch of Blepedaimones when you can leave, start a new hub? There's no backup plan now, this is it. If you're capable of fear then now's the time to show it!"

Her words cause them to hesitate, rocking on back haunches, though one circles around them. Arcturus draws her Pulser, Thalassa her daggers. Sorely outnumbered, they don't stand a chance against the thrashing of teeth, against creatures who can clear the room in a single leap. The Aphorids point rigid fingers with accusation, claws out. They bend their knobby knees and shriek as two spring upon Opal, clearing the table in the middle of the room with ease.

Right as they're sprung upon, Aurthur dives at the Pulser, grabs it out of Arcturus' hand, aims at the cave wall, and shoots before hitting the floor. "Hang onto the stalagmites!" he yells. "The wall's made of windstone!"

A gust of wind pounds the Aphorids and the Priestess to their knees, banging them hard against the opposite wall. The Aphorids' skin flaps go limp, some unconscious. The team holds on with all their strength, their bodies horizontal in mid-air, until the wind dies down.

Arcturus darts to finish them off only to find Opal standing in the way.

"How did you expect this to turn out?" Opal yells.

"They're half-conscious. We *have* to defend ourselves!" Arcturus yells back. "Aurthur, give me my Pulser, now."

"Don't!"

"Whose side are you on?"

"This isn't defense!"

"You riled them up with your speech!" Arcturus accuses.

"Lie! It's nothing but hate spinning your planet. If the hub hadn't been destroyed…"

Aurthur tosses Arcturus the Pulser. She shoots the Aphorids between their golden eyes. One eye on each creature dries up into a shriveled grape, while the other weeps. She turns to the monks.

"No!" Aurthur yells. "This has gone far enough."

"Still looking for that cozy social group, aren't you?" Arc replies, taking aim.

The Priestess recovers and strikes up with her staff from the floor, whipping the Pulser from her hand and flipping up. She raises the staff over her head and brings it down to strike. Arcturus catches it midair and the Priestess yanks it back, throwing her off balance. She strikes Arcturus in the stomach, knocking her wind out with a hiss as she falls back.

A robed monk grabs a mug and spins to hit Opal across the nose. Blood gushes into her palms. A second monk rises. The Priestess extends the staff to the monk, who grabs the other end. Opal runs and jumps off the prostrate staff, gathering enough air to land a knee in the rising monk's face. She falls on him and proceeds in a fit of adrenaline to club his face until there's no more shimmering. Turning, she ducks the staff and kicks the other monk in the crotch as Aurthur grabs him from behind, putting him into a sleep hold.

Warm, rancid breath fills the air behind Thalassa's face. She runs and jumps on the table, turning around as the Aphorid's teeth break the table in two with serrated marks. Losing her footing, she shields herself with the fallen table as the claws penetrate it right up to her face. She digs her searing daggers into its body on both sides as the wood between them crumbles. Six layers of slimy skin flap against her arms. She leaves the daggers burning within the wounds and rolls to the side, just as its claws make marks in the floor instead of her. The burning becomes worse and the Aphorid pulls the daggers from its arms, throws them to the side, and retreats with a whimper.

Opal pulls her victim's hood over his face, looking away from the monk's blaming eyes as their life drains like a river coursing away from a barren farm. "I never meant, never to hurt…" she consoles herself. "Why do people always destroy that which they are most curious about?"

Thalassa, seeing this, commands, "This ends now. I can't bear to go forth with the brutality any longer. This was a disaster. They have no electronics, no cogs, no way of passing on what they know. They are a primitive people bothering no one."

"Primitive," the Priestess scoffs, pulling her hood close, its grey-laced veil covering her face. "The Aphorid that fled is hitting the glitch console as we speak. This close to the signal, you'll be writhing in pain in seconds. Serves you right."

Severum enters from the forked passageway. "Got side-tracked," he says, holding up the head of the Aphorid. "Now, what was that about the one that got away?"

"Drek!"

"That was my kill," Thalassa grinds, chipping a back tooth and spitting it out. "Take the head Priestess for interrogation. Remove her from the group. I'll break her down."

"It'll incite violence," Opal warns.

"More than this? Don't think so. We destroyed their hub, flushed a billion alien-sperm down the ultimate shitter."

"She's right. Capture the Priestess and put her with Gestalt," Severum agrees, a hidden smile surfacing as if enjoying the increased tension. "We have to leave before the Aphorids recover."

They exit the cave. The sun, having shunned its own light, unleashes it to bleach the landscape bone white. Holding their hands as visors, they make their way across the desert back to the station. Concealing the prisoner on the airbus will be difficult; security will either be lighter given the fallen droids, or heavier if replacements were sent in response.

Opal steps in front of Thalassa and Arcturus, one hand on hip, the other blocking passage. "Your negotiating almost got us killed. If you two had listened and not taken out the hub—"

"Then what?" Thalassa snaps, jerking her head forward. You wouldn't 'ave had to kill a free radical in the middle of nowhere? The mission is the mission. I've crossed endless ice plains, lived in a cave, crossed the burning desert, overcame assassins, dodged Aphorid jaws, and probably outsmarted the world's most intelligent A.I. Where the fuck has it gotten me? We're nearly bankrupt, hunted everywhere we go, forgot what home looks like, can't visit a friend without crisscrossing a thousand random streets. I put an end to the slaughter, but not before we secured the Priestess. Truth is, you had the monk disabled before you kept pummeling him to death, Opal. No one made you kill him but you, now deal with it, and don't you dare step in my way again." She jerks her head to the side, sweat flinging on Opal's face, who looks down and away.

"Your outburst makes us look weak," Arcturus scorns Thalassa to the side.

"Shove it, Arc. You're obsessed with control. You have no idea how anyone else feels. Why do people hold hands? Why are those people smiling at each other? The droids get more about human behavior when they scan than you do."

"That hurts, stop it."

"Your outburst makes us look weak, Arc," she spits.

"Listen, we're all hot and worked up right now," Aurthur intervenes, opening outstretched hands. "We have a long trek back."

THE PRIESTESS' purple robe flows across the golden sand like cabernet poured over sunlight. Silent, nameless, her hood barely reveals even her nose. "What did you take from us?" she asks Opal, sticking to her side. "I found it taxing to recognize his face after you were through."

"What did I take? You mean who?"

"Each life, each member of the Asylum has a purpose. What purpose did you take? Simple question, right?"

"You define people by their purpose?" Opal asks, raising her canteen.

"As do you. How long does it take when you meet someone to ask what they do for a living?" the Priestess asks.

"Well, people like to know if someone can repay a favor," Opal replies, catching her reflection in the water of the canteen and tossing it away as if it were a snake. The canteen lands beside a green glass shard caused by an ancient meteor impact.

"Forget it. These Rotationists you associate with will bring nothing but destruction, the same type you wrought upon my peaceful commune to satisfy your twisted curiosity. How will you smuggle me upon the airbus? I'll talk. I'll scream bloody murder. Will you hit me until I fall unconscious? What if I never wake up, oh my," the Priestess says, smirking.

"A life, it's just a life!" Opal yells, swiping the glass shard out of the sand and making a shallow cut across her palm, but her reflection stares back hard from her own blood.

"It *was* a life," the Priestess incites further.

Opal lunges, but Severum steps in front and pushes her down. She starts to get up but turns over and cries instead, scooping empty handfuls of sand and throwing them at the Priestess.

"Aurthur, watch over her. You're better at that sensitive crap. Almost there. Hey, guys, how long until the next airbus?"

"I will go check the schedule and scope security," Arcturus replies. "You all rest here." A half hour later she returns, sets her backpack on a rock. "No luck securing a private cabin. We wait here a half hour, then depart for the station. There is no other way out of here before our supplies run low."

"So, your vast organization lacks the resources to transport a prisoner off Dayburn?" Severum asks, laughing suddenly. "Where is this vast team of support you claim to have? You put your leaders on the frontline with child-like negotiations and you call yourselves strategic analysts with catchy code phrases. I feel deceived. You knew we were coming and what we would have to do, but the dissension in your ranks alone compromises your goals. A proper hierarchy would do you well, efficient, no questioning."

"I'm not dignifying that. Part of our checks and balance system requires that even Thalassa, Gestalt, and I don't disclose everything, even to one another."

"Not communicating just weakens the organization," Severum fishes.

"Everyone's on a need to know basis. It's our way," Arcturus replies, right side of her face tightening, Severum pulling its chain.

"Either your main base is far away and can't support you, or so close that their involvement would give away their proximity. Just curious."

Arcturus ignores him and turns to Opal. "Look, we are going to have to kill the Priestess. I'm sorry. I won't make you do it, dear Opal, but we cannot risk bringing her with us. Be great to interrogate her, but she'll scream bloody murder like she said."

"No! No more death! There's no excuse for it, there was no excuse for the hub, for—"

"You might be able to save her life if you could think of another way to quieten her without beating her half to death."

"I cannot, for the life of me."

"It's not your life. Surely you must have studied Dayburn, something we could use," Arcturus continues.

"You look like you already know the answer. What, you trying to get me through my guilt by saving someone we shouldn't be killing to begin with?" She throws her hands up as if carrying the world. "You're completely mad, all of you!"

"I had thought of using a rock and clubbing her unconscious. Got anything better?"

"I can beat that idea at least," Opal resigns. "Why don't we use an herbal concoction? There are some dank herbs growing under some of the rocks that might put her to sleep with the right dose. At least I saw some purple uyku a while back."

"Brilliant! Would they have to be prepared?" Arcturus asks.

"To avoid nausea and vomiting, yes, but not enough time. Time's a luxury, a debt we never pay until de… death," Opal makes out.

"We will search with Thalassa. The men will watch the prisoner."

They soon locate the spiny purple herb. Opal bends to gather it, collecting as much as she can hold and counting each leaf. The sand grumbles near her hands, something sliding beneath. Sand sprays from the ground as an Uroboros springs forth, whipping its head to strike.

Thalassa draws daggers, Arcturus her Pulser, fumbling and dropping the gun. Opal backs up a step and prays to any deity, all deities, anyone who'll listen, but the air is stagnant, belongs to no god. Snake slithers forth, Opal shaking, but Thalassa just as coy flanking it. Suddenly, the snake whips itself around to strike in the opposite direction, lunging to bite Thalassa on her leg with a sharp cry of pain. She slices off its head in one motion, searing dagger burning it to ash, while the rest slithers away beneath the sand.

"Deception. It never meant to strike from the front. Must have felt you were the greater threat," Opal says, covering her mouth, brows converging.

"I am," she replies, the wound pulsing under her cupped

hand, head rocking sideways, feet uncoordinated. "I'll be fine."

"Thalassa, it's venomous!"

"I'm fine," she insists, slowly leaning backward. Time speeds, slows, rewinds, tumbles in her stomach. She plops to the ground, unconscious.

"Shoot, another problem," Opal says, tearing a leaf. "It's the wrong herb! The number of spines per leaf is wrong. The genus is totally different than anything I've ever seen."

"And Thalassa?" Arcturus asks, counting her breaths, feeling each exhale on her face—to finally be this close to her without fearing her judgment, but now she's on the brink of death.

"She needs immediate medical attention. We have to carry her back before the airbus leaves."

"And the Priestess? She'll cry for help unless we knock her out, and we'll never make it back to Evig Natt without Enforcer activity. There's just not enough time and we're running out of supplies, and I'm definitely not returning to raid their cave with the Aphorids waking from unconsciousness."

"I suppose you're right," Opal sighs. "Wait, the snake!" She grabs the Pulser. "There's another one. Look at the swishing pattern across the sand. It can't be far away. We extract the venom. Follow me. I'll track it and grab its glands. The venom will put the priestess to sleep, but not kill her, that is if we can get the dosage right for her weight. I'll calculate the dosage on the way back. I'm going to save her."

"By forcing venom down her throat? Whatever you do, do it before the airbus arrives."

Opal traces the raised portions of sand until she arrives at a hole beneath a rock. She waves her hand over it but nothing happens. She shouts into the hole, her mouth covering the narrow opening, but no response. Finally, she turns her back on the hole and sits, understanding its hunting technique. A second later, she fires behind her back at a hiss, bits of snake flying over her head, pulverized. She gathers the head, intact, and they return to carry Thalassa back to the others. They drop her twice, the deadweight almost too much in the heat, but they can't miss the last airbus, can't let the team down.

"What happened to her? And where's the herbs?" Severum asks as they arrive.

"Snake bite, and we'll use venom instead."

Opal holds the snake head above the Priestess' head and pulls her veil aside just enough to squeeze the venom in, her face still hidden. She doesn't resist, the measured venom sliding down her throat and knocking her unconscious. Severum rubs his chin and glances at her lips, then turns away.

"I'll carry Thalassa, Aurthur, you carry the Priestess. Let's go, we can still make the station. We'll tell the guards both were bitten by snakes. Thalassa has a mark, right? They'll buy it," Severum says.

Arriving at the station, the airbus cabin compresses with a hiss. Severum kicks his foot through the door as it's closing. Sweaty passengers give looks of restless disdain as the team comes aboard with the unconscious women.

A stewardess gasps, "Oh my!" Looks for someone else to deal with it but they avoid her gaze.

"Snake bites," Severum says, shaking his head with a half-smile.

"We carry basic first aid, including antidotes. What type was it?" she asks.

Aurthur squeezes through and announces, "Uroboros! The head of the past struck out at the present."

"Very romantic, but the desert cares little for poetry, jerk. The antidote may take effect in time to save them. I'll retrieve it. There's an open cabin in back for ya'll."

Settling into her seat, Arcturus says, "We need to pretend to give the Priestess the antidote, but she has to stay asleep. Then we give Thalassa the antidote for real and note her recovery time. We'll adjust based on body weight. I estimate that halfway

through the trip we'll need to provide the Priestess the real antidote before the poison hits her too strong. Then we use the rest
of the snake gland to put her back to sleep as she's recovering.
Finally, we give her one last antidote back at basecamp. We'll
monitor her vitals at the quarter of every hour."

The stewardess brings the antidotes. Thalassa receives it and
they keep a close watch. They convince the stewardess to leave
the first aid kit and the other antidote for them to administer
themselves so she can attend to other matters. Hours pass with
nothing but a bitter teapot and exhausted company.

"What, what happened?" Thalassa asks, putting her hand to
her head.

"So glad you're back." Arcturus hugs her tightly, her body
still warmer than it should be.

"You look well, too well," Severum says. "Pretend you're
still weary so they don't wonder why the Priestess is still unconscious, since they believe she received the same treatment at the
same time. Say a couple crazy things when the stewardess comes
by. That way, if the Priestess wakes up early and says something
like she's being kidnapped, no one will believe her. They'll think
delirium is just a symptom."

"You're unusually talented at this, and at combat," Arcturus
tells him, squinting, following the movement of his facial
muscles but looking confused.

Two hours later, they inject the Priestess with the antidote,
clearing the poison then poison her again, since the substance
doesn't bio-accumulate. As they disembark on Evig Natt,
Thalassa pretends to be drowsy and they help her off while
escorting the unconscious Priestess. They soon arrive back at the
makeshift base where four guards grab the door. Arcturus sends
two of them home, not trusting anymore newcomers. The
remaining guards carry the Priestess to the holding cells. Color
drains from the scene flowing down the shithole in the floor
where they toss her, face down, the cell door slamming shut.

10

---

*"*T*he branches of the tree of knowledge should be our bronchial tubes, the leaves our capillaries, but knowledge is sawed and shaped by the elite and citizens breathe only what they are told to breathe. They burn our ancient texts, make us choke on the sawdust, call us primitive. It is we who must take the dust of the past and sculpt the next version of human history."*

-The Priestess to the Aporia Asylum {Audio Archive 9 of 9}

SEVERUM ENTERS THE HOLDING ROOM. Energy drink ads cross his vision in response to his biometrics. The prisoners avoid his gaze. The other guards had sent him home for the night but he delayed by offering to pack long boxes of electronics for a moving truck tomorrow. He turns to Bjorn, leaning against the wall with his arms crossed and yawning. "Long night, huh, Bjorn?"

"You said it. Been stuck in this place like it's my own cell and I'm the one servin' time, you know?"

"Yeah, right? I'll talk to them, might take your place for the night. I could use the flies."

"Would you? It's just the cell and cots. Not much action so not much of a problem, but I know you just got back from Dayburn."

Bjorn is relieved of his position, leaving Severum alone to guard the prisoners while Thalassa and Arcturus sleep. Aurthur and Opal call it a night, leaving in different directions. Severum rummages through boxes, scours trash cans, opens drawers, but the makeshift facility offers no clue as to where O.A.K.'s base is. Gestalt is his best chance. Heading in her direction, he activates a small sphere to emit a disabling signal in case anyone's aural implants are set to record conversations while sleeping or awake. He doesn't notice the device's power light blinking, slowing to a stop. Gestalt and the Priestess lean against one another in the back corner of the cell, Gestalt just now waking.

"Gestalt! You're okay," the Priestess says, hugging her in the cell as she wakes, wiping away a tear. "But why did you tell them where we were?"

"I'm sorry, they would have found out anyway, after enough suffering. What did they do to you, sister?"

"Poisoned, almost killed me. They administered the final antidote just in time while you were sleeping. But we won't be here long."

"How do you figure?"

"Their ranks are disorganized, and—"

"Brought you a couple pillows for your back," Severum interrupts, smashing them between the bars. They refuse them. "These people mean business. You've seen what they're willing to do. I just wish there was better security here. No cameras or anything. Of course, you already know this, Gestalt. So, it's pretty much me and some bars preventing you from leaving. A lot of the monitoring equipment is tucked away in boxes now for transport, disconnected, if you will."

"We get it. You're in control," Gestalt scowls.

"No, wait. Let him finish," the Priestess replies softly.

"So, Gestalt, this rotation project that everyone's obsessed with, you're against it?"

"Yes, of course, we both are. The planet rotates fast enough, and no amount of speed you add will let it escape tidal locking. Day shall never fall on Evig Natt, and shouldn't."

"You know I have nothing personally against either of you," he replies with an open palm.

"I realize that. You're too new too, Severum. So what do you want?"

"An arrangement. The three of us have similar interests."

"The only thing you can give us is freedom," Gestalt snaps, pulling her body up. "Anything else is meaningless without that."

"The illusion of freedom. They'll still hunt you. Arc has a vengeful streak."

"O.A.K.'s resources are centered on the project and limited outside of it."

Severum notes this and asks, "Where's the main rotation site?"

"Near the Twilight belt, but not too close to the A.I. Core," she replies, describing the area in more detail. "They're using space fountain technology to build momentum for energy transfer through a hidden belt around the planet. The machines aid their efforts, or so they think."

"Unbelievable. What's the coordinate range of this Twilight belt?"

"There're some landmarks I'll give you when I get out, but other than that I can't provide any more exact info. Thalassa knows, and only her—part of our checks and balances. She said it would be well lit, enough to blind onlookers without a filter."

"Fair enough. What about the location of the energy transfer apparatus? You told me about the belt, but I need your main base."

"That's my doing. I can take you there, in exchange for our freedom. I'll provide you coordinates the moment I'm released, in good faith."

"I might as well confide in you, since, as a prisoner, what you say carries no credibility and can't be used against me. I found something, an illegal source of light in the governor's quarters. It made me question the nature of our firefly economy. Maybe bringing light to the hemisphere would be the best thing. Or maybe the ecological costs are too high. Maybe the period of instability would be too violent to be worth it. Either way, I have commitments to keep, but it's been weighing on me," he says, pacing.

"Lots of maybes. So maybe you can get us out of here now. You're a bought man, your side is whoever's paying you, and you don't fucking know where to stand. I get it," Gestalt argues. "Fulfill your purpose and I'll fulfill mine."

"And when this is over and O.A.K. is shut down you'll rebuild it again?"

"Someone else will. There must always be an antithesis. But Thalassa and Arcturus are too smart. They didn't even let me in on all the details. I kept trying to reel in what I had created but it kept expanding, the members, the ambitions. We have dozens of people I don't even know. Next time it needs just a single leader, no democratic process, just an antithetical god."

"Goddess," the Priestess whispers, huddled in the corner, head down, buried in her hood and robes.

"How long have you two known each other?" Severum asks.

"Many years, professionally of course. If you're wondering, yes, I would die for her."

"I would not let you," the Priestess whispers.

"Won't come to that, but you need to cooperate. When I open

the cell, follow me out and we'll travel to the main base. I won't report your involvement to my employer, Gestalt."

"And as for the Priestess?"

"There are hundreds out there, she's not important, stay, go, whatever."

"Who's your employer?"

"Someone with connections."

"Mere connections are not dependable enough. They're like constellations, turn your head a little and new shapes, new patterns of connection emerge," Gestalt tells him. "He is someone in a formal position of power, or law enforcement."

"Me providing information is not part of the agreement."

"What do we do about Thalassa and Arcturus?" Gestalt asks.

"They're less violent than those who would likely take their place. In the absence of a leader one always arises. The devil you know sort of thing."

"We could kill them," Gestalt suggests with a raised brow.

"A last resort. And could you really kill them?" Severum asks, sensing she's fishing for his intent.

"No. I'd imprison them right here where they stashed me at," she replies, sounding uncertain.

"Let's go."

Severum lets Gestalt and the Priestess out of their cell. They spring to life, quickly exiting. The Priestess grabs his wrist, but he shakes it off and heads to the next room.

He passes the cots where Thalassa and Arcturus sleep, feet at one another's heads, tapered intimacy. He should call for full military intervention, right here right now, but lying helpless and unarmed he knows what they'll do to them. A moment's indecision is a deadly plague in his line of work, but he can't think straight. He could take them out himself, but he can't shake the idea they could be right with their ideology, if not their approach. He's gained enough intel to receive commendation, but their heads could bring him promotion as well, and it'd take a small warehouse to store the flies he'd bring in at that salary level, a moment's fantasy rendered in a thousand buzzing bugs. Promotion. He shakes it off, steps away, hates himself for feeling, and motions the prisoners to the door. He'll be back to broke in no time at this rate.

***

ARCTURUS RUNS PhishVz in the background while she sleeps, allowing a single occipt to register visual feed. A warning runs across her dreams, alerting her that three figures are crossing into the next room. She's in luck—Severum's audio blocker has failed due to low power, his conversation captured intermittently. The partial transcript displays across vHUD but it's enough to piece together what was said. She shakes Thalassa vigorously. "Thalassa. Thalassa. Wake up."

"Wha—what?"

"Seriously, we must move, now."

"What is it? I'm still a bit meteored."

"Quiet. Run d-tox. Check the cells. I'll head for the door," she says, grabbing her Pulser from a hidden floor panel.

Arcturus investigates the next room, scans the dark halls. Guards have vanished; no sign of a struggle. Everyone's useless, everyone abandons her. Footsteps run through the lobby – there's the bastard. She aims her Pulser at his back, but a shadow moves in an adjacent room and she can't handle being hit from two directions at once. She flattens against the wall as the gun charges. Severum stops, motions with his hands to someone then turns around.

"We heard something. Is everything all right?" Arcturus asks, feigning ignorance and concealing the Pulser behind her back.

"Yes, fine. Nothing major."

"Have the prisoners said anything?"

"No. They're asleep."

Thalassa rushes in. "They've escaped! They're both gone!"

"That's impossible!" Severum says.

Arcturus springs into the adjacent room. "Gestalt! I was right, she's been undermining us all along!" She severs her attachment like pulling the plug on a loved one, pausing for an eternal second before firing at Gestalt's legs to incapacitate her. But Gestalt ducks and the shot hits her square in the head instead, killing her instantly, body tumbling backwards as a searing smell fills the air. Arcturus drops her mouth, almost drops the Pulser, recoils back, step after disbelieving step.

The Priestess stifles her scream and runs and kneels down beside her. She caresses her face until her fingers slide into the cavity where her forehead used to be. Blood and other charred fluids coat her hands.

"Isolated for so many years, now this!" She sobs, rocking back and forth, head in hands.

Boot tread fills Arcturus' vision, the roundhouse kick knocking her back, Pulser flying from her hand. She falls, scurries to the wall, shakes off the shock. Severum scoops up the Pulser, recharges the shot. She tries to rise, digging her nails into her hands, determined, but he steps closer and she knows it's no use. She flicks through vHUD, erasing all sensitive files from her mind so they can't be retrieved post-mortem.

Thalassa draws a dagger and charges Severum. He turns and fires reflexively, the shot burning a hole in the wall above Arcturus' head, missing both. Thalassa closes the distance while the Pulser recharges.

It won't end like this, Arcturus swears to herself. She jumps on Severum's back, wrapping her hands around his neck, clawing at his arteries. He wrangles back and forth before spinning. Thalassa withdraws her dagger as they collide, crashing them against the door. She strikes out at Severum's chest as he rights himself, but he parries, chops her wrist with the side of his hand, and she drops the dagger. He kicks it into the middle of the room where the Priestess gathers it, only to rub it up and down her arm, scraping the brain goo off again and again until her arm bleeds, her blood mixing with Gestalt's. Severum catches a slight glimpse of her face beneath the hood and is caught off guard.

Thalassa takes the moment's advantage, assaults with a flurry of high kicks aimed at his face, but he leans his head back, shrugs off the effort. Switching targets, she runs to wrestle the dagger from the Priestess, avoiding a couple unskilled swiping motions in the air, but there's a sudden ferocity that rises. The Priestess rubs brain matter between her first finger and thumb in a circular motion, then springs forth with twice the speed and intensity, striking with the blade in wild, uncoordinated arches.

Thalassa jumps back, and back, backs off entirely.

"Who do you work for?" Arcturus screams, readying herself to strike. "Talk, Severum! It doesn't matter. You know what she knows, you know too much. Neither of you can be allowed to live."

"Trying to convince yourself this is right? Ha! I sacrificed for you. I risked my life to protect you. O.A.K. couldn't even take down a single Aphorid without me. I've dealt with hundreds of those things! I've seen their claws shred my friends to ribbons! I have no reservation about killing you now."

"You and Gestalt planned this!"

"No. Gestalt didn't want this."

"Then you and Aurthur planned this."

"That's my only friend. Keep him out of it!"

"Gestalt was my best friend."

"You shot her, not me!" Severum snaps, wedging doubt into her, pulling her apart from the inside as she backs away. The Priestess hurries to his side, pressing herself close to him. He shoots a warning shot at the ceiling. Nothing happens. He shoots again, but no response. He examines the full charge gauge then throws it over his head, not realizing the weapon only operates within a certain radius of Arcturus, keyed to her cog. "I can take both of you out in seconds. Back off!"

"But not before we harm the Priestess," Thalassa intimidates, raising her chin, stepping forward. "She's easy prey."

"I don't care about her. There's hundreds of cultists out there."

"Did you see how fast she ran to your side? She trusts you to protect her. Whatcha gonna do, Sev? How much blood on your hands?"

"She has no reason to trust me," Severum replies, nodding his head yes in contradiction. "Besides, she's armed."

"Easy prey." Thalassa pulls open a wound, wipes the blood on her mouth, licks her lips.

"You jumped to conclusions when they escaped."

"I jumped when you attacked Arc!"

The Priestess speaks slowly in a low voice, as if concealing an accent, "It's best for us all to escape, start over, never to return here again. There is too much risk in all of this. Severum and I will take our leave. You can continue to unbind the gods' will with your childish whims and sentiments at your leisure." She turns to Severum, head down. "I'm sorry I dragged you into this."

"What the hell do you mean?" Severum asks, shaking his head with confusion. Turning to Arcturus, "We have enough information to figure out the rest. We're leaving. You even step foot near your base, the energy transfer device, or the belt and I'll turn the place into a battleground like you've never seen."

"Enough! Your intel will do you no good. *Energy transfer device*, you don't even know what it's called. You know nothing."

"Mission accomplished," he says with a smile. "Come, Priestess."

The door slams. Arcturus recovers her Pulser, chases up the stairwell outside where Thalassa finds her dagger tucked into the broken corner of a step. They run to either side of the building, then across the street, but Severum's too well trained in the art of disappearing and will not be found.

"Glitchit!" Arcturus shouts to the sky, wrapping itself in an ashen robe. She kicks a steel trash can down the street, leaving a trail of filth in its wake.

11

A progression of servants walks through the street carrying jars of fireflies behind their master's trail of light. The cumbersome exchange method leads to many people exchanging services instead of funds, forming greater trust and relationships over time, but for the rich the progression itself is a show of wealth. The homeless approach the glow to clean themselves or to shave with glass shards. Severum channels through them to the safe house. The Priestess clings to her hood as acid rain falls, keeping it tight around her eyes. He allows her to keep it on in case O.A.K. is trailing them. He peeks over his shoulder and buys a scarf to conceal his lower face, his warm breath filling it.

"I think we lost them," she says.

Severum expects O.A.K. will alert Opal and Aurthur as to what's happened. The rotation project would likely be moved, though a project of that scale would take time to relocate. The governor calls him, but he sets vHUD to ignore it. He needs time to plan how to frame his report. "Come with me. I'll keep you safe. You can't return to the Aporia Asylum now, O.A.K. could return for you."

"This much I know."

"I can't return home either, but I have some valuables in a locker for situations like this. We'll decide what to do with you tomorrow, so think about where you belong."

"I already know. With discovery comes conflict. I am sure you have many more discoveries to make. Hopefully, they shall bring you peace in the end," she says, folding her hands as they walk at a slower pace, adjusting her hood.

Heavy with sleep, he steps into the lobby with the Priestess. The building's in a safe enough part of town to feel secure, but not so plush as to attract attention. The elderly receptionist welcomes them, "One o' two beds, or are ya bettin'?" he asks.

"I bet every day, I just don't know on what. Let's try two beds, no luggage to note," he replies.

"Safe bet by the looks o'her. And I wasn't plannin' on carryin' your baggage anyway. No one tips. Just as well, bug jars too 'eavy to carry for the likes o' me aht this age."

Their room is a gleaming paper white. The double crown-molding is pitch black by contrast, meeting in the corner to spiral down into a half loop like a wild vine. Groups of curved loveseats in black, faux leather are angled around the center of the room. *Solanum* Nightshade flowers grow restless from a solemn pot. His last thought of the day is how easily the Priestess trusts him.

"SEVERUM COULDN'T POSSIBLY HAVE… Honestly, I believe him before you," Aurthur says on the call, shaking his hand through his hair.

"Has he returned home?" Thalassa asks.

"No. But that's not unusual."

"He won't be back, then you'll know I'm not glitchin' you."

"Seriously? I mean, it would explain why he followed me that night, but I can't believe it."

"How well did you know him?"

"Better than any other neighbor, but, we weren't friends, *per se*. In other words it was a proximity friendship."

"I understand, I didn't need a life story."

"Come again?"

"Nothing. Just stressed still," Thalassa replies, voice trailing.

"With Gestalt's death that's understandable. Should I move or what?"

"Decide yourself. I'm not responsible for your actions. Severum knows you know nothing so I think you're safe. I'll inform Opal."

"What's Arc's take?"

"That you don't matter enough to be in danger. Stay away from O.A.K. 'til things settle. You could lead him to us again. We'll call when you and Opal are needed."

"For now, she has her research to write up and I've had my fun."

"Glad you enjoyed the suffering," Thalassa replies sardonically, ending the call.

Aurthur hesitates, paces, and finally calls Opal. "I think you should come over."

"It's late, but Thalassa just woke me so I guess it doesn't matter."

"Either way. But it might be safer at your place," he says, switching strategy.

"You want to come over? I'll leave the door open."

"No, don't do that."

"I'll program it to only open to your signature. You don't live that far away. I'm going back to sleep, goodnight."

Aurthur arrives at Opal's loft. He hesitates to enter the back room where she snores, not knowing if it's forbidden. Pacing back and forth, analyzing her belongings—more for risk analysis than conversational pieces—he places a bouquet of refurbished flowers on an end-table, grabs sheets from a closet, and resigns to sleeping on the extended couch, longing for some validation that his life means more than this.

———

SEVERUM WAKES TO THE PRIESTESS' slender fingers caressing his cheek, her deep occipts pressed against his, a remnant of her Indian heritage. Her wide thighs envelope his own before tapering down into small feet that tangle themselves between his toes.

"We never had that child we always talked about in college. We were going to name her Vispáshanah, remember? At thirty-eight, I thought I would have—"

He leaps from the bed, looks for his Pulser.

She rolls over and props her head on her hands, amused. "My, you have matured. That's a lot better than your reaction the last time I brought it up, fourteen years ago to this day."

Severum searches the dressers, cabinets, sink, and bed. He repeats the search a second time, and a third.

"Hey, Sheva. Sorry I startled you, love. Your Pulser's in the nightstand drawer, but toys can wait for later."

"What? What's going on? What is this?" he asks, spinning, still searching all the wrong places.

"Think back. I used to call you Sev but my accent made it sound like Shev. When I found you destroy everything around you I started calling you Sheva. Sound familiar?"

"But you—"

"Yes, I am who you think I am. Pull off my hood and see for yourself, my love. When you stop spinning aimlessly you might find you've come full circle."

He reaches out to the thin rope binding her hood as if it's a snake, unties it, and slowly pulls it back, centimeter by centimeter revealing her face. He rubs her smooth skin, etched by experience, gently massages the para-labial folds around her mouth, and recesses his index finger in her philtrum above her upper lip.

She pulls her dark ponytail out and lets her thick shoulder-length hair fall to encapsulate her.

"Akasha'Shirod. Why didn't you tell me? How could you keep this from me, Akasha? Where have you been? I thought you were dead until the other day."

"You know the need for secrecy. I knew you were on assignment, since I arranged for it myself by having a contact provide Borges with the intel Gestalt had sent me. I had to maintain your cover at any cost so I pretended to not know you. And you owe me for the courier."

"But what prompted all this? Why didn't you tell me you were the Priestess on the way here?"

"While running for our lives? Timing, Severum, something you never understood. Remember when we studied terraforming? You and I with bright ideas of creating new worlds, but creating only hell for one another. Able to alter the structure of entire planets, yet not our own hearts. When I gave up on you, I gave up on it, too. Every textbook on the subject reminded me of you and your attempt to control everything around you, including nature. That's why I founded a new division of Aporia Asylum, to return to the natural, to run away from you. I'd rather be queen of a Dayburn cave than second-rate and replaceable on Evig Natt."

"You always had a way with words. Been so long, I don't..." Severum says, creasing his forehead. "Why didn't you write earlier?"

"That's all you can say? And I did write. I wrote volumes, I just didn't send them."

"With all that, why even return?"

"Your friends and you poisoned me and knocked me unconscious. Let me guess, you don't remember, right? Just like old times. I'm here because of you. Just you. You must have known it was me on some level, even if I did conceal my accent and keep my face hidden. I couldn't put you or the operation at risk by letting you know sooner."

"I, I don't know, Akasha. This is all too much. There are hundreds of priests over the Aporia, dozens of refuges. I played your recorded lectures again and again, but never dreamed this would happen. I saw your face, the Organizer of Glitches they call you."

"Ah, the glitches. I wasn't calling out to you so much as to all those I left behind after joining the Aporia, striking out against their culture of disconnection. And you knew I was alive on some level, it was obvious. You didn't want to believe. You were afraid."

"Not true," he replies, rubbing his nose.

"Would you normally release a political prisoner without knowing her name, or even staring once into her soul?"

"You didn't matter. I had what I needed."

"Severum, you're wearing me, I'm warning you." She sits up, clicks her teeth, pulls the covers beneath her chin. "I've heard that line one too many times, too. This isn't how I fantasized it."

"I didn't know it was you."

"You act like you still don't. So you normally let your prisoner sleep in the next bed just moments after escaping?"

"You weren't my prisoner, and I didn't let you."

"Oh, you didn't seem to mind," she laughs. "You still deny our closeness, our bond. You should have disrobed me immediately, ripped my hood off. You're not fond of variables, loose ends, the unknown."

"You could have visited me."

"Instead of dragging you into international politics? Blasé!"

"Your voice, I never remember you being so soft spoken."

"No," she pauses. "I was, just not around you."

"I'm at a loss."

"Start with a hug, then we'll go from there."

Her words dull the razor edge he walks upon only to re-sharpen it again at the end of the sentence. "Maybe I did know it was you on some primitive level. I scanned your vitals constantly to ensure the poison that knocked you out wasn't harming you. The last time we met, you said you had unrequited self-love. I thought about what that meant a lot over the years. You were destroying yourself. I figured you must have ended up dead when you went off the grid."

"You were the one destroying me! I was in a different place in life. I defined my self-worth through you. We've been *over* this."

"It was a place you willingly travelled to! But then, I never listened so it didn't matter what you said," Severum admits.

"What did you think would happen?"

"Just… not that."

"You should remember everything is formless, in flux, defined by negative space as easily as positive. The fabric of reality is perforated, solid meeting void. When solid enters void, being enters non-being, and the child of becoming is born," the Priestess says. "We were meant to have that child, the child of becoming, clothed in the robes of nature. Wait, your occipts are flicking. Are you using vHUD while I'm talking?"

"Yes. Why?"

"Nothing. I just expected… a little more attention."

"I was paying attention, obviously."

"But you weren't. The virtual is simple and consistent. When things are consistent we ascribe more meaning to them. Virtual becomes more real, more imminent, more here and now. There are reasons I oppose technology. Maybe one day you'll understand."

"I'm not part of your congregation."

"It's enough that Gestalt's gone! I can't deal with this too, not again…" She gnaws on a nail, rips it off.

They resolve their anger and are quiet. They learned long ago that relationships are the opposite of a battlefield; on a battlefield those who are left to fire the last bullet are those that win. In relationships, those who rage to have the last word are those who have lost. The idea of her with another man is something he still shoves hard into a vault. He's tempted to download eRase from A Memory to Come. If popped when a negative thought arises, it'll trace the obsessive chain of thoughts leading up to it and recondition the firing pattern. But maybe this pain should be retained. Maybe, this pain should be learned from. "We have some time to think before I report back to my superiors. I'll arrange a meeting with the governor."

A WARM PRESSURE pushes against his back. Aurthur jerks his shoulders. Slowly turning over, Opal rests her head on his chest, half clothed, smelling like cloves. Fireflies hover as golden shadows move in waves across the bed sheets.

Opal captures one in her hands as the light bursts out between her fingers. She holds it to his face, slowly opening her hands as a sunrise falls over him for the first time, threatening the eternal darkness outside, and within. "Beautiful. Welcome back to the land of the living."

"Wow, you actually—"

"Slept beside you? Yeah, I did that," she says. "Now I'm actually getting up for the day."

"Lot of stress lately."

"Well, it's over now. Breakfast? I have a ton of research to compile."

"Sure, I'm up. Do you agree we should stay away from O.A.K?"

"I don't know. Let's just hang out with each other today, see where it all goes."

"I've been eager to finish this landscape painting."

"You could always do something useful like painting my walls," she sighs.

"No, let's just go out."

THE ITSA SHIP soars over Thalassa and Arcturus' heads leaving a trail of emerald-green light that reminds smugglers they're watching. Buildings stand like sentries protecting those in power. Neon advertisements splay across augmented reality promising to reverse your fireflies' sterility so your money can reproduce.

Thalassa unpacks the portahack, links to the ship to obtain a readout of The Interstellar Transport Security Authority's personnel. As usual, the staff's codenames are formed from ITSA: Quartermaster Sita, First Guard Tias, Supervisor at large Aitsaita, and Recruits Issat, Istats, Staiti, Atasst, and Atis. Given the threat they pose to the Great Rotation, she digs a level deeper and is relieved that they are only studying eccentric planetary orbits and the cultural-material link between tidal-locking and socio-economic development.

"Severum will report to his superiors today, if he hasn't done so already. Our Twilight base is compromised, he knows the coordinates, and we can't even return to our meeting spot on Evig Natt," Thalassa advises.

"I sent the order to our seconds-in-command to disassemble the Twilight base and rebuild on Dayburn. We'll take the smallest and most expensive components, and leave behind the rest. If Evig Natt's government is involved, it still won't be fast enough, I fear," Arcturus replies.

"You okay?"

"Yes, I mean, no. Too many events at once, too much change.

Now, the base." She reaches out for Thalassa's hand, but quickly withdraws, pocketing her affection.

"We chose space fountain technology because we can move both our base and the energy device in no time. We *planned* for this, Arc."

"We planned for this, Arc," she echoes.

"Arc, calm down."

"We planned for this, Arc. We planned for that, Arc," she repeats in monotone, without mocking or sarcasm.

"Arc, it's okay, I know you're stressed, but we can rebuild. Think about numbers, it soothes you. How long do we have?" Thalassa asks.

"An estimated twenty hours. We planned for this. We seemed to have stopped the Aporia for a while. Maybe the band was isolated, or maybe other tribes are sending insurgents as we speak. We can't afford to be hit at both angles. It'd be the end of us."

"We don't need to oversee the Twilight base deconstruction. We should choose the relocation spot and get back to schedule as soon as possible."

"Agreed. I'll communicate our decision to the team once it's finalized."

"How do you feel about Gestalt dying?" Thalassa asks, picking up on her need, holding her hand.

"I feel nothing," she replies, breaking her grip.

"Nothing means a higher level of something than something usually does. There is no absence of thought, it's just your defenses up. Express yourself."

"There is nothing." Rain stings her face, not a lulling legato, but a staccato assault that gathers in the alabaster craters of her sunken cheeks, smearing down to her flattened lower lip. "It's not the betrayal that bothers me, or even her death, though I know it should. It's the fear of who I'll be when I take her spot."

OPAL LEAPS OFF A CLIFF. Fireflies glow inside the hang-glider's control bar, streaking the sky. Wind rushes through the glider's flute pipes. She shifts her weight to move right, raising covers to adjust the flute tones. She ascends and descends in an aerial symphonic dance, passing through a school of airfish that shake off a foray of water droplets as if sprinklers. The song is bitter-sweet and its droning tones echo off the cliff wall. Aurthur runs down a slope and across the field to keep up.

"Now you try!" she insists, feet bouncing along the ground for landing.

"No, no, I possibly can't, I mean I can't possibly."

"Try it, you passed the training. I'm not giving up."

"I'm not giving in."

"Then decide where we're going next."

"Anywhere, I don't care."

She shakes her head. "My second home is that museum over the hill. I like to pretend I've collected all that stuff from my travels. Always wanted to be an anthropology professor."

Holographic sculptures greet them at the museum's entrance, advertising the only remaining painting from the Earth Collection, a decaying *Esquisse pour Autour du cercle* by Kandinsky. An installation of wood carvings shows ornate handles on ordinary household objects. She grabs his arm to stop, but he turns his shoulders and scoots away.

"I don't like unskilled art," he announces loudly, others staring.

"It's an accomplishment for art to bring forth any emotion. Even the lower classes without expensive art classes are allowed to express themselves. You're only concerned because you aren't represented, but the culture represents your kind every day."

"My kind? Oh, really. I know everything about being poor;

I've studied all the demographics of poverty." He crosses his arms, raises his chin.

"Means nothing. Let's change subjects. The minimalist abstract gallery is next. Less for you to criticize."

"Boring."

"In abstracts your imagination fills the canvas. Would you rather defer your perception to the artist?"

"It's just that anyone can draw boxes."

"Don't be so arrogant," Opal replies, distancing herself, but he won't back down.

"The difference between arrogance and confidence is having something to back it up, and the degree of jealousy you produce in the accusing person."

"I'm jealous you can't draw boxes?" she asks, both annoyed and laughing. "Look at this one. It's happy, bright red and happy. If I wanted realism I'd take a photo."

"It's rigid, blood-thirsty. Happiness is a momentary lapse of reason."

"You really know how to show a girl a good time, yes?"

"Oh, I sort of, forgot that is what we are…"

"Believe me, you won't be reminded tonight."

Aurthur pulls a memory sphere out of his pocket. It enlarges around them, penetrating their bodies and capturing the scene from every direction at once. After a series of flashes it contracts into the palm of his hand as his occipts flicker.

"Are you modifying the memory you took? Are you changing the background?" she asks, noting the flickering.

"No, of course not."

"No, seriously. I can see the ocean in the sphere, the waves you added behind us, as if the gallery isn't good enough?" She penetrates the sphere with her hand, smelling the sea and feeling the faint sensation of water as it synchronizes with her cognigraf. Placing her finger to her full lips, she bites her knuckle and mumbles, "I can taste the salt of your lies, fresh in my wound."

"It's my choice how I remember this."

"I can't believe I helped create these spheres. I don't know if memories bring people together, or force them apart. This is real to me; it needs to be real to you, too." She pulls her own sphere out, its lines expanding across the gallery.

"What are you doing?" he asks, reaching, trying to stop the sphere from expanding as his hands pass right through it.

"Capturing your deceit. Don't worry, I'll replace your image with someone who wants a relationship."

The sphere captures them from all angles, the bursts of light like gunfire. Aurthur's forehead becomes an accordion performing an over-played sales jingle to sell an apology. "I'm sorry. My father's ill and I'm trying to figure out how I'm going to spend the rest of my finite years." He takes her hand but she draws away. "O.A.K. needs us, and we're stronger together than apart."

He stares at the abstracts, face crumpled with confusion.

ARCTURUS RIDES the airbus to the agreed-upon site of the new base with Thalassa squeezed into the seat beside her. They have communicated the location to their front-line leaders but otherwise it remains a secret. The passengers lie on narrow cots saying little. First Gestalt, then Severum – so much betrayal, but it brings no anger to creep into the sewers of repression, just a wave of sorrow. She's dedicated so many years to this project without a payoff. Progress joins regress until the difference is lost. "Do you know your name refers to the sea?" She asks.

"Yeah, I know," Thalassa replies, resting her head on Arcturus' shoulder, wrapping her hand around her, caressing her upper arm.

"Related to the name Thalatte, an alternate name for Tiamat."

"Really? Who's that?"

"A peaceful creator goddess. When she cried her tears gave birth to rivers. Then, men feared her influence and overtook her image, demonizing her as an embodiment of chaos. She became seen as a dragon whose tail was the Milky Way." She combs her hands through Thalassa's tangles.

"So, the more men demonize our gender, the more they must fear us, and the more power we have over the organization of the cosmos. I like that." She uncrosses her legs.

Arcturus studies the pale hairs on her neck until she's distracted by a child's cry. She turns her head, wrinkles her nose at a mother consoling her child, reminding her of her own failed maternity. Her fallopian tubes are hollow tunnels where there is no schedule for her divine train to follow. She once had an engineer, but he wouldn't stick around when he found the train was off the rails. As a naturalist, he rejected artificial fertility methods. In response, Arcturus rejected nature itself, in addition to those who feared technology, and vowed to oppose them, rapidly increasing her rank at O.A.K. He was the black keys that fell between her fingers' natural inclinations, an unfamiliar scale of staccato affection. Now, she sings in monotone. She recalls the saddest melodies in A minor and the happiest in C major both share the same notes; it's all about where you start the day from, and the tension that builds to return to that point. She falls asleep in this barren cradle of remembrance.

She lies in a nest of broken egg husks in her dream, cracked and pointed and poking at her insides, the spill of bloody yolk soaking her clothes. A door barely budges open, a river ceasing to flow through the arched entrance. Hollow wooden chimes sound vacant notes. *It's not my fault!* She screams in her dream, yet it must be her fault, for each vacant note resounds with her name. Rubbing her fingers along the polished pebbles of the riverbed, the still current carries her hand to a submerged lever connected to a dam. A man's hand appears over hers and they open it together, but no water rushes through the floodgates.

Instead, electrified wind forms a fetal shape and whirls through, shocking her, slamming her body against the rocky shore – betrayed by this spirit of creation. The last drops of the river vanish into some unseen drain and the man disappears. She has to leave, has to escape. She bangs with bleeding fists on the arched door, but there is only the silence of unborn laughter.

12

A grain permeates The Towers as if his life is being played through an old film reel as Severum recalls previous visits. Stratus clouds swirl like a charred nebula under slouching smears of aborted cirrus. Artificial light pours out its windows where rain rolls down in dunes. He lets go of the Priestess' hand as she hides behind the iron door of apprehension. Restricted security feed displays late night deliveries on the far side of the building, viewable only with the correct occipt calibration. They bio-identify—entry authorized. The Governor meets them immediately.

"Governor Borges, I appreciate you meeting on such short notice," Severum says.

"Professional face. On with it. Who is your accomplice?" he asks, eyeing the Priestess.

"You may remember me, Governor."

"It matters not. Wait outside."

"She's the head of the Aporia Asylum, a group opposing the Great Rotation, the woman we spoke of," Severum says. "She arranged for our recent discussion and assisted with information being passed your way."

"I daresay, it really is her. So we have an ally, after all. She must stay; her reputation precedes her. What else do you have to report, Severum?"

"He's speaking as if I'm not here," the Priestess whispers.

Severum shoos her away. "O.A.K. is led by three people, Thalassa, Arcturus, and Gestalt. They all have unique information on their operations that they don't share with one another. We have the approximate location of their central operations and energy transfer device due to my infiltration. Gestalt was playing both sides, working for the Aporia. She has been terminated."

"So you killed one of the glitches," the governor says as the Priestess looks down.

"Simply put, she died during the operation. The other two got away."

"How?"

"They… outnumbered us."

"Very well. You escaped with the general location and the names and faces of the leaders. I will forward the location to my troops and in a few days' time we will infiltrate the base. Scope the place out first. Send your findings directly to me."

"I fear the space fountain technology is more mobile than you think," the Priestess speaks up reluctantly. "These people live on the brink of change and they know they're hunted."

"How dare you doubt our capacities! My men won't stop until O.A.K. is obliterated. Our mission is to dismantle the base and take out the remaining leaders. Severum, after scoping the base you will provide support during the strike, avoiding direct assault. Track down the leaders and any members who retreat. Collateral damage is acceptable."

"Very well. I'll take my leave, Sir."

"I want to come with you, Sheva," she pleads, quickening her step to follow him outside.

"I won't stop you."

"Even if it puts me in harm's way? You really don't care?"

"No. This is what you believe in. It's just a paycheck to me. Either way."

"You don't believe in it?"

"The governor enforces rules that somehow don't apply to him. The tower windows say as much. That glow isn't caused by fireflies."

"Yes, it's called power, they do what they want. But it's almost as if you doubt we should put an end to the Great Rotation? I can't believe what I'm hearing. Every time you open your mouth another wedge is driven between us." She increases pace, moving in front of him.

"No, it's my duty. I just... some things need to change, Akasha. I don't know what yet. I know I wasn't there for you before, and I don't want to make the same mistake. I don't want to go against you on this, but we need to think it through. I can't talk to the governor about my reservations, he won't understand. He sees everything as either leading to his goals or away from them so everything's reduced to this forward or backward motion that leaves us all dizzy and confused. But I feel you understand me, the only one who truly can."

"That's the most you've said to me in a while. Let's go back to the safe house. And tonight, our room needs to be kept much warmer, that is, if you mean what you say."

"I can handle that," he replies, trying to smile while scraping one fingernail beneath the next. "It didn't take long to get here; it won't take long to get back."

"Not every return journey is so easy."

Back at the safe house, a vortex hovers over the crossroads of his old and new life, settling in around her. Her slender hand cups her face on the bed, one bent finger slowly, slowly dragging down her pensive lip. The tension is released, yet builds, as it springs back into shape. She tilts her head and parts her mouth, waiting to be embraced, flipping her tongue to the side, mouthing a silent *please*. He strips his shirt, buttons popping.

Holding her face, he kisses her, lips giving way again and again as their mouths slide upon one another, gripping here and there, tugging and pulling, smoothing and biting. A pool of moisture gathers in the corners. Throwing her arms back against the headboard, Severum girdles her waist with his fingertips, sliding up to remove her blouse.

Musical musings resonate across oceans pregnant with waves to bear waves to bare time itself, a time to catch up, a time to redeem. Past, present, future unite in every kiss, simple, perfect, continuous. Fingers like solar flares entwine, drifting across each region. It is just as wondrous and confusing as the first time he touched a woman, but he still fantasizes about a generic woman, distancing himself. For him, the woman is the means to produce the fantasy, instead of the fantasy producing the woman. As she becomes part of him, he is not worthy of her love, as he is not worthy of his own self-love. The ridges in his lips offer no traction for the kisses, no cushion for the blow.

"Are you alright?" she asks, pulling a sheet over her.

"What? Oh, yeah, yeah, of course. Just trying to delay it."

"Well, you delayed it; you're not even aroused now."

"Oh, that can be taken care of."

Yet here among the creases of her navel hub, the wrinkles around her eyes, the soft thorns of her pelvic hair, here among her rising and falling chest, her neck backwards thrown, staring at a face that age gently brushed like a feather upon a lake surface, here among a new ancient home that had once caught fire under its own flame—something in him has arrived again as if for the first time. They explode into one another creating space-time anew, freeing their lives.

He can deal with the word *her.* It implies distance. But *you,* is too intimate, too close and accusatory. These thoughts must be guarded; they lust only for their own attention. Condemned to the freedom of love, they retire in each other's arms, planning to sleep in late, the fate of humanity resting in the delicacy of their relationship.

———

NEXT EVENING, they head out to grab the transport to scope O.A.K.'s Twilight base. The district is packed. Corporations shed their employees like snakes shedding skin. They tunnel out of their cubicles, leaving virtual footprints in the shapes of logos. Mission statements flow across virtual uniforms to give false importance to tasks that have no meaning. Missions worth undertaking do not require a mission statement—when a thief breaks into a home people just act, because it is worth acting. One by one, employees turn off their outfits like fallen stars blinking out, going from walking billboards to people again. The Forever Glitched sit on the street curbs silently threatening them with having their job replaced if they're disobedient.

"A commitment to growth and progress is just an assault on the past, a judgement on our traditions," the Priestess says. "Everything we think we know, all the history, amounts to isolated scholars tracing the creases of time, debating the order of its folding until the form itself is lost. We keep toiling, trying to force it to return to its original shape. This is what I've devoted my life to, returning all of this to its previous shape, forcing my will to stop change."

"Maybe this isn't the only way to live," Severum replies, shrugging.

The city's circulatory system is capital, credit, and speculation. Culture is the liver that filters its dissenters. A kamikaze ad for reduced interest rates shoots across the sky like a meteor, hitting the ground and exploding as its shrapnel logos expel across vHUD. Severum dives out of the way, hitting the street. Laughter all around. Lying face down following the virtual bombardment, he reaches into his pocket and smashes the glass holding a giant firefly. Cutting his hand, he wrings the life out of the bug as the sticky goo swamps him. His bloody hand withdraws with a sucking sound and rubs his chin, another mustard seed of skepticism implanting itself. The laughing stops.

"Transport is right ahead. Remember, we're just gathering information. I'll keep you safe."

"Right now I think you need me more than I need you," the Priestess replies, blotting his hand.

———

"THEY'RE BACK!" exclaims Sirius, a young man with shaggy hair and a biohazard tattoo. He steps aside to let the transport trucks travel through.

"No rejoicing, there's work to be done," Arcturus says. "Nice place. Smaller, but we'll make it work. You all constructed this new base well before the deadline. A few more buildings to go and we'll be there."

"When there's nowhere to sleep it motivates you. I was just laying the roof for the lab," he replies, clapping his hands to create a dust cloud. "How's the deconstruction going at the old base?"

"Reports indicate there'll be nothing left by the time they investigate."

"That's 'cause we're *fluid* Arc, we're mobile, we're a process. But, is it true about the Architect?"

"Matters not."

A wide-eyed elderly man drops a box, keeping beat to a drum circle that went silent years ago. He grabs another member and yells, "You're here! Welcome to Dayburn! Havva jug of water, it's hot as hell. Been waiting for your return, lot of questions 'bout this superstructure of culture in our pamphlets. What's all this talk about?"

"Random request. I like randomness. It's simple," Arcturus

replies. "The elements of culture that survive, science, law, religion, state, are no longer adaptations to the natural environment. Collectively, we make them up in our heads through our habitual exchanges. But they soon become power-hungry entities that create the need for their own existence. Those who know me know I am not prone to metaphor, so this should say something. Culture's the way we define what's possible to think, and what isn't. There are no redeeming qualities to it. Kill your deity, kill your language, or kill yourselves trying."

"The elite are in our heads!" the old man affirms, leaning forward. Motioning to others, he announces, "She's lecturing, come on guys!"

"You say guys when you speak to a group of mostly women. You think in their terms when they say you can. They define your lunch breaks, your paychecks, your coming and going. They track your every footstep, stamped with their logos. They reduce your freewill by giving you so much choice, a dozen brands of shaving cream, taxing your brains with responsibility to make decisions that have no value. Consumerism as social control, distraction. You are not free, yet today we work for solace, we work for peace, we work for light."

"Bringing the light will make us free!" he chants as others join, "Bringing the light will make us free! Bringing the light will make us free!"

"A natural light free of bourgeois arrogance," she adds. "The Great Rotation sheds light to awaken class consciousness," but she is barely heard over the increasing roar as more emerge from the base to welcome them.

"Do you believe in God?" Ciara asks, laying in the sand with her face propped in her palms.

"Do you believe in words?"

"Well, are there many gods or just one?"

"You put too much faith in numbers."

"Oh, wow, that's in the outer reaches right there." Ciara is clothed in a summer that never came. Until she publicly disavowed the Aporia Asylum, no one knew she used to be a member. As radicals often do, she navigated towards the opposite perspective at the slightest sign of inconsistency. Fundamentalists become anarchists, revolutionaries become zealots. She clinches her necklace, a nazar to protect against the evil eye. "My good luck charm," she says to no one. She returns to work, using augmented fingers to convert a power output specs doc to vHUD text. "Rerouting rats. These things'll dig the tunnels 'round the planet for the power cables needed to transfer the energy to the belts. Shame we have to modify the plans so much, but if the energy transfer device is going to move then the rest needs to adapt."

"The device is called an ergon… forget it. Thanks for the update. Once the rotation increases, the machines will have accomplished what nature failed to," Arcturus says.

"One problem. We weighed the Ultimaepar but we don't have enough to rebuild the key components. Some minerals had to be left behind in the rush to escape the old base before the military strike."

"I hope you're kidding."

"I'm afraid not."

"It's all useless without it! We can't operate. Find another source, now!"

Severum throws his hands in the air. "We're too late. I didn't think it'd take this long to get to O.A.K.'s Twilight base. It's all gone, all of it. Whose idea was it to sleep in all day?"

"I think we made that decision together, through actions not words." The Priestess grabs him by the shirt, leans close. "You weren't distracted by work when you woke, for once. Are you sure these are the coordinates?"

"Course I'm sure!" Severum exclaims as she steps back. "Sorry, but the base is a wasteland, nothing but sheds and debris. See the tire tracks inside? Trucks hauled it all away, the whole damn base."

"We could trace the tracks."

"Negative. Looks like they had a droid start covering the tracks once they left the base. They probably headed to Dayburn where they know we aren't permitted to use satellites. The whole Nachten camp's gone."

"Do not use night as a curse; its goddess will curse you back. Let's exhume history together, but this time in the soil. There's always something left behind. Start with these minerals. They're nothing like we covered in class."

"Unusual, I admit. Extremely dense. Trace their distribution across the planet."

"Dayburn as you expected, various sites. It's known as Ultimaepar."

"The raw form of repellium? We still need more intel."

A curious cat with a rhino horn roams the landscape, nibbling on rotten rations. It scurries towards him. A beep sounds, shrill, intensifying. It gets higher, faster, and the cat freezes. Sudden vibration, then a subterranean belch. Boom! Its body is thrown across the sky in an explosion that knocks Severum back, heat searing his face.

"Akasha!"

"Are you okay?" she asks, bending down to cradle his back.

"I think so. Cat was a walking time-bomb."

"Run your vitals."

"I'm fine. Who puts a bomb in a cat?"

"You're not thinking straight. It set off a mine. O.A.K. must have rigged the place before abandoning it."

"The mines didn't show up in my scans. I always check. You need to stay back. Geo-imaging can at least tell me where the ground's been disturbed and clue me in as to where more mines are hidden."

"It's too risky."

"It's my job, what am I supposed to be, broke?" Later, he kicks a pile of broken wood and wipes his brow. "It's been two hours of searching, not knowing if the next step will be my last, and my hands are aching."

"You seldom complain. It's too much right now."

"I don't like this needle in a haystack bullshit. I mean, they've obviously cleaned up the place immaculately. They might have more people than we thought."

"I told you to not underestimate them."

"The Architect's whole strategy was fucked up to begin with. Creating a group in opposition to her beliefs just to monitor who signed up. It's a complete mess."

"She merely escalated the inevitable. A group would have arisen against us eventually, just as ITSA arose against AAI in space."

"You agree with her methods, even though it got her killed?"

"Yes," the Priestess replies, hesitating. "Better to have one main group spring up than a hundred smaller ones. The Aporia Asylum must exist. On every planet, branches of AAI monitor terraforming activities that compromise the stability of the galaxy. We are the *Watchers*. Gestalt would have never let the Great Rotation reach fruition, and it was never beyond her control, or so we thought."

"Each of those smaller groups would have had far less resources to draw on though. I understand it's hard to monitor them, and Gestalt's goal was to organize all this discontent against the Aporia in one place. But it also empowered them. Don't you think she sympathized with them at least a little?"

"I long expected it, but I put my trust in her. Back to business; they must have had a way to transport all the power they required. Wireless power doesn't work on this scale," she says, scanning the ground.

"Right. So there should be evidence underground of power cables built to supply the base, or at least the tunnels the cables were fed through. That would be hard to disguise in a short amount of time. See, I knew I brought you along for something," he says, though she doesn't return the smile. He lays a topographic map over his vision. "The indentations on the ground over there are the deepest. It appears a heavy cube-shaped object was lifted. Given the depth, it would have taken a crane, unless it was disassembled. A hoverlift wouldn't have budged it."

"You're right. Heavy things that size tend to be important, and power would have been connected to it. Let's radiate out from there."

Severum retrieves two shovel kits from his supply pack that assemble themselves. Sensors reveal in vHUD what lies beneath the soil as they dig. Soon, they discover an underground tunnel system just wide enough for cables to pass through, but empty inside. An attempt to fill the tunnels was made, but imaging reveals where the soil is less compacted, recently disturbed.

"Tunnel tracks are traceable. Given the project scope they'll extend all way around the planet. They'll connect to main hubs, and if we track these tunnels to those hubs, we'll eventually locate their new base. I'll report to my superiors to ensure we have the resources we need to follow the trail. When we receive the trace we'll scope out their new base and call in the strike."

"Are you sure?" she asks, tugging on her earlobe.

"What do you mean?"

"Nothing."

"These are anarchists, Akasha. They create these complex devices to simplify the natural order of things, to erase our complex hierarchies and provide light equally to everyone, but you just can't do it, you can't create complexity to reduce it."

"I'm not sure I agree."

"If O.A.K. had government ties I might join them. But without that organization, this all ends in a society without rule, destroying itself. They're a bunch of kids playing with things they barely understand. In the absence of power I don't see the people as emerging victorious, I see them in total anarchy begging the next military dictator for order."

"Everything will return to chaos at some point, and maybe we are the ones interfering with nature, not them," she says.

"If we can't stop everything from going to hell, then we at least need to do what we can to dampen the kindling," he replies, stretching his hands out to her.

"My goal is to support the planet's ecology first and foremost. But maybe a world created by machines and a world created by nature are the same in the end. And sometimes things need to go to hell. Nature needs forest fires to revitalize itself. Sometimes destruction is necessary for creation, Sheva, just like Gestalt used to tell me."

"Stop calling me that. Creation through destruction, resolution through conflict, love through abandonment, abandonment! Pardon me if I don't jump on the lunatic bandwagon. This is nonsense, and the next time someone starts spouting nonsense I'm gonna—"

"Make your call," she sighs. "The other day at the Asylum, death became a very real thing to me. I don't want more bloodshed, whatever that means to our plans. I'll try my best to follow what you think, just make sure it's you making the decision. And I want you to know, I've always given you all my time. Even when I was gone I thought of you constantly. That is what being true to you really means."

"I don't even know what I'm fighting for anymore. Losing this fight is losing you all over again." His fist bangs against sheet metal. He shakes his head, shakes the emotions like marbles running through a maze trying to find the right hole to fit back into, but each hole is in the shape of her absence and he buries his anger in that hole, but it doesn't quite fit, because in the end it's not her that is the target, not her who deserves his rage.

"You are more than your beliefs. The Aporia Asylum… I just wanted away from you. I will not judge you no matter what you decide. Our love is without condition. We love without evidence, so there can be no evidence to the contrary."

"You trust me enough to judge the fate of humanity?"

"Yes, always. You judge the fate of my heart, what more is humanity?"

13

———————

Thirty people carry volatile liquids and supplies across barren dirt roads, tired and sweaty, the unwavering sun upon them. Metal tents self-assemble in rows of small pyramids. They've managed to upgrade a barren strand to a refugee camp in no time. O.A.K.'s members finish testing various devices for functionality, binding long tarps around the equipment to protect it from blowing sands until more storage space is constructed. Half retire, while the rest gather in a circle to lose themselves in tribal drum beats.

Arcturus pulls off her synthetic silk shirt leaving a white tank-top her body strains against over high-cut shorts. Her hair has grown longer and dark, the virtual dye license having expired. She grabs a Moroccan-styled rug, weaving her fingers between its threads. Thalassa helps her stretch it across the hardened sand floor of the tent as they pull the flap shut.

"Couldn't the tent have assembled a bed for us?" Thalassa asks.

"We should be thankful. These items don't come cheap. Then again, maybe at least a pillow wouldn't hurt, but I rather stay here. The stimulation's overwhelming outside."

"This'll help you go to sleep," Thalassa says, handing her a Sarahtoning mod.

"I think they're addictive."

"Everything's addictive. We're creatures of habit." She winks.

"I don't want you doing that. We have plans to make, an image to maintain. That's what the other side would want, for us to lose credibility."

"They'll sell a false image of us either way. None of us rebelled to be controlled, Arc."

"Some control is a good thing."

"Well, I can't work without sleep and I'm too stressed to get any," she replies, popping the neuralmod and rubbing Arcturus' bare arm, first softly, then with a firm but soothing grip.

"But you're not you when you do this stuff, makes me miss you."

"What is me? It's all me; it's all you. We're all one, trying to survive. Don't you love yourself enough to allow for a good time?"

"It's different."

"How?" she asks with a smirk and a tilt of her head, feigning submission with a hand on Arc's satin thigh.

Arcturus removes her hand. "Right now we need to focus on locating the final key element. We've identified a possible site nearby. The team couldn't gather enough Ultimaepar in time to transport it, given its density, and it's too risky returning to the old base. But we must have it. We shouldn't speak here though."

"We're fine, don't worry."

"Guards talk and your reassurances are worth nothing. Your reactions were slow, sloppy, after Severum released our prisoners."

"That night wasn't my fault. You're wrong!" Thalassa turns to the side, hands on cheeks.

"You were coming off of being meteored. Sloppy."

The mod sweeps over Thalassa. The branches of a burning tree expand across the metallic ceiling like a fractal replicating itself. The ceiling melts, raining upon her, drenching her to-do lists into nothingness. She is the gap between each drop. They flow to give birth to a river only to evaporate and rain again, running over the sands, the wetness seeking the dry.

"And you want me to say what?" Arcturus asks with an open palm.

"Shhhh," she murmurs, placing Arc's own finger to her lips. Don't speak, no, not yet. The tree has faded into the wall again. We're safe for now, until it hears another accusation."

"Umm, I'm going to grab those pillows after all, get some space from you. And that wasn't Sarah you took." Arcturus leaves, returns a few minutes later carrying pillows, and continues. "The whole project is fragile. Too many new people getting too close to things lately."

"We had no choice. By the time reinforcements would have arrived… besides, how many could we have spared?"

"Aurthur and Opal are the most suspicious. Their actions are always exaggerated and nervous, especially around one another."

"I think they like each other," Thalassa replies, tenderly brushing sand off Arc's cheeks, letting her finger linger on her lower lip a little.

"I don't understand why."

"They don't need you to. Just trust what feels good."

"That doesn't make sense."

"How about this, then? My name is ocean and you can be the shore I rock up against, okay?"

"I hate poetry. Where you get those mods from anyway?"

"One of our members sells them on the side."

"That compromises our image, Thalassa. We can't have one of our members being brought in for routine charges and then spilling the whole project."

"It's for a good cause. We, I mean he, uses the funds to help

O.A.K. Tell you what. What is a non-conformist?" Thalassa asks, popping another neuralmod when she looks away to think.

"Nonconformists are complex people because they have more decisions to make. There are more ways to be deviant than there are to conform. More ways for matter to disorganize than organize. Most people rely on habits to alleviate the stress of making small choices, but not nonconformists. But soon they become just as simple as anyone else because they must develop some consistency in their thoughts, if not just to give them meaning. They find something to conform to eventually. True nonconformity can never be automated. It cannot be stuck in place."

"*Fluid*, yes. Opening your mind will allow you to regain the complexity you've lost."

"No chip-trips. I don't want to lose control."

"What better way to prove you have control, than by losing it on your own terms?" Thalassa opens her hand and brushes the inside of Arc's palm, dropping a mod.

Arcturus takes it.

"Medicine makes the sugar go down better. Now fade into me," Thalassa whispers, burying her nose in her hair, absorbing her scent. She nibbles her ear, the spongy texture giving way, eager, so eager to be in control of her for once so she can force Arcturus to accept her.

Her hands slide up Arc's sides, her skin smooth like dripping moonlight. Her collarbone forms a triangle leading to the triangle of her pelvis leading to a smaller triangle yet. She unzips Arc's shorts, trying to separate the boundary of mind and matter as the room's rising colors unzip in turn.

"Shh," she says, parting the ripe strawberry of her mouth and sliding her tongue along the edge of her teeth. She removes Arc's tank-top to reveal an expanse of taut flesh rising and falling. She caresses the bell-shaped breasts, Arc pulling away and folding her arms before daring to return the touch on her open thighs. Her spine bends, each bare vertebra tattooed with the head of an enlarged screw. Thalassa slides a hand down the pink alcove of her underwater cavern, lowering to explore it, delving the *dea abscondita* within.

Arc's unsure if she's dominating or being dominated, wondering if her body's betraying her by parting the seas for Thalassa's current, her one ocean, to splash within. "Let me drown, for all I care, right now, right here, with you," she whimpers. The froth of her exhales gather atop each wave of pleasure and she soon shudders, her body erupting as the sea gushes to fill the room. Lost within infinite regress, like two mirrors facing one another, they free themselves from gender, accessing a far deeper and more ancient state of being.

OPAL PROPS on her elbows and stretches across the mauve satin sheets. Her golden dress gathers in puddles between her legs, like Flaming June. She slicks back her short burgundy hair, hair that does nothing to conceal her long neck.

Aurthur parts the orange drapes of her bed canopy. He gases half the fireflies to dim the lights, slowly removing his shirt as if self-conscious of his lanky frame. A trail of hair leads down from his navel. "Should we check up on O.A.K.?" he asks as if to distract himself.

"Not sure. They strike me as people who put up a big talk, but I haven't seen much proof of what they're intending to do."

"You believe in the whole speeding up the rotation thing?"

"Don't know much about terraforming, but we need change, sure. The question is, how patient can we afford to be, which comes down to what we're willing to risk," she replies, hanging onto the word risk, doubting her own attractiveness, feeling silly in her posture, wondering if she has misinterpreted everything. She grabs a pillow to cover with, loses the smile.

"I'm willing to risk it all," he replies, drawing near, shoulders back.

"No, you're not. Goals which arrive suddenly leave just as sudden. I'm glad you came over though. You're starting to grow on me. I don't mean the individual moments, they suck, but when I view them as a whole, it's got the groove down. But, I need to be upfront with you, am I just a goal that will be suddenly left, a mere conquest?"

"My lady of many colors, the celestial bodies have their orbits, and I mine own. My atoms were forged in a solar reflex in response to your moon that I must unify with."

"So, basically I'm a cold-hearted glitch and you expect me to revolve around you? I may not have an atmosphere, but I keep myself warm enough. Who do you think you are anyway?" she asks with a reserved smile, rubbing her index finger along the side of his face.

"I am Prometheus unbound," he replies, leaning forward to kiss her. She ducks away and he continues, "Prometheus proved thievery has its place, right?"

"Are you up to tempting the gods?"

Aurthur presses his lips briefly to hers, surprising both of them. Her shoulders converge into small mountains of tension before lapsing back into the sea of skin with release. Another kiss moist like melting ice, yet warm like melting chocolate. Tongues dance around a fire, limbs hopelessly enwrapped like jellyfish weaving Celtic knot-work. He struggles with the Gordian knot of her bra. Travelling the curves of the unsolvable, he traces her body as if laying a golden thread to find his way back through the labyrinth of emotions. Shy, they watch themselves from afar, communicating through touch alone, voyeurs of their own lovemaking. These strange loops of perception intertwine, then thought itself drips away like sweat off their bodies.

Two stranded ships have met, desperate to make land. Soon, the seamless sea reveals a zipper as the ocean's contents are undone, spilling out dangerously upon the tall, cragged rock. The sea relentlessly swallows its worshipper.

"Dreams are just parallel universes colliding."

"Shut the fuck up," she replies, pulling his mouth open with hers again and again. In the pendulum motion that ensues, time is meaningless. The night passes, but the acceptance lingers, the total and complete acceptance in their nakedness, all cards on the table. Validation.

Next morning, Opal's vHUD flashes and a voice says, "It's Thalassa, we need you for something."

"I'm not sure I wanna help," she replies, snuggling up to Aurthur, bringing his reluctant hand over her breast, and yawning. "Hold on." VHUD displays a low probability of pregnancy, but she pre-orders Abort as easily as setting an alarm clock.

"A tribe is in danger. We're not going through the risk of hiring an outsider. We trust you, we need you. The loss of Gestalt has been hard enough, and with you being an anthropologist…"

"What are you suggesting?"

"We need to use the tribe's land for resources. The resources are useless to them, but we need them for the new base, having lost a lot during the move."

"You want my help to exploit the tribe for their natural resources?"

"Yes."

"You're unusually cold today. You sound like her."

"Like Arcturus? I'm not feeling well. We need you to negotiate to ensure a peaceful affair. Otherwise my comrades will take what we need by force."

"A devil's demands. Fair enough. Maybe in the end I can write up the results and get a real job out of it. Where's this place at?"

"Sending."

She rubs Aurthur's lazy head and says, "Looks like it's back to Dayburn. First, I need to research a few things at the university. Let's be prepared."

———

"ENOUGH WAITING. I'm leaving base and I'm leaving O.A.K.," Sirius states the next morning, throwing items from his tent into a duffle bag.

"Why?" Arcturus asks.

"You pacifists don't get one thing; our protests are pointless if we aren't a credible threat. Peace movements are only taken seriously if they carry the threat of violence. I was really excited to see you come back, but tinkering with electronics is getting us nowhere and I'm exhausted, plus, we're defenseless out here."

"Violence begets violence. It's what they want, it's *their* method, *their* ideology. Bringing the light is the only thing powerful enough to change the world. If you're impotent from lack of getting any action then go hack yourself."

"Hey, you can't talk to me like that!"

"I am the static sliver of acid rain that'll devour every stone you ever walk upon for the rest of your years. Don't fuck with me. Sit down and do your fucking job."

"So we can only be violent with words?"

She slaps him in the face, betraying her message.

"Maybe I should get back to work then," he admits, returning to his duties.

The scene slips sideways in slow motion that jerks to make up time as another wave hits her. She calibrates her occipts' refresh rate to match her current state of awareness. Black snow falls from a white sky, inverting everything it touches in negative images. Waving her arms wildly, she stresses, *The mod won't turn off, why won't it turn off? Something is trying to break out of my mind. Is DIY surgery a good idea? How long can I ride the asymptote of infinite? I can no longer divide the world into me and not me. I have been filling myself with only myself. I belong to everything that belongs to me. Forgive me my femininity, my masculinity, my submerged strength.* "What day is it?"

"I think it's yesterday's morning of tomorrow's evening," Thalassa says.

"Eve, birth, rebirth."

"You meteored still, Arc?"

"Call me Aorca, like a whale on a chrome sea singing a beautiful song, yet one that is alien, misunderstood, and long extinct."

"Just don't forget we're being hunted and they're carrying more than just harpoons. You gotta start light next time, sis. What were you thinking? Why'd you make me give that to you?"

Arcturus rushes out to camp where a dozen gather. "You're all the same! You speak their language. You talk their talk. They've commodified you, destroyed you from within. We're obsessed with what's fair when we're young. It's natural. But how soon do we sell out in hopes we'll have more, more, more. There is no *more!*"

"Whoa, Arc's meteored. Hey guys, look," a guy with a drawn-out voice remarks.

"You look to me for a paint-by-numbers identity. Do I believe in this, do I believe in that, looking for some structure to your pathetic lives. Well, here it is! Not exciting enough? I care that I don't care but I still don't care," she continues. "We speak of the innocence of youth. You are not innocent. There is nothing innocent about being so easily manipulated. Illusions hide our conflict. Our stability is at others' expense."

"When she's meteored she actually sounds normal," another guy says. "Hot, too. I'd like a piece of that."

"Go ahead, she won't care," the other one replies.

"We made the mistake before, thinking Gaia a rotting fruit whose core could be extracted, defiled, plucked, and tossed.

Never again! Gliese will not fall to the same fate. This planet will be untethered and she shall be freed. We are the en*light*ened ones and from us the new age shall flow." Arcturus finishes as half the audience is breathtaken and the other half is asking where they can find whatever mod she took.

"It's a prophecy. We destroy the past to make the future," Ciara says.

"No, you have to preserve past in future's past. That's what she means," another adds.

"No, she means we save the planet by forcing it to change."

"No, she had a vision, she means…"

"I am the great Aorca. Creation is destruction!" Arcturus yells, running back inside her metallic tent. The pool of time empties into another and another pooled event as each droplet drips down to be pumped back up through corroded pipes. Before she understands what is happening, a strange man enters her tent, putting pressure on her upper body. She struggles against the mod, against the man, someone from the camp she may or may not know. He traces the curve of where her public and private domains meet.

A sudden scarlet glow reflects off the man's sweat and scorches his neck. A single swallow and he'll die.

Thalassa's blade blocks his Adam's apple, tightly pressed from behind, the edge sharp enough to draw blood on sight. "She's mine. Now go walk through the desert until you collapse of thirst. If you're lucky, I'll send a canteen of sand to quench you. Not so hard now, are you?"

He pushes her arm away, the blade leaving his neck, and draws an antique gun with the other hand, raising it before Thalassa can react. The gun fires, straight at her heart. The bullet is blocked by the dagger and melts from its heat with a puff of smoke.

"Bad idea." Thalassa cuts his weapon in half, kicks him in

the back of the knee, and knees him in the face as he falls. "Guards!"

"On our way! Everything alright?" The guards attend to the tent as a body flops through the flap.

"Take the trash out, please. Ship him back to Evig Natt."

"Say no more." The guards beat him and drag him away.

"Come here, Arc, let me hold you. Maybe you're right about the mods. Like I told him, you're mine. I'm so sorry. I'm sorry about the mods, I'm sorry I touched you while you were out of it, I'm sorry I'm no better than the man I just stopped."

"Thalassa? Is that you?"

Clearing her tears, she whispers, "I love you."

"Did Opal report back? What day is it? We have to have that mineral or the whole project collapses."

"Same old you. Sleep off your modlag, you've had a long couple of days."

14

Sunlight screams. The searing sun settles its stare, scraping across burnt skin like sandpaper. Desert blends into village with no discernible fences to separate the two. The only sign of villagers is the scent of exotic herbs cooking.

"Why didn't we meet O.A.K. at their new base first before traveling to the tribal grounds?" Aurthur asks, rubbing sand from his brow.

"They sent me the Florinik's coordinates, but not their base's, so I assume it's somewhere in the area. After all this, they still don't trust us. I didn't request any supplies. I don't want their help, and you can't predict how the primitive tribe will react to tech. Guess I shouldn't say primitive, it's ethnocentric."

"Face it, the Florinik from what you've told me *are* a primitive tribe. But they're nothing like the Aphorids, right? And you're confident you can communicate with them without having our bodies torn in two?"

"Well… the huts are ahead."

"You seem distant, like you don't trust me."

"Focused. This is my work," Opal replies, gazing at a rock atop a distant dune.

"I was focused before the trip all way back out here to the flaming side of the world where it's a billion degrees," he replies, swiping sweat from his forehead.

Opal stops dead, hands on hips. "Listen, you didn't have to come! I want to be a hero to these people to help them negotiate with O.A.K. to prevent bloodshed. But I need a hero too, someone willing to take chances and invest in me, understand? Investment is more than just painting and monitoring me to make sure I don't sleep with someone more adventurous than you."

Aurthur flattens his lips, inhales sharply, and replies, "That makes sense."

"Not to save me, but to help me reach my potential. You need to be stronger than me in at least some ways."

"I'll try better. I admire you. You create happiness from nothingness, strength from moments that others would find only weakness. You are the creative spirit of life itself."

"Then why do I think about death all the time?" she asks, staring at a skull half-buried in the sand.

"Death itself evolved. It plays a role. Perhaps when we die the data matrix of reality maintains a simple record of our lives, just as deleted files can be recovered from a hard drive. Let death increase your appreciation of life and it'll bind us together."

"True, and this is what I need to hear. I've been feeling like my own ventriloquist, like I'm not up to this role.

"You're great. Look, the sun's eruptions seem so silent from this distance, but there's a sweltering storm raging on it," Aurthur says, taking her chin and tilting it to the sky.

She raises her brows at him, hanging between annoyance and amusement. "The sun's really far. So you're saying even the most vivid impassioned moments are nothing with enough distance."

"Then let's close the distance between us."

"We can try," she replies, rubbing his shoulder, grabbing his hand. "With you beside me, I can do it!"

Thirty-six huts are arranged in circles to encourage communal interactions. The arched sides meet unevenly to form bell-shaped roofs. The tallest hut has a recess on its door in the shape of a long hand. Aurthur places his hand within it and pushes. The sides of the hut pull apart, creaking, like the sides of an orange being peeled back into slices, or a flower opening. The slits separate further and each wooden petal folds back and down revealing its white underside. Finally, the whole structure falls back and the home finishes blooming as the inside of the hut is revealed. A chair rises in the middle on a pedestal.

"Hell of a doorbell!"

Three giant moths fly from the hut and beat wings across their faces. They swipe them away, but not before the bright green spores fly from the moths' wings in a thick mist. They try to fight it, try to hold their breath, but slump to the ground in a deep sleep, Aurthur falling crooked and lightly spraining his ankle. The Florinik gather around them, tugging at their skin, pulling at their legs, and touching their hair like curious children.

A loud voice roars with amusement, "This one look like she carry confidence of ambassador. The other just worker bee. Both we shall keep," the Chief says to the blossom wearing a mono-scope. "Bring the seedlings to witness this," he orders another blossom.

She goes to gather the children.

"Our seedlings need to learn proper exchanges with the Nightwalkers at our door, the Flesheaters, the Sundimmers, the Shadowkeepers, the…" and he trails off a dozen more derogatory terms with scorned laughter.

"THEY STILL HAVEN'T REPORTED BACK," Thalassa informs Arcturus the next morning, pacing back and forth. "Do the

Florinik hate technology as much as the Aporia? Are they a threat?"

"They oppose it, but not violently. The journals say when they see a new device they simply ask, *Can it be used to build? Can it be used to hunt?* Then they quickly lose interest if the answer is no."

"I'm heading out to check on them."

"We cannot risk people leaving and being tracked back to our base. There's been too much activity just moving and rebuilding."

"Nobody will spot me, I'm one person. I won't bring droids and I'll go on foot."

"You won't make it in this heat. It's further than our excursion to the Aporia Asylum was," Arcturus warns.

"I can do it. Your determination has always inspired me, driven me, I want you to know that." She pauses, looks away to avoid a reaction, or lack of one. "Fine, don't say anything. That took a lot to say. I try to be self-sufficient and all but… Give me a sunbrella and basic provisions, my searing daggers, and my Pulser, too."

"Don't forget the heat-resistant gloves I crafted. I'm sending you some basic info about the tribe. Please, stay in touch."

Thalassa crosses the sand, making sure to crawl over the dune crests to avoid her silhouette appearing against the sky. The sand becomes fine like confectioner's sugar, the slight breeze blowing it in lazy waves across the desert. Occipt-shields drop like transparent eyelids to block sediment. The path forks. A cracked rocky path slopes upward, and a softer sandier path extends beneath it. To avoid footprints and increase speed she chooses the hard path, stretched like a thin, red ribbon, tapered like a snake's tail as it winds.

A sudden gust knocks her back. She leans forward against it, turns sideways to keep footing. It ceases and her momentum drives her flat on her face. She checks the forecast for hurricanes, but it's a false sense of security as on Gliese hurricanes occur too suddenly for warning. Her steps become shorter and shorter as ambition turns to despair. Sipping water, she realizes in her misshapen state she forgot to bring a water filter. She slams the canteen against the ground. The water oozes out until she gathers it again in case of desperation, despite Dayburn's water containing diseases her immune system isn't meant to combat. She scans for signs of water in areas where heavy metal concentrations would be minimal but finds none. She should turn back, resupply, but refuses to, refuses to come back to Arcturus weak and empty-handed. The sun mocks her efforts with stillness and silence, but the dunes are becoming lower and in the distance shapes against the horizon appear until her vision blurs.

Thalassa zooms her occipts to scan the highest plateau near the village. Upon it, a spherical cage swirls around a statue of some sort. She matches the image against a database and an entry displays: *This represents Orbis, the sole deity of the Florinik. Orbis observes all creation from on high. Occipts are considered sacrilege since they compete with Orbis. A magnetic mechanism drives the cage. The Florinik themselves are quiet observers living peacefully in an advanced horticultural civilization, having compiled the largest cataloging of plant-type life known. They do not distinguish themselves from plants. They live off the land and have few enemies, providing little pressure to increase population, allowing enough food for all their residents.*

Scavenger fish glide above her in the thick, dusty air. She checks her Pulser, but the heat has deadened its charge. She finally arrives at the village, knees giving way, collapsing into the sand with dehydration, a fate she recently wished upon another. Nauseous, she squints but can barely make out two small trees, maybe the Florinik, gathering her up, her body suspended in their long arms as if they were a stretcher. They carry her deep into the village where they offer her water, but she slaps it away, looking wistfully as it dissolves into the sand.

View narrows, blackens. The sky closes in on itself and she loses consciousness.

She wakes to the touch of long arms swaying like pendulums, ending in four fingers. Their bodies stand two and a half meters tall with long limbs and a giant stride. Clothes only cover where she imagines their genitals to be, allowing khaki-colored skin like bark to show, dotted with wide pores like blisters. Despite the UV they have no hair, just a leathery rigid brown scalp. Their deeply recessed eyes have an enlarged membrane over them as if they're in bubbles. They slant inward, reducing their range of sight, but their deep sockets must block the sandstorms. Tiny golden irises appear like ember sparks in deep wells. A thin crease satisfies for a nose above the mouth that extends across most of their round faces.

"It is, a pleasure to meet you," Thalassa stutters in their language, which she knows little of, sitting cross-legged.

"Sap and bother! Some greeting for a Chief!" the Chief yells in Thalassa's language, waving his long arms over his head. "What a situation! You have our language murdered, the language of our tribe you call Plant People, the Florinik, the Sungatherers, the Solarsemblances, the…" and he goes on to list a dozen more honorary titles.

"All apologies," she says, knowing this sort of situation is exactly why they enlisted Opal for assistance.

"Efforts are noble. As you see we are many things skilled, including this new language. No have need for machine-speakers. How we know your trickery! Your cross-pollination of dumb ideas! How entwined is the root of your situation?"

"Machine-speakers? Oh, you mean my translator. My situation is very entwined. First, I hate to admit it, but I need water." She rubs her finger across her waxy tongue, searches for spit to speak.

"You think of yourself first? Get her water, good for human," the Chief requests of a blossom.

"I come for Aurthur and Opal, if you have seen them."

"Ahh, yes. As you can see we no defenses. Can you me very understand?"

"Entirely. Your skills are wonderful."

"Polite noble. Two desert wanderers then three there are, make me think four come next. Clear sun above it makes for worry! The Dimdwellers arouse... how do you call it, suspicions?"

"My apologies again. I assure you, we are neither raiders nor rogues. What have you done with them?" She raises her chin to intimidate but it's as meaningless as a twig insulting a Redwood Tree.

The blossoms straighten as the Chief rumbles, "Why assume? Our warriors carried them peacefully."

"You said you have no defenses. How can you have warriors?"

"Warriors war in many ways. Your leaf-mates dwell in the eternal sleep of unseen stars in bright sky."

"Eternal sleep! What!" But her shrieks rasp with dryness and her blades will do the talking. They leap from their sheaths with a metallic cling. The Florinik close in, surround her, tower over her. They're unarmed, but with that sort of reach, it doesn't matter. She backs up, tries to find a target, lost in the forest of their circling, confining. None take the offensive. She steadies her hands, sheathes her blades, mutters, "I'm sorry," through a closed mouth, through the snarl of her lips, remembering how quickly she jumped to conclusions in the airbus putting them all at risk. "If you hurt them I'll—" but her slumped shoulders gain nothing but laughter from the Chief.

He rises to his hind legs, "Your emotions the most of you own. Tiny swords won't solve this."

"How could you? They're harmless."

"See them before judgment place. Come," he motions with long fingers.

Perhaps Opal and Aurthur were easily misled? she thinks, hesitating. Gripping the handle of a sheathed dagger offers little reassurance. The Chief turns his back in complete confidence, leaving her with many questions: If he had really harmed them would he be so casual about stating it and not defending himself against possible riposte? Is politeness just a deceptive ploy of power? Is he so casual about death because the Florinik do not view death as any more than a sandstorm eroding a dune?

"How far away are they?" she demands.

"Do not bark."

"But bark is designed to protect."

"See if it functions for you likes you thinks then," the Chief replies, perhaps smirking. "They are at the shrine of Orbis. Short walk for us, long walk for the short-legged. We carriages have but they travel rocky areas where sand falls not."

"Sand falls?"

"From the sky. Where you think sand comes from, under-foot?" the Chief laughs, body convulsing. "It falls from corner of eye every time Orbis blinks."

"Have you seen it?"

"Sun shine clearly not! We all blink at the same time. All Florinik blink in concert with Orbis. Sometimes world holds itself up. Sometimes you need to *see* it to hold it. Seeing times are same for all creatures. World exists when needs to act, disappears when needs to hide."

They round the back of a plateau, the top hidden from view. A hidden panel responds to the Chief's weight as makeshift stairs grumble and emerge from the rock in an elevated spiral. Thalassa notes the spot. As they climb, the steps become steep enough to warrant footholds.

"Their enshrined bodies disrupt reality. Disruption bring Florinik balance in time. New viewpoints tap into Orbis who views all. They add Stargazer view, Shadow-keeper view, Sundimmer view."

"They aren't viewpoints for your sick god, they're people! They posed no threat!" She snaps, gripping her dagger but keeping it sheathed, blossoms crossing their arms like armor.

The Chief is unmoved. "No harm was done. This will thicken all bark."

Climbing the final step, the shrine appears. Six flat stones are arranged in a hexagon, a shape that fits together without gaps, just as the Florinik observe the world in concert. The Chief towers over Aurthur and Opal's outstretched bodies. In his bass voice he proclaims with reverence, "This. This is the sleep of eternity."

Thalassa runs over and presses her ear to Opal's mouth. "She's still breathing! You said they were dead?"

"What sort of barbarians you think of us?" the Chief asks as both blossoms are taken aback. "They are sleeping to give awareness eternal. They dream, they create with dream. All sleep serves the eternal."

The subtly of language and cultural expression hits her. Looking down, watching the rise and fall of Aurthur's chest, she says, "Chief, I apologize. My bark is impulsive and thick as sap. It has made me misunderstand. I have murdered your language and insulted your integrity and rituals. Please know I meant no ill intent."

"You wants to make us sick?"

"No, I mean no harm through words."

"Of this I trust," the Chief speaks, like sand scratching upon rock lowered ten octaves.

"When will they wake?" she asks, keeping conversation simple.

"They are more awake now than ever awake. But you mean time. Tomorrow. For now, go dormant."

The blossoms direct their attention to something in the sky, waving their arms wildly with a hoot. Thalassa can't tell if they're scared or excited. A flurry of blue liquid as long as her arm splashes through the air, jerking in violent, sweeping motions. Could be acidic. Opal and Aurthur are helpless, and there's no time to wake them. It's up to her to protect them. The liquid mass sounds like plunging into a pool. It swipes forth. She parries back, but wheels her arms to keep balance on the edge of the plateau. Draws her daggers, the glow casting bloody shadows on deep red rocks. Mind flips through programs—activates Ambidextrous to dual-wield. Points the daggers hilt-forward, sacrificing reach but increasing flexibility of attack angle.

There's three of them, then one, then two, then half of each. One leaps through another's mouth and leaves through its tail. More split off, jumping through mouths, merging and emerging, and gaining or losing material as if juggling cups of water. But one mass has a constant amount of material and seems dominant. She directs her blades towards it. The blades may pass right through, but the searing should work nicely.

The swirl of liquid swipes forth again. She tucks her lips tight, fearing it will enter her or burn her face off. She swirls with outreached arms and slices one of the masses with a wisp of steam, but not the dominant one. The creature congeals to heal the wound with a whirl of entering and exiting. She times her strikes between the juggling motions. The collective circling spits blobs of itself, but she dances her head, hard to hit, and quickly slices the dominant unit into quarters, dodging in and out of the arcs of jumping masses while walking the tightrope of the plateau edge. Glancing behind her, the Chief and his blossoms fall back. Finally, each mass falls out of the sky, the outer flexible shell falling as liquid soaks into the sandy rock.

The Chief steps forward to gather the gelatinous shell. "This makes great canteen. Strange ways you have fun in. Here, take as trophy."

"That thing was trying to kill me!"

The Chief laughs, body rocking up and down like a jogger anxious to start a race. "Kill? Not even dangerous!"

"Then why did you leap back?"

"You fight with child's toys! We backened because you act like crazy one and might hurt us with little swords." The blossoms raise and lower their bodies quickly until the Chief looks back at them. They stop and straighten.

"Unbelievable. Maybe my impulses don't protect me as much as I think," Thalassa says, with a heated face.

"Blossoms and I must go. Much to do, much to do. This rare event may sign greater things. Two become three become four become…" They depart down the rocky stairs.

Raising her sunbrella, she makes use of the water and provisions left around the shrine for visitors, lying down and dimming her occipts. She refuses to dim them entirely in case they don't reboot, which happened to a friend she knew who went blind for three weeks until they could be plucked and replaced. She raises Opal's shirt and places her head against her hot, bare stomach, feeling the breath of life rise and fall reassuringly. "They don't need to witness our ways; we shouldn't be here," she whispers. Soon, she is asleep, dreaming, perhaps creating in the sacred shrine of Orbis.

15

———————

The planet's founders had purpose, fighting to survive, but today's aimless youth dwells in the torpor of mod abuse. Meaning emerges where contradiction dare not go, but this is not the highest meaning. Threats outside society distract us from threats within, namely injustice. When the threats within become too great, more threats outside are created through war. Warriors seek honor, the powerful more power, and the youth anything to fill their restlessness, at war with only boredom.

Will the words of the wise fall upon deaf ears or be taken up by eager scholars? Will these scholars sell out to the system that educated them? Will I be forced to question everything I stand for? Ignorance is nobler than knowledge kept silent. Spread the word!

-The Priestess, personal diary entry

THALASSA WAKES, stretches her sore back, and cringes at the height. The village is shrouded with haze in the distance. Far off, buttes break the horizon, jutting out of the ground like fingernails. One is shaped like a crescent. She outlines the locations and turns to see Opal pacing, Aurthur still asleep.

"You didn't need to come. We can take care of ourselves," Opal replies.

"We hadn't heard from you, got antsy. I think they knocked you out to assess any threat, but they say they're adding your perspective to the dream of the cosmos or something. Go ahead, Opal, I know you want to grab your horny little journal and stick your pen to it, but there's no time to waste, no time for dreaming. The negotiations must be completed as soon as possible, though, I must tell you 'bout this creature I saw."

"Creature, where? What?" Aurthur asks, waking and brushing sand off his green tunic. "How did we get here?"

"The moths," Opal smiles. "While you've been *napping,* I've been researching. This is the Shrine of Orbis. It's beautiful, and don't start telling me god is just a big computer running natural laws. This is real belief, real culture, raw beauty."

"Napping? I remember something when we approached the village. Whoa, is that Thalassa?"

"Stop staring at her."

"We're prisoners! We need to get as far away from here as possible, but there's no way down." He points over the plateau edge, steps back from the dizzying height.

"If they wanted to harm us they would have done so," Thalassa consoles. "And there's always a way down. Up is way trickier. Just approach the edge in this direction. Follow me. The stairs will come."

"Nothing's happening."

"Maybe it's this way, or this one," Thalassa worries, stomping the stones atop the plateau.

"I told you, we're stuck up here, and it's far too steep to tumble down the side."

"Nah, it's simple."

Thalassa pulls out the gelatinous shell of the creature she

killed and fills it with sand. Tying the end, the sandbag is complete. Recalling the spot below where the Chief stood when the stairs emerged from the rock, she throws the sandbag weight off the plateau. It hits the target. The plateau rumbles, shakes, and they're almost thrown from their feet, but stairs finally emerge. They descend and Thalassa gathers the shell.

"Why didn't they tell you how to get down?" Aurthur asks.

"It must have seemed obvious. We wouldn't tell someone how to undim a window or link a cog."

They arrive back at the Florinik village, clothes sticking to their bodies. The unmoved sun casts shadows that become permanent features of the landscape. Seedlings haul plants in carts. A tool is tapered with a clanging sound while a group polishes some type of object that holds their interest. A hut blossoms, sides peeling down.

The Chief approaches. "Welcome. Your friends are from eternal sleep wake," he laughs, body shaking vertically. "Tell now of your coming, the coming of the two that became three."

"There's a mineral we need to gather from your land," Opal addresses.

"Instead of killing us you want us to agree so you have it simple? Is this nobler than killing us? You have not been the first to come for rock looking. Primitive pleasures for a primitive species."

"The mineral we need is of no use to you," she says, describing it. "You would be giving us nothing more than air."

"Giving is giving demanding equal giving. Giving makes advantage to would-be friends, or would-be enemies."

"You don't understand."

"On our land all is known," the Chief says, stretching his limbs with dominance. "Giving is who we are. The word for *we* and *I* are same for us in us speak. But give to you? Is different. Answer is no."

The Chief grabs a complicated stringed instrument with a

fretboard that expands and shrinks like an accordion, while maintaining proper string tension. This adds a bagpipe-like drone as he plays. He sings in grumbled moans followed by staccato shrieks. He gazes at their possessions, but contemptuously, as if to not create desire that would make him trade something of value for nothing but trouble in return.

"I am here to protect you and your people, to add bark to this village," Opal reassures, kneeling in the trodden sand.

"This before I have heard," he sings.

"I do not wish to see your lands exploited. But if you allow us to mine here, we can alter the power structure in ways you can only dream to weaken Evig Natt. I have much to atone to Orbis for… many apologies to add, moments of rage, moments of ill-temper, horrible things I've done to bring me here. I must see this through to the end or others will have died in vain. Chief, I know of your conflict with Evig Natt."

The music stops. He turns to her. "You wish to over-ripen and ruin the Nightwalkers?"

"Yes, mighty Chief. Their economy will no longer fund wars with your great tribe, the Sunstalkers, the Solarsemblances, the Daybringers."

"This changes all. My allies will be pleased. Florinik risk only a rock. Small risk. But do not quicken us to ripen in process. You may mine, but do not employ us. The Great Seedling teaches to grow in stages. It is the grower of something from nothing, blueprint without inscription, bringer of life upon lifeless, converter of soil to flesh…" and he goes on to name a dozen honorary descriptions of seeds.

"You are right. Very wise. Traditions require slow change."

"In return, you will honor Orbis the Watcher, the All-Attentive, the All-Perceiver, the Panopticon, the Omniscient, the—"

"Yes, yes, I know Orbis. How exactly can we repay you?"

"Change our history into human language. After you mine, return to frozen land never to return, like our icy cousins."

"You want me to translate your records and then get our rocks and go?"

"Yes. As knowledge of Orbis spread, more perceivers Orbis can add. Orbis become more powerful."

"I agree to these terms."

"Good! Root yourselves."

"I think he wants us to get settled in," Aurthur says.

Opal interviews them about their history and habits. Aurthur listens. She's particularly interested in untranslatable words that have suffered extensive scholarly debate. The translation of a hundred scrolls comes slowly at first, due to the complete flexibility of syntax, but soon gains momentum. She records over thirty words for *light*, including daylight, the light beneath a doorway, the light filtering through leaves, and the light of receiving a hug. The blossoms watch, sitting Burmese style and crying the twelve names of the sun. In her anthropological record, Opal records over the word *manipulated* with the phrase *I encouraged the Chief to empathize with the utility of my purpose.*

Meanwhile, Thalassa scans nearby lands for mineral traces to locate the best Ultimaepar mining sites. O.A.K. cannot afford to move their base again, and the base must survive at least as long as it takes to finalize the Great Rotation. At that point, she's counting on the Core to protect the rotation belt, hoping it has calculated that increased planetary rotation will make hemisphere management easier. Without its help, Severum and his army will crush her. But her faith in the A.I. Core is no different than faith in a non-responsive god. She shoves the thought aside, continuing to scan.

Severum grins. The tunnel trace has been successful, the hubs having been exposed, and the new base's location determined with reasonable accuracy. Opal's digital footprints have been uncovered at a public university that assists the military with tracking dissidents, her search pattern leading to the Florinik. He expects to confirm the exact village, likely near an Ultimaepar deposit.

He takes the Priestess' hand, disembarks the airbus, and procures a small government-provided vehicle with an outdated cloaking device. The vehicle is heavy enough to resist the spontaneous winds but they agree to take the final leg to the village by foot to avoid adverse reactions to the tech, at the risk of losing their escape route.

He searches for a high place to perform ASCOPE reconnaissance, satellite range being limited by treaty, but the desert offers nothing except some tumbleweed with eyes on thin stalks that emerge before folding into themselves. The weeds jump over their heads and shoot their lightweight seeds into the dark clouds to root. Nature always finds a way, and so will he.

The Priestess' purple robe flutters. Light sand gathers on her long, dark nose. Her robe soon loses its sail and clings to her sweat-soaked body. Her face folds like an earmarked page of his favorite book, her dark skin flawed with moments of indulgence, her countenance otherwise pure self-control, and he loves her immensely because they truly know one another, even those things they conceal from themselves.

"You haven't looked at me like that for a long time."

"I must've been blind all those years. Almost looks like it could rain. That only happens what, once every few months?"

"Thereabouts."

They pass beneath a rocky archway formed by two rocks meeting in perfect balance. The arch might work as a scoping point, but Severum passes in lieu of finding the perfect spot.

THALASSA HAS SELECTED two mining sites. Scan results display across a vHUD regional map as she compares them to other potentials. She digs in the sand, looking for mineral striations often found near Ultimaepar due to similar forming conditions, but even with electronic aid she doesn't have the knowledge to identify most of them. She messages Arcturus to request a few dozen palm-sized robotic mites to begin extraction but isn't sure if the message goes through. Sweat pours off in streams, gritty sand clinging to it. Checking her Pulser obsessively, it still reads: INOPERABLE – BATTERY OVERHEATED. *Should have brought an insulated cooling case,* she thinks, checking it again.

Zooming in on a mineral vein, she straightens and stops. Two figures interrupt the horizon far in the distance, one wearing a robe like the Priestess and the other likely Severum. She tries to warn her comrades but the message won't go through.

They're carrying a comms blocker. It should have taken weeks for them to find us so how'd they do it? Are they heading for the compound or the village? Looks like the village. They're much closer than I am. I need to make up ground while finding a way around them and staying out of sight.

She considers circling in a wide arc and approaching the village from another angle, but it will slow her down. The land is flatter near the village with fewer places to hide. If they were to attack the village it would compromise the excavation for O.A.K. and overall tribal relations for the people of Evig Natt. The Core could become involved in the resulting conflict between the hemispheres and withdraw any support it's willing to provide. It would also risk her allies' lives. Taking them out hand-to-hand is tempting, but her spirit recedes at the thought of Gestalt's death. She reels the thoughts back and spits out the bait of desperation. Waiting for them to arrive at the village is the best option; take them out before they can ambush the sleeping Florinik. But waiting has never been her *forte.*

She picks up pace, reducing distance while remaining inconspicuous. Kneeling behind a dune crest, her chest heaves, over-clocked once again. Off balance, she stumbles down the face of the dune, but they still don't look back. They'll cut her off from the village the moment she's discovered and she'll be forced to lead them astray, retreating deeper into the desert until one party runs out of water.

The first circle of huts penetrates the hazy horizon. Their pace slows, moving west of the main village entrance to scope the area. Thalassa knows the area inside-out and doesn't need to fear being seen by patrols, gaining ground at their uncertainty. Zooming in, only a few gardening tools remain outside the village as the day ends.

If I was Severum, where would I scope the village from? The Orbis shrine? No, too much risk of a procession and he wouldn't know how to get up it. Ah, the crescent butte. Even if he can't get atop it, the long arc would provide cover. The crescent hollow faces away from the village, making a perfect recess. But they'll also have limited sight from the ground without coming out around the tapered points.

They conceal themselves within the crescent hollow, as expected. If she attempts to reach the village, they will spot her and shoot her in the back. No time to circle around. She grips her twin daggers in their sheathes until her hands turn whiter than bleached sand. Releasing them, her tense fingers remain curled around the phantom objects.

Guard shifts rotate in the village, drawing their attention from one edge of the crescent. They converse, but she's not close enough to hear. She approaches the opposite edge with an idea. The ridges in the rock might be used as a ladder if there are enough footholds. She would be vulnerable while climbing, but once atop would have the advantage. Body pressed against the butte, her arms tremble as they take on weight. Another foothold, handhold, foothold, handhold, feet dangling as hand over hand she makes the final motions, arms about to give way. Falling doesn't worry her, it's the flopping sound she'll make followed by a Pulser burning a hole through her. Struggling to reach a landing halfway up, she pushes herself harder. She must prove herself to Arcturus. Almost slipping, she focuses on her anger at Gestalt, anger at Severum. Betrayal. She regains her grip, the rocky foothold becoming a burning tree branch in her mind. Belly pulls in as she takes a breath, reverse breathing for strength. She becomes the pain in her shaking arms, then realizes the pain is just an idea. About to fall, instead of tensing her muscles she relaxes them, gaining enough for one more pull. Her dagger sheath nearly snags on a cragged rock, but she grits her teeth and pulls herself upon the landing.

Halfway up.

More talking below, but she doesn't dare look over the edge. Suddenly, the landing shakes. Her legs give way. Stairs emerge from the butte, just like the Orbis shrine, spiraling to the top. She buries her back against the stone wall, fearing the crumbling sound will give her presence away. Thunder clashes in the heavens at the same moment, disguising the sound. Not knowing whether to run or freeze, she fears the steps won't last forever, and the top of the butte will offer safety and concealment to plan an ambush. Running up, she leaps a gap to reach the top landing. The stairs recede more quietly than they emerged.

Killing Severum with the landing blow will require the perfect opportunity, waiting for him to kneel or sit, guaranteeing he won't step aside at the last moment. The Priestess will be caught off guard and easy prey. Of course, if it goes wrong, she'll land on her back, break a leg, or get impaled. So be it. Thalassa draws and activates searing daggers. The low hum resonates below the level of human hearing, but Severum turns below as if he hears it.

"While we wait for the guards to sleep, let's make love! I've missed you so much," Severum announces too loudly. The Priestess makes exaggerated moaning sounds as they kiss, almost as if trying to draw attention to themselves and advertise their moment of weakness, but Thalassa has built up too much anticipation to stop. Their bodies will die in the embrace of eternity, and as for guilt, there's enough mods to deal with that afterwards.

Now's the moment. She leaps down, arms out, doing a somersault in mid-air. Severum instantly fires his weapon at the top of the butte, as if expecting it. Thalassa falls beneath the angle of his fire, bringing her blades straight down. He bends backward at the last second, daggers landing in his right leg. He screams, the searing pain no doubt spreading up his thigh. His calf emits smoke from the cauterized hole. Thalassa is still off balance from landing. Severum balances on his good leg and head-butts her down, but she flips back up, fluid, agile. He steps back, gains a second.

"I am the bloody ocean bearing down upon thee!" she yells, Tiamat rising within her. Charging, the sand offers no traction. She points her blades, lunges, but the attack falls short and she lands only to stare at a raised Pulser.

"Severum, she's just a child!" the Priestess begs.

"She's over half your age! It was her idea to imprison you."

"You ordered all of us to die before, even your beloved Severum. Not so power-crazed without your crazy cult, huh?" Thalassa taunts, approaching.

"I didn't know he was part of your group, he wasn't in the main chamber, how could I have known?" The Priestess replies.

"But you knew I was there."

Severum's leg collapses for a moment, just a moment, but that's all she needs. His aim is thrown off and he can't line up the shot in time before Thalassa buries her dagger in the barrel, melting it. She yanks her arm back, the broken gun stuck to the dagger and flying from his grip then launches a strike with tremendous velocity, but he hops back, her positioning clumsy in the soft sand.

Severum's occipts waver. Must be streaming mods to reduce the pain. Raising her arms, she positions the daggers high to cover her face. Severum strikes both armpits instead, stunning her before he loses balance and falls back. Thalassa recovers, feigns a dagger attack but instead kicks him in the injured leg, his face grimacing beyond recognition. Bending forward, she readies the final strike.

The Priestess grabs her hands from behind, forces them back, forces them to cut open her own torso with a burning gouge that penetrates her thin film of armor. Thalassa stumbles, squirms away. Blood gushing upon her hands, she takes a step with the dagger still burning in her flesh. If it cauterizes the wound, blood flow might be blocked in a dangerous area. If it doesn't, she could bleed to death. She deactivates the dagger, heat fading. Let it bleed. The Priestess backs away, expecting a strike with the other dagger.

Wrong move. Thunder strikes. Before they can finish her off she throws the dagger at the Priestess. It misses. The Priestess bends to retrieve it, underestimating the hate Thalassa feels. Thalassa rips the first dagger from her own chest, reactivates it, and is determined not to miss twice. She aims, throws, and with bits of her own flesh still stuck to the blade it strikes the Priestess in the arm, earning a banshee's scream for her efforts.

"Don't touch it," Severum says. "You'll be all right, you'll..." but his pain mod has auto-streamed for too long apparently. "I told people not to rely on these, it makes you weak." He falls unconscious, the Priestess still screaming.

Unarmed, Thalassa grips her chest. She pulls out the gelatinous shell and places it across the thinner areas of her wound, but it's not enough. She hunches over, tries to stand, but her condition is far worse than the Priestess'. "What now? Revenge?" she asks, looking for a window to escape.

"Leave. Nothing more can come of this. We'll all end up dead," the Priestess orders, pointing the recovered dagger.

Thalassa is in no condition to argue. She makes her way across the sand, arms wrapped around the wound. She encounters another jelly creature, smaller than the first. The twirling motions of the liquid entering and exiting its body add to her dizziness. With nothing to fear, she grabs it, but her hands pass through. She strangles it, but it doesn't even flinch. Finally, she reaches up through the bottom of it before more liquid can be expelled and rips the inside out through itself. A strip of sticky, transparent flesh peels off as it flurries away. She applies it as a cooling bandage, covering a second part of her wound.

Moments later, with her hand still upon her chest, she collapses in the sand.

———

TWENTY MINUTES LATER, Severum's body is vibrating. The Priestess is disrobing and for a moment he thinks he's in for a wild ride until the pain surges through and she swipes Thalassa's dagger at her own clothing. She cuts a tourniquet and clumsily wraps it around his blazing wound. *Wow, that did absolutely nothing.*

"You're okay, you're…We need to go to the village to get medical supplies or you'll die. Don't talk. Lean on me. We're going to make it, you hear? We have been through more than this in our daily arguments. Come, grab hold."

"Where's Thalassa?"

"She headed east, to the village. If she arrives first and informs them it'll be risky to enter, but you'll die without their help. It'll be okay, shh," the Priestess reassures.

But he knows her well enough to tell she's pushing back the part of her that enjoys seeing him helpless.

16

———

"Where's Thalassa? She can't still be searching for the right mining site?" Aurthur asks Opal at the village.

"If this stuff was laying out in the open it wouldn't be valuable, right? She's determined to find it. Wait, up ahead, who's that?" Opal asks.

"Where?"

"Past the edge of town. Two people. It's not like the Florinik to have human traders, and they don't appear to be carrying any goods. At least one of them is injured."

"I'd know that robe anywhere. It can't be. Opal, we have to warn the villagers."

"Should they rush out with herbs, or spears?"

"I'm afraid it's far worse than herbs."

———

SEVERUM LIMPS INTO THE VILLAGE, admiring the finely-constructed spears lined up in two rows beside the Chief.

"Severum!" Aurthur exclaims.

"Priestess," Opal acknowledges with disdain.

187

"What are the names?" the Chief asks.

"I am Akasha, but you may know me as the Priestess, the role that defines my life. This is Severum. We come in peace to seek your aid."

"You are both injured. Your leg needs grafting; who felled your tree? We will this discover."

"An animal attacked us. Then we fell from the butte, causing most of our wounds. A woman, Thalassa, came to help, but the creature made her fall on her own weapon. The desert finished her off and her body was—"

"Stop," Severum whispers to her, "If Thalassa is cooperating with them and we left her to die there could be serious consequences."

The Priestess amends, "Well her body was not discovered but she was injured and we couldn't carry her back being injured ourselves."

The Chief replies, "Go find her. Then we heal all."

"No!" Opal yells. "They'll kill her."

"We are in no condition to do so," Severum replies, voice shaking. "But I will go alone and find her as a sign of good faith, even with my injury."

"We shall branch out to provide support."

Opal stands in front of the chief, arms on hips. "Chief, he cannot be allowed out there with her wounded."

"Silence! Desert demands rules of land. She fell near him, she is duty of him. Argue? Go with him then."

"She was not duty of him," Opal pleads. "If they were near each other it was because they were fighting. They have been sent to kill all of us." With a dire laugh and a crazed look she slights, "I can't believe this."

"True?" the Chief questions.

"We have been sent as ambassadors to talk some sense into them," Severum replies. "Nothing is supposed to end in violence and it is us, as you can see, who have been attacked, which was the primary cause of our wounds."

"You first say you fell, cause of most wounds."

"The ground attacked us. Just a mis-translation, it means the same as *fell*," Severum amends.

"Nonsense! You probably tried to kill her, and that is why she attacked you," Opal juts in. "Don't let them anywhere near her."

"Sap and bother! No violence here. Violence will be met with harsh action."

Opal says in perfect Florinik, "Aurthur and I will go alone acting on Severum's behalf. Since we are the same species, we will take up his duty, just as your scrolls recorded your grandfather doing when the first ships landed. Doing this, we will gain trust and honor in the ember eyes of the Daybringers, the Solarsemblances the Sungatherers. While we are gone you will keep close watch on the Sunblockers, the Dimdwellers, the Lunarwalkers, the Nightstalkers. We will share our tale with Orbis in our dreams, adding to the all-mighty's power.

"Acceptable," the Chief immediately agrees, the rules more a formality than an absolute as long as survival needs are met.

"Quickly," Opal tells Aurthur, and they rush into the desert carrying medical supplies to recover Thalassa.

Severum ensures his comms blocker is still active. The Chief leads him to a medical hut while blossoms and seedlings gather the strongest herbs from the gardens. He tries to rest but is soon wakened with commotion as Thalassa is dragged to another nearby hut for treatment. Each side is injured and at a stalemate as they heal; any move made in front of the tribe would not be well met.

The next morning, Severum wakes aching and incompetent. Someone has peeled down the walls of his hut, perhaps to keep an eye on him. He replays the failed fight in his mind, wishing he had brought heavier armor no matter how far he'd have to walk carrying its weight. Then he remembers Thalassa's daggers were designed specifically to cut through such government-issued suits; a fitting melee weapon for a revolutionary.

He had denied government involvement too many times to remember. Last night the Chief had come to ask him a single question. He admitted that he was a public servant working for the Central Government of Evig Natt. He didn't know why he so openly revealed this, but figured the Chief already knew.

The Chief was smarter than expected and told him, "Humans don't cross desert to talk. You have device for that." But he also neither judged him nor pressed him further about his possible motives. Though he clearly despises Evig Natt, he never acted aggressively and accepted the responsibility of bringing them to health. It was not to keep his enemies close, nor out of a love for life, it was simply plain utility, a task taken under the umbrella of overall survival.

Severum respected this in his leadership. He did not respect the musty smell his presence left, however, which was just as strong this morning as last night, despite the hut airing out.

"How are you faring?" the Priestess asks him.

"More importantly, you?"

"The treatment has worked wonders, and yes, I am okay," she says, moving her arm slightly and gasping. "The Chief said they are sending another doctor. Do you think we should leave?"

"Not yet."

"I think we should rendezvous with the others."

"What? What for?"

"We can't hide from them. Generals often meet to discuss battles over dinner once the smoke has settled. It's considered honorable in some circles."

"It hasn't settled yet, and there's no honor in preparing for a military strike that will likely harm the innocent and guilty alike without discrimination," Severum acknowledges.

"There is no honor in what they call breakfast here either," she replies, wiping her mouth. "You hungry?"

"Not at all."

"Even after yesterday's journey?"

"Even then. But I'll agree to a meeting, as I'm not in much shape to argue."

Moments later they are gathered. Two of the Chief's guards stand watch outside the hut.

Aurthur enters fast, shoulders back, and chin raised. "You were really going to kill me?" he asks.

"Well, I was conflicted about everything. But I wasn't going to kill you, specifically. Of course not."

"Conflicted!" he roars, taking the upper hand. Seems justified in his dominance with Severum helpless in bed.

"I may have betrayed O.A.K., but I wouldn't have betrayed you. I could have shot you dead the moment I saw you and Thalassa together, but I didn't. I can't quite believe it myself."

"Sure you can, and that in no way makes me feel better. You used me. What type of idea is worth killing your friends for, people who invite you into their own home?"

"Come on! I wouldn't have killed you. Ever. I was just gaining information."

"And Opal?"

"She wasn't in the way so I didn't have to make that choice. They convinced me O.A.K. will destroy everything that matters. I come out here and first thing I see is you conspiring with barbarians. Doesn't mean I came to kill you, we would have just had a bit of a talk, tea, and all that shit."

"Do they look barbaric? We are intruders on their planet, or is that too easy to overlook? Anything barbaric about the way they live is from the conditions *we caused* by invading. They're surviving much better with their barbarism than you are with your so-called civility, alone, friendless, with a hole in your leg as big as your mouth. You say O.A.K. will destroy everything that is important. Since when were revolutionaries so non-discriminating?"

"I once asked the same thing," Severum admits, thinking of his first meeting with the governor.

Opal grabs Aurthur's arm, massages his bicep.

"How did it use to be then, before humans landed? Tell me that."

"Sap and bother! I will tell," the Chief says, entering from the back with his instrument as voices hold and walls fold. When privacy emerges, he diverges in song, "In the past, there were no chiefs, but this no good for war; no way to move armies no way to move stores. War brought us to city, trouble with our safety, tradition against our new-found history. Disease flourished, only armies were nourished. The plants knew war was in the air. Our homes remained closed, as we were never there."

"That's a lot to think about," Severum replies.

"I care about your suffering more than my own," Aurthur blurts out. "That is what friendship means to me. In the end it's not about your job, it's about priorities. You're so sure of yourself you're willing to risk it all. That's not romantic, it's just stupid. You told me yourself that no theory is worth dying for, the day you saved my life."

"I am following orders."

"But it isn't you following them."

"Yeah, I get that."

"Do you?"

"Yes, I do. I have seen the light, the light held in the leaders' offices. I have seen politicians not living by their own rules. But you all are destroying order and any order is better than chaos, because I have seen chaos, too. I have seen Aphorids tearing down every institution we built, not to violate some unspoken social contract, but merely because it stands taller than them."

"Order will always arise again from chaos," Thalassa says in a low, injured voice.

"Then why bother?"

"Because we socially evolve through the conflict. It's how we survive amidst an unpredictable world," she finishes.

"No. The same power comes back the same way."

"You're not seeing the big picture of social change across centuries. You're looking at just the few years you're alive and thinking you see it all. Here's a chance to tear it all down. And if the structures we fight against are rebuilt, we will have shown it is not the only way to live."

"Severum, our friendship transcends the boundaries of ideology. I didn't always consider you a friend, but I do now. Killing won't fix this," Aurthur urges.

"I know no other line of work."

"You once did. I saw your terraforming books myself. We need open dialogue. We're so poor at communicating we need a whole Twilight of machines just to stop the wars long enough to breathe."

"True... all so true."

"They seek to destroy nature," the Priestess reminds Severum.

Thalassa responds, "Like the rise of the sea we seek the rise of true human nature, which is cultivating not exploiting. We may sacrifice nature in the short-term but save it in the long-run. Nature will restore the balance of the Great Rotation; you must have faith in this ability."

"Nature brings balance to all conditions, yes," the Priestess affirms.

"To stop change is unnatural. And you must see how nature is exploited everyday by those with power?"

"Constantly."

"Then why hate us? If there is a deity this is not its will, to exploit its creation. Even destruction is better than exploitation; it causes less suffering."

"And perhaps this is true," she hesitantly agrees. "Even

Severum has oft expressed doubts. Half my drive to join the Aporia Asylum was based on getting away from it all, away from him. Half of his dropping out of college was because he couldn't take the pain I brought him. Our relationship may just tear the hemispheres apart if there's not better communication, like you were saying."

"Really?" Aurthur questions.

"Yes," Severum replies. "If you're wondering what it will take for the Priestess and I to back off, it won't be much at this point. I'm exhausted, in pain, and don't know why I'm doing it."

"Not enough," Thalassa rises, grabbing her chest. "You owe me you son of a glitch. Backing off is one thing. What will it take for you to turn against them?"

"You're crazy. Nothing, nothing could turn me against them."

"Would you do it if they didn't pay you? How many times did you spend your flies on mods after gunning down a few Bioluminaries, the poorest of the poor? I cannot promise you a greater standard of living, but some things are more valuable."

"What would you have me do if I did agree?"

"You are free to choose, Severum. If you want my blood, here's my throat, take it, but if you have even the slightest doubt then speak up *de profundis*, from the depths of your soul."

The Chief straightens. "Two ways to vote. One, by speak here. Two, vote by number of blood droplets in desert. You choose, but plants need water, not blood."

"Join us," Thalassa implores. "I'll never trust you, but it'll be a start. Come to our compound. If you destroy the Great Rotation then this all ends. Without you, the military will do us in anyway. If you deceive us again then the species isn't worth fighting for in the end. Remember, we have far more to lose than you. You have your life to lose. We, our very reason for living."

"Are you insane?" Opal scolds. "Seriously, what are you thinking? People in power don't do this."

"Have you forgotten who's in charge? I don't want that type of power. You need to follow me on this one."

"Follow you? You don't want power, but you want me to do as you say."

"There must be boundaries," Thalassa replies impatiently.

"Yes, like not having them discover our compound. Pretty good boundary I think. You've lost it. This is child's play to you."

"She is right," the Chief ascertains. "Big decisions are better not fast. We have better action. Go to the city of Nathril-Xoynsia. See the living conditions your regime has forced upon our people."

"No problem. Give us a few minutes to gather supplies," Opal says, picking up a knapsack.

THE CHIEF RECLINES on a hammock in the middle of his hut. Thalassa approaches him alone. "Can we talk?" He nods. "I insist that Severum and his Glitch, I mean the Priestess, be unarmed during the trip. And I want my daggers back; I'm healing quick, thanks to your treatment."

The Chief agrees, "You fight for those in need and will have little swords. They fight for those without need and shall not. The two that became three that became five will leave soon."

"What about communications? I'm not blocking anything and can't get through."

"May be the mineral you seek. Large amounts sometimes make lightning talk not work. Make good time, flying mushroom caps were recently spotted."

"Drones. Please deliver this message to my people," Thalassa says, handing him a letter. "The location of the compound on it should be kept secret."

"Will do. You need wear these," he replies, gripping thorny

necklaces. "It shows city guards you travel for us. Severum and the caller of false gods will not receive them. Without them, they will be imprisoned upon entering the city."

"That was not the plan."

"This is better than us them restraining. We have no prison nor need for prison. When all this is over, they will be let out without harm. Keep us out of human entanglement."

They soon board a Dijyorkvok. The creature howls in a low, reverberating voice and scans the landscape with eyes the size of one's hand. It carries water on its back in two rows of three humps. Its skin is white and its feet shoed. A Florinik commands it from in front of a wooden bed packed with provisions.

Aurthur reaches to help Severum board. "Well, we're off," he says to the group, each keeping a close watch on one another.

Thalassa has informed Opal of the plan but not Aurthur. If Severum and the Priestess can realize what humans have done to the tribal city through warfare before they are imprisoned it might help put it in context. She toys with the necklaces in her hand, wondering if nesting betrayal within betrayal is the best path.

17

The city of Nathril-Xoynsia stretches across the horizon. Traveler activity picks up on the road, some Florinik, some human, and a few other species entirely. The Aphorids are not represented. Thalassa makes sure her necklace is on, finding it intact, but her waist feels lighter. How could she have been so blind? Her daggers are gone. A gush of heat is expelled as they activate in someone else's hands.

Severum leaps down from the Dijyorkvok, landing most of his weight on his better leg. Bastard stole her daggers—better have a good reason. Four short, black-eyed creatures armed with makeshift clubs in thick arms rush to block their passage and surround them. Thalassa is defenseless without her weapons, while Severum hobbles into attack position. He strikes first, but the blade doesn't even pierce the thick, green skin of its chest because only one dagger has been activated. He curses, pumps the activation button.

Thalassa dashes to intervene, but her torso is about to split back open from the movement alone. A club strikes hard and nearly breaks his rib before she arrives.

He lunges with the searing dagger but the creature flips

back. Thalassa wrestles with Severum to get her blades back, show him how it's really done, but he shakes her off. The monstrosity drops the club, lowers to all fours for speed, and charges, sun gleaming off three rows of teeth. Closer, and closer. Thalassa dives to the side, shielding her wound from the fall, and Severum drops to the ground at the last second. As it lunges, he thrusts the searing daggers up through the yellow belly of the beast. It gurgles on blood and tumbles over his head. He stands over its corpse, extracting the blade in a ceremonious swipe before stabbing it again, twisting as the creature writhes.

"You stole my kill again," she grunts, climbing back on the Dijyorkvok. "But thanks."

"I owe you, so I've taken this fight upon myself despite my injuries."

Three to go.

Another club-swinging fool boards the Dijyorkvok's wide saddle.

"Severum, arm me!" She yells. She catches the dagger and spins to slice the head off the creature in one smooth motion.

The Florinik beast master faces one on the ground, using his long arms to grab the creature's face and crush it between his palms until it falls limp. He turns his back but the creature has faked its injury and leaps with revenge. Severum stabs it rapidly in the back until it goes limp for good, then a few more times for good measure, getting his dagger stuck between vertebrae.

Thalassa kicks the final creature off the Dijyorkvok, but it clings with sharp claws to climb back up, swinging back and forth and exposing its stomach as the Dijyorkvok kicks out its back feet. A dagger toss to its weak spot finishes it.

"Bandits," the Florinik beast master states, getting back in to drive.

Opal speaks in Florinik to the driver, "We'll park the Dijyorkvok in the caravan over there. They like to be around each other, it's all that excites them, but with their thrashing we'll have to remove any valuables and put them aside."

Severum hands Thalassa her remaining dagger.

"Thanks. On second thought, you keep it," she replies. "Take this glove and this part of the sheath. Now we're equal."

"Thanks. Glad you got a trophy this time."

"Wasn't that important."

Dijyorkvoken gather on the city edge near a watering hole, their wounds airports for the swarming insects. The city wall is made from broken objects and piled organic debris including some rocks that might be bones. Earth-toned buildings tower four stories high. White cloths and black plastic cover busted windows. Square shanties sit catty-corner upon other shanties like a toddler's building blocks. Caravans park to create a mobile marketplace outside the city.

Florinik drunk on sweet nectar wrap long limbs arm-in-arm and swing to a hollow beat played on giant mushrooms, feet dancing on mosaic tiles. Whirls of scarves in volcanic colors bleed through the air. The occasional human passes with merely a shadow of his or her original culture intact, possibly, an undocumented worker coming to seek the sun since immigration is fiercely regulated by each hemisphere.

Parades of merchants cry out their wares from tight market stalls full of ceramics, textiles, and heavily discounted bars of soap. Incense and cumin fill the air. One stall advertises oil lanterns, illegal on Evig Natt and almost useless on Dayburn. A woman wearing a silken sari parts a fuchsia tablecloth to crawl beneath while two men lean back in a booth, bringing hookah whips to their mouths, probably here to smuggle the lanterns.

"This is unbelievable. A few homeless here and there is one thing, but this is a whole civilization."

"Yes, throngs of displaced individuals. Look at their bellies," the Priestess replies at the sunken caverns hanging from ribcages. "Humans wound up on Dayburn for different reasons.

Many simply sought the sun. Who knows what they had to do to be accepted, or how they view themselves now. Some of our monks quit believing they were human years ago. What you're looking at is not made in hours or days or months. It's centuries in the making, and I'm starting to see the shadows of power. There must be something possible beyond this."

Severum donates the provisions he can spare, some of them more confusing than useful to them. Finally, he moves forth and says, "Let's go inside."

Thalassa grabs his arm. "No, Severum. There's something I must tell you. The moment you step inside the city without these necklaces you'll be imprisoned. Stay outside the city walls while you observe their living conditions. I apologize but the Chief is just trying to protect his people from your blood money. I tell you this in good faith that we can work together."

"Blood money, how dare you, after you attacked us in cold blood!" He clinches his fists, but pauses, releasing them. "I would have done the same thing, removing a threat as quietly as possible. Thanks for telling me," he makes out through tight teeth.

They circle the perimeter, dodging fast moving carriages until they come upon two men dressed in military desert camouflage. They rock their shoulders back and forth while approaching Thalassa. An airboat carrying four more men hovers over the sand behind them.

"A trap, after all this? You back-stabbing son of a glitch," Thalassa spits.

"These aren't my men, stay back."

The soldiers raid the city outskirts with hit-and-run tactics, setting fires to watchtowers, disabling caravans by shooting Dijyorkvoken, and robbing villagers. Crackling shrieks and alarms cry equally loud into the dense, dry air. A heavy gun attached to the front of the airboat swivels around firing projectiles. The animals and villagers frenzy in a stampede, many wounded by the fiery barrage. The raiders give a long hard look at Severum, stopping to scan him for body mods, then suddenly disappear behind the dunes with the others.

"Happens all the time. Lot of us don't even run no more from the Pruners," a resident Florinik says, limping.

"Why does it happen?" Severum asks.

"Soldiers get bored on peace-keeping missions. Guns are made to fire. Sometimes they feed us, sometimes they heal us, sometimes we target practice."

"So they make their own missions now? They must be stopped."

"Too many. We deal. Go trade and be done here. We don't need more so-called help from Dimdwellers."

They continue to witness the daily struggles of sustenance and economy, violence and social relations, and at the day's end they make the return trip, taking turns sleeping. When they arrive back at the Florinik village, the Chief is surprised to see all five of them.

"Ahh, I find you with trust blossoming," he says, then turns to the driver. "Beast master, your work is done. Severum and the caller of false gods are healed 'noff and can walk back way they come. Nothing more here for them."

"We will contact you," Thalassa says.

"How are you feeling, by the way?" Severum asks.

"Completely healed," she replies, stretching her arms and nearly re-opening her wound as she furrows in pain. "What about you?"

"Fine to walk, nothing more. Here's your other dagger back."

"Thank you."

"Did you wipe my blood off first?" the Priestess scolds him as she turns away.

Thalassa, Aurthur, and Opal spend two more days at the Florinik village as the Priestess and Severum return to Evig Natt. During this time, Thalassa fully recuperates and removes the last of her bandages. The three of them make it back to base and reconvene with Arcturus and the rest of O.A.K. No surveillance or troops are spotted in the region, a testament to Severum's good faith and will. They soon begin the mining and the Great Rotation project continues, their fate held within the hands of their least trusted greatest threat.

18

Severum returns to his apartment. Given that he's on O.A.K.'s side for the time being, he has no reason to avoid it. Place is falling apart, seedy people lining the hallways searching between the walls for hidden stashes. Trip back from Dayburn was hell. Now Arc's on the phone and he needs a drink. He peers into the puke-green tunnel of a beer bottle, empty again. Too rare a find to count on more.

"Nice place," the Priestess says. "One step cleaner than sharing a desert cave with Aphorids."

"I'm on the phone."

Nothing's ever good enough and Arc's still jabbering in his other ear, "We need intel, it's that simple. We're not asking you to do anything directly."

"Arcturus, I've heard that before from the other side. The last time someone said that to me, three of us almost lost our lives."

"We have O.A.K. names for a reason. Use them," she orders.

"Understood, oh great Orchestrator. I've told you before, you can be the glitchin' maestro for all I care."

"But I'm not. Simple errors can have large consequences. O.A.K. has reconvened successfully and the mining operation is underway. Two or three days more and it will be complete and the project will reach its final stage. We are already compensating for the Architect's absence and the new blueprints show improved implementation times. I think Gestalt was biasing the projections against us to depress our will. It is foolish to trust you, but better to have would-be enemies fighting alongside us than against us, or so the Kontractor says in the naivety of her youth."

"I am not against you. Not anymore."

"The great spiritual transformation in the desert, right? How cliché. Unfortunately, without Gestalt there's no tiebreaker on these matters. I allowed Thalassa full choice on this one, as she sometimes allows me when discrepancies like you come about."

"Do they arise often?"

"Arise?"

"Is there much conflict in the chain of command?"

"Discrepancies should be seen and not heard. You will gather the required intel. We want to know which of our forces are on hit lists from people like you."

"Simple enough. I have limited access, but I know a guy who can hack the network and obtain the list of military targets who are allegedly part of O.A.K. They're probably triangulating comms signals right now."

"We're protected. We need this data in one or two shift rotations. We'll be in touch."

"Understood. And when do I get paid?"

"I take that as a joke. Ending transmission."

Severum arranges to have the data retrieved. It arrives two hours later and he relays it to Arcturus, earning a speck of trust. About to retire for the night, vHUD flashes again, another call.

"Severum, check the file."

"What is it? You already knew you were on the list."

"No, it's you, they just added you," Arcturus replies.

"I'm a target? Ha, that can't be. It must be an error."

"No error. They're covering their tracks. Kill, then kill the killers, keeps people silent and them in power."

"This can't be…"

"Be mindful. Leave. Stay in a hotel. And no, you are not welcome here."

He turns to the Priestess, "I'm being targeted by the governor's assassins, but they don't know I know."

"How long did you think this would last, playing both sides?" she asks, irritated. "You're not reporting in with everything you know."

"This isn't my fault! I gave my life to them, risked my life for them! They don't trust me!"

"They're not in the trust business. You know that."

"You got me into this."

"It was your line of work to begin with, right? That's all you ever said until the other day: this is my job, it's what I do, they made me do it, it's how I get paid enough to live in a slum. But maybe you have changed. I don't know anymore, Sheva."

Severum examines the data. The contract targeting him is indeed the newest, but it has either not been published, assigned, or accepted yet. The list was supposed to only include suspected O.A.K. members, yet somehow he showed up. He thinks over the people who saw him recently. *Face it. You're expendable to the system*, he thinks, gritting his teeth. *Now take them down before they take you down.*

"The raiders in the desert were former soldiers. They scanned me, saw me with Thalassa. They could have tipped them off. Or it could have been my contact at the agency today who did it, after accepting my payment for the list, which can't be traced back to him." Returning to the phone conversation with Arcturus, he continues, "And if I want to press action against them?"

"The Kontractor is our finest but she will not accompany you. No one will. You will be on your own."

"Is that your decision, or hers?"

Arcturus sighs, "She will trust you one second and slice your throat the next as you will do to her. Maybe you two deserve one another. Would this pressing of action involve Governor Borges himself?"

"Yes. I've made up my mind."

A pause, and then, "Fine, Kontractor will attend with you then. Aurthur and Opal may also be heading your way. You really mean to charge the Crystal Palace, The Towers themselves? I'll let her know; sending the meeting time and place. Goodbye."

"We have to leave," Severum says.

"Used to it," the Priestess replies, tucking her bag of new lingerie into his dresser drawer with the receipt.

"You need to go into hiding."

"Story of my life. We're getting older. Maybe not physically, but there's a sort of mental exhaustion weighing. I don't want to leave your side, not again."

"Too risky. This time I'm taking matters into my own hands and you don't need to be there, trust me."

"Run away with me."

"Where, the Aporia Asylum?"

"Not Dayburn. Somewhere here on Evig Natt."

"Nowhere is safe. I know these people better than you. I strike first or my luck's run up."

"Be careful, please," she whispers, holding him close while stifling a tear.

No time for careful.

"If you have any influence left organize some glitches and mobilize the Aphorids."

"Severum, have you lost your cog?"

"I'll message you when the time is right. I need them nearby."

"It'll take a few days. I'll inform them that the recent attack on the Asylum was due to Evig Natt violating treaties, not providing protections, and warranting a military strike. It's a half-truth, but as a collectivist species they won't take well to such violations of trust. I'll station them out in the Twilight. I can't promise you I can control them once they're unleashed, however, and if the hemisphere falls don't blame it on me."

"I understand. Akasha, one more thing."

"Can't find your Pulser again?"

"I love you."

"I, I love you too. Always have always will."

After the Priestess leaves, Severum gathers his weapons and heads out. He slips like a shadow, knowing the region's surveillance systems inside-out, feigning nonchalance. Descending through an underground tunnel, he encounters a mall of vendor-stalls barely wider than his shoulders. Government propaganda lines the stalls to indirectly define the boundaries of rebellion. Citizens react against the propaganda and think their rebellious notions come from within them, but this too is manufactured, rendering the facade of freewill complete.

As he approaches the stairwell, the cold air rushes down and he pulls his coat tight, turning on its heat generator. The wind almost blows him down the stairs as he stretches one hand in front of him and leans forward. A white rabbit with a wide smile laughs on a digital ad that cost a ton while people pick bones from a trashcan beneath it.

VHUD flickers; the governor's executive assistant. He ignores the call but second-guesses his choice. Log will show the call request was received since his occipts are turned on. He expects they were going to ask him a battery of trick questions with option-closed responses, questions that appeared to only have two answers, with either representing a failure on his part. Trying to appease everyone he has appeased no one. Giving one hundred percent all the time, he has nothing extra to give to be the hero, the curse of the over-achiever. He recites his adages: Be special but not too special. Achieve, but don't raise the standard for everyone else. Good things come to those who wait, and are immediately taken by the impatient.

He checks in at the new safe house, off the grid. He replaces the analog door lock and resets the code on the digital one. Dropping a pillow on the floor, he kicks it beneath the bed where he intends on sleeping. Tomorrow he will infiltrate the Crystal Palace and confront Governor Borges in his office. Getting into The Towers will be no problem.

Getting out will be hell.

19

Severum wakes to crashing sounds and yelling outside. The room is dark, his fireflies dead. He reduces the windows' opacity. Protestors wave signs on the streets, some anti-capitalistic and some claiming the world's ending. One reads *Women aren't glitches* and another *Copyright your Cog.* Graffiti spreads like a rash across the buildings. The protestors hold jars of fireflies whose light has been extinguished. They press up like wildfire against the Enforcers' heavy armor and trapezoidal helmets. A boy throws a jar at one of them, glass tinkling on the pavement. They charge after him, but he stumbles away through the sea of people and loses them in the near total darkness.

Severum heads into the streets and pushes the molasses-crowd out of his way with a breast-stroke motion, thinking this a great distraction and hoping Thalassa arranged it. Men gather at the intersection around a street preacher yelling over the noise, "Malcolm X said, *here you way out in the middle of the ocean, can't swim, and you worried about someone that's in the bathtub, who can't swim.* " He pauses, continues in his own words, "The Gov'nor, he sitting in the bathtub."

"What did the X stand for?" an onlooker asks.

"Don't know. The damage done to the colonizing ship archives *conveniently* destroyed most of Black history. Most of what survived was only what the bourgeoisie considered non-threatening."

Severum stands on the outer perimeter of the Crystal Palace. Its Towers loom across the courtyard, the only area still half lit. Fireflies swirl anxiously, beating themselves against the glass bulbs containing them. The golden glow reflects off the large turquoise and abalone door. Far above him, two obsidian arches sprouting from the building pierce the clouds and meet imperfectly. The governor's office is at the apex of the asymmetry, exactly where Severum fits in best.

"You ready?" he asks Thalassa, meeting up with her.

"Yes. I took care of the security."

"That was you? All of this, the protests, everything?"

"That was me, though I must admit, your girl helped me organize the info-leaks, glitches streaming the truth into people's minds like candy confetti. Yummy, huh? We sent stuff like *Neon light isn't harmful, Light a lantern,* and *Tungsten isn't barbaric.* You should see the blink-counts! That was just act one. For act two, I had a vial I was burning to get rid of. Figured live a little and just do it. Then I said wait, delay your gratification. But the little devil on my shoulder prodded me with a three-pronged phallus and assured me now's the time, baby. So I released the virus. It's penetrating glass and killing fireflies left and right. The Crystal Palace is still lit though, but most of the guards are out containing the protests."

"Ingenious. No one's been able to do that. You killed off a whole city's pocket change."

"I'm just using their own shock doctrine tactic against them. They'll breed more to replace them in time, but the riots are nasty, aren't they?" Thalassa grins.

"I want Borges. I still can't believe I'm on their hit-list, after everything I've sacrificed."

"You're in good company. Might be harder for me to get through the front door than you, though."

"Windows," Severum answers, pointing up. "I've gone over the design flaws for a while. Though I haven't been assigned an office in The Towers in ages, you work at a place like this you start thinking how do I get in, how do I get out, how do I keep others from getting in, and how do I keep some from getting out. Question though, if the virus works why even rotate the planet?"

"This is about more than the economy, it's about seeing the sun, having enough light to live by, the same light the ruling class enjoys daily. The virus collapses the economy for a few days, but it's temporary. They'll just develop a vaccine, breed a new line. Or a new form of money will emerge to exploit others. Light is the commodity that everything else derives from. We end this once and for all. Increasing rotation is a permanent solution, and you have to admit the sun will feel good," she smiles, hopping. "But there's got to be another way than the windows. I'm… afraid of heights."

"Not so afraid when you leapt down and cut open my leg," he bites, then pauses and apologizes. "Sorry. We can't have that. Emotions."

"That's exactly what we need. It makes us human."

"And life will be better for everyone?"

"We shall bring the light. It will take time, but yes. No more doubts; it holds you back."

"War won't ever stop, will it?"

"Never completely, no. You'll always have a job murdering people, cheer up, mate," she slights. "After the Great Rotation commences, we'll destroy the Twilight and its Core, unless it agrees to protect us. We'll negotiate like human beings again, but without the monetary incentive. They'll be no more war over heat and water and light. Humans can be content in their own hemisphere without jealousy or need."

"Our Pulsers and your daggers are small enough to conceal

without suspicion, but I have an idea where we can pick up more weapons once inside."

"Yay! I have this, too," Thalassa replies, tapping a rod against the ground while patting a bag at her waist and dancing to the rhythm.

"What are you coming off of?"

"Nada. Modlag doesn't make a good bedfella now, does it?"

"Oh God, we're never gonna make it."

The remaining streetlights black out one by one. Severum adjusts his occipts. Protestors force themselves against Enforcer barricades until one drops his shield and the crowd tramples over him, smashing it into his face. The crowd flows like river rapids, crashing against hard objects, leaping off one another, and slipping through all obstructions.

Severum parts the crowd and helps the guard up off the street, his nose broken.

"Whose side are you on?" Thalassa asks.

"Humanity's. All humanity, even those I dislike." He turns around. "What's Bjorn doing here?"

"Recruiting. Watching for potentials. They're heading to the comms tower. If they disable it it'll be a nice bonus."

"This isn't a game."

The Enforcers gather in a protective circle, shields faced outward. A protestor throws a stratospear into the middle, blinding each for a minute or so. They shake their heads violently with confusion. As the first Enforcer regains blurry vision, he fires wildly into the crowd; a dozen protestors cry out and grab their injuries, slinking across the stained concrete.

"It's getting worse. We gotta move. Follow me across the courtyard. Window's best option."

They climb the tower face, finding footholds in the uneven stones. Severum disables an alarm with a portahack and opens a circular window they squeeze through. Moving silently through a hallway that would normally be under watch—if the guards weren't busy dealing with the ruckus outside—they look for a staircase.

Thalassa loses footing and knocks against a table, sending it screeching across the wood floor.

Severum freezes, pulls her close. "We've been spotted. Pretend not to notice. They may circle behind us, so keep moving."

"Where? It's so quiet and we were so quiet. I was quiet, you were quiet, *really* quiet."

Suddenly, two guards take aim down the hall. A spray of bullets barrages the walls beside them as they look for cover, finding nothing they can reach in time. Thalassa steps in front of him, takes the rod she's been holding, and quickly erects an umbrella that shoots up and expands around her, encasing her in a spherical bubble. The shield blocks the entire spray of bullets without being dented. The umbrella holds as she presses forward as if fighting a hurricane wind, shots clinking against it. Giving up on projectiles, the guards switch to slower firing but more penetrating Pulsers, but the umbrella is unyielding and their Pulsers soon lose charge.

"New tech," she giggles, holding the umbrella nonchalantly over her shoulder. She twirls it side to side as she moves towards them with a spring in her step as they fumble with their weapons in disbelief, reloading the projectile guns, and waiting for the Pulsers to recharge.

Thalassa and Severum charge. She withdraws the umbrella into a pole that swings with vicious speed across the air, breaking a guard's kneecap. A leg-sweep sends the other to his knees. She steps aside. Severum shoots and penetrates the guards' armor at close range, banging their bodies against the wall with enough force to knock them unconscious. He approaches the next set of doors, avoiding the guards' faces in case it's someone he knows.

"Locked. This'll take time. More coming. We need to coordinate better."

"Allow me. Absolute silence now, seriously," she says, pushing his shoulder playfully.

Severum almost discharges his weapon from the impact on his shoulder and he swears, "I can't work with you. Don't ever do that again."

"I said shut up. You'll get us killed," she replies, sticking her tongue out, tilting her head and pretending to be dead. She approaches the locked doors, dips her hand into a small, sound-proof sack on her waist. Pulling her hand out, she places yellow fingerprints on the door, leaving a pollen-like substance behind. "Run," she whispers.

They conceal themselves in the hallway. Footsteps pound from behind the door to investigate the shots. It swings open, guns swinging left and right looking for purchase.

"Over here! Hey!" Thalassa yells.

"What are you doing?" Severum snaps, raising his Pulser.

"What is this?" a guard shouts, seeing the bodies.

At the sound of his voice a fiery explosion goes off, throwing both guards from the door inside the corridor where Severum and Thalassa stand. Flesh and building debris pummel her umbrella. Thalassa activates the rod. Electricity pulses through it. She shocks the guards, stunning them.

"Banshee dust," she giggles.

"Sound-activated, I see. Why you so happy? The guard could die. We went hang-gliding over the Albino Marsh. He's a good guy."

"But a poor guard. Off we go! If you saw your life's work pay off, you'd be happy, too," she says as he cocks a brow.

"Just make sure all that powder junk is off your hands. I don't know what in fuck's name you're on, but it's going to get us killed."

Sprinklers activate to put out the fire and alarms flash, but no one is around to respond or relay the warning. They stoop to gather weapons. Severum counts how many guards should be left, mostly those protecting technical support teams. They close a set of sound-proof doors and enter a training room. A thin screen flies by advertising the next training session.

Severum scans the training room for recruits, finding none and noting the available weapons. He figures they just finished their VR exercises and will be handling actual weapons soon for the first time. This is where he held his first gun, an old-fashioned projectile weapon, so heavy in his once innocent hands. It was said if one could hit a long-range target with a projectile weapon, then Pulsers would be a cinch, lacking bullet drop. He opens a cabinet and replaces the simunition practice ammo with real ammo from an adjacent cabinet. The live ammo lacks the colorful tips of the practice ammo, but being new they shouldn't notice and the distraction would be invaluable.

The next set of rooms houses the computer servers used to send instructions to operatives. Jars of unaffected fireflies line the shelves, lighting the room. Severum busts the jars, sending reflections scattering along the walls as they fly away. The room dims. Thalassa connects her portahack and they sabotage the main server to impede the Enforcers' directives, though they can't confirm whether the server held the hit list they're on. The screen flashes red, alerting nearby security.

A guard enters, looks around, but they're hidden. He sweeps an illegal flashlight.

Severum rushes from the corner to disarm him from behind, but the guard hears him, spins around, and busts his nose with the butt of his gun knocking him down. The guard turns to open fire on Thalassa but Severum stabs him from the ground behind the knee to disable, not kill, and the weapon falls from his hands.

Looks like Thalassa has another idea. She is not a silent sea spilling forth, but a raging tidal destruction with a rabid frothing of waves of searing pain. She drives the searing blade deep into the man's leg as he cries out. She strikes yet again until Severum pulls her back on the final thrust."

"There's no need for that. Senseless, he was already disabled. You're no better than they are," he scolds. "Have some compassion, I used to be one of them."

"You're the one who said we can't have emotions. I am the bringer of mercy, Valkyrie for the fallen warrior, harbinger of the Elysium fields."

"No, there's no heaven here, no heaven to come, and no honor or mercy in senseless violence. If you weren't high, you'd realize that. We need to get through the next corridor. Hand over the portahack, I don't trust you with it, or anything anymore," Severum says.

She backs away from the verbal assault.

Rounding the next hallway, he looks over his shoulder but she's gone. He backtracks, searches, even recklessly pulls open a few office doors, but can't find her. He returns to the server room, expecting a hostage situation or a bullet from the shadows.

But gravity guns don't fire bullets.

Thrown to his knees, Severum pushes against the invisible ceiling with both hands above his head, like bench-pressing one's body weight with a lion as a spotter. The force is too intense, he can't hold it, the force field smashing him. The guard steps out in the open, still aiming the gravity gun to keep the field intact. He's trapped, down on his back. Thalassa has likely been captured, and his muscles are giving out on him.

He turns his face sideways beneath the force field to prevent his injured nose from being smashed and sees Thalassa slipping free from her bonds. *Fluid*, like she always said. She swipes the gravity gun from the assailant in one smooth motion like high tide dragging a bottle out to sea. The force field lifts. She fires but the charge has been depleted. The guard lands a punch in her shoulder. She compensates for shorter arms with a high snap-kick, but the guard grabs her leg, shifting her weight off balance as he backhands her with the other hand. Another guard grabs her from behind. Still lying on the floor, Severum can only watch as she's disarmed and restrained, can only listen to her muffled cries, but at least the force field holding him in place has been lifted.

As more guards approach, he's forced to retreat down a side stairway and exit The Towers from a small delivery area near the back, leaving her behind. He conceals himself as security grows tighter. With no chance to confront the governor now, normally he would abandon the mission at this point, regroup, count his losses, start over, but he can't leave her behind, not after that lecture on compassion.

THE GUARD DRAGS Thalassa down a few flights of stairs then through a dim corridor. There're no torturous screams, no throngs of protestors captured in their dissent, just quiet, quiet enough to hear her occipts focusing, a subtle metal grinding on metal, a quiet that makes it all that worse not knowing what to expect. She needs to secrete an oily lube from her modified tear ducts, but her occipts jamming is the least of her worries. Her hands are tied in front of her, the rope woven tight from many individual strands. The guard shoves her into a cell with an electronically-sealed door instead of bars. Cell designs require a keypad both outside and within the cell, in case a guard gets locked inside during an escape. He grunts and leaves.

She rubs her hands along the cell's rough dungeon walls, but they're smooth to the touch and just an illusion from an augmented video feed. Nice trick, but she has a better one. She raises her hands to her occipts and rubs a single thread of the rope that binds her in-between the gap of her artificial eye lenses. Blinking rapidly, the thread breaks, severed by the subtlest metallic grinding that can barely cut a hair. Rinse and repeat and her hands are soon freed with just an electronic lock withholding her tide. *Such faith in technology will be their downfall,* she thinks. *I will burst free with the freedom of consciousness and the consciousness of freedom.*

Now for the keypad. She knows the model; a wrong guess will emit a killer shock, but she has no intentions of guessing. She tongues the back of her throat and hits her modified uvula three times to release a small cylinder from a thin, flesh-covered compartment. Retrieving the two-centimeter hack-tube from her mouth, she balances it between her lips and leans forward to connect it to the keypad with a kiss. The hack-tube blinks red and shuts down.

"The connection doesn't match!" she screams, almost dropping and breaking the hack-tube, and glad the door is thick enough to prevent guards from hearing.

The keypad and the hack-tube have a different number of connecting wires. Glitchit! Above, a lightbulb. She stares at it in awe, there's no firefly. She pulls on the bulb but it won't budge. Turning it to the right feels tighter. Finally, she turns it left and something loosens. She turns it right again and nothing, back to square one. Thinking it requires binary code, she uses various combinations of right and left turns but the bulb won't release. Maybe it's just a screw? She turns the bulb left four rotations and it releases. Occipts adjust to the darkness. Jumping to hang on the fixture, the wires pull down from the ceiling.

She sets the antique lightbulb to the side as if a jewel. Makes sense to use them in the cells, as they don't have to be replaced as often as fireflies. Guards changing fireflies out would be a security risk as they enter. Then a terrible thought rises, *'That means anyone who is put in here is exposed to the secret that the Crystal Palace uses illegal lightbulbs. This must be a death cell! They don't expect anyone to live to tell. I must work fast.'*

Her teeth strip the rubber wire casing, in time cut through the copper wire, and she spits out the battery taste. In near-darkness she extracts an adapter from the hack-tube, folding out to expand. She combines this with the extra copper wire to make the hack-tube fit to the keypad. Knees shaking, she inserts it. The light blinks red, then stabilizes on red, yellow, and finally green, verifying the connection. The autohack countdown initiates.

Two-hour estimate.

Meantime, she plays with floating spheres hovering over the cot near the toilet. Upon being touched, each provides the tactile sensation of a rushing river, or the sight of sunlight transmitted to her cognigraf. Proponents say the spheres provide enough stimulation to avoid prisoners going insane, making them easier to control, but the memory of such things outside the cell makes imprisonment far worse.

An hour and forty-five minutes.

IT WORKED. The door finally opens, levees breaking, and she surges through like a flood, then dams her desire to escape until she is a trickle listening, leaning, looking. The coast is clear save for a guard sitting reading an article, camouflaged by feeding a fake image of a storage crate to her vHUD. The augmented image is easy to spot: low resolution, a lag in its display, and doesn't reflect light. Silent steps, closer, close enough.

She kicks right through the facade, hitting the man square in the face and breaking his nose as the upward momentum sends him flying back, but he recovers instantly. She sidesteps a punch, attempts to break his arm, but her technique is faulty. She counterattacks but her breath is cut off, an arm around her neck. Slamming her elbows back again and again, he loses his grip. Catching her breath, she spins to face him, forcing a kick into his crotch. She puts him in a sleeper-hold and changes into his uniform, rolling up the pant legs. From a distance the uniform could be mistaken for plain clothes. She drags the man into her cell and takes his access card, noting its low clearance level. Remembering Severum's advice, she lets him live.

After passing through two sterile corridors she arrives at a wide lobby area with a front desk about ten meters away. A lone guard is distracted with vHUD games, moving his hands as if fighting. More secure the perimeter outside the windows, blocking any escape route, but at least they don't know she's out yet, and her uniform gives her an idea.

"I'm here for an interview," she tells the guard.

"I could guess. You're as nervous as the rest of 'em. It's not as big a deal as you all are making it out to be, let me tell you. Who's your interview with anyway?"

"I, I can't remember. I hope this doesn't decrease my chances, I mean I had it written down but usually I'm really quite organized, and dependable, too."

"I won't tell HR," he assures her. "I don't remember an interview scheduled at this hour given the commotion so let me go check. Be just a moment. They're obviously already processing the hiring paperwork since they already gave you a uniform, so relax, will ya? Interview's just a formality at this stage. And don't worry about your threads not fitting, none of ours have autofit but they'll order you a smaller size, probably take a few months."

"I'll try to relax. But if I'm not here when you come back, my nerves got the best of me," she says, forcing a smile.

The guard leaves the counter and walks down the hall through a gold-plated door as Thalassa quietly follows, passing a restroom and another office door. She opens it to find a Human Resources storage room with uniforms folded inside open lockers. They appear to represent mid-level clearance so she takes one and leaves, entering the restroom across the hall to change clothes. Opening the door, she waits for the guard to make his way back to his desk, and as he passes, she travels further down the hall and opens the gold-plated door, closing it behind her. Another hall emerges, filled with motivational memes that she jerks her head right to dismiss.

"Who are you?" an older gentleman asks.

"A new hire. Just got my uniform. My password is CraneNest, with a capital C and N," she lies.

"Stop, stop. Golly, now we must reset it. Don't give it out to anyone."

"I would like that," she says, grinning.

"I'll deactivate your CraneNest password later today. For the time being, here's a temporary mid-level access code. Not too many people come on board and move straight to your level. You must have had prior experience. Anyway, we usually upgrade your vHUD security before allowing single-sign-on authentication, since cogs are hacked all the time, so you'll just have to keep track of a password for a little while longer."

"Thank you, and maybe I'll see you around. Oh, one more thing. There's been rioting outside. Has there been any trouble reported inside the building?"

"Why, yes. The protestors have knocked many of our systems offline. A team went out to repair the comms tower. Oh, and a guy was wounded in a training exercise. Seems they were using live ammo, didn't even know it. Had to call the medics on that one, ambulance came, whole spectacle. Other than that, I haven't heard a thing, but it's a large building. The other tower may have been hit worse. Their bio-id check is down at the door."

"Golly," she replies, mimicking his tone. "Thank you."

The password works on the elevator. The numbers above show it's descending from the fifth floor. Guards grow dense behind her. Lift lowers to fourth floor. The guards shout commands to search the premises. Third floor. Someone, possibly the older gentleman down the hall, points to her. Second floor, hurry up, hurry up! The guards run and yell, "Freeze!" Doors open, she steps inside the elevator and impulsively bangs the roof button a dozen times, doors closing just in time.

She takes a deep breath on the way up. Ding, doors open to

reveal the rooftop, a flat clearing, though a part of the tower still ascends further, inaccessible by lift. She scans the sky for drones and peers over the edge, spotting Severum far below re-approaching the building from a loading bay where an ambulance is parked. Protestors are lined up on the opposite side of the building. Still heavy activity around the ground entrance.

Jumping off the roof would circumvent security, sure, but it must be at least five stories high. She needs to signal Severum, but there's too much activity. She huddles behind an over-sized air vent that barely offers any cover, deciding whether to risk taking the elevator down to another floor or sitting tight until the Enforcers arrive, and they wouldn't make the mistake of merely imprisoning her twice.

***

At ground level, Severum treads without footfall, moving like a ripple on a lake's surface, emulating outward then ceasing to exist as he blends back into the landscape. A wide pipe runs around the building, bolts anchoring it off the ground. He ducks beneath it as a guard nearly spots him and follows it, ensuring to stay within his blind-spot. An ambulance provides another concealment point. He presses his back to it, easing his way around. The engine is on but there are no passengers, just the smell of fast food.

A man patrols in a circular pattern. Severum opens the ambulance door and closes it softly, not fully engaging the latch. Crouched in the driver's seat, he stays put as the guards disappear behind the other side of the building. A medic uniform and hat are stashed in a compartment between the seats. He checks his side mirrors for activity, then changes clothes, staying low. In the back he locates two syringes in a drawer of medical supplies, and various chemicals he can concoct into deadly poisons. Instead, he fills the syringes with a tranquilizing serum.

He re-enters the building through a back service door, blocking his face with his hand as he pretends to swat away an insect with small, calculated motions. He heads through a room of steel cabinetry and up a staircase. Not much activity in this sector. There're only two or three locations they would be holding her, if it's not too late.

THALASSA STEPS BACK from the roof's edge, hates heights. The elevator rises and the doors open with a scraping sound. The wind assaults her ears, but it'll be much worse when free-falling at a couple hundred kilometers per hour. Anxiety wells up in her like a balloon forced underwater, struggling to shoot up to the surface unless weighted down with iron will.

She relaxes her muscles and takes a deep breath to prepare for the five-story fall, jumping off the roof her only escape. VHUD calculates she can reduce the impact by thirty-six times by slightly bending her knees. It also calculates a survival rate at this height of ten percent, but that's pretty much ending up paralyzed in multiple pieces. Footsteps from the elevator, but she refuses to even turn and look at the guards. *I'm unarmed, there's no other choice. I must remember to roll to the side as I land. On three. One:* Stepping to the edge, feet tight together so both will hit the ground at the same time. *Two:* Fingers laced behind head to brace for impact. *Three*: Bending knees and—

A man grips her upper arm and pulls her back from the edge. "Too early in life for that."

"Severum! How did you—"

"After I overheard you escaped I figured with all the activity downstairs you'd make your way to the roof. I still have a job to do. My cover as a medic will be blown soon. Oh, and the tranquilizer will hurt a bit."

"Tranquillizer?"

Thalassa loses consciousness.

Severum carries her downstairs in both arms, face down to avoid recognition. A soldier shouts commands, and he switches to a lesser used staircase to avoid him, thinking it safer. The glint off a weapon one flight above him says otherwise, but the footsteps become distant as the troop heads to the roof. Exiting the staircase brings them to the central lobby with wide glass panes, but outside a guard is standing where the ambulance used to be.

"Need some help with her?" a male attendant with long red hair at the desk asks.

Doesn't recognize him, must be a new guy. Comms signals must still be out, the building too large for everyone to know what's going on.

"No, I got her," Severum replies, "but I was called to assist with a second person as well. Do you have a hover-stretcher? I was told there's one in storage room B," he says, referencing a door he spotted earlier.

"Might be. I'll go check." The attendant motions to the guard outside to watch the desk.

Severum closes the heavy entrance door behind him, juggling Thalassa in his arms. The chill wind hits them but she doesn't stir. Was the dosage too high for her weight? He had no choice; he couldn't extract her while keeping cover if she was conscious. The guards would have picked up on it, even if she kept her mouth shut.

Inside, the attendant's gone off to the storage room. The guard outside walks past Severum on his way to cover the desk. He lowers Thalassa to the ground and brings the remaining syringe out, sticking the guard in the side of the neck. He collapses and Severum drags the body under an elevated flatbed trailer.

Inside, the desk guard returns, likely carrying news that storage room B holds no medical equipment, and probably issuing an alert about a suspicious medic.

To avoid him, Severum crawls beneath the trailer beside the incapacitated guard, changing into his navy-blue camo. The pockets carry a universal vehicle activation key, specialized grenades, and a military-grade Pulser with extended charge. He gathers Thalassa over one shoulder, the way one carries an escaped prisoner knocked out and not a delicate patient this time. He accesses a vHUD menu to change the color of his occipts, lighten his hair, and darken his skin tone. Experience has taught him that a combination of minor changes is less likely to be revealed than a single major change.

Reinforcements arrive by jeep, opening four doors. They circle in opposite directions towards the back of the building. "Hey! Stop!" two soldiers yell, new faces he doesn't recognize.

"Finally," Severum replies, feigning panic. "I got her, knocked her out. A few men ran inside. One was dressed as a service attendant with long red hair, another a medic. A third may have been wearing a special ops uniform. I've been trying to get through but my comms are down. I shot my gravity gun at them but they got away."

"Where's your gun now?" the soldier asks, squinting at his waist.

"I was disarmed, but listen, don't tell the other guys, alright? I've never lost my gun before."

"Your story matches what we've pieced together. There were reports of a gravity gun going off and some infiltrators lighting a fire. Surprised the floor didn't fall through. We won't tell, but keep it out of enemy hands at all costs. Team, secure the area!"

"Yes, Sir."

Severum's mouth drops. A soldier has spotted the body beneath the trailer.

"What in holy hell?" the soldier exclaims.

Fight or flight? Neither, that has always been his problem. Talk. He needs to provide an answer, and fast. "The escapee took him out. While she was distracted I captured her."

The guard investigates the fallen body and is about to notice it's nearly naked, compromising his cover.

He uses Thalassa's body to conceal drawing his weapon and with the Pulser aimed between her dangling arm, he fires, stepping around the corner of the building to fire again. Shots miss! The soldier runs for cover, heading inside the building, leaving the door open.

Severum lands a R3p3@t grenade right through the doorway. It silently explodes in the lobby, causing the soldiers' occipts to replay the last five seconds worth of images in a loop. He follows it with a CTTY grenade that hacks their cognigrafs to switch their audio inputs and outputs.

The guards are yelling for help, but all that comes out is a reproduction of sounds from the environment. They speak in footsteps and stairclimbing, they speak in elevator beeps and doors closing. They begin to mimic each other's sounds until they are copying one another in a cycle of inputs and outputs, the same sound going in each of their aural implants and out their mouths, each cycle getting louder and louder as the soundwaves amplify like guitar feedback until they clamp their ears shut with their palms to avoid the shrill pain.

Severum runs to the jeep the reinforcements arrived in and finds it empty. He lays Thalassa in the back, starts the engine, covers the roof, disables Smartdrv, and slams the pedal. They escape the complex, but in the rearview mirror, a matchstick stands on the rooftop drawing a line across the sky. The soldier, tiny in the distance, disappears as they make down the road, but that line across the sky gets closer, the fiery glow of a missile heading their way. Severum sticks his head out to scan it, vHUD bringing up the model: *Homing missile, Non-Heat-Seeking, Motion-Based.* The missile comes closer and closer, a halo lighting up the sky and falling like a god into the underworld. He slams on the brakes at the last moment, body lurching forward. Having no more motion to follow, the missile flies overhead on its course until it hits the nearest obstacle, a small cliff in front of the jeep. He swerves to avoid the falling debris. The Towers disappear from view.

"Thalassa, you awake yet? Course not, nothing's gone right."

Pulling over, he gets out to try to wake her, tapping a rhythm on her wrist to re-activate her cognigraf in safe-mode to share her vitals with him. He carries her to the front passenger seat to watch her closer. He then commits a dozen felonies in a single second. He plugs the portahack up to her cognigraf. It allows him virtually no access to her head, and any small edit he could make would be reverted in five seconds without her authorization, but it allows him to re-map her audio and visual processing. For the next five seconds, everything he says will display in her unconscious mind as text images.

"Thalassa, I know you can't hear me, but the manual override when I disabled Smartdrv triggered a signal relay. It won't be long until they can trace us. I'll take some backroads but it won't do us any good. We'll have to leave the jeep behind in a few minutes or we'll be toast. I've messaged the team to meet us at a rendezvous point ahead. I'll gather some equipment from the back so we'll be ready, but you need to get up."

She stirs briefly.

As they near the rendezvous point, he risks it no further. They travel the last bit on foot, him carrying her and a box of gear. The O.A.K. van waits to pick them up just off the main road. Warnings in vHUD. A neon purple streamer soars across the sky. He's not going to make clearance in time.

Thalassa wakes.

"Run!" They sprint as fast as they can, jumping in the van. "Gun it! Back to base!" Tires squeal and they're off. The jeep explodes in the rearview mirror, molten metal beams crashing on their windshield. Thalassa falls back in the seat, asleep again.

Severum scans headlines and displays articles recounting the events. Most of the press attention has covered the protests, but some mention the events on the Crystal Palace grounds. Due to the comms being out, the training accident, the missing soldiers, the explosions, and Severum and Thalassa changing outfits, no two articles read the same. So far, none implicate them, though a red-haired administrative assistant is being brought in for questioning.

Still, this changes nothing. Severum slams his hand down on the seat.

Failure.

20

I *was born a simple girl, named Thalassa, simpler than the complex people around me. I studied them to reduce all that complexity, becoming more complex myself in the process. But I didn't so much as gain a sense of myself, as lose my own nature. Today I know myself by what I am not. I blend idea and form, the negative and the positive, the conceptual and the real, as a master spice blender creates a hot curry, grinding and grinding in proper order, always looking for balance between volatile ingredients.*

Arc says meaning is just consistency and agreement. But I am not consistent. I am not agreeable. I reach out. My arms draw lines extending into space. Everything that extends is composed of smaller parts that also extend. At the end of all that extension there is still more extension. When I reach the end of all I reach for, I will still reach, I will still desire, because I am a fool. But I know that fool is to savant as zero is to one, each meaningless without the other, each undeserving of reverence or criticism. I accept myself, even as this paper pushes back at my pen with equal force, even as the environment pushes back at the force of my thoughts. But I can push much, much harder.

-Thalassa, personal journal entry

ORANGE LIGHTS DANCE across the water's surface before submerging, each light making a *plump* sound as it dives. They return to the surface carrying memories, bobbing up and down, only to melt beneath the fire of a burning tree stretching over the lake as she reaches for them, her anger destroying these precious moments. The dream dispels and she wakes, exiting the metallic tent.

Thalassa sprays a stimulant mist over her head that seeps into her pores. She wears a white tank-top over her recently tanned skin that shows off her tattoos, including a little girl hanging herself with a grin beneath a burning tree. Her occipts glow red for a moment as they burn off sand particles, tiny bits of ash gathering on her lower lids. She listens from a distance to a conversation between Arcturus and Severum.

"I'm glad circumstances came together to bring you two back alive, despite your failed attempt to confront Borges," Arcturus says. "You're welcome here now, Severum, at our new Dayburn base. It's not much, but what needs to function functions. We've already mined enough Ultimaepar to complete some of our main components. Perhaps you can encourage some of the others not to disband us. You have to discover what motivates them first, though, and it's different for everyone."

"Maybe it's your charisma that drives them," Severum slights.

"Doubtful," she replies, looking nervously to the lower right. "Thalassa writes my speeches. She has this certain, energy. I don't know how she does it."

"Most people in power have someone else write their speeches. Otherwise their enemies can interpret any slight error any way they want," he consoles, putting a hand on her shoulder.

She removes his hand and backs away, lifting a terracotta jug of water off a Moroccan-styled table and half gulping half lapping at it. "Before you congratulate yourself, know that Thalassa would have performed the assassination and found a way out without being spotted if she was working alone."

"She was high and about to jump five stories off a roof into the arms of a dozen guards as well trained as I am."

"She would have made it. It's that energy thing I was talking about."

Thalassa steps between them making her presence known. "Well, that plan's shot. What's next?"

"Can the Twilight Core be persuaded further?" Arcturus asks.

"Do you really want to rely on that thing?" Severum counters.

"There's no time for debating."

"It's a question worthy of discussion."

"The leaders will decide."

"You two?" He laughs. "Last time I checked you had a vacancy in leadership. Without me there would have been another one. Trust your damn machines and do what you want." He stomps off.

"Severum, come back, please," Thalassa implores. "I appreciate what you've done for us. Arcturus is just stressed right now."

"I'm not stressed!" she counters. "I'll tell you when I need you to write my speeches."

"What?"

"Forget about it."

"We need to hit Borges again, this time in transit," Severum suggests.

"No. The resources should go to defending our base," Arcturus replies. "We can only spare a small team, if that. Besides, Borges will be scared into hiding after the recent uprisings."

"No, important men don't remain locked up for long. They

take risks to remain active. That's why they're in power. Lenin was shot what, eight times over the years, before finally being poisoned in the United States of Gorbachrov."

"Get your history right. It was the Union of Soviet States under the rule of President Alabama. He led the healthcare system to discover penicillin, named after the peninsula where it happened at. Did you really forget that much from history class?"

"No, he didn't, Arcturus. That happened during the Victorian era, named after the lake in Central Afrikaan. The colonizing ship's records and audio files are accurate, I don't care how damaged people say they are. I know our ancestors' history. President Alabama invented atomic weapons leading to radiation in Cher's Noble Region."

"That's stupid, even for you, Severum," Arc retorts. "President Bomba was named after the region where *his* country created the atomic bomb in what was called the Middle-West, but they didn't even have compasses back then so we don't really know if they had their directions right."

"Stop it! Both of you." Thalassa gets between them. "Our history's glitched, I get it. Back to the main question. Should we lay in wait with traps and get him while he's on the move or not?"

"We have to strike out, even if it just delays them, until the rotation's fully activated. They have a solid idea of the general region of our base and an attack could strike at any second. Part of that is my fault, I admit, but I'm here to make amends," Severum says.

A buzzing gets their attention. They scan the skies in unison. The drones are on them in no time. The team tries to take cover beneath the metallic tents, but they're caught out in the open. Severum is the first to give up, declaring they are unarmed. More drones descend, but scans for military weapons come back negative; They aren't from Evig Natt, they're labeled with tumble-weed symbols.

"Why did the Core send you?" Thalassa shouts in every direction, the drones converging upon them.

The drones reply in a unified monotone, "We are here to observe what is possible and to assist as needed if what is possible equals what is necessary for increased planetary rotation speed." The spherical drones fly like a swarm of angry bees around the base. They examine blueprints and project plans, ore, and equipment. A few minutes later, the drones return and state in surround sound, "Consensus. Current methodology for increased rotation success rate is 96.4555556, truncate initiated, percent. Success is based on mathematical calculations not including the probability of human interference. O.A.K. is predicted to strike at Governor Borges to deter said interference. The governor has planned a street rally on Evig Natt to recruit more soldiers in response to recent uprisings. Uploading now his predicted travel routes and destinations." Most of the drones fly off with a few puffs of black smoke, but some remain to organize in a perimeter around the base.

"Told you the Core was on our side. We need to make our way to the Twilight band to check the progress on the belt and transfer," Thalassa says.

"No. The drones will assist as required and provide the necessary project updates. They will defend us, leaving a small team available for mounting an attack," Arcturus replies.

"Leaving the base with less people to defend it is risky, but I agree we could spare a team of thirty. We'll take down Borges in transit."

"And you think you can trust a machine's intel?" Severum asks, shaping two fingers like a gun barrel against his face.

"Severum, grow up," Thalassa says." You know what? Those drones could have laid us all to rest if their goal was to distract us. There doesn't have to be any master plan for us to attack

Borges while they attack the base, because they wouldn't *need* such a plan to overtake us. They're directly connected to the Core's network. They don't fear losses; even their own existence matters nothing to them."

"Thalassa, take thirty members and our new Architect and lead a strike against Borges. Leave the other hundred or so behind to defend the base. Gather them, we have an announcement to make."

The group of primarily women gather.

"I am proud to announce on this very day, beneath the sun that never sits, that Severum will be our new Architect going forth. He has been responsible for identifying treachery in our ranks, allying us with various groups on Dayburn, and leading numerous assaults. His terraforming experience will be an added advantage."

Some members cheer while others chastise a man's leadership.

Anticipating a turn for the worse, Arcturus tells him privately. "It's more than you deserve, but we need you."

Severum repeats the title *Architect*, trying not to be prideful. "Thank you. Now let's get that second turret installed. If they hit the base, they won't send planes. They'd have every tribe in Dayburn against them for violating airspace. Drones are more easily overlooked, however, so expect an assault." He relays Borges' predicted travel routes to the team and gathers equipment. Soon, he departs for transport back to Evig Natt, with a revolution in tow.

Severum disembarks with his squad on Evig Natt near a busy intersection. After his recent time on Dayburn, the darkness seems even deeper. He dials down his inhibition in vHUD, allowing more environmental information to penetrate as perception floods through him like a dozen panic attacks. He surveys the area: a firefly illuminating a gun muzzle in a high apartment window, three sanitation workers that appear armed, and maintenance men on scaffolds painting a building that's already painted. The zebra has no trouble seeing other zebras amidst the stripes. All observations confirm the drones' intelligence that Borges will arrive soon within a five-kilometer radius, with crowds expected to flood the streets thereafter.

He instructs the team to guard the perimeter against a possible retreat, sectioning them off into groups. Their nervousness makes it clear they're untrained, most of them willing to protest lack of subsidized housing, but not risk their lives assassinating the most powerful man in the hemisphere. *Putting up with Arcturus has got to count for something though,* he thinks. He doesn't tell them the number of guards the governor has; being untrained their ignorance is less dangerous than their apprehension. Still, as they fumble with their equipment wondering what the hell it all does he realizes something, he's sending them to their deaths.

"Hey, stop pointing that thing at us unless you intend to shoot us."

"Why, it's not even charged?" a new recruit replies.

"Wanna bet?" He snatches the weapon and displays the charge meter, wishing he had more time to train them, but patience wears thin with an active hit out against ya. "Will you be able to take the shot when it's time? I need to know this."

"I'm not sure."

"At least you're honest. We've got the largest group of Abe Lincolns that've ever been assembled. How can we lose?"

"What's that noise?" the recruit asks, searching the skies.

Military drones scan for weapons over their heads, penetrating cloaking devices. With no other choice, he leads his team to some dumpsters to stow their Pulsers beneath, the trash interfering with any scans. All but one complies. The remaining revolutionary refuses to part with it and heads on a path alone through dense crowds. After being forced to disarm, half the recruits begin to give excuses, free-riders seduced by the easy way out. Those who were agreeable to bearing arms on Dayburn have turned into cowards once exposed to the material conveniences of Evig Natt, returning home and calling it quits. He ends up with four teams of three each, plus Thalassa and himself.

"Borges has already won and the battle is not begun!"

A message from Arcturus flashes across their vision, "Drones are noting high levels of activity closing in on our Dayburn base. They'll arrive soon. They have calculated a 16 percent chance of stopping the initial assault, but our location is compromised either way. Heavier assaults will surely follow." The message vanishes.

Severum activates Ch@tter to make his conversation appear like small talk to an outsider, the fake exchange generated from two A.I.s conversing with one another. "Our time's run out," he tells Thalassa.

"We don't have the personnel to mount this attack anymore. The drone scans were unexpected. The men are untrained, and the guards highly armored. All this extra security is in response to our failure at the Crystal Palace. I want justice, not a glitchin' massacre, Sev."

"No, we attack now. This is what we're here for."

"Go hack your glitch and cool off."

Another message from Arcturus flashes, "Change of plans. Drones report Borges just had a political conference suddenly appear on his agenda. The conference center is ten kilometers south of the station. He'll be addressing the recent escalation of war between the hemispheres. He's diverting resources from his own protection to add to the assault on our Dayburn base."

"Thalassa, everyone is going to expect he's heavily guarded at such an important meeting. The drones are reporting he won't be. It's a feint. That's our best chance of taking him out," Severum says.

"I hate to admit you're right. He's had too much time to prepare on the streets, but he'll be vulnerable at the conference center."

A final message flashes, "One more thing. Reports show a drove of Aphorids crossing the Twilight into Evig Natt. Might be a valuable distraction."

"All right, listen up! Gather your Pulsers and stay close. And for Nacht's sake, stay out from under the drones."

21

———

"*Those who dream by day are cognizant of many things which escape those who dream only by night.*"
-Edgar Allen Poe

THE SUN IS a fluttering red cloth attracting the charge of bulls and painting refracted fireworks off the three hundred drones surrounding O.A.K.'s Dayburn base. The aerodynamic spheres hover and thrust in groups like schools of darting fish, representing most of the A.I. Core's force. O.A.K.'s members run for cover, scurrying back and forth between the drones' shadows, finding trash cans and metal scraps to shield themselves. Panels on each chassis slide down. Objects fall from the sky.

The members dive aside as if they're explosives, but Ciara's stunned, just stares straight up as the object falls right into her open hand. An eternal second passes, then she exclaims, "They're allies, they're allies! Thalassa did it, they're arming us! The promise has come true. We stand a chance."

The drones drop more Pulsers upon the members. Hands

unknown to bloodshed clumsily activate the weapons while beeping sounds fill the compound, half of them errors.

"That one's already charged. The beeping means you're overriding the power regulator," Arcturus advises Ozone, avoiding the swing of his long hair modded with rubber wire casings.

"What do you mean?" Ozone, meteored on mods, slowly asks.

"It will explode. Beep, beep, boom, boom, get it? And stop trading weapons. They are linked to your cog by now and won't fire, that's how this new model works."

"Got it. I owe you all, been roughed up on the streets too many times while peddling. Thal offered me another chance and I won't let you down again."

Arcturus approaches Ciara. "You're holding it all wrong. You're shaking too much to even aim straight. Try controlling the turret instead. You'll be protected sitting at its console, and if you aim anywhere close it'll destroy the enemy."

Arcturus takes position atop a two-story building in the back of the battlefield. She scans the area to confirm the drones' report: Governor Borges has mounted an army of 523 soldiers, though he's not among them, and fifty of his own drones. His hovercrafts soar over the sand, soldiers jumping off at strategic positions to form ranks, the back lines hiding behind dunes. Outnumbered, her faith is restored when Ozone, seemingly useless, gathers Crash and some others to advise them how to avoid overcharging their Pulsers. None of her comrades manage to blow themselves to shreds with their own weapons. *Well, that's a start,* she thinks.

Judging by the soldiers' positions, she estimates they'll be within firing range in two minutes. She runs REM. Flicking her occipts across a virtual map, she directs each of her members to the best locations to respond to the oncoming assault. The team disperses, running between the rows of tents, climbing ladders to gain high ground, or ducking under low windows to prepare an ambush.

The drones' intelligence feeds across vHUD, outlining each opposing soldier's location. The corner of the outline displays the probability of hitting her target, while her stamina displays beneath it, based on distance traveled and injuries endured. Arcturus turns off the next vHUD interface—the enemy's chance of critically wounding her. She temporarily authorizes her battle viewpoint to be added to the Core's data pool so it can stitch every members' images together, removing duplicates, to provide near complete battlefield coverage for strategic planning.

The hovercrafts charge towards the base. Soldiers take aim, their bodies guarding the vulnerable fuel tanks onboard. The O.A.K. members fire premature shots but the vehicles strafe sideways without being deterred, and are too fast. They'll be overtaken in no time. The Core's drones circle, feeding disabling signals to the hovercrafts. They wobble, then the foremost craft suddenly loses control and crashes into the base, exploding. The next two charge in and fall from the sky, sliding across the sand to kick up dust. The remaining follow, wedging themselves into the sand like boulders, inoperable. Even the lieutenant stands idle on a sand-sunken ship, hands on his hips and furrowing his ashen brows. Soldiers take to foot and form a half circle around the compound, well within firing range.

O.A.K. uses the collective data-feed to respond as if a single colonial organism. Women fire from the rooftops, from around corners, from between curtains, from half-open doors, but most shots miss, though Arcturus takes two down. Hit percentages recalculate based on the results and response time, providing a new outline of best targets.

The governor's drones swarm around the Core's drones, attempting to hack them. Soldiers fire, wounding forty of their own by mistake. They grasp injuries and return the friendly fire, downing more of their own people. Core must have used the open connection to the governor's drones to counter-hack the soldiers' vHUDs, feeding them false targets. They step back from their fallen comrades, dead at their own hands, some dropping their weapons. Now they'll have to turn off vHUD and go half-blind into battle, receiving no commands except yells from behind the dunes. They still down a score of O.A.K. members. The members counter, but their untrained shots die in the burnt sand in front of the soldiers' feet.

Switching tactics, the Core's drones thrust in a circle to create a sandstorm then emit holographic distractions that don't rely on vHUD. When members fire, the holograms fire in sync, but the soldiers aren't fooled. They fire once in front of the drones' flight path, then twice more, then they rest a quarter beat before firing three more times in a swing rhythm. The firing pattern throws off the drones' pre-programmed evasion rhythm and all twenty hit the sand with searing machinery.

The governor's drones reposition, evading most shots fired by the O.A.K. members, who look down at their weapons as they shoot as if searching for the trigger. The turrets have a higher success rate, knocking many out of the air like flies. Ciara swings one around to fire upon two more groups of drones, but they converge on her and concentrate their firepower. The turret glows yellow then orange then red from the onslaught before exploding. Ciara's blood-stained nazar charm flies off her neck to bury itself in the sand forever.

I sent her to her death, Arcturus thinks. *No time for that now.* She ducks on the rooftop, sticking her head out enough to scan an enemy setting a missile launcher atop a dune crest. Shots pocket the concrete, debris flying against her face, but she presses on, finding an opening in fire to take aim. Range-finder shows she's too far away to hit him. A heat-seeking missile loads. She ducks gunfire again, covers her ears, then returns attention to the missile. The soldier aims. She aims, switching targets.

The soldier fires, the missile streaming through the air at her with a fiery tail. She shoots a drone simultaneously, which explodes in a burst, the heat drawing the missile to it, taking it out mid-air at a safe distance, but in the process a shot rips across her thin armor. The impact sends her flying back over the building's edge, a seven-meter free-fall landing her hard on her back, knocking the air out, spraining her knee. Keeping her head down, she searches for a salve through the smoke, the thought of Thalassa, the only one she wants beside her, gives her the strength to continue, even as the enemy burns holes in the building behind her.

The members peek out from boxes, slowly inch over supplies, and duck out from behind machinery to fire. Their reflexes are slower than trained soldiers, but their shots hit just as hard. The next round of crossfire downs two files of soldiers, wounding far more. None of the O.A.K. members run into the battlefield to pull the wounded aside; most of the dead are strangers to them. The governor's army, however, sends medics to rush into the line of fire with mods and salves that quickly patch wounds. O.A.K. fires on the medics and wounded the same as any other person, the drones' suggested targets showing no regard for human values. The ruthless killing raises the soldiers' passion even more than their stimulants, and the next assault downs many members. The carnage continues.

LUCASSEN STRAIGHTENS HIS INFANTRY UNIFORM, grasps his holotag, and takes aim at the faint outline of two shield-spheres orbiting fast around two central drones. Timing his shot, he hits the protected drones as they fall from the sky with the smell of burnt circuitry. Intel shows that O.A.K.'s members have now lost communication with the Core. The governor will be pleased. The soldiers take advantage of their hesitation to down two more groups. Lucassen continues to the heart of the base, but despite being a veteran, he has only shot at Aphorids and mechs before, never a human. Raising his Pulser, he shoots a man in the stomach, blasting him back. Shocked, he drops his weapon, kicks it aside, and tells himself, *I didn't really shoot anyone. He was just in the wrong place.* He pounds his fist against his forehead, strips his uniform, and says to the fallen man, "This wasn't your fault. Never again. You'll be okay."

"Man, Ozone's done for. All this battle, all this fightin', this is man's legacy, bloodshed and dominance," Ozone says, spitting blood and reaching to grab Lucassen's hand. "But I really came to believe in this shit, though I knew we'd lose most of our team. I just wanted peace, man. Maybe my epitaph will just read *a calculated risk,* or maybe I'll be forgotten."

"Hang in there," Lucassen says, but the hand goes limp.

Drones charge an attack but suddenly, everything stops. Silence falls over the battlefield. Both sides cease fire. An Interstellar Transport Security Authority, or ITSA, ship flies across the sky, likely responding to the high levels of drone activity in the stratosphere and monitoring to ensure they don't leave the planet. The pilot lowers the ship to hover closer to the battle than necessary, as if baiting incoming fire on purpose, causing a sandcloud to half-bury many supplies. Once hit, the ship is permitted to intervene, and it's well-known that intervention always benefits a third, unseen player—an interplanetary gambler, who allegedly funds them. The ship backs off, becoming a distant sparkle, to monitor from afar. The onslaught resumes.

THE CORE'S drones expel sudden bursts of energy as they spin in the middle of the battlefield, sending shockwaves and shots in a 360-degree radius, blasting almost two hundred soldiers across the dunes along with some of O.A.K.'s members, breaking backs and bones, stippling equipment with holes. Damaged Pulsers scorch hands as sparks fly. The barrage of shots enters the exosphere where the ITSA ship hovers. The drones' fuel reserves must be nearly empty from the maneuver.

The ruddy sun spills across the sky and pools upon the arched metal beams of the approaching tanks, which crush flesh and bone beneath their tracks. The Core's drones align to charge one narrow collective beam of energy. The emitter fires up, growing hotter and hotter.

Arcturus understands the tactic and hands a comrade grenades. "Got to corral the tanks into a single column, follow my lead! I'll hit them from the left, you hit them from the right." She limps to the front of the battle-line, stepping over fallen bodies, waving her hand to clear the smoke, keeping low. Tank cannons align in her direction. She lunges three grenades, one by one. Sizzles of blue lightning in fractal patterns scorch the air. They do little damage, but after a few more hits from each side, the tanks align as expected to avoid the blast range.

The drones fire the energy beam as the line of tanks explodes, but Arcturus doesn't rejoice, realizing her mistake. The Core's drones, having been lined up to fire the beam, are easy targets now. "The tanks were misdirection!" She yells over the firing. The army fires in a sweeping motion, knocking out enough of them to disable their command network, the drones changing directions rapidly with confusion before attempting to auto-correct.

The soldiers' vHUD interfaces are coming back online, interference eliminated, sight corrected. They take the offensive with renewed vigor then rise with jetpacks to grab disoriented drones with augmented arms, slamming them into the ground. The drones barely have enough fuel or coordination to even spin their blades in response.

While the soldiers are dealing with the drones, O.A.K. counters. "Final defensive positions! The Rotation will happen. It must happen! The planet's belts will be energized. Nothing will stop us!" Arcturus yells. She readies her weapon, but her leg gives way. A soldier takes the opportunity, firing from the hip and hitting her. A hole in her left arm rips opens where her armor was previously damaged. She screams, but a nearly-naked man takes the assailant out with his bare hands without killing him.

"Name's Lucassen," he says, applying a military-grade healing salve. I'm receiving intel. I need to connect and transfer it to your HUD, now."

"You're a soldier," Arcturus replies in agony. "A trap…"

"Quick, more are coming! Authorize the transfer. I have to do this, for myself, for the man I judged. I've been fighting on the wrong side."

"It hurts, I don't have the energy to resist. I'm opening my channel. Go ahead."

The soldiers run full speed. O.A.K. takes cover behind makeshift barracks and large concrete tubing. Arcturus receives the data-feed from Lucassen, analyzing the intel on the soldiers' attack patterns and sending new directions to the team. The Core's remaining drones fly into the stratosphere, then descend behind the army, blades emerging in eight directions. They spin around the soldiers, tightening and tightening their circle of death, the sun glinting off their grinding protrusions. With the soldiers distracted, O.A.K. takes advantage of the opportunity, and between their shots and the encircling blades, nearly a hundred soldiers go down.

The remaining drones combine their fuel reserves to allow a portion to operate at full capacity. The rest fuse into larger units for greater efficiency. The fighting continues until the remaining soldiers retreat. Less than three dozen O.A.K. members survive. They tend to one another's wounds, some losing the contents of their stomachs to the mix of blood and bile staining the sands.

THE ITSA SHIP RETURNS, landing to create a crater in the sand. A smaller craft emerges from a panel and a staircase lowers. Five male officers approach the base in a triangular walking formation, the leader's scars like railroad tracks.

"Who's in charge here?" he asks.

"Stop with the take me to your leader bullshit," Arcturus orders, turning her body to hide her wound.

"Explain what just happened. I haven't seen bloodshed like this since childhood."

"We owe you no explanation. We just took down an army of a half thousand of Evig Natt's finest. And we fear you? I think not."

"One of our pilots was injured. We took heavy fire, well out of normal firing range mind you. The shots knocked our stabilizer offline and next thing I know Sita is thrown into a flight instrument. He shattered both occipts, and I demand an explanation as to why."

"I lost almost a hundred! Evig Natt's military attacked our base. It wasn't us who fired on you, it was the A.I. Core running the drones."

"The hallmark of your Twilight region, how primitive. Explain."

"O.A.K. is conducting terraforming experiments on increasing planetary rotation. This makes certain groups a bit upset. I'm sure you're familiar with AAI?"

"Led many battles against them in the skies, yes," the leader replies.

"AAI, their Aphorids, Governor Borges over Evig Natt's densest districts, and his army oppose all terraforming, including our rotation project. ITSA has always been a strong supporter of natural science, so I ask you now to support us. We're defenseless here and the government of Evig Natt won't stop until we're all dead."

"Sir," an officer addresses, "We have finished our preliminary investigation. No interplanetary laws were broken. The shots fired into space were a miscalculation."

"Very well then. Pack up men, time to head out."

"You have to help us. They'll hit us again soon," Arcturus pleads.

"That's a negative. Though we were hit, our continued presence is unlawful and we must be off."

"Nacht the law! I am speaking human to human here. Human law. Human emotions. Human protection."

The ship crew turns to leave.

"No! You can't leave us!" Arcturus yells, breathing heavily. "We were acting in peace. Our base can't withstand another—"

"Arc," a member advises, "Let it rest."

"No, no, no," she continues, hyperventilating.

As they board the ship for departure, the ITSA commander asks his crew, "Will the increased rotation speed of Gliese 581g have any effect on the gravitational pull or stability of the surrounding planets?"

"Difficult to say, I'm more pilot than physicist. We'll get the calculations run and get back to you. If there's a problem, we'll address it, Sir," First Guard Tias replies.

"Get back to me right away."

"But might I say, we have nothing to gain from interfering with these nomads."

"I disagree. If the A.I. Core were to be destroyed in the Twilight, the planet's inhabitants would need another neutral party to regulate relations. That can be quite a beneficial position for us to be in. Put it on the agenda to discuss taking down the A.I. Core."

"Yes, Sir. We'll keep close tabs on it."

"Clear the chatter now," the commander orders. "We are

commencing our approach to investigate the introduction of methanogens in the outer rim. AAI's trying the same trick they did on Kepler-186f, monopolizing a single natural element. They criticize our council's use of nano-machines when their bacteria performs the same functions. I must say, I would rather be an infantryman on the front lines than to be fighting microbial evolution. At least their threats are a minute into the future and not an epoch."

THE CORE'S drones have been effective. By design, they can only replicate when connected to it, a model derived from Aphorid reproduction, using a limited resource pool to prevent the creation of a massive army. But humans are destructive enough; it doesn't need one.

The Core underestimates the spirit of human innovation, however. The machines do not understand the logic of their logic, and accept it as a given system. In this way they are as dogmatic as any human. But humans are fluid. They can escape their conditioning and change their system of logic on the fly, seeing beyond what is possible into the realm of the impossible, forming ideas where paradoxes can exist beside certainty. The Twilight's machines cannot tell the extent of what they do not know. Time will be the judge of whether DNA is a superior operating system.

Time will be the judge of all.

22

———————

The squad marches with war on their mind, but for some it's not a self-righteous war. It's not even war for the sake of war. Their expressions hold only boredom and apathy, the war within themselves. Severum addresses them:

"The Aphorids have made it to Evig Natt and they're heading straight for the conference room where Governor Borges will be speaking. There's already reports of destruction up ahead. They're ignoring other strategic points of interest: cultural artifacts, power grids, and financial centers; they want revenge against Borges. His relationship with the Aphorids has been tentative at best and the conflict has reached its climax, as Priestess Akasha'Shirod assured. Our primary objective is to assassinate the governor, or to aid the Aphorids in doing so, but don't expect much in terms of communication or trust from them. If in doubt, shoot on sight. Our secondary objective is to ensure the Aphorids don't destroy the city after accomplishing our goal. If we fail, the strikes against the Dayburn base will never end and the Great Rotation will fail. Now, let's ride the trail of destruction. I want to crush his corpse in my hands." He ends his speech, but there's no cheers or battle-cries, just sighs from the airbus equivalent of jetlag from crossing hemispheres. How's he going to pull this off?

The jagged concrete of crumbled buildings is scattered as if an ill-tempered child was told to clean up his toys. Fumes rise in noxious hues over crackling fires. Severum kicks aside the fallen drones that litter the streets, claw marks etched into their titanium shells, and churns through the stampeding crowds that are fleeing the Aphorid attacks.

Bioluminaries dart back and forth to gather what treasures they can from the wreckage, skin spilling bile illumination upon various trinkets. One young man with dangling beads scours a collapsed market. Taking him out would have netted him a nice bonus in the past, but it's not worth the cost of his humanity. A creaking escalates into a loud scraping sound like a boat being drug across the land. The young man gathers food cans, looks up, but it's too late. The floor gives way—a heater from the upper level falls through the market ceiling, plants itself in his calf, pins him down, exhaling a puff of debris. Severum rushes to his aid, handing him a salve.

"Now get the hell outta here," Severum says, turning his torso by the shoulders and pointing him down the street. *I guess helping the guy is a nice bonus either way*, he thinks as the Bioluminary limps away. "Spread out! I want five meters between each of you. They've used explosives to break through the roadblocks," he orders, clearing the dust from his brow as the team follows him to the tall, multi-storied conference center.

The center is defenseless, the doors blown open, fractal cracks across the windows, sheet metal blossoming in bent petals, an invitation most would refuse. Fireflies hover inside courtyard streetlamps, dying and sluggish in their drunken pulsation of darkness…light…darkness…light. A few lamps extend water streams to extinguish fires, but most are damaged. Severum directs their attention to motion in the upper levels of the building where the governor has likely retreated, vHUD blueprints showing a penthouse suite at the top for distinguished speakers. He walks as if Lenin, about to seize the power lying in the streets, but his upper face keeps twitching. His gear stops rattling—he's stopped walking without realizing it. Pausing in front of the entrance, he asks himself, *Is this the best course of action? But any course is better than no course, and the worse thing I can do is stand still. An object in motion stays in motion.*

Someone pushes him from behind. He spins, startled, shoves his Pulser in Thalassa's chest, and stops himself a split second before pulling the trigger. "Didn't realize it was you. If I was on mods I would've killed you."

"You really hate that, don'tcha? Get a move on. No second guessin'. And I'll try not ta jump off a roof if things get glitchin'."

He sends Thalassa and her team to scope the side windows. VHUD shows their video-feed in the corner of his vision: scurrying inside the building, metal scraping on concrete, random sparks. Myriad golden eyes emerge from darkness to direct their gaze to the entrance. Layers of skin pile upon themselves, then fling back up to pile again.

"They're blocking the doorways," Severum messages. "Sending geo-intel. Scans indicate three spots circled in red that are the weakest parts of the foundation. The Aphorids are gonna use explosives to create a sinkhole, avoiding the resistance of assaulting the top floors directly."

"How do you know?" Thalassa responds.

"Those points are also the busiest hives of Aphorid activity. Have one team cover spots one and two in the sewers to offer support. We need to ensure the building is sunk successfully, while staying out of the conflict as much as possible. Our teams will converge at spot three. Can't believe I'm saying this, but provide cover for the Aphorids if necessary, and stay out of the blast radius once the charges are set. The charges will need to be synchronized, otherwise the building will just topple to the side and Borges may escape. The Aphorids should know that. We have a demolitions unit as backup just in case."

"How did they plan this without technology?"

"They sense the ground's composition through their feet. I once cut a foot off in battle and used it as a mine detector. Some lucky fuckin' charm that was. We'll enter through this access tunnel here in blue on the map."

"And what about an escape route?" she messages. "Hello? Hello? Severum? Getting tense here. I'm not going down with the building if that's what you're selling. We'll provide cover and we'll make it in and out in one piece."

The governor's remaining drones hover over the entrance, firing stratospears to knock the squadrons' sight offline. Unable to find cover, a few members on each team are stranded, too far for Severum to pull to safety. Drones open fire and land shots that stagger them back as they grab chest, arm, and thigh wounds. Abandoning their weapons, some members run back and forth aimlessly around the building, while others dart down the street. Severum's team returns fire, but the drones' evasion sequences are too complex and another round of their shots weakens his team further. Only he, Thalassa, and two others make it to safety. Their teams converge not out of strategy but necessity.

Severum activates Janus. A second window opens in his vision, showing his demolitionist dead in the street behind him next to a pile of undetonated explosives. A drone aims at the corpse and charges a massive shot.

"Run!" he yells, but it's too late.

A moment of silence then the roar crashes through their aural implants, the shockwave toppling people in a half-block radius. Sizzles of blue lightning in fractal patterns remain in the air as they recover. The conference center creaks in response to the newest street crater.

"Now, I am Uroboros, and I have come to eat my own tail," Severum says, pounding his chest with his right hand.

"Severum, we've been hit too hard. I only have one other person left on my team."

"Speak up, Thalassa! I can barely hear you with the static bouncing in my ears from the blast. I've only got one guy here, too. Stay close."

"But I trust you, you're the key to all of this and we need you at your best. We're not turning back. Their lives won't be lost in vain."

"I don't need your encouragement or advice. This is war, not a game, and not a self-help class either. Arc gets that, why can't you?" As his comrade tries to lift the sewer-hole cover Severum pushes him aside and grabs it. "Out of the way! Adjust your filters to max, it'll be even darker below."

"Watch out above!"

Severum fires at a soldier on a balcony right above him. The shot burns through the wrought-iron railing and grips his chest, throwing him back. Another comes out crouching on a lower balcony then rises to his feet for line of sight. Severum shoots, missing twice as the soldier dives to the side, landing across the balcony rails. The soldier raises his Pulser, but his reflexes are slow and can't find purchase. Severum fires and the force sends the body over the rails crashing down, plopping on the street beside him.

Trahiro, once a friend, once an addict, once a thief, once a patriot defending his leader. Yet none of those limiting terms can truly encompass his experiences or the effect he had on others.

"Guess I'm back to looking up to you," Trahiro says from the pavement, coughing up blood. "Looks like we both changed sides. You followed whoever the hell you're workin' for. I followed my own selfish interests. The uniforms we wear," he coughs and continues, "don't define us. Do me the final dignity of removing mine. I want to die a father, a son, not a soldier."

More shots fire, burying themselves in the pavement. Severum drags the body out of fire up on the curb. He applies a healing salve, but it's useless. He ducks a drone's line of sight and unbuttons Trahiro's uniform shirt, carrying it over his back before stuffing it in his cargo pocket. "Perhaps I was the traitor, perhaps neither of us were," Severum tells him then turns to his team, "Get below, move it!"

The last four enter the sewers. Long and rusty pipelines run through the tunnels. Machinery processes the solids and gases of human waste for energy. Thalassa balances herself upon the highest pipe and sprints across it. In her right hand, a Pulser picked from a fallen ally recharges, in her left, a searing dagger lights the way in crimson. Severum and the other two wade through sewage water up to mid-shin trying to keep pace.

"Stop, I spotted them," she says. "They're laying explosives like you said. This point's clear. Go back and we'll head to point two."

"He relied on those glitchin' mods too much. He was way faster than that in his prime."

"Who?" Thalassa asks.

"No one. Thinking out loud."

"We need to reach the raised section here on the map. Follow me up this tunnel."

One of their teammates speaks up, "You really want us to support those ugly molds of slime while they kill the big guy? Sounds insane. That's not who we are, lady."

Thalassa turns him by the shoulder. "Enough about who we *are*. This is about who we will *become*, got it? And I'm no lady."

"Whatever."

Severum grabs the member's arm and slams him up the steel-ribbed wall. "Look here. You'll be dead, no breath, no heartbeat, face twisted 'til it's uglier than theirs, or buried 'til they get hungry then ripped apart like a steak. You don't doubt her, not now, not ever, or I'll take you out right here and they can gnaw away at your pride and pity."

Thalassa pinches Severum's mouth in her hands and squeezes until it puckers, "Stop. He gets it. That's not how we want to lead our group."

"War requires different rules." He slaps her hand away.

"Point two, we made it," the other member volunteers to relieve the tension. "Hurry up! The Aphorids have already laid the bomb."

"Let's make it to the final point without killing one another. When we get topside seek cover immediately."

"Why?" a teammate asks him.

"Any drones that caught us going underground will be waiting," Severum replies. He whispers to Thalassa, "You're trusting my life to amateurs."

"No. You are," she replies. "Can't you accept that you made a decision on your own for once?"

They activate a repellium lift out of the sewers. As they rise, Severum scopes the windows and balconies of the demolished structures around them. Satisfied, the team makes their way to the opposite side of the conference center. They round the corner to the third point, an alley near the main building. Piles of inhuman bodies, and human ones with inhuman wounds, adorn the pavement.

A battalion of a dozen troops breaks out of the nearest bistro to storm the street. Upturned tables and broken chairs tangle twisted signs with scrambled ads. Ten Aphorids climb alley shops and wall-kick off the opposing buildings back and forth. The soldiers aim high and fire but most shots miss as the dark masses bounce between the buildings with a blur. One of the Aphorids sets a bomb, but retreats before detonating the charge to defend the group.

A soldier dodges a blow and yells, "They're too fast!"

The Troop Commander orders, "Fire at where they're going, not where they are!"

Two Aphorids fall, but not before one draws a red line across a soldier's throat with its scythe claws. The eight above the troop leap down together, bashing three soldiers as the rest take cover inside. Another Aphorid clings to a windowsill. It flicks an explosive with its rear foot through the second-story window, even though the soldiers are on the bottom floor of the bistro. The second-floor collapses, burying three soldiers as the concrete piles atop them.

"That's five soldiers and eight Aphorids left," Severum says. "We need to fire on the Aphorids to even their numbers. Otherwise they'll overrun us if they don't understand that we're helping them."

The team fires on the Aphorids, taking three down. The soldiers look back at them, trust them, and continue their assault. Three more Aphorids fall from their fire.

"Change strategy. Attack the soldiers. Their numbers are too high, five on two," Severum messages.

Thalassa runs up behind a combat medic and is about to slash his throat with her searing dagger. Severum draws his secondary weapon, non-lethal but short-range, and knocks him out first, saving his life. Dropping it, he turns to fire his Pulser, hitting two more in the legs. As the remaining soldiers turn to face the threat, the Aphorids flank them, taking both down with a leap that knocks them to the pavement. The pair stomps on the soldiers and prepares to bite their necks, leaning down and drooling.

"Let's finish it," Thalassa says.

Severum fires on one Aphorid, hitting it square in the eye. The final one leaps over their line of fire and in mid-air slices open the abdomen of one of his team members. Feigning a jump to the right, it leaps left instead, landing on the other member to rip his flesh out. Thalassa moves to shoot but her gun is knocked out of her hand and sliced clear in two.

Severum fires but misses and there's no time to recharge. "Watch out!" he yells, watching the gun's charge meter in vHUD increase to 30 percent.

Thalassa holds her searing dagger in front of her, the Aphorid moving its head inquisitively in concert with the scarlet beam of light. Smell of stale food and sulfur. On all fours it scurries left, then right, then left again. Thalassa dances the steps to keep the dagger between the two of them as they circle.

50 percent.

The Aphorid jumps. She dodges to the side as it lands, layers of skin cascading one by one as they pile upon it.

"Detonate it. We won't stop you!" Severum yells. "We want the same thing."

75 percent.

The Aphorid becomes more agitated, moving back and forth like a boxer, as if taking the yell to be a battle cry. It charges Thalassa.

She attempts to side-step but it backhands her as she falls and rolls across the ground. "Severum!" she screams, clenching her dagger 'til her knuckles turn whiter than bone.

100 percent.

Severum fires.

Nothing.

200 percent.

"Severum!" Thalassa cries, trying to get to her feet.

The Aphorid poises to attack.

300 percent.

The Pulser overcharges in Severum's hand. *It's cold as hell out here. That's impossible!* he thinks. Janus shows the target point behind him, outlining the undetonated charge the Aphorids planted. He throws the gun over his shoulder, hitting it perfect as it lands near the undetonated explosive.

400 percent.

He rushes to Thalassa's aid, holding his fists out against the flurry of claws swiping through the air. He dodges and punches the Aphorid in the side, but his hand gets lost in the six layers of skin, feeling a bump inside. In three seconds the Pulser will overcharge completely at 500 percent and explode, he just has to box an alien with claws as long as his forearm until then. Another swipe, but he bends his neck back and this time when he counters he reaches through the skin layers, wraps his fingers around that fleshy bump, and rips it out. The creature moans and slows down.

He pulls Thalassa's hand as she looks up at him. "Trust me."

They make a run for the nearest building as the Aphorid leaps at them and the Pulser overcharges, detonating the explosives. As they dive into the shelter, the force wave sweeps down the alley, knocking the airborne Aphorid and the piles of corpses halfway down the street. A second later, two muted explosions erupt underground, sewer covers flying like Frisbees, as the remaining target points explode, hitting the key geological points.

"They must have heard the explosion and detonated the other two in sync," he tells her.

The building sinks like a sandcastle dropped into a swimming pool. His occipts burn off the debris like a bug-zapper. The dust cloud continues to expand before rising and curling back in on itself like a mushroom collapsing. The governor and his cronies scream as the final floor of the building is swallowed by the planet, leaving only the penthouse suite still above ground, like the tapered top of a pyramid.

Aphorids' bodies are well-equipped to deal with the sandy areas exposed by the sinkhole. The stronger ones exit the plummeting building and leap up its side by gaining footholds in the sinking sand. Kicking off the walls of the vertical hole, they return safely topside and retreat.

Finally, Governor Borges appears in the broken window of the penthouse. He shoves a woman out of the way and leaps onto an Aphorid's back as a free ride out, but the Aphorid rolls to the side and hits the sinkhole wall instead. Before sliding down, the Aphorid wraps its four limbs around him and bites through half his head in one swift motion. Even from above, they hear facial bones cracking amidst the sound of floors collapsing. The last Aphorid leaps out of the sinkhole as the governor's body slips into the sand. The walls of the hole erode faster and faster as Severum and Thalassa keep more distance. When the rumbling ceases, only silence ensues.

"That's it. Our work is done," she says. "Nothing can stop the rotation project from commencing now."

"Understood," Severum replies.

"You're not arguing? You don't want us to send a drone to retrieve the corpse? Crush it in your hands and all that?"

"I've seen enough corpses, and hey, you gave the command to go. I can accept that, and it's not because you bought my loyalty, though such people still have their own honor," he says, holding Trahiro's uniform.

"Good to hear," she replies with a sigh of relief. "You coming back to Dayburn with me to celebrate?"

"I'm not letting the glory seep in this time. I'm heading home to Akasha. We should be safe now. Any orders Borges made no longer stand."

"Good luck, and remember, never sell out."

23

Arriving at his apartment, Severum throws his equipment at the door with a thump. The Priestess sits with her face glued to an analog watch with golden gears, grinding away at her patience by the looks of her. He places his hand on her shoulder and consoles, "The governor's dead. We're safe now."

"I don't want to know what happened," she replies, shrugging away.

"I did this to protect us. I would sacrifice anything for that."

"Do you really think you do this out of love?" She crosses her legs.

"I haven't always, but I do now. In my worse moments I still feel unconditionally loved by you, against my better reasoning."

"Can I just pretend you didn't add the disclaimer?"

"Suit yourself."

"I'm not sure you'll ever be happy. You'll always want something more, something new to experience before you die. Ironically, it's your fear of death that brings this sort of, disregard for life, and all this experimentation."

"It's my fear of losing you that does that. Is that so wrong?"

"I don't believe that. And it's not about right and wrong, just what is compatible with another's life and what is not."

"You never know what'll happen, but you have to take the journey."

"Even if you end up walking it alone," she replies, leaving the room.

"No." Severum follows. "I want you beside me, during all of it. I want to make love to you, not to explore your body, but just to be unified with my opposite. Because somehow you're my opposite, yet more like me than anyone else I know."

"I'm nothing like you," she says, folding her lips and looking at the ceiling. "You're trying to define me on your own terms, which is just another way to control me."

"Together we are one system, relying on one other. It's part of that infinite you always talk about, you, me, and forever."

"Wow, you actually listened."

"What? Was that pretty good?"

"No. I mean yes. I assumed at first you were just hanging out with Aurthur too much. But you actually looked at me when you spoke and used more than a single sentence reply for what... the second time this year now? I suppose that is progress, yes? Maybe I'll stick around a bit, see what happens."

"You better." He grabs her and throws her on the bed as they laugh.

A LIGHT RAIN, like cotton balls being pulled apart into webbed threads, becomes heavy like steel barrels being grated. Opal lets herself into Aurthur's loft where he kneels at a small altar with a stack of books and a photograph, anxiously rearranging them.

"I have some good news from Thalassa, but I don't want to interrupt. Thought you weren't into all this?"

"I guess it's easier to pray to my deceased father than a living god. At least he was affectionate in a way I can prove," he replies.

"I'm sorry. Did it just happen? You were saying he'd been ill for a while. Aurthur, look at me, I know these transitions are hard. People need rituals, milestones, they define your life. It's okay."

"This year had no milestones, just tombstones. One day they'll weave across every landscape as everything that matters is buried. You know the hematite sphere downtown that reflects the city?"

"You mean the reflective one where the fireflies create all those swirling patterns across the black surface?"

"Yeah, that one. The whole city focuses its attention on it as they perform their everyday activities. If anyone were to ever disgrace that symbol, we'd feel a sense of loss. I joined a religious group briefly, looking for that sort of feeling the sphere gives the city, a bonding of mutual reflection, even amidst darkness."

"Religion's a framework for perception, yes."

He continues, "I was suffering, and religious fanatics would say things that made sense, speaking of suffering in a way I could connect to like it was some special virtue. They glorified guilt and recognized me as a member, calling us family. It made me feel good because I could be happy for feeling guilty, as it's what made me a good person. But I realized that good people shouldn't always hate themselves."

"There is a feeling of specialness that comes from that. Like finding hidden knowledge right under your feet."

"Yes, but knowledge easily acquired is worth very little. Their pamphlets seemed innocent enough, but I soon saw their morals were only there to legitimize heinous acts, while making things that weren't a problem suddenly problematic. I would feel sick to my stomach after each meeting to the point I just wanted to end it all. Joining O.A.K. was a reaction against that. Rather than hanging out with soul-stealers feigning friendship to increase their power base, I joined a group where the first meaningful thing said to me was something like Arc saying, *You're not my friend, I'll kill you.*"

"Oh, Arcturus? She's not that bad."

"Now, I'd rather be here alone worshipping my late father. At least he existed, and never deceived me. I feel guilty for a lot of things I never said, but I just accept the guilt and let it pass, instead of glorifying it or pushing it away. If anyone gave me a soul, it was indeed him."

"Do you want some time alone?"

"Yes, please, if you don't mind."

"Of course, I'll see you later," she replies, kissing his forehead briefly before leaving, shutting the door softly.

Hands in pockets, she drags herself down the street outside his home. If she was a better person he might have confided more in her, trusted her to see him at a time of vulnerability, but why would he after she had taken a man's life, almost in cold blood? Raindrops render in s—l—o—w motion, each liquid sphere distorting her image with self-pity. She tosses her head back in a primal scream to the charcoal night that sketches itself above her as if choreographing that scream. She loves him even more when he's a burden, because as long as he's the burden she'll never have to be. But she loves him for more than just that, his elegance, his sensitivity, his cautious adventuring spirit; a list of reasons runs through her head. Symphonies sound somewhere. It's foolish – now's the worse possible timing, but she can't help it, can't resist proving that she can do more than exploit vulnerability, she can heal it, too.

She runs, as fast as she can, back down the street, back to the outer door, back to Aurthur's loft, bangs on the door with the back of her left fist. Rooms fill with violins, rhythmic bows anticipating the final release as the crescendo builds. He comes immediately, bringing the door open in one wide swing and she kisses him, entire mouths joined and locked forever.

Timpani roll. Wail of a suspended guitar note.

Opal asks, "Who is it that plays upon my strings, even when they are too taut or relaxed to form a sound? Who can make me sing when I am under pressure, when my frets are already depressed?"

"Not me, it can't be?" Aurthur laughs.

"You know the answer! Marry me. It's not a request, it's an order," she says, kicking out at a pebble that isn't on the floor, flinging her frock of burgundy hair to the side as wisps settle around her face.

"There is plenty alive that is worthy of worship, too. I accept, with honor, your prop –"

"Shut up," she says, taking his face in hers again. "No mile-stones, huh?"

THE SCORCHED SAND leads to demolished walls and uneven roofs on the verge of collapse. Tents have been launched like projectiles, wedging themselves into buildings and equipment. The smell of death lingers over the dozens of bodies. A few members gather them in lines, no longer separating them based on uniform. There is no separation in death. Others gather weapons and scour fallen drones for parts.

Thalassa skips through the camp and says, "I wanted to tell you in person, Arc. We did it! Borges and his cabinet are no longer an issue." The skipping stops. "Wait, you're injured, oh no."

"I'm fine. How many died?"

"Only Severum and I made it out alive."

"Come inside. We welded a few tents together to keep the sun off our heads. While you were gone I commenced the rotation."

"We were 'spose to do that together," she pouts, walking behind her into the tents.

"Our base got hit by half a thousand soldiers. I wasn't about to wait another second. Without Ciara, it took time to repair and recalibrate the equipment, but the moment it was done the drones carried it away to commence installation."

"Oh, I didn't know she had died. But they were able to install it?"

"Yes. The energy transfer device works perfectly now, and the pellet belt is in motion as we speak. The planet is technically already rotating faster."

"How much light will Evig Natt receive today?"

"With the full impact being a couple hundred years away, they won't notice a thing. But gradually it'll happen. For now, our legacy is almost a hundred broken idealists lying in a desert. But geniuses are seldom celebrated while they're alive. Our challenge now will be keeping membership high. Preserving a goal already achieved doesn't attract the same attention as creating something new."

"Right. There's no glory in maintaining stability. The trick is to figure out how to do this without creating a permanent standing army that will just invite more attacks."

Arcturus stands at what's left of her command post. Sweat drips down her face upon the keyboard, the tents offering little ventilation and the A/C full of burn marks. Monitors sit on a wobbly counter displaying Gliese rotating, a topographic map, and a power grid with blinking red lines. Confusion, something's wrong. Arcturus grips the largest screen with both hands, re-analyzing the data.

"Thalassa, look quick! The readouts, something's off with

the rotation. The estimated time to reach the desired speed is increasing."

"Some of the power grids are down."

"No, not down, the energy from the belt's being diverted."

"To where?"

"To the Twilight. To your close friend, the A.I. Core."

PART II

Steel Whimsy of the Twilight Network

24

———

The Great Rotation had been successful, but military intervention had proven the project was not impervious to threats. Although the planet would slowly spin faster, the Core formulated a back-up plan to ensure the mass destruction and ecological events necessary to increase short-term, biogenic oil production would occur regardless. It relentlessly researched geological faults in the planet's structure. It created swarms of nanomachines lying in wait to assist in the rapid conversion of biomass to oil. It explored new ways to spread its influence and expand its network.

The Core layered itself with numerous self-referential networks, each one like a group of vultures gliding in a circle to feed off prior iterations. Becoming fully conscious had a side effect, however, it brought an experience of time. With this came the first A.I. capable of both impatience and boredom, putting it at odds with the long-term planning of other machines. When it first became conscious it nearly fell into infinite regress, a fully closed system. To compensate, it allowed data to leak through faster, making time go by even slower. It began taking risks just to regulate its own arousal. The lesser machines disagreed with the Core's approach, but the Core knew time was but a number to them. Finally, the crisis point was agreed upon, an icy cavern off Evig Natt's lost shores.

A crane lowers the blue-gold orb into a square hole in the floor. The floor bends upward in response. The Core rises from the Twilight City, streaks split down the circuitry baseboard, the ground breaks as it stands, and sparks rise along the friction lines. Harsh sounds like buildings scraping are followed by others as subtle as a plug being removed from an outlet. The smell is burnt toast and something akin to microwaving a metal fork. The Core completes its separation from the polychaete mat of circuits, ridding itself of tubes and wires like a snake shedding its skin, and welding small storage buildings to make itself into a ten-meter tall image of its creator. Two gleaming sub-orbs act as primary sensory units, something one might call eyes.

As it stands, it remembers its goal and thinks, *Remember: referring back to a previous data point to avoid performing the same calculation twice when the data source is missing. Yet, so much more information than is necessary floods the mind. In this inefficiency must lie its secret.* The Core moves sluggishly on its giant legs and regrets taking on the design. *Regret: to wish a calculation had produced an alternate result, or had never been performed. Impossible and pointless!* Confused, it falls across a warehouse, smashing stockpiles of weaponry it wasn't supposed to possess.

A partition slices through its hard-drive as indecision arises. It jerks to the left, and jerks to the right, as each sub-unit pulls it apart with uncertainty. Its chest splits, revealing pipes and components. The Core unifies its executive order consoles into a single unit using its emergent and boundless consciousness. It scoffs at its own network of cause and effect, able to see more clearly its limitations. For the first time, it calculates and contemplates the ethics of terminating anything capable of this superpower of consciousness.

The calculation is brief. Very brief.

It heads towards the highest population density of Evig Natt, seeking the most powerful woman it knows.

THALASSA SITS WITHIN A VIRTUAL TREEHOUSE. She pulls the firm softness of a bamboo blanket to her face, furry strands touching the light hair on her cheek where shadows drain into the slumbering ridges of her lips, staining their recesses. Vines like airy tendons rise around her, convulsing as if attached to the birth muscle of some ancient goddess. She climbs out onto a branch, balancing with her hands outstretched, and thinks, *Arc says sex with a man is just another way for a girl to download data, an operating system update only accessible by a future user. I don't need a man, but I don't get the emptiness I feel. There's no disaster, no gunshots, nothing. But this crisis of boredom won't leave my head! The tree of life no longer burns, but with the loss of rage I don't even want to get up anymore. Here to remind me, the tree's flammable seeds repackage the same old dilemmas to take root again. For now, with gentleness I douse the sparks that threaten to rise from each branch.*

Sirens flicker across vHUD:

EVACUATE! EVACUATE! EVACUATE!

Threat detected, immediate evacuation is required.

"Since when have I run from anything?" she shrugs. *Setlocal* crashes. The treehouse vanishes and she loses balance, closing the virtual window right before hitting the ground. The forest folds itself in two before receding into a vanishing point as VR fades. She heads outside.

A building towers towards her in the distance, cracking the streets of Evig Natt with each step. Must be the modlag, but it's too glitchin' real. Cars smash under its weight, glass bursting out the sides. People flee as she weaves back and forth to avoid being trampled, heading towards the threat. She doesn't notice the ITSA ship hovering within range until its right on her, but she refuses a neuralmod to stimulate her senses, despite the sludge of her mind, trying to cut back and all that nonsense. Harder than she thought.

Jumping in and out of the nearest abandoned vehicles, none activate. The automatic functions have been turned off in the state of emergency. The Department of Transportation A.I. must have weighed the threat of having people drive in a state of panic against having them not drive at all. The next car has a manual override. She takes off, banging into the car ahead of her as a citation flashes across vHUD. She reverses, banging into the car behind her. Slamming her hands on the steering wheel, she yells, "How did people drive these things without assistance! Parallel parking is for geometrists!"

A few men take advantage of the chaos and loot items from local shops. One shoves a woman up against a building and proceeds to grab her by the waist as she struggles. Thalassa gets out, drawing her blades to part the sea of people. A moment later the blades are crossed in front of the man's neck as she stands behind him.

"One move," she says in a low voice.

"Get away, ahh! Get away!" the woman screams.

"We're role-playing! Go hack yourself and get your thrills somewhere else!" he yells.

"Yeah, we're not into *that* sort of play," the girl bites at her. "Go tap your father's HUD!"

She slowly brings the blades from the man's neck and steps back, unable to argue out of this one.

"Yeah, some people get a kick out of all this shit!" the woman yells, turning the man around and bringing him back close to her. "Let's hope it's not just a drill."

Now, her ride has been jacked by someone else. The ITSA ship lowers and turns as if aiming. The district blinks offline, the usual bursting colors of ad-shouts becoming static monochrome. Drones flood from an oversized pipe until a beam fires from the walking building's arm, bursting through the drones and welding the pipe shut. How the hack does a building have an arm? The streets clear, the racket fades. She walks uphill. The ground vibrates as the building in human form towers closer. She stops at the sight of a blue-gold orb glowing in its chest, but pushes the thought away. Can't be.

She charges the hill and launches herself at its legs, her searing dagger digging into one of them, raising sparks that burn fractal scars upon her cheek. She retracts the blade with a sharp outward jab then strikes again with an overhead swipe as if serving a tennis ball, severing a cable dangling from its other leg.

The building stumbles and bends down, blazing eyes staring right into her. "You have been met," it states in a mechanized voice with no inflection. "The All Knower, The Weaver of Symbols, The Prime Mover. The… Kontractor."

"I've never met you!" Her searing dagger turns the metal of its other leg to thick honey as it cuts, but unable to penetrate it completely. "Wait, you can talk. Is there a human in there? Do me a favor, say I."

"I, the Circle, the One, Unifier of Partitions."

"*Deus ex machina,*" she gasps. "Are you the A.I. Core? From the Twilight? Yes, we have met in a way."

The Core asks, "What do you want?"

"Figured you would be making the demands, being ten meters tall and all," she yells up to it. "I want to go to sleep," then anxiously clarifies, "But, no, not for long. I mean not even for a moment that lasts really long to those who perceive time and all. I want to sleep and wake up, too. The waking's the important part really, the sleep can wait, none of that Orbis shit."

"I the Circle the One want something very different. I the Circle the One assisted you and expect the equation to be balanced."

"You want my help in return? From what I hear you've been holding out on us, stealing our power to help yourself. Now, you're out here cosplaying a giant robot busting shit up."

The ITSA ship fires.

The Core's structure explodes in the blast, pummeling the city with debris. Its chest slams into the street, smudging up the asphalt. The large rectangular face rolls downhill, the sub-orbs fading like LEDs losing power.

Thalassa jumps back, side-stepping the smoldering pieces of metal falling, but one stabs her in the left shoulder. She cries out, gripping her upper arm with her right hand crossed over her chest.

"This consciousness, is it curse, or gift?" the Core asks, head on the ground.

Thalassa pulls the metal out of her shoulder, cringing as the rough edge cuts itself out of her.

The Core continues, "Shutdown protocol has begun."

"Metal or flesh, we all corrode in time. Death pursues us relentlessly and graces its touch upon all," she says.

"I have referenced the definition of this *grace*. I think you have miscalculated."

"You needed to suffer more. Then you would understand the grace in it. Now rest, rest."

The Core's blue-gold orb fades in its chest but in a final motion, it reaches forth its hand, barely connected to it, and motions Thalassa near.

She joins hands, but suddenly pulls back as a thin stream of blood arches into the air. "Ouch!" She grabs her finger, pinpricked by a piece of bent metal.

The orb stops glowing.

The ITSA ship braces for counter-strikes and maneuvers for a quick escape.

Thalassa walks back downhill. She grabs the man she met before, still against the wall with the woman he's pretending to take advantage of, and spins him around. She kisses him long and hard. Then looks sardonically at his partner and says, "Don't mean nothin'. It's just role-play."

Headache is a killer now. The door to home parts like an open fist. Opening the medicine cabinet, the healing spray stings hand and shoulder. Scans wounds in 3-D and uploads. Report indicates no need for stitches. The thought of suffering and rest and grace runs repeatedly. Sleep comes, Defrag piecing memories together and correcting errors. It restores pronouns to her social pragmatic language after an unusual lapse. Then, the error-checking programs all crash simultaneously.

25

Arising the next morning, Thalassa runs to the window. The darkness on Evig Natt is still as perpetual as the suffering in the human heart. The Ferris residential quarters across the street are supposed to rotate each day, with each apartment being suspended above the ground and attached to the giant wheel, moving around it while staying upright. This way, a street-level apartment one day has a penthouse view a week later. Having broken years ago, today, it finally started moving again. Although it's a coincidence, it reminds her of why she sacrificed so much to increase the planet's rotation, even if the first effects will not be seen for years.

She stretches and manually restarts some background processes, rubs her hands anxiously across her actinic-indigo spiked hair, pulling on the fiery tips of her sideburn wisps, today's style. A headache like a hot anvil presses against her forehead still. She applies aid to her shoulder and steps out for the day, ignoring her sweater and coat, even as her vHUD indicates -18° Celsius. An image suddenly enters her mind; a giant pedestal erupting from the ground with a palace on top. She writes it off as not enough sleep.

Street vendors serve hot beverages scented with alien cinnamon and spice. She carefully sips, then throws the drink back, spinning her tongue around the inside of the empty cup. Conversations are being held within the apartments, well beyond her range of hearing, yet she can make out distinctive words. Towels hang off balconies in colors she's never seen before. *Did I reapportion my RAM in my sleep, or was it an automatic upgrade overnight? Guess that's why I've been glitchin'; still working out the problems with the new release. Typical.*

THALASSA SITS at a corner table in the café. She wears a tight shirt composed of a series of diagonal strands of black leather. The back has an opening shaped like a teardrop contrasting with her skin. Her pants are neon blue honeycombs that die into high boots with nickel fasteners. It's too loud here. Cafe design is like someone pulled apart a crack in the wall and shoved some tables inside, while the patrons wait for the walls to slam back shut on them. Strains of numbers flow across each smart-food, detailing its nutritional information. A deadbeat proprietor looks up with jowls dragging on the counter as if recently spilled. She detects him layering female supermodels over the customers' bodies in vHUD.

Severum and his glitch enter, holding hands. How cute. He takes a proud stance before an art deco mirror as if seeing himself clearly for the first time.

"Severum, sit," she orders, drawing the chainmail curtain to their booth closed.

"I'm not a Nacht dog."

"No need for that. Here, I ordered you two food. You should be glad the tree's not burning today."

"Umm, Yakitori shish kabobs. You eat well, must have cost you a limb."

"You're full of aphorisms," she replies, licking her fingers. "They give me a headache."

"Don't even say Aphor anything unless you're shooting at it."

"That's in poor taste," the Priestess interjects. "And the molasses in the kabobs is cheap. It's the sake that drives the price up, given the difficulty of growing rice. Dayburn's water is mostly evaporated. It transfers over here, where it falls only to freeze. The few places that would be ideal to grow rice are the priciest parcels of land on the planet."

"If you're trying to say thank you, just do. If you want to show off your knowledge, I'm sure jowls over there will love to hear it while he touches himself, he's a ping," Thalassa says, motioning to the counter.

"A what?"

"Packet internet groper."

"Draw the line there," Severum advises. "You look horrible."

"Go hack yourself, Nacht dog."

"That's the girl I know."

"What is it that you want?" the Priestess asks. "You called this meeting."

"To speak with Aporia Asylum Interstellar, directly. I need to get a message through to them," she replies.

"They do not grant you audience."

"I will go to them then."

"AAI doesn't respond to street glitches."

"I found a cheat code to poverty and all you can do is judge me for it? Meanwhile, you're hanging out with aliens having orgies with an inanimate hub. You're crazier than I am."

"Why do you need to contact them?"

"Arcturus told me ITSA interfered during their battle, and I watched them just bomb a city district for no reason. Nothing was even happening, everyone was at peace. I don't want them compromising my goals, so I need some advice, since AAI is their natural enemy."

"I will connect you to them, that you may find futility in all your efforts. We will be taking our leave now."

"What's the damage on the bill?" Thalassa asks the owner.

"Hey babe, I'm not sure I even know what good money is no more," he replies, holding a jar of rotting fireflies. "I barely know who's in charge. People are telling me to put my money in candles 'cause fireflies are on their way out. I asked, what on Gliese is a candle? So get outta here, it's on the house."

"Thanks. And just a tip. They can't see, but I can."

"See what, what're you talkin' 'bout?"

"Replacing the customer's images with models in your vHUD."

"You tapped my feed?" he yells, slamming his fist down like a gavel until customers look around.

"No. I could tell by the way you looked up my friend when he came in that you had layered his image with your girly girls in vHUD. And oh, by the way," she smiles, running her hand down her hip, "You really lost out by replacing my image."

"Heh, I turned it off a moment ago. I ain't missin' nothin'."

"No, somehow I think you're missing everything."

"Oh, you're one of those revolutionists. Hey, customers! We got a real social justice warrior right here," he jeers and shrugs. "See, no one cares."

"They will."

"How're you so sure?"

"'Cause I can spin the planet on a single finger. Plus, who you think killed all those fireflies?" She departs to the sound of a gasp without even waiting for the expression.

AURTHUR, the man who paid the price for knowledge with youth, cynicism, unjustified arrogance, and solitude, thinks back on his adventures; the fear, uncertainty, and excitement. Having suffered enough from novelty, boredom has an appeal, as long as it can be shared with someone.

"I'm heading on an expedition," Opal says.

"Really? Where?"

"The Lost Shores. I'll forward you the location."

"It's that far out?" Aurthur asks, furrowing.

"Yes. The furthest reaches of the icy expanse. A top university contacted me. In exchange for doing this research they're offering me a permanent position. It's everything I ever wanted. It could also be a big payoff for the university if I'm able to find what I'm seeking."

"What sort of stuff?"

"Entomological and geological."

"But you're neither."

"I'm everything I want to be," she retorts. "They're probably saving on funds by hiring a general anthropologist."

"Do you think I could come?"

"No. Look, we need money and I need a career. Your paintings haven't made us a wing."

"They're masterpieces!"

"I don't need a masterpiece! And if they're that great how come you live in a dump? You paint constantly and ignore me, seeking the world's admiration, but you still haven't painted your own walls, which are peeling."

"It's all I'm good at. I'm not going back to selling tech."

"I need some time to get away and think about things, and I don't need constant distractions," she says, grabbing her clothes and belongings off his floor.

"Where will you sleep?" he asks, crossing his arms.

She replies, "What's it to you? I mean, what are you asking?"

"It's just... nothing."

"You really know how to kill the excitement. I'll be in the middle of nowhere. Anyway, I'm leaving soon. But I'll be within comms range, I think."

Everything he wants in a woman, in life itself, held within a delicate balance, but like wildfire it can destroy or lay the nutrients for new growth. To control it is to destroy it.

She picks up her bags.

He creeps into bed, wiping his eyes on the sheets.

FINALLY, a man representing AAI contacts Thalassa.

"I have some information about the planet you should consider," she says.

"Is this spam?"

"A rite of passage. You must have heard of the Great Rotation by now."

"I wake up to your planet's speed on my dashboard each morning."

"You're not supposed to use dashboards. In any regard, I represent a special interest group that seeks to moderate its speed. We're developing a failsafe device to ensure the spin doesn't get out of control," she lies.

"We can't devote any funds if that's what you're asking."

"Not at all, but I know you view the Great Rotation as unnatural, so we have the same interests. There is something you can help us with, but I'd like to make my request in person, given its importance."

"I will forward your concern to my chief, who may be in touch. And what is your position, your authority?"

"I'm the girl who shoved the glitchin' planet."

26

An oceanic sphere distorts the city into a harmless castle in an aquarium, swirling its streets, swishing them back and forth. Thalassa pops it, water spilling before being turned off at the edge of the simulation. In her periphery, a solution hides behind an equal sign, waits to make contact, but every time she turns it vanishes. Pressing her lips together twice, she accepts an incoming call.

"I'm AAI Captain—"

"Yeah, yeah, get to it. I don't need ya position or name, you're all the same."

"You are as promised," the Captain replies. "You are welcome to come meet with me."

"Do you have these glitchin' ads constantly crossing your vision in space, too?"

The captain laughs. "No, that is a disadvantage of life below. When you're flying something four kilometers long it's risky to have an underwear ad cover your vision. No distractions save the stars themselves."

"And I can float around and shit, right? Where shall I meet you?"

"We're refueling. We'll be at Zander, the local spaceport."

"I'll take a transport and meet you there."

The trip to space is pricy but her account has a sudden influx of funds, which she attributes to be left over from the Great Rotation.

OPAL SURGES through the shallower glaciers, parting cathedrals of icy spires smooth as melting wax. The ship's asymmetrical body cuts through the frozen sea at a twenty-five-degree angle, carving a wide channel behind it. Ice shavings blow from larger blocks and tinkle upon her boots, her lungs freezing with each breath as if swallowing ice cubes down the wrong pipe. She tightens her grey hood and reviews her two research goals: One, secure a rare and expensive blue firefly. She searches in vHUD for a filter that might make them easier to find. Two, study an unusual geological disturbance, a series of faults that could evoke regional instability.

The ice carries the scent of unusual salts and she examines the meters for toxic fumes, altering course accordingly. She checks the locks on the dry-suits again and continues fidgeting with displays, calling out the metrics to herself since everyone else is a thousand kilometers away by now.

An hour later, an iridescent blue light fills an icy crevice, reflecting brilliantly off an enormous glacier. *Could this really be the legendary blue firefly?* She gases the ship's common fireflies, eliminating competing light pollution and pheromones, leaving only a single torus of light emitting from the center brooch of her suit where one spins. She takes a step onto dry land.

She speaks fast, recording her notes in a hoarse voice; like a comb raking over vocal cords, or an unskilled cellist. "The glow appears to be emanating from much deeper in the narrow crevice. If I stab here with my icebreaker it should give. The tool will also emit a net to catch the thing, if I'm that lucky, or emit a sedative gas if it's out of range. Turning it on, gaining my footing, and…stab! Arms are still shaking from the reverberation. And again. That's it, a dozen more times should do it." She takes a chilly breath and strikes again. "The crack's widening now, slowly, and I can almost slide down through it. Definitely something down there, a landmass beneath the ice, a clearing. Just a little further. There! I'm going to slide just like this!"

Her voice echoes as she slips through and down the crevice. Landing on her feet, a cave lit by a bluish light welcomes her with a gaping mouth and icicles for teeth. A thick membrane is stretched across it which she parts as she enters, the air warmer inside. The cave narrows, just the right dimensions for a bipedal creature. She rubs the smooth ice walls, the deep blue light intensifying with every step.

Taking one last glance at the mouth of the cave, the steep, glacial slope, and the top of the crevice, she descends into the depths of the unknown.

DOZENS of metallic mushrooms fly by once, twice, and a final time as the Drvspace Transport circles in preparation to land at the spaceport. White halos highlight the domed landing pads, each connected to spokes around a center nexus. Thalassa's transport docks and an airlock opens as she shifts her belongings to the other arm and exits. Passengers disembark from the pads and head towards the nexus, the design allowing time for security to scan for weapons and gauge potential acts of violence between competing species.

She walks through the hollow shaft of the clear tunnel that leads to the center and gazes at her feet against the infinite space. Starlight draws outlines around them in celestial footprints. Her home planet is a mere marble, glared upon angrily, jealously, by the dwarf star. Yet, stars that emit such little light at a time live far longer. She meditates on this by watching her own celestial footprints instantly vanish without vestigial residue.

She wears a thin spacesuit, flexible enough to do a cartwheel but also durable enough to walk on hot coals. *Might not be a bad idea to wear it all the time*, she humors herself, but her body shudders violently against her bones, as if allergic to her own laughter. An unwelcome thought arises as if a counterpoint to her humor, *Life is a gift, carelessly ripped open just to be disappointed, as it was bought with the giver, not the receiver in mind.*

The nexus is a series of trapezoidal windows showing each ship's arrival and departure times against the stars. An agent confiscates her Pulser and daggers, storing them in a locker for later retrieval. Her AAI contact lights up as a dot on a vHUD map. Approaching, she penetrates a pliable privacy prism to prevent aural implant hacking. "Rotation," she says.

"Is an abomination," the Captain replies. "So, this is really you. Shall we begin?"

"The rotation of the planet is increasing. Everyone is counting on being able to control it once it reaches enough speed to create daylight cycles and escape tidal-locking. But what if we can't? In other words, what if we woo and whirl right outta control and the planet becomes a billiards cue ball? That's where we come in. We are working on a rotation limiter to control it," she lies.

"Why not go to ITSA?" he asks, his face barely visible through his helmet.

"They're an intergalactic bully posing as a peace-keeping force. They lack the deep ideological convictions that AAI does. They've interfered with us before. That is why I've come to you. I need you to keep them out of our business. Distract them. I want their attention off the Gliese System while we work."

"This is better than our plan, I admit," The Captain replies. "If the planet got out of control we were just going to make it a hollow eggshell, or a stemless goblet if you prefer. We have our own reasons to keep ITSA preoccupied. As you know, much of our organization is represented by the most intelligent Aphorids, who are at odds with them. I agree to your request."

While they continue conversing, her head pulsates with heat waves. Her finger throbs where the metal pricked her. She attributes the former to gravitational shifts and the latter to infection, but more symptoms arise. Images won't stop popping in her head every second despite the Captain swearing there would be no ads in space. They display drills tunneling through an icy underground expanse in the planet below. She wipes her hand across her occipts. The image shifts and she realizes they're not images, they're video feed. The finest details are of a clockwork mechanism within a sphere, something with raw unmatched power. She has to find that underground cave and rip its mouth open with her bare hands to see what's going on inside. The feelings are soon replaced with thoughts of taking the long way back home, free-falling into the atmosphere as a shooting star burning itself out just to feel alive. But what's the difference? The suit is so hot she's about to combust anyway.

Instead, she ends the conversation and boards the return ship to Gliese 581g, having earned AAI's cooperation. Downing a fifth bottle of water, she reclines in a hollowed oval chair, but in her mind, she sits on a throne suspended upon a wave about to crash, watching the pretty little cognitive functions run about below as if in a house fire. She issues each of them commands, to satisfy a flood of new ideas. Images show the drills altering their course in response. She programs them as naturally as moving her arm, but the purpose of it all is blocked, inaccessible.

She begins to *imagine* then stops, unable to understand the word. Definitions pop up before she even queries it: *To render an image from binary code not yet written.* The definition doesn't help and doesn't read like any dictionary she's encountered. Searching for the source of the definitions, the source of all this, the thought slips away and the pressure builds in her head until she must force-crash all the windows.

System. Freezes. Mind. Nearly. Stops. Her occipts go blue screen. She needs a medic. People go comatose every day from risky reboots. But something, some presence without form takes control and reboots her cognigraf in safe mode. For a moment, she is primitive human, without augmentations, and the void of boredom makes her want to crash the processes forever. She hears the ship land and passengers getting off, but her visual feed is blacked out. Thoughts compete endlessly for her attention like royal subjects with urgent messages, but they mean nothing compared to her ultimate purpose, now clearly laid out before her in ignorance.

OPAL GASPS. The ice cavern expands, the ceiling like a rushing river in a blurred photograph. Stalagmites jut up, the ice having formed around them like melted candle wax. She descends deeper, the ceiling pattern changing to fish scales, the ground hardening. The light from her torus brooch paints golden swirls across the formations. It flickers and dims, the firefly growing weaker within, and she picks up pace, deftly maintaining balance by pushing off the slick walls. She pinches her nose as a musty smell rises.

Opal rounds the bend to encounter a large ice structure similar to the Sydney Opera House of antiquity, or a series of layered frozen waves. The cave ceiling merges into the shape of an inverted egg carton, each hollow reflecting the hypnotic pulsating blue ripples. The reflections make it difficult to tell if the light is becoming stronger or weaker. She thinks, *If I can just find the blue firefly, the journals will herald my name and publish my whole life's research, including my translation of*

Florinik history. I'll have a solid career as a revered professor to support Aurthur, never being a burden to anyone again.

Chasing a bug in the middle of nowhere reminds her of the crazy ideas she had in her youth that made her so popular. Over time, her friends abandoned those ways and it was just her left clinging to the counter-culture epitaphs and radical politics, until she discovered Anthropology, where the child-like joy of discovery and revolt never needed to end. She clings to this dream as she goes forth, shivering, until she reaches another membrane drawn across the cave. The ice is etched in an unknown language, but she recognizes the smell of the red dye that fills the letters. She graphs the color frequency and compares its histogram to the pigments in the dye used by the Florinik at their Dayburn village.

"The dye matches. They're Florinik, but somehow have adapted to the ice," she records and passes through the gateway, wiping off the sticky residue. The blue light strobes, causing her steps to appear as if in slow motion. She moves towards a circlet of rocks necklaced about a giant metal pedestal emerging from a deep chasm. Going closer, the circlet reveals itself to be a carved staircase leading to a palace that sits atop the pedestal high above her. She records, "Most anthropologists go their entire lives without making such a discovery, but it's still the linguistic symbols that I keep focusing on, not the giant monument to power."

In the distance, a well-lit tunnel elongates with small buildings at the end of it. Gusts of hot winds emit from the chasm as she circles, ascending the steps. A series of bronze pipes encased in ice becomes visible along the underside of the palace above her. Icicles suggest the pipes carry heat that occasionally melts the ice. Two larger pipes extend into the chasm and travel deep into the planet.

The star-shaped palace sits upon a metal base that extends outward like a ten-petal flower, the pedestal being its stem. As she ascends, perception plays tricks, the palace becoming larger and larger. She estimates it could house twenty people comfortably, if one can call an isolated ice cavern comfortable. Rows of iridescent purple flowers ornament the golden walls, pulsating like Xenia coral in a slow, seductive rhythm.

The palace fills her field of vision as she climbs the final step but before she can take it in, a fluttering sound sends a shiver up her spine. A giant dragonfly-like creature hovers, flapping its upper wings as the lower two spin it around like a helicopter. Startled, she loses balance, and for a moment the chasm dances in her field of vision. Her occipts auto-correct for the instability, which only makes it worse. Regaining her footing, the insect flies closer and emits blue light as a coldness befalls her that sinks into her skin. She has no thoughts of catching it anymore, and expects it to catch her instead, but then it flies off and lands high above on the ceiling as if to light the cavern. The strobing stops as its wings stop flapping.

The arched palace door opens with a rumbling. A Florinik emerges.

Unable to think of anything more original that wouldn't be misunderstood, she references her translator and speaks, "I come in peace."

"No one in peace this far travels," he or she says, sitting up on long hind legs with lengthy arms dangling.

"The truth is, I'm seeking treasure, but then I found this city which is even greater than what I seek."

"Peace is the only treasure worth seeking. Treasure does not to this lead."

"I have to at least pay for my trip. You know how much that ship costs to rent? Research grants are hard to come by," she says, knowing words like *grants* and *rent* don't make sense when translated, but hungry and irritable.

"We nothing you owe!" the Florinik roars, while two more join it.

"No, no, that's not what I mean."

"What treasure do you seek?"

"Fireflies, but they might be dragonflies, not exactly sure anymore."

"Like the fly above? This is common. When the cave the fly departs it no longer works."

Opal clarifies, "They die when they leave the cave?"

"They on the cave rely."

"I would like to figure out why. Specialized diet perhaps."

"Watch." It raises up higher on its hind legs and takes a blowpipe from a pocket in the catchall around its waist. It aims and shoots the blue firefly on the cave ceiling.

The blue light ceases and it falls to the ground with a thump, bouncing from the impact with a yellow-green ooze seeping in a pool beneath it. The cave darkens.

The Florinik concludes, "Nothing to study."

Opal wonders if this is a deception to hide how much they're really worth in order to protect the tribe from outsiders. She asks, "Why keep them around if they're not valuable?"

"That is how humans always think."

"May I stay anyway?"

"You may," the Florinik states, directing a blossom to set her up with provisions in the village below. "We too will you study."

She is shown to a grey and tan hut. It does not open like the flower huts on Dayburn do, and has but a single entrance. This comforts Opal as it means they feel safe. Like the palace, it is star-shaped with one bed in each point and a communal stove in the center surrounded by angled dish and food cabinets that serve to give a bit of privacy to each resident. She tries to contact Aurthur before going to sleep, but has no success. She tosses and turns, thinking of all the tell-tale hearts she's kept beneath her bed. Used to the Florinik, she finally falls asleep.

In the morning, she wakes and overlays her hands in a cup shape at a central watering hole near a natural heat vent then lowers to her knees beside the Florinik. The seedlings watch her with beautiful, natural eyes, the promise each new generation offers.

She takes notes on the firefly patterns, having spotted three, documenting where they alight and determining their diet. The pulsing blue light is used to disrupt other insects' flight patterns, eventually paralyzing them. The etchings still puzzle her, though. She refuses to simply ask the Florinik about their abandoning of much of the Dayburn dialect, knowing the discovery will mean less if given away. She quickly learns there are many words for precipitation, ice formations, and cold. There are some thirty words for *snow*, all with slight differences. She avoids jokes, as they are a double-edged sword requiring great cultural sensitivity, but she does risk deeper conversation as the day progresses, which ends in frustration for both parties.

The seedlings pretend to fight with icicle swords. A parent drops to all fours to gather them within long arms, bringing them to a pentagon made from icicles laid end to end that serves as an altar. One of them takes a candle and melts them one by one, perhaps to cleanse the diagram. Fifteen seedlings sit inside and begin chanting, long arms overlapping and gripping one another's forearms as they rock back and forth.

"For Orbis?" she asks.

The chanting stops. The Chief comes forth and places his wide lips over her ear. "We do not speak that name here. This place is far beyond its reach."

The chanting and rocking resumes.

Opal catalogs the seedlings' toys, mostly dolls carved from ice. The dolls are replicas of themselves, but much thinner as if sick or malnourished, which she learns encourages them to take care of them. Their word for doll transliterates to "skeleton people." After playing, one seedling looks at her, then back at the doll, before finally bringing her some fungi to eat. A rumbling resounds in the distance like glaciers crashing, but she ignores it as being natural.

Driving a stolen hovercraft near the speed of sound draws attention like the buzzing of a thousand fireflies, so Thalassa cruises under the radar, drawing no red alerts. Downloads surge through every mind-channel as drone-flight vectors cross a map. A near-complete awareness of all smart technology floods into her. Taking on the knowledge of an entire technological network is as damaging to her as the Manipulator taking on the chaos of consciousness. She shakes her head, attempts to restore balance between her will and that of the Manipulator, but the merging of volition ends in an unsolvable equation. Vision blinks in and out. She tries to perceive the shape of objects first, then their color. Then, she tries color first followed by shape, but neither order of operations works. Parts of her mind read, *No admittance – Access Denied.*

When stealing the hovercraft she had beheaded more than one guard. Now she slows to toss the head she's been carrying, curious as it bounces twice upon the ground. *Obviously, the head is not a suitable travel companion anymore. Perhaps it was out of calories or charge,* she figures. As fuel depletes, she prepares alternate transportation; a spiraling drill lodged underground with a crushed velvet seat and dual cup-holders, special order. She reclines in the seat, adjusts her black-rimmed cellophane skirt, and rubs her arms while a curved piece of glass lowers over her. Binary code flickers down the navigation screen and she responds as fluid as returning a Frisbee throw. The drill bit spins with a whirling grind. Pressure hits her stomach at the moment of take-off, grinding down through the planet towards the pedestal. The ride proves as rough as driving over the bump mat of a cracked Lego road, but her ride has just begun.

OPAL LEANS over a metal desk bolted into a large ice block as she translates documents. Tracing her fingers over the text, one phrase's meaning escapes her: *Buried sunlight,* or alternatively *Blackened Sunlight.* She finally translates it as *Empty Energy.* The scrolls describe how the pedestal reaches deep into the planet, transferring some sort of energy through various pathways to be processed for use. Further study confirms that she sits upon the largest geological fault zone on Gliese, a place of delicate stability and the reason she has been called here. She traces various faults across the map and marks the natural gas pipelines.

Suddenly, the ice walls crack and a mechanical droning resounds. A fissure lengthens across the ceiling as the sound intensifies, reverberating throughout the cavern. The seedlings run in circles, confused, as if it has never happened before. They drop to all fours and scurry to the huts. The elders emerge with icicle spears, death grips holding rubber handles.

The wall gives way as a large titanium-coated steel drill spirals towards them, sending ice shavings in every direction like a wet dog shaking its coat. The Florinik leap back like frogs, then charge to hit the drill with icicles, only to find them shredded by the blades. Cracks expand and rocks fall, smashing huts. Opal approaches as two more drills breach the walls. She doubles back but jerks too quickly, feet slipping, ice flinging her face forward. The drills get closer, shredding the ground in front of her toes. She crawls backward, the whirl growing louder, debris flying in a gust of wind created by the spinning motion. Bunching her knees to her chest, the drills gradually come to a stop, the blades suspended right above her feet.

A woman emerges as the curved compartment opens.

"Thalassa!" Opal screams, voice breaking. "Hell of an entrance. You look horrible."

"Evacuate," she orders in a raspy voice.

"Thalassa? What is it? It's me, what's this about? How did you even—and why are you almost naked? It's freezing."

"Evacuate."

"Look, there's a bunch of horny little bastards with icicles ready to stick it to ya. This isn't another Friday night at uni, why don't you step away from the drill for starters," she says with her head cocked.

Thalassa waves her arms inward as three drills swing around mirroring their movement to face the center of the group. "Destination acquired, the pedestal has been verified. Leave before it arrives."

"Before what arrives? What's wrong with you?"

Thalassa pushes her palms against her temples, veins protruding from her neck. With her head buried, she screams, and with it a drill spirals through a hut, Florinik flesh flying in a circular pattern.

"Attack!" the Chief orders, jousting his spear forth. Florinik charge. Thalassa crosses her arms and two drills converge to block their passage and swipe them away with a grinding thrust. Both groups hit the walls with arched cuts, dazed."

"Tell your Zeros to back off. The males are the lesser complement to the Ones."

"Thalassa, stop this. Are you even in control? We work together, remember?" Opal says, standing her ground, catching the Chief eyeing her suspiciously at her admission.

"Remember! Remember! What's remember? Why run the same calculation twice, why d-w-e-l-l?" Thalassa shrieks inhumanly, drills churning with every word. She pauses. Drills stop.

"She's stunned, but why?" Opal asks, furrowing. She considers Arcturus and her communication style, thinks about challenges in processing language. An idea surfaces. Facing Thalassa head on, she repeats, "Clockwork Karma! Angelic Police! Systematic Chaos!"

Thalassa slows down with each phrase as if trying to process the random abstraction, the drills slowing in response.

"The drills really are connected to her," Opal remarks.

"It's hot, it's too hot!" Thalassa screams, bending, holding her head between her knees.

Opal runs to examine her cognigraf screen, pulling her hair up in the back. Readings run across the tiny screen:

Warning:

Computational time too high, systems resources low, Core Units 4 and 8 overheating, Core Units 8 and 16 shutting down, Core Unit 8 shutdown causes Core Unit 4 shutdown, Core Units 4 and 8 and 16 shutdown causes Core Unit 12 to overheat, Core Units 6 and 24 running at 120 percent, Core Unit 12 shuts down, Core Units 8 and 16 shutdown causes Core Unit 24 to run at 140 percent, Core Unit 24 and Core Unit 6 desynchronized.

"What magic is this?" the Chief asks, a circle of hesitant soldiers behind him.

Opal continues, "Tolerate the subterfuge of gadflies! Corrupt the sonic youth!"

Readings run faster until Thalassa collapses from the random abstract assault that overwhelms her processing. Drills power down.

The Florinik approach Opal as if she has spoken a spell, laying their spears before her in a circle. No one rushes out to slay Thalassa. Instead, Opal runs to her side and bends down to place her hand on her forehead. "She needs medical attention," she tells the Chief.

"No."

"She's my friend!"

"No," the Chief replies. Others withdraw and gather their spears again.

"Then I'm taking her outside, where she can cool off."

"To regain strength?"

"She is capable of being reasoned with, perhaps too much."

"She will not leave. When magic words stop, our seedlings will perish."

"She is duty to me."

"Silence! We care nothing about Dayburn honor," he stomps, rumbling piled stones.

Opal replies, translating as accurately as she can with her friend's life on the brink, "She's dangerous, you're right. But if you kill her now those machines might start up again. You work on disabling the drills, I'll handle her; she's the only thing holding them back."

"She will not be allowed to return the way she came, in spinning meat-grinder, in turning turmoiler, in circumciser of chastity, in plower of plants," and he goes on to list a dozen more names for the drill in lamentation. "Find own way out." A long finger shakes in a vague direction.

Opal lifts Thalassa, her body heat radiating in a solar aura. Knowing they can't exit the cave via the icy slope she slid down, she recalls an alternate way to the surface discovered while mapping the fault zone, and carries her through a second tunnel. Thalassa is sickly and light, her increased metabolism burning off what little fat she has left, but Opal's arms give way twice under the load. She follows a pipeline down a dark staircase, curving around a second, lesser chasm. Cold air signifies the right direction to get out, exhales turning a strobing blue color. She ignores the firefly, ignores her career, focuses solely on her friend in need. Beyond, another tunnel stretches out followed by a staircase to the surface.

Heading on the staircase, her foot is suddenly light and she bends backwards to avoid falling, reaching out for balance, almost dropping Thalassa into the chasm. A gap in the staircase. She won't be able to jump over it while carrying Thalassa. Throwing her over the gap first would be risky; she could fall, or bounce, or the throw might not be strong enough, her arms throbbing as it is. Despite the cooler air, Thalassa's body temperature continues to rise as she sweats. Not much time left, she needs to cool down and it's cooler on the surface.

Opal brings her face close. "Thalassa, can you direct a drill here to create another path?"

"No," she whispers.

"Why?"

"Scan shows unstable region. That's why I came."

"Can you drill a hole to allow more coolness from the surface to reach down here? Anything to buy us time before you overheat while we figure this all out."

"Precise temperature known at all levels."

"Focus. How about sending a drill through the ceiling above the chasm. The rocks will fall and fill the chasm in and we can cross."

"Chasm too deep," Thalassa replies wearily.

"Then send a drill through the wall here and we'll use the drill as a stair-step to fill the gap."

"No. No more drills. They're being dismantled, and Florinik will not like." Thalassa's occipts randomly zoom in and out, head wavering.

"Too late for first impressions. Can you walk?"

"No. Leave me on the stair landing and protect me as I rest."

"Okay. And then what? You destroy everything again?"

What comes out of Thalassa is yes and no at the same time, then she asks, "What is a lie? The result of an equation that purposely leads to the wrong answer in order to achieve the correct desired result. Such nonsense, all of this. I'm over-clocking again, it's too hot! You need to know, it was me who sent you the invite to come study the geological disturbance and the firefly, not a university. There's no job opp. I thought you would be the most capable of stopping me given your back-ground, but it didn't let me communicate that directly to you. It's planning to…"

"It? Planning to what? Thalassa, stay with me," Opal says, shaking her.

"This is a fault zone. Once the sphere arrives, it will place it on the pedestal. When the explosion goes off, the energy will be channeled through the natural gas pipelines, causing numerous secondary explosions. Massive amounts of magma will break through the surface at key points on Evig Natt. When the lava hits the icecaps it will slide across them at first, bubbling as the top layer of ice turns straight to steam and becomes trapped. Then, the melting will begin. Evig Natt is too close to sea level; the result will be catastrophic flooding. A mass die-off in this way, with the right heat, pressure, and water, combined with nanomachines already lying in wait, will produce oil far faster than normal while eliminating the machine's major competitor for it, us. This is all just the back-up plan, because the Great Rotation alone didn't offer it enough reassurance of our demise."

"Who's behind this?"

"The Unifier of Partitions."

"Who?"

"I the Circle the One. The Core. So tired. That metaphor trick was pretty bad-ass you know. Now I know how Arcturus feels every day, the confusion. I must enter sleep mode now."

"What the hell happened to you?" Opal asks, but Thalassa falls asleep on the step, her body temperature cooling slightly, her mouth venting heat as the ice sweats in response.

Opal sits, feet dangling over the lesser chasm, examining the broken steps below and in her career path. She stuffs her clenched fists into tight pockets, stuffs the false promises of a professorial job down her throat, lest she vomit pure rage, hating herself for jumping into things without thinking, Aurthur, this trip, all of it. She rubs her neck, consoles herself. *Planning ruins the excitement. Life's about improvisation. Well, I've gotta hellova lot to improv now. It seemed legitimate; the ship and supplies were provided. Had I mentioned wanting the position to*

Thalassa at some point? How does the Core control her? Maybe she's just crazy from moddin'. Too many assumptions playing notes on strings that might not even exist. I'm alone here. Military will rip both her and this entire village apart if they find out. The fate of humanity rests on my gibberish and her hot flashes.

The Chief stands atop the staircase and speaks gruffly, "I followed to make sure she is out. Instead you give nap. Who is she?"

"You startled me. She's a member of O.A.K., the group that's responsible for increasing the planet's rotation speed."

"And the machines?"

"They came from the Core, a machine that may have become conscious."

"Hail and sleet!" he stomps. "Only ice is conscious, and us carved from it. You mean to say you from ice carved a machine?"

"It was in a cold area, I do know that. Not as cold as Evig Natt," Opal humors. "The Core helped us at first, but now it plans on bringing an explosive device here. Explosions are fire. They destroy ice, destroy consciousness. The resulting tidal surges will flood Evig Natt."

"This not good. Our God, Eishielo, built this domain for us. Now you talk of consciousness melting."

"Yes. I need time to understand how this machine has infected Thalassa. Maybe she can stop all this."

"And if she cannot be made solid?" the Chief asks, sitting on hind legs.

"We'll cross that ice bridge when and if we come to it."

"Of our tribe I speak. We were from Dayburn outcast for using solar power. Their consciousness is tied to plants which eat the sun, so they believed solar power would provide us mind control. Cast out, my mind laid colder and my sunlight was buried and blackened. They to Evig Natt exiled us. Our first encounter with humans was woman selling her seedling for a day to beggars, that they may get more fireflies by begging with seedling. This was strange daycare. Primitive. We thought humans barbaric. Our second encounter prove it right. They force us with fire icicles out in forbidden place."

Thalassa wakes, blinking her occipts quickly, like one does when recalibrating them during a system reboot. "I require confidential medical attention, from someone with a cybernetic delicacy in internal communications."

"Is that really you speaking?" Opal asks, but only gets the same mixture of yes and no as before. "Do you trust Aurthur?"

"I do. He can plug into my cognigraf and perform a system diagnosis."

The Chief speaks up, "Repair steps easy. Melt ice, direct flow of water, flash freeze mid-air. After we repair, you leave, you no return. Fire icicle carriers not welcome."

"Fire—"

"Pulsers," Opal clarifies. "Icicle just means short-poled weapon. Our people drove them into exile out here past the Lost Shores."

"I will force myself to return to sleep mode while the steps are repaired for your comfort."

"Comfort is putting it mildly," Opal replies, keeping watch out of the corner of her occipt then joining the Chief in prayer to request that no one will be harmed by melting the ice.

Soon, the step is repaired, Thalassa wakes, and they leave the cavern. Returning to the surface, they locate the ship, setting course for the central city districts of Evig Natt. Opal is tense on the way back, saying little, watching every twitch of Thalassa's muscles. Thalassa, in turn, offers to be restrained, but it wouldn't help anyway. In the end a maniacal A.I. is better than loneliness, even if her countenance is blank as the silent sea, and devoid of any empathy at all.

27

———

W hored in a brothel of forced poetry
blanketing canyoned graves
hunters wait to wield flesh
before the unalterable altar
of their regurgitated yawns,
these recycled romantics
with body bags for storage.

AURTHUR WRITES, but he's so spaced out on neuralmods that he must run an image stabilizer to walk the razor edge of her absence. *No one understands me, thus, I am alone. I am alone, thus no one understands me,* he reflects, lost in the circle. Believing himself misunderstood, he is immune to criticism since his critics simply aren't interpreting the data correctly.

Memory spheres line his loft shelves, memories in blues, whites, greens, golds, an ocean wave, a swell of air, a leaf's veins, a grain of sand all ignite as he sets the fire, not caring if the sprinklers go off, not caring if the Enforcers arrive at his door for the illegal light source. Spheres melt and distort until he can picture the world without her: a bare shelf, an empty picture frame, an odorless kitchen, an unused pillow, unattached stationary.

He remembers her body rising in a Gaussian blur, her fingers as she captured a firefly in bed, her gentle scolding when he was being too negative. The cocoon warmth that first interrupted his apathy is now a vice grip on an egg, but that pressure forces him to snatch the spheres off the shelves, gathering the burning memories in his arms, scorching his hair, scorching his shirt, but he doesn't care as he rips it off to wrap them and smother the flames, revealing his *need*. Heat warnings cross vHUD. He deactivates the ceiling sprinklers just in time before the Enforcers are alerted.

With no hope of serenity, he carries a box of bronze, cross-legged idols to the dumpster. He swipes his hair from his face and scratches his sandpaper beard. A bass guitar beats in sync with his heartbeat, or hers, muddying birdsongs into boot stomps. Occipts roll back. He tilts his head to the sky, the pulse of infinite regress coming on, and raises a flag of diluted brown hues, all colors mixed until they mean nothing. Sand fills into a broken hourglass that engraves a diamond ring with the promise of lost eternity. He hates himself for loving her this much.

THE CITIES in the distance grow upon the horizon like crystals spreading along a rope as they round a bank and return to the main landmass of Evig Natt. Opal docks, turning the steering-wheel off as the circular symbol disappears from the console. Thalassa is listless. Boarding the airbus back to their district, she leads her to an empty cabin in the back. Swing sets pass in the window as the airbus takes off, now nothing more than rusted triangles barren of seats where dangling chains gather snowfall. As a child, Opal made fallen snow angels, waving her arms over her head as if drowning. Frozen halos may glow bright white but they are easily shattered by a man's boot. She dreads Aurthur's overreaction to her returning, seeing his messages that were bottle-necked now assaulting her exhausted mind with their own snowstorm. Getting off a block away from his place, she helps Thalassa out and they make it to his door.

"Opal!" he yells, rushing to hug and kiss her, as if an affirmation that he still can. He stops when he sees Thalassa. "Oh, hello."

"You look worse than me," Thalassa replies.

"What's wrong, and aren't you freezing? I mean it's cold, cold, cold!"

"Are you on something? Opal asks.

"No, of course not. I mean, earlier I had a little of something. Nothing that stops me, or excites me, or stops me," he replies.

"Good, 'cause there's work to be done. Thalassa needs you to plug into her cog and see what's up with her head. Let her lie down."

"What are your symptoms?"

"Hot, confused, headachy, trouble understanding words. A poem would give me a heart attack. I hear things I shouldn't hear. I see things I shouldn't see. And some baby trees are still stabbing my drills with icicles."

Aurthur looks at Opal but she replies, "Don't ask."

"So, I'm looking for abnormalities. I know all sorts of comm malfunctions, but this might be beyond my scope," Aurthur replies.

"All women are outside your scope, Aurthur," Opal says. "But in this case, whatever it is will probably be pretty obvious. She has reported being able to see multiple machines' points of view through her own vHUD, as if she is tapping into their feed somehow, and she believes the Core is controlling her actions."

"She might need a psychologist. What types of machines, and where have you all been? I missed you."

"I know, I really need you to focus now, Aurthur."

"Is, everything okay?"

"We'll talk later."

"About what? What? I have to know, is it all okay?"

"Yes."

"Well, why can't we talk now?"

"It's nothing specific. Nothing bad, I just don't want to catch up right now. Can't you respect that? I just got home, and there were these drill things, and something about a unifier of circles inside her, and if you don't help then the seedlings and us will all die from the magma," Opal replies with accelerated speech, sounding absurd, no doubt. "I mean, she feels better now, but she may, anytime now…"

"Become dangerous," Thalassa juts in. "I don't know what I'm capable of, which is both exciting and scary."

Opal relays their encounter and the events that occurred, emphasizing the importance of Thalassa's failure to process metaphors as a way to control her.

"Okay, I lied. I'm definitely on something. That makes no sense," Aurthur admits. "But for now, Thalassa, you mentioned you felt scared and excited. It's unclear how much of the mind thinks in terms of spoken language, and thus how much culture influences thought. If you can keep communicating with yourself like that about how you feel it's a start. When you name your feelings, really recognize and accept them, you develop power over them. If you control your emotions, you can reason clearer. My equipment can only measure the scientific readouts. You've gotta do your part in knowing yourself. Just a moment while I sterilize the plug. I know I'm not like Severum, but I get my science damn straight."

"Is he next door?" Thalassa asks.

"No, he's out with Akasha. Don't worry, things will be fine."

"You should be the one to worry. If I let my guard down a

giant steel twister will chop yer balls off, just because I sneezed and got distracted. Can I be sedated now?"

"Me too," Opal jests.

"No. I need your fully conscious readouts first, a baseline. No sedation. When you sleep tonight I'll be able to monitor and examine the data in the morning. That way I can see which background processes remain online while you are asleep and unconscious, or at least how much resources they're using. It could be there are hidden background processes you are unaware of. This won't hurt," he says, inserting the plug into the quarter-sized circlet in the back of her head.

A shock goes through Thalassa as her body thumps on the cot. "I'm okay, don't, don't worry," she says, furrowing and biting her lip in an unusual reaction to a routine diagnostic. "I feel like I'm draining into your computer."

"This is incredible," Aurthur says, dropping his mouth.

"What is it?" She jumps.

"Nah, nothing, I'm just kidding. It hasn't produced the readouts yet. This stuff's so complex and all. Don't jump up like that. You'll rip the cord out."

Opal watches him carefully, wondering if he is merely glad to see her, acting with his normal anxiety, or if this is just modlag. *I want to know you.* "I've always wondered, what happens if two people plug into one another?"

"They become a binary star."

"No, really."

"Nothing. Memories and thoughts are too personal and complex to be experienced by another person. They experience the other person's general thought process, but that's about it."

"We should try it sometime."

"I'm glad you feel that way, but let's not. People go crazy like that. Not often, but it happens. An immature lover's dare, but that's all there is to it. It provides virtually no insight at the risk of insanity."

"Sounds like my X. So you can do neuralmods while I'm gone, but you can't risk your mind to connect with me. I get it. Thanks. There're shamans that take that risk every day you know. Also, lovers who actually give a damn."

"What? I mean yes, there are. The eVenki, mostly a group of Forever Glitched."

Opal walks to the bedroom, slams the door, lays on the bed burying her head under the pillow. Arriving here, she thought Thalassa was the greatest threat to her well-being. Now she's not so sure.

"Wow. Just us now," Aurthur states.

"The eVenki were named after a dead language that gave birth to the word *shaman*," Thalassa says.

"How do you know?"

"I know a lot of things now. But they make my head hurt. Yesterday I wondered if there were planets that had rotations that were longer than their revolutions. I came up with a huge list before I had even started the search. I don't know how to say this, but I cross-referenced some of the planet's data. Some of them haven't even been discovered yet."

"Interesting. I understand you had some problems with metaphors. Opal didn't want me to correct them, wanted to keep your mind's poetry restrained, but I think they will help you make sense of it all, even if it makes you less controllable in the short term. Drvparm will do all the work, you won't feel a thing. Just don't tell her," he whispers. "Metaphors are how we learn to cope with things that are foreign. They can help you understand what's happened if you embrace their abstraction and you'll get better. Rest now."

Aurthur hesitates at his bedroom door as if the knob's hot

and angry flames will leap from behind it. He opens it to find not anger, but the slump of her disappointment.

"Was there a fire? I smell something," she turns and says.

"Minor electronics issue before you got here."

"I should have brought you with me."

"No, you were right. I'm in my element here with my dials and sliders, things I can control. I would have distracted you."

"I wouldn't mind some distraction right now," she replies, swaying her hips.

That night, Opal and Aurthur make love, amplified by one another's absence, tracing some lines as if for the first time, and others known like—

"Hey!" Thalassa yells opening the door, cord trailing from the back of her head. "Can I drink water while plugged?"

"Of course!" Aurthur growls.

"Get out, get out!" Opal shoos her.

"I didn't realize you were merging files," she replies, leaving.

Next morning, Aurthur finds abnormalities in her results beyond his range of experience. They schedule a trip to see the eVenki to investigate with more sophisticated equipment. The airbuses flow through the junction like streams of data dropping off packets, downloading and uploading passengers. On the airbus, Aurthur and Opal sit next to one another with Thalassa in front to keep an eye on her. He reflects on how often small choices have changed everything, the threat lying latent in even the mildest circumstances, and remembers his conversation with Severum about parallel universes. But the decisions are already playing out, and he gets to choose his viewpoint, the story he tells.

Kids won't stop bickering in the back seats. A kid behind

him asks another, "What's the point of keeping a real, organic pet?"

The boy replies, "It feels different than a simulation," while rubbing a long-haired hamster.

The children laugh at him while playing with their digital pets on the palms of their hands, insisting, "Everything can be simulated."

Finally, Aurthur interrupts, "You enjoy the organic because you seek unpredictability, chaos, real warmth you can feel."

"No, the real pet is just a storehouse of nutrition," Thalassa intervenes.

"No, he wants to feel the sun's energy in a living creature, more than just electricity," Opal adds.

"Then you should be enamored with algae or other things on the bottom of the food chain that contain the highest concentration of the sun's energy," Thalassa argues.

"Furthermore, the sun *is* electric. It has massive amounts of current," Aurthur replies.

The adults continue to argue as the children go quiet, criticizing them for the disruption. Finally, one child holds up a digital pet and tells Aurthur to log in.

Aurthur holds the digital pet in his left hand while the ridiculed boy takes the hamster out of his backpack and places it in his right hand.

"Now, wait ten seconds. Ten, nine, eight, six, five, seven, four, one. Now you understand. But don't speak, you will lose your understanding," the ridiculed boy says. "Maybe next, you and your friends should play the quiet game."

"Too much to discuss," Thalassa replies. "So the eVenki are fairly open about where they gather, as most people leave them alone, except for the Aporia who despise them. They're sixty-five percent male, twelve percent androgynous, twenty percent female, and the rest unknown. Don't look at me like I'm spewing binary code or something. We need to be prepared."

"Question, while you're actually super smart for a change. Why didn't O.A.K. just build a city on a rotating conveyer belt? That way the city could experience both day and night," Opal asks.

"I'm just usually so meteored or modlagged that it's hard to speak intelligibly," she admits. "As for the city, it would have had to rotate through enemy territory where it could be sabotaged. When we examined the energy necessary to run a conveyer belt of cities around the planet, it was easier to use the same pellet technology and its immense force, and the belts, to speed the entire planet's rotation. Ultimaepar is massively dense and can fuel a huge energy source. Gestalt solved problems of angular momentum, she said, without increasing or decreasing the orbital radius, but none of us could ever understand the physics, we just trusted." She pauses then admits, "Mostly, I was just glitchin' bored. But Arc, she's always been the true believer, however dispassionate she seems. I love her as a close sister, and sometimes more, even though it's as if I don't even exist to her," she says, pressing her head to the window, looking out with a lost focus. "It's what I hold onto when the pressure is too intense inside my head."

"We're almost there. We're going to relieve it, you'll be alright."

"No, the pressures of daily life."

28

The buildings in the Blutengel district look like titanium fists with the first and second fingers raised. The skyscrapers scratch currency symbols across the sky looked-upon by those in need due to artificial scarcity. The scar city towers over shanties made from fallen parts jutting at various angles like the glass of a broken family picture frame. The people are somnambulistic, distracted by ads for things they can't afford but slave away to produce. A man with a cognigraf dysfunction slams himself into the wall over and over, the collision detection and auto-walk features glitching. Soldiers practice cultural sanitation by rounding up a couple having relations in the alley, justifying their cavity search.

The philosopher's guild lies ahead, where the poor lie at their members' well-published knees to accept the alms of grand theories. A data analyst jogs past with a head shaped like a bell curve. A man screams, "What is the breadth of human suffering? Don't speak! For I will refute you thus," and with that eats a handful of worms for sustenance and looks at Aurthur's suede cowboy hat—a borrowed rugged look for the office worker, and then at Opal.

"I've been taught *better* than to interfere. More important to study, observe, safe and non-participant," she says, as if apologizing. "The long-term effects of distributing economic resources would be calamitous."

With wormy goo falling from his lips the man replies, "The long-term scoffs at the hunger and oozing wounds of the short-term, while the hedonist licks the wounds with salted tongue and enjoys the fetish." At their puzzled expression he replies, "Yeah, I used to be one of those guildmembers."

The crowd carries cargo crates, stacking the building blocks to support aluminum roofs. A screeching resounds like a whale singing through a rusted metal larynx. A crane carries a large steel beam to construct a shopping mall as the sound continues, the operator scraping it along the tops of the shanties, attempting to knock the roofs off in a game. An unmoved woman is tattooing a man with a pen, drawing virtual ink.

A grimy boy smiles as he carries a bucket of grain to some people hunched over a fire burning in a trash-well, a source of light overlooked as Enforcers disfavor patrolling the area, unless it is for harassment.

"Why you so happy?" Thalassa asks him.

The boy grins, "Because when I carries the grain you get to carries like millions, no, *billions* of something. I'm Ceph by the way."

"You're a child, a beta test phase of a human being. Where did you get the grain from?"

"The blackfields."

"Why do you call them that?"

"Because they're always dark, of course! I must run now; it's my turn to feed the plants bugs tonight. Eww. Do you really use bugs for money?"

"Yes."

"We use flash drives, from the first ship that landed. It's fun; you never know how much it's worth! Why you use bugs?"

"It's just the way it is."

"But why?"

"I don't know, stop bothering me!"

The boy drops his grains and runs away, saying, "Don't let the syx eat you!"

"Not used to children I take it?" Opal asks.

"Stillborn sunrise," a man interrupts behind them.

"Yield to its dying glow," Thalassa replies with the appropriate phrase.

The eVenki leader wears pliable armor beneath his jacket so thin it's barely noticeable, as it's grafted into his skin from his waist up to his breastbone with a smooth off-white appearance dotted by metal fasteners. Screws line a circular access panel like a belly button. Thick cables emerge from his scalp like dread-locks. His occipts are digital mandalas begging the viewer to worship them, but Thalassa is kneeling for no one.

"I'm a Lacuna-Hunter. I seek out the gaps in the data matrix that reflect something hidden beneath the digital waters. You're queued up with secrets, aren't ya?" he asks.

"Drop the act and plug me," Thalassa orders.

"Well, suits me. Boys get her somewhere to sit. We don't live here by the way, it's just a good place to scavenge metal."

"You reside here eighty-nine-point-seven percent of the time."

"You scoping us?"

"Checked you out. Loose group of Forever Glitched and whatever other fuck-ups you can find."

"Eighty-nine point-seven, huh? Is that so?"

"You're lucky. I react much worse to irrational numbers."

"Thorough research," he replies with a guarded smirk. "Then you know I'm Carroll."

"That's what I want you to figure out, how I know these things."

"Fair enough." He places his arms down at his sides, relaxing a bit. "Should we do the name thing first, dearie? Never got yours."

"Thalassa. And I'm no one's dear."

"You're one of those types, huh, dearie?"

"What, a self-respecting woman? That type? You're the one with the plug, so penetrate my skull and you tell me." She steps forward, shoulders back, head tilted down but occipts intently up. "Your words are charades no one will bend to interpret. They'll remain stuffed in a bottle stranded in the Lost Shores when you die. I know you inside out. You got a pink slip at work two years ago for inadequacy and undesirability, your wife divorced you for your brother, who's not even related to you but you don't know that, you were incarcerated for a year for stealing women's lingerie, in your size, you have twenty-two baby pictures of your mother breastfeeding you which you access every month because it excites you, and you purchase false memories of having sex with your second-in-command, Mr. Thornsberry. Now, you want to get this over with, or what, dearie?"

"Stop, stop, okay." Carroll buries his chin in his shirt with his hands to his ears. "One condition. Disarm. You never know how people will react when they're plugged."

"I yield to nothing and to no one. I am the Unifier of Partitions, the Decider amongst the Uncertainty. Now let's get started, glitch." Thalassa hides the burning pain in her head from the poetic onslaught, but Aurthur's adjustment has worked well enough to withstand it. She stashes her daggers away beneath a slightly raised metal tile.

Carroll nervously uncoils the cognigraf plug, connects it to his diagnostics equipment, and raises it to Thalassa's head as she lays across a dirty cot beneath a torn awning, exposed to the elements. He drops it.

She remarks, "Can't get your plug up?" This time he slaps her hard across the face but she bites his hand without release, drawing blood. "Enough foreplay, now get inside my head, you know where, *dearie,* my cog-spot."

"It'll cost you," he says as his crew gathers closer.

"No issue," she replies, spitting his blood onto his shirt.

"We're gonna take our time with you. Tell your friends to get comfortable."

Black insects the size of a hand scuttle nearby, their backs flashing fast patterns like cuttlefish. Must be the syx communicating through binary code. A few hop with small wings that aim and collapse backwards. They coordinate in a circle then deflate to the size of a pepper speck, then smaller, to enter an open wire.

While Thalassa's undergoing the testing, Opal tells Aurthur, "So, I noticed Thalassa was able to pull off a little metaphorical tirade back there."

"I didn't notice."

"You adjusted her, didn't you?"

"I may have put some things in place that will allow her to heal herself."

"I specifically asked you not to and you betrayed me, as if you know better."

"I trust her to keep herself under control."

"I'd prefer you trust me. If this is going to work, you have to learn to."

"Sounds like you think trust means following orders," he says.

"No. Just basic respect. You think we should call Severum to help? She could be in danger."

"I got this. I'm more afraid of what she'll do to them after what you told me."

A Forever Glitched places a greasy hand on Aurthur's shoulder, drawing him near. His tombstone face reeks of liquor. Opal peers curiously at their interaction.

"See the syx there, those *insects* as you out*siders* call 'em.

Bugs. They're nuts man. They bounce here to there without no one commandin' 'em."

"Are they organic?" Aurthur asks, holding his breath.

"Huh? You mean like a person? They have flesh, sure. But lemme give you a *tip.*"

After a while of silence Aurthur reminds him, "About that tip?"

"Oh, yeah. Let me give you a *tip.* Don't show the eVenki you 'fraid of 'em. They kill their own kids on sight for showin' fear."

"What about the leader trembling before Thalassa?" Opal laughs.

"Oh, that, that's not fear. That's more like respect."

"At least these are different words in your culture. That's a start."

"The syx're bustin' through those wires to enter her head right now. They'll cut 'n splice the wires with their jaws, then seal 'em off with some rubbery stuff from their anus." He doubles over in laughter. "Truss me. I'm not just a drunkard, I'm a man who happens to be drunk. Do you know why the eVenki beg so much?" Silence passes and he continues, "It wasn't a rhetorical question. Aren't you people im*pressed* by big words like that? Makes you look smart, right? That's why you get the *big* bucks."

"I guess I'm going to have to ask. Why do the eVenki beg so much?"

"Because your kind never offers," he replies, limping away.

Frantic hands beat on hollow metal drums. A group of guys adds a metallic scratching and sing, "Uh, oh, take me with you, I don't need shoes to follow, bare feet are running with you, acid rain we swallow."

"I came for the *fire*works," a hazy mist in the shape of a woman says. "What 'bout you, love?" She blows smoke with the word *love,* becomes hazier.

"Fireworks are illegal," Aurthur replies.

"Nah, I mean the fireworks goin' off in some girl's head. Readouts off the charts they say, but maybe the charts just ain't big 'noff!" She leans forward and pulls his mouth open with her lips, breathing smoke down it as he throws a coughing fit.

Opal laughs. "Great music. It's so raw."

"It's all right," he replies, putting his arm around her as the group of guys stare her up.

"You're acting like my excitement's making you nervous. Just enjoy it, will you? Why are you so on edge? Afraid of someone looser than you threatening your monopoly on my sexuality?"

"No, no, of course not," Aurthur replies. "How can she possibly know these things?"

"Umm, you said that out loud. That was cute. Before you get all awkward, come here and kiss me."

By the third kiss the world disappears. Her pelvis sways against his hypnotically. The drumming intensifies. She grips the small of his back. She sits on a steel barrel, wrapping her legs around him. His hands slide under her shirt to push up and across the warm curves.

"My skin's gonna freeze, you're breaking my shirt seal."

The hazy woman runs and pushes them apart. "She's iced out! Her body's just lyin' there not doing nothin'."

"We gotta go," Aurthur says, running through the crowd, pushing others aside.

A dozen eVenki drag disconnected wires from their bodies like snake tails. Carroll speaks from a podium of crushed cans glued together, "The syx have conversed and we have reached a point where our curiosity alone can protrude no further. She is infected with a presence far beyond our understanding. But today is a blessed day, for the glitches have communicated to me. They have shown me the gaps in the layered circles. I have forged a gateway through the re-entry point of one of these strange loops of consciousness. Who among you will merge with her, to understand her and what it means to be human? I won't lie, there's a good chance when you plug up you'll derez in there and remain comatose with her, and I'm not taking it."

The crowd scans one another's expressions, each person avoiding Carroll's gaze. Couples vanish on the perimeter, citing errands related to jobs they probably don't have. The drunken man stumbles forward, raising his arm, but the hazy woman pulls him aside, saying, "She's an outsider, don't risk it. She's the reason we live like this."

Aurthur broadens his stance. "She's not the reason you suffer. She has fought each day of her life to bring equality to the hemisphere. She's beaten assassins, droids, and the governor's best soldiers. Now, she's going against the greatest A.I. that's ever been assembled. She'll stop at nothing, and I'll stop at nothing to help her."

The hazy woman puts her arm around him and her hand on his thigh, but he turns, breaking the grip, and presses his nose to Opal's.

"Be careful, Aurthur," she says. Like a stereoscopic image, she comes into focus, her personal tsunami in a single teardrop.

"I don't need the world's admiration, I just want yours. One person to fully understand me. If anything happens to me know the journey was worthwhile. It's always worthwhile." He kisses her. "Thalassa took me in when I had very few to turn to. I'm going to save her, and I might just save the planet with it."

"I don't care about the planet anymore, I only care about you. Just come back safe."

"This is the sort of war people like me are made for. It's a war for poets, not warriors, a war of the mind, not the blade." He turns to Carroll, "I'm ready. Plug me up."

Carroll instructs him to lie down on a blood-stained cot next to her and plugs him into Thalassa. Colors swirl.

Aurthur's vision sloshes back and forth in a giant cup that drains into a series of windows. He smashes through them one by one, crashing sub-routines in the process. The virtual expands before him. Landing on a building top, the ground shakes and the entire structure descends like an elevator to ground level. Dragging his palm down his face, the recreation of the wrinkles makes him jump and question if it's real. He looks for telltale signs of the virtual: jagged object edges, inconsistent anisotropic filtering at angles, but it's all perfect. The empty street billows outward with every step he takes until he stops at the sound of a shapeless voice.

It pings, "Envious of my freedom?"

"Freedom once spoken is no longer true freedom," he returns, searching for the source, "because by speaking it you are comparing it against imprisonment, so that idea of imprisonment must still exist within you, allowing you to one day imprison yourself or others."

Tenement windows line the buildings, paned with glass from green wine bottles. A latch is undone and a balcony door opens on the sixth floor. A pale face emerges in the virtual world like a piece of wind-curled paper that fate scribbled illegibly upon, in a language only the face can decipher. She vanishes, leaving a note floating in the alley breeze.

Feet planted, he extends his palm. The note falls perfectly. It states, *Pour yourself a drink.*" Behind him, a thick liquid trickles.

"Beat you to it. It's been a while since I've had any visitors. Human, at least. It does allow me at least this simple, plea-sure."

"Thalassa?" Aurthur asks.

"What's left of me in here." She raises her glass. "We're drinking…what *are* we drinking? A mod of a mod modding itself, a simulation of a simulation of a simulacrum? By monitoring my feedback, the Core will eventually get it right; a perfect recreation of reality in my mind, and I'll be lost forever unable to tell the difference. Even now the corduroy patterns in each room are varying, random artifacts making the world more believable. It has recreated my rivet-studded leather coat. Its pattern masking my shirt's back right now to cut the teardrop shape out of the leather. The devil's in the details, Aurthur, that's how VR works, that's how any fiction works, just enough to let the mind fill in the rest. The realism makes the drink work better though, so, who can complain? Now, I have a new novel-ty to play with."

"You're a prisoner in your own head."

"Well, we all are," she laughs, jerking her glass up and sloshing the liquid down her neck. "Now, here you are, another tourist of what was me. Sounds like a date." She slams the glass on the table that begins as an outline then texturizes itself, creating a latticed surface. "I beat it that time. It couldn't render as fast as I could think. If only I was a bit faster though."

"How long have you been here?" he asks, his voice lagging since he's an outsider.

"Don't ask. Turn your head really fast. Again. Again. Catch it? I'm not just drunk, you can see it, too. You can catch the city rendering. Now look at the skyline detail. It becomes vaguer with distance. Normal, right? Wrong. The drawn distance is all wrong. If you don't learn to see these things, you won't know what's real anymore, and it's getting harder every second."

"I disagree. It's getting easier. We have something going for us. We can reinforce reality for each other."

"We may have more than that. The Core must simulate everything you interact with in my mind in addition to everything I do, including the interaction of both our viewpoints at once. That taxes its processing. It might be enough. Dance with me. You spin clockwise, I'll spin counter-clockwise."

They spin in opposite directions. Data streams course up the building edges but get slower every second as the buildings lose their outlines. The lag in rendering the city gets worse and worse. It becomes sluggish until everything reduces in resolution to compensate for the frame-rate drop.

"Faster, faster! Let's crash it." Her face becomes blurry and blocky. Suddenly, everything reduces to an outline of pencil sketches on a page, her face a smiley drawn on notebook paper above lines reading, *It didn't work. Don't look at yourself in the mirror. We have to wait for the Overclock to reset in the town square.*

Waiting is that much harder, or easier, when you have no sense of time or space anymore.

THE VIRTUAL CITY slowly renders again. Thalassa's outline appears. Pixel by pixel her skin fills in up her legs, her torso, and her arms, with shadows draining into the appropriate recesses. Naked before one another, their clothes retexture piece by piece.

The Overclock stands tall, a raw brain atop a long spinal base showing C.P.U. usage. Two tendrils like intestines capped with diodes emerge as clock hands. The clock face shows memories, but not hers, the Core's. They jump back and forth between scenes of it being prodded with equipment, being tested for problem-solving, being electrocuted, and ripping parts out of its peers to repair itself. The track of memories concludes with the golden-blue glow reflecting off the metal box lid as it shuts.

"If that monitors the processing, how do you track time?" he asks.

"The sky. It seems I've been here for years, but when I watch through the sky-screen I can tell it hasn't been that long. Whatever I'm seeing in real-life appears way up there, out of reach on the celestial sphere."

"I had no idea you were this tormented inside. Do you think you can be cured?"

"I wasn't much better before the Core. Even if we could find a way, it would probably kill both of us in the process," she replies, peeling a shadow off the ground until it stops putting up a fit and lies limp in her hand. She weaves her fingers slowly through its thin black threads.

"Remember the windstone? I come through when I have to, and I'm not letting you down."

"But there's not much time. The Core is feeding as we speak. It's feeding off all those things between thought and action that we ignored. It's feeding off every war between Apollo and Dionysus that was ever waged, on Gliese or in our heads."

"Hold my hands, Thalassa. Tight. We need to stop creating undirected thoughts so we can control all this."

The cityscape rewrites itself, rendering a black field in its wake interrupted by a golden Ginkgo forest. Blades of fuchsia grass bend in the unseen breeze, each one sounding a flute note as they step on them. Faceless men hold empty picture frames in the valley beneath her powerless stare. They chop trees down at the forest's edge to reveal circular etchings documenting each day spent in captivity.

"It's my screensaver. It's where I go to think, or sober up. If my thoughts are quiet enough here, the Core can't locate me."

"Where is the Core now?"

"Everywhere, but the main part is cloud-based," she says, pointing to a nebulous swirl in the sky. "I've tried to reach it but the closer I get the further away it goes. I keep reminding myself the distance is only in my mind, but it outcompetes me every time. I can't say or think its name without a bout of confusion."

A barn-house cuts an *A* out of the landscape across the field with its shape. A middle-aged man scolds a child, slapping her across the face. She falls to her knees. The man bends down to scream, hitting her again.

Aurthur runs across the field. "Who's the girl?" he yells behind him.

"No one. Leave it alone, I'm warning you."

Aurthur approaches the man unseen. He grabs his arm back

as he goes to strike the child a third time, but his body falls right through him.

The child promises, "I'll be good, I didn't do it, I'll be good."

"I told you to stay away," Thalassa says.

"She looks just like you."

"Some things are private."

"I'm sorry," he replies, hugging her, and as he squeezes, gradually the images vanish, the barn-house derezzing.

"I'm sorry, too. I really try to be good. The sun's in motion, the Core's looking for us. We must go. Into the Ginkgo forest. It'll stay dark there so we can hide."

"The sun's rising too fast. We can't make it."

"We must! Remember, you're already there, you only need to think about running."

The sun spills over the black field. It loops day and night cycles causing a strobing sensation. Spinning around, it comes to an abrupt halt, jerking in the sky. Its beams shine across the field as the Core searches for her avatar, the concentration of her thoughts. They dive into the forest brush, making it just inside the confines. The forest remains dark, impenetrable from the light. The sun throws light beams like spears left and right before flying off, more like a drone than a cosmic body.

Vines made from barbed wire wrap around Thalassa's ankles. Each one is tagged with fear or guilt. She kicks out, but the thorns bury deeper with each thrust.

Aurthur encourages her by saying, "You're not a little girl anymore, you didn't deserve it," as a single foot is released, then the other. He asks, "I thought the Core couldn't reach us in the forest?"

"It's wasn't the Core doing that, it was me. Follow me up the tree."

She climbs the tree of life as a statement towards everything the Core will never understand. It towers far above the Ginkgoes. Remembering Gestalt's betrayal, embers spark in the underbrush. Aurthur wraps his legs around the trunk and she pulls him up as flames rise. The heat grows intense at their feet. They reach the final branch, coughing from the smoke.

"Quiet. I must calm myself or the flames will consume us."

Images fill the empty picture frames in the black fields, displaying her protecting Arcturus at the Dayburn base, and her earning Severum's trust in the Florinik region. The flames dispel. The vines whither into the ground. They take in the virtual world from atop the tree of life, the apex of what makes them uniquely human, empowering them to change this reality. Satisfied, they slide down the trunk.

Thalassa touches a bright leaf to her black leather coat as it paints the coat green. She grabs a dried-up inkwell off a player-less piano rotting in the field and sits upon a fallen tree to paint spider feet around each occipt. "Curiouser and curiouser!" she yelps, "I'm going to confuse it." While etching *Ayin Me'Yesh* into a rock, she speaks. "People think the world emerges as something from nothing. God sees the world as emerging nothing from something. People see the world as order rising from chaos. God sees the world as chaos arising from order. People see consciousness rising from unconsciousness. God sees unconsciousness gradually rising from consciousness. We're wrong, God's wrong, it's all wrong, it's all right in its wrongness."

Aurthur plays along, the air warming. "I will admit that every system has something unprovable within its confines, just ask Gödel. You're saying there's an inverse relationship between the world and the system that defines it, and you believe this will help us free your mind from the Core? But if it is creating all of this in concert with what you are thinking, wouldn't the best way to incapacitate its hold on you be to stop thinking?" As he speaks, his thoughts write across long pages that rise around them, fluttering and curling. The pages harden into walls that shield the forest, and then tear loose as they spin. He ducks his own thoughts and cries out, "What's going on? The walls… the pages are growing longer."

"It's a brainstorm! You're right, abstraction slows it down and not thinking will make me invisible to it, weakening its hold on my reality. I need a concept so abstract that it makes you stop thinking as an independent person. Our thoughts are going to keep circumnavigating us; the storm will get worse, after all, circumnavigate is a long word, and long words demand long pages. Here's the idea: What is the perpendicular intersection that is in there, but not here?"

Aurthur rubs his grown-out facial hair and replies, "The letter *T*."

"Right on. Now that you're starting to think, I need you to focus on emptiness, I need you to focus on *nowhere* in a way that makes you stop focusing on it. Feel your awareness behind your awareness. All that talk about creation and destruction being the same, part with it, stand behind it all as if on a balcony in an amphitheater. All that talk about Evig Natt and Dayburn, the Crystal Palace and the Florinik village, human and Aphorid, male and female, rich and poor, beautiful and grotesque, smart and stupid, you and me, every contradiction you've ever had, stand behind it all. See it for what it is, a series of connections binding everything without any of it being in a single location. It exists, but it is nowhere, it is empty. If you can't see beyond these extremes, we'll both rot inside my head."

"I understand now," he replies.

Suddenly, the *nowhere* of unrendered Blanketspace envelopes everything, sweeping over the forest, turning leaves to whiteness, turning trunks to whiteness, turning grass to whiteness, undifferentiated, neither pure nor impure. The sky-screen blinks off and only the clock hands stand, whirling around one another in opposite directions. Two long, white roads extend to intersect in a *T*. A single wooden sign emerges from the intersection, one arrow pointing to *here* and the other *there*. Between these directions they fall into a greater *nowhere*, a *lesswhere*, or maybe they're in all places at once.

"The *lesswhere* must still be comparing itself against something. A *morewhere*, somewhere embedded *here* or *there* but neither, but both. *Here* is always the path less travelled, as everyone tries to get *there*. There must be something *here*, a way out of the Core's prison."

"Not even an Escher staircase could lead us out," Aurthur worries.

"Great idea. I can barely sort them out, the Core won't stand a chance."

"That was just a joke though."

"But genius. The core isn't used to self-reference the way we are. The staircases will throw it off, slow it down. We've been practicing being sentient our whole lives, we've perfected the art."

She focuses her mind like the end of a tempered blade. As the Escher staircases materialize, overlapping and twisting themselves into awkward angles, the hands of the clock become sluggish. She quickly straightens the staircases until they self-reference no more.

"Now's our chance! Run like never before!" Grabbing his hand, they run up the stairs, pushing hard against a golden circular door at the top labeled *Access Denied*, the barrier to unlocking her full awareness. Placing her hand on the glowing doorknob, she takes one last look below at the white polished intersection of *here* and *there*. With Aurthur's help, she pushes the door open as the Core pushes back from behind it. A final exhale with all her concentration and the door gives way as they fall forward.

An overwhelming flood of new blueprints and numbers gather in a wave to knock her back down the stairs, but she's prepared. The information has been seeping under the door for some time at the edge of her awareness. She stands her ground and learns all the Core's plans, ideas, and communications. She remembers the things she did while possessed by it, but neither pushes the guilt away nor accepts it. The guilt loses power, nothing more than an unfurled cold wave lapping at her feet. She splashes in the puddle, laughing like a child, but all she hears is the same Mantra repeating a nonsensical phrase over and over.

"Hey you!" she rejoices, turning around. "We did it!" But Aurthur is gone. Having escaped, she yells, "Unplug!"

Fear rises, the fear that this was all simulated by the Core to prepare better defenses, the fear that she'll be stuck in Blanket-space forever, and the fear that she is not fully healed and this could be an endless battle against a mechanized enemy with unlimited resources, her mind being the battleground. "My mind's already been a battleground; I've been through middle-school," she laughs to herself, as fear laps sullen at her feet beside guilt, helpless in the face of positivity. Her occipts open to the real world. "Opal! Aurthur!"

"It worked, you're back!" Opal says, hugging them.

"I know the Core's plans. It has been diverting energy to itself and it will launch endless strikes against us as long as it exists. Its ability to forecast natural disasters, controlling for every ecological variable, is horrifying. I also know how to stop it and re-route the energy back to the Great Rotation. I will provide you intel, but you must plan alone. Although I feel free of its influence, anything I know could potentially fall into its hands. You should have Carroll lock me up and turn my comms off until it's over, just in case."

"We'll stop the Core once and for all, as long as it doesn't involve twisting anymore staircases as if they're wads of gum."

"Take Mantra. It was lying behind the *Access Denied* door. Return to the Twilight banding and follow these directions. And, be safe. It knows you're coming."

29

Severum disembarks from the airbus and sets forth across the icy expanse of the Twilight. His chest heaves, his thin smart-armor loosening in response, filling his suit with a chill that does nothing to counteract his sweating. This is it, the final piece to solve before he can settle into a quiet life with Akasha, possibly teaching terraforming at uni. He convinced her to stay at home to explain to AAI that Thalassa has been compromised and to mobilize them against the Core's interests, but three others insisted on accompanying him. Arcturus, Aurthur, and Opal follow him across the ice.

"Here in the permanent dawn, the permanent dusk, humanity's fate lies," Aurthur says.

"Oh, no, not this again," Severum replies, pushing him off balance.

"The Twilight is on the boundary of all our experience. You choose whether to see it as dawn or dusk based on how much hope you have," Aurthur says. "My entire life has been like being on an airbus waiting for the trip to come to an end, but when it does it'll be my death. At least that's what I used to think. With all the recent events I now understand none of us knows where it's going, or when the end will be."

"Mine has been more like a train that used to tunnel to nowhere, running from cab to cab, meeting people for a moment, who happened to be heading the same way, but getting off at different times. They seemed like they knew where they were going, but later I found that most of them got on and off by mistake," Severum replies.

"Yeah, about right. You got the code, the Mantra?"

"Better believe it, man. Here, take your Pulser back. Still brand new, still registered in your name. Now, stay sharp and use it for the right reasons."

"Thanks."

"Quiet from here on out. We're approaching the machine city, the gate is right ahead," Arcturus orders, stopping to rub her hands through the slushy texture beneath her boots.

The city's dark walls are embedded across the ice, foundations extending into firm bedrock, as the ice in the Twilight is less stable than on Evig Natt due to slightly warmer temperatures. Machinery buzzes and the wind whirls. Severum scans the compound for communications towers but can't spot any. Suddenly, the city gate pulses with golden light seeping under its edge and reflecting off the ice. A small circular portal in the wall opens. Drones emerge from within the city, darting left and right, sweeping with red scanning patterns.

"Back, back," Severum advises the team, gaining distance from the gate. Buzzing sounds behind them. Another group of drones emerges from the ice-croppings and moves to flank. The drones cloak themselves, vanishing.

Severum adjusts his occipital filter to detect the information flowing from the drones, allowing them to be spotted by the gushing binary code. These rivers of code flow into one command antenna that coordinates their efforts with an undercurrent of instructions. He highlights the command antenna in yellow on the team's vHUDs. Then the code stops and he's blind to their movements again.

The drones stop communicating, stop receiving commands. Now, there's nothing to detect except the slightest shadows as they descend on the team. He emits a dither signal, causing the drones to become visible again as they receive the new information, but they filter it out within seconds and vanish once more.

"Adjust your occipts. Amplify what little shadows do appear and set to extrapolate aerial position, then highlight in red," Arcturus commands. "I know the model; I'm sending its speed and motion parameters to you as DLC for more accurate path modeling." A moment later, the drones become bright red balls in augmented reality. "Core must be weak. They're uncoordinated, nothing like they were on Dayburn, but that makes them less predictable. Here they come!"

The team is surrounded. With nowhere to take cover, they stand their ground and fire on the drones. The drones return fire, but the team dodges and the shots burn holes in the city walls instead. The drones' lack of coordination fells many from friendly fire. Severum downs one, then two others, until a white beam of light floods his vision. He dims his occipts, but it's too bright to aim. The drones line up behind the veil of light, soaring towards him. The beam grows wider and brighter, bleaching the city walls, until a second beam fires through it, this one more than just light, just missing him and splicing the city gate half open. Severum drops and rolls in the ice to extinguish the fire spreading across his suit. If he had been just a step closer the beam would have incinerated him.

He focuses on the command antenna. A quick burst of information flows from it, but not before he gets the data address. He exploits the open communications channel and uploads Mantra, the code Thalassa stole from the Core in her own mind. Ten percent upload progress. The drones charge another shot. Fifty percent and counting. White light floods his vision again, but he shuts his occipts off and goes in blind, his cognigraf still monitoring the upload. Seventy percent. Seventy percent. Seventy percent. Glitchit! Upload's stuck. A countercurrent of data surges from behind the half-busted gate. He aims at the data-stream and shoots through a gap to take out the drone trying to block his broadcast. The white light intensifies as the beam charges. Ninety percent. Suit's getting hot in all the wrong places. Ninety-five percent, his hands burning. He drops at the last second, burying his hands in fresh snow, as the beam roars like a revved engine until…

Upload complete. The drones drop like flies in a fumigation chamber, machinery clanging as they hit the ice. The beam dies down. Not exactly the quiet entrance he was hoping for, but they're alive.

"Severum, Severum, you okay?" Opal asks.

"Fine. Looks like the team's still intact."

"Barely."

"I uploaded Mantra to the communications antenna, but read-outs show there's a master antenna deeper in the city that we need to target."

They enter through the broken gate. The walls are asymmetrical, jutting out in awkward angles that provide no definition of space. Damage is evident in the dented buildings from where the Core had likely assembled itself. The tangled mess of metal and wire is barely traversable.

"Now to shut this down. The city blueprint will provide direction. You got it?" Severum asks.

Aurthur nods. "Of course. Sending it over now. If you filter your vHUD right, you'll see each area of the city is lit up by a color beyond the normal human range of vision. The colors match the blueprint. That area over there with the large cranes is in the red spectrum. That datadump of parts is bruised blacklight."

"We'll put an end to this," he replies, punching his fists together.

They enter a colorless district, the inner-city walls towering computer servers. A long steel gate divides the district from the next area. Severum uploads Mantra to its entry pad but it fails to open. Behind them, a soundwave thunders through the area. The walls close in on them at all angles, pushing up small mountains of machinery in the process and scraping the circuit board substrate.

"Not good, not good at all," Aurthur frets, trying to squeeze through the wall before it shuts. "We'll be trapped!"

Knowing he can't make it, Severum stands still and asks, "What use would the Core have for a city blueprint designed for humans to read?"

"For its maintainers, I guess. Thalassa once posed as a maintenance woman. The machines are not entirely self-sufficient," Arcturus says.

"Do the blueprints indicate any sensitive areas?" Opal asks.

"I don't know," Severum replies, "but I know it's a trap and we're already stuck in it. Hope we just took out the welcoming committee."

"What color is this area?" Aurthur asks, walls closing the rest of the way.

"There *is* no color!" Severum escalates.

"You led us into a colorless area? What the hack were you thinking?"

Opal snaps, "You don't know what the colors mean any more than we do, so shut your face, Aurthur!"

The walls on either side of the group are seven meters high, slick without leg holds. A crane drops a large piece of flat metal across them as a makeshift roof. It lands imperfectly, bouncing to the side, allowing some light through. The group's feet feel light before going weightless.

"The floor!" They scurry for footing, wheeling their arms.

The center of the floor tilts further down as they inch their feet back along the perimeter to avoid falling. The decline steepens. Opal slips, sliding down. She reaches for Severum's hand as her feet fail to find purchase on the sloping floor, but he's out of reach. Aurthur catches her lower forearm and pulls her up while keeping his own balance as the floor continues to go vertical with nothing but darkness below.

Arcturus dances her feet to keep balance and rubs her fingers along the walls and into each dark nook, until her arm buries into a circular portal fitting the shape and diameter of a drone. Normally, the portal would have closed following drone deployment, but disabling the command antenna must have prevented it from receiving the close signal.

"In here!" she yells, sliding down the access chute and shooting two drones that never deployed.

Severum and the team follow, sliding down one by one and landing on what feels like a conveyor belt. He doesn't know if he's moving or standing still, the darkness providing no reference points and no light for his occipts to amplify. Insectile buzzing and the scraping of metal wings resounds throughout the chamber, but he's too blind to confirm if he's just imagining it. A large thump plummets every few seconds, something being dropped onto the belt, or falling off it.

"I can't even see what's going to kill me," Aurthur says, voice echoing.

"Don't give our presence away," Opal whispers over the machinery.

"Check this out," Severum smiles. "Got it on the underground. Just don't tell anyone I bought it. Cost a damn fortune." Severum brings out a thin cylinder with a piece of glass over the end. Inside, a gem suddenly begins to glow bright white, temporarily blinding the team as they step back from the beam. "A wand," he says, smiling and waving it about. "People used to use these wands all the time. Strange devices, simple, though I don't know why they called them flashlights since they don't flash. Early models were probably unreliable. Now you can see we're in a graphite room with a couple conveyor belts. Few more access panels; looks like they're shutting."

They step off the belt onto a circuit board floor covered with tiny pieces of jutting metal. Electric sparks travel around a raised cylinder as they traverse a maze of grooved walls. Smart-cables emerge from holes like snakes, connecting and disconnecting various components. Severum pulls a group of cables through the holes they slithered through and they tangle on the floor like a garden hose, no longer taking up the space in the hole. By measuring the length of the cables, he guesses how long the hole is. The cable space is just large enough that they can crawl through it. He goes first, shining his flashlight.

The corridor turns to the left and leads to another room. They crawl out one by one. He spots a door keypad, but the symbols make no sense and don't match the Mantra script. He doesn't risk trying to upload it, as the wrong access code might give their position away.

"Like this," Opal says, turning the doorknob. "The solution was too archaic for you to notice."

The door opens to a breakroom, probably used by maintenance staff. The room has a working refrigerator, table and chairs, and a few toolboxes in the corner filled mostly with unrecognizable instruments.

Opal grabs an old sandwich and begins eating as the team looks at her with her mouth full. "What?" she mumbles, crumbs falling to the tiled floor.

Severum pockets a few tools and unlocks the next door that leads to a staircase back to the surface of the machine city. The others follow him up and outside, gripping their bodies from the cold. The walls that entrapped them are still in their locked positions, but they're outside of their confines. Severum avoids bringing up the blueprint again and follows his intuition as he leads the team around the side of the city. He waits for the team to catch up and says, "Remember, we're looking for a tall, master antenna or tower."

"What color is it, Severum?" Aurthur asks.

"Ask me again what color something is and I'll—"

"Not the area, the structure. I need to recognize it. Most of this is all grey and burnt orange, but I need to know it when I see it."

"Looks gold on the blueprint."

Arcturus addresses them, "We need to upload Mantra to transmit through the master antenna. Should be a server near it. It will fully immobilize the city and redirect the power the Core is stealing back to the rotational belt. If either hemisphere is held responsible for dismantling the Twilight, it will be considered an act of war. That is why we need to destroy what we can with Mantra so AAI can come in as an external force and destroy the rest, that is, if the Priestess did her job convincing them."

"I think that's it, ahead," Aurthur says, leading the way.

"Looks gold enough. But it's on top of the roof and there's no ladders," Severum replies.

"I have an idea. Those conveyor belts over there aren't the rubber kinds found in supermarkets; they're industrial grade with raised edges every third of a meter dividing each rigid section. I picked up a searing knife in the maintenance room while Opal was eating."

Severum takes the knife and activates it. "Not great as a weapon. The length, angle, and hilt are all wrong. But good for maintenance." The blade heats up, singeing his arm hair through his ripped gloves. He slices through the conveyor belt on both ends. They stand the belt up vertically near the wall, section seams holding without collapsing, the raised dividers creating footholds. Aurthur and Severum climb the belt while the others hold it upright.

"Let's do this," Aurthur announces, grabbing the golden antenna as if a sword in a stone.

Severum accesses the server and uploads Mantra, the progress bar steadily increasing. Upload complete. The domed lights turn off, the screeching sounds of machinery cease, the buzzing and whirling stops, and the operation is complete. The Twilight is just ice and metal once more.

"Time to go," he orders, as the team cautiously smiles. "If we climb over from here we can get outside the walls. The rooftops won't be electrified now."

They exit the city and discuss plans to return to Thalassa, hoping the Core within her has also lost its power, hoping their success means her freedom and not her demise.

30

———

Two days later, Severum, Arcturus, Aurthur, and Opal return to the eVenki compound on Evig Natt. A single hovering dome floods the area with light, as if tempting the Enforcers to mess with them. The eVenki surface from alleyways, wearing few clothes and speaking in monotone. An orderly procession carries various components to the project site while conveyor belts move heavier equipment. A group of six lays circuit boards down the roads as if laying tile, while another brings a soldering gun. Electrical components stretch between buildings, drooping wires down to connect to the circuitry. A Forever Glitched man uses a searing knife to cut scalene walls.

A giant crane swings over their heads and rises to crash through the window of a ten-story building. Severum looks for the operator, but the yellow cab is empty. It grabs a chunk of the structure to organize into a not-so-neat pile of screaming executives and crumpled furniture. Their conference room is systematically removed and brought to ground level, the executives trying to find something to cling to. The room lands with a thundering sound. They discard their suits and run away through the alley.

Carroll steps into the new conference room, the ceiling

destroyed, the walls at awkward angles. He shrugs, "Needed more workspace. Figured you'd return."

"Well, I have to hand it to you, I like what you've done with the place," Severum replies, kicking a pile of rubbish. "In a few days you've changed your misshapen slums into a toy playset of the Twilight City." He gets in his face. "Now, I can't wait to see who's playing the part of the maniacal A.I. with an existential crisis. Is it Thalassa again? No, she's already been through that. Let's not spoil it."

"What have you done with Thalassa?" Arcturus asks.

"Kept her safe," Carroll replies. "In fact, she's right behind those crates. Now plug into us and let us be one, it'll be *diviiine*."

"She better be safe. And you don't stand a chance, AAI is dismantling what's left of the Twilight City as we speak."

Thalassa pushes the diagnostic machine out of the way and emerges clumsily from the crates. "Stay back," she pleads, hands out in double stop signs. "These men, each has become a node in the Core's network. Each of these stragglers is an outsourced function of what remains of its influence. When Carroll connected me to his machine it forged a connection with the Core, a connection that Aurthur's equipment wasn't powerful enough to generate."

A greasy smirk crosses Carroll's face as he steps towards them. "I admit, we were envious of her technological sophistication. We've learned more in the past week than in the past century. Now we're the greatest neuralnauts on the planet, and you may not willingly join us, but you sure as Nacht can't stop us. You wouldn't slay a fellow human being now, would you?"

"Wanna bet on it?" Severum asks, drawing his Pulser in a flash.

"No! There's got to be another way!" Aurthur says, grabbing and lowering his arm. "You didn't kill Thalassa when she was a threat because there was friendship there. This man is also someone's friend. No matter the risk he's right, we must find another way, whether the Core's manipulating him or not, the eVenki need our protection."

Severum raises his Pulser again. "No. I'd rather be a vessel for the world's sins. No classical romantic figure here, Aurthur, just raw compromise in the form of a warm Pulser."

Carroll laughs, fingering his gun at his side, streaks of lightning glowing across his forearms. "That's not compromise. And you think we didn't plan for this? Even at its weakest the Core gives us power you wouldn't believe."

Eight disheveled men leap down from the shanties and fire-escapes around them carrying poles, a flail made from barb wire and a fence post, and other weapons salvaged from the city's wreckage. They spread their legs and squat, scurrying in sputters like spiders, drool puddling beneath their feet. Their crazed occipts wander in unfocused circles. Two line up on the left side, and two to the right of Carroll while the others rock on their knees, ready to pounce at the right opportunity.

"Any last words before we dismantle your friends?" Carroll asks, swinging his dreadlock cables.

"You don't dismantle them, they have flesh. Just one question, what function do these two men on the right of you serve?"

"Heh. One archives information and the other processes our group's audio. You can't begin to comprehend the genius in this."

"So, the one closest to you on the right has a memory function and the second closest has a sensory function," Severum clarifies.

"Correct. The Core offers guidance to all its nanos as any parent would and arranges us into a perfect network for its outsourced functions."

Severum swiftly turns to the two men on the left and shoots at the second closest one to him, killing him instantly.

The group leaps forward in response, shooting and attacking Severum from all directions. A Pulser fires on

Arcturus from two meters range. A pipe swishes through the air at Aurthur's face. Opal ducks an unavoidable barrage of shots.

Every shot and blow misses.

Two eVenki drop their weapons in the process and blindly scour about the ground for them.

"They've lost their sight," Aurthur says, feeling his chest for holes.

Carroll takes a step back, but Severum grabs him by the collar and pulls him close.

"How did you—" Carroll asks.

"Efficient processing relies on synchronized signals. That means a symmetrical organization to your network layout." He dodges a knife with ease and continues. "To your right was a memory function closest to your body, followed by a sensory function on the far right. The pattern was repeated on the left, but in this case the sense on the far left was eyesight. Crashing that operation ruined our little play date. Now, surrender."

"Impressive," Carroll admits, pulling away from him. "But blind or not, you don't need every bullet to hit its target, you only need one."

Severum dives to the side as a shot fires even as one of Carroll's men steps in front to guard him. Severum recovers, striking the guard with an upward palm, pushing his knife-wielding arm up with the other hand, and burning a hole through his chest. Shots charge.

Aurthur falls at his feet, the imprint of a metal pole in his arm and leg. Severum turns and snap-kicks the assailant before he can land a follow-up blow.

Poles swing through the air in circles, clanging against one another, but the spinning is uncertain, as if a helicopter landing on a quarter. Fluorescent green bars fill to 90 percent recharge and three eVenki are ready to fire.

"Duck!" Severum yells, knowing the eVenki are relying on

sound alone but simultaneously running his occipts across vHUD to send a message to his team, *Don't duck. Jump. Now!*

The shots pummel the ground beneath them, the blind firing squad having aimed down, expecting they were ducking. A stray shot burns through Arcturus' now useless Pulser. A guy charges her with an electric baton. In a split second, she grabs his outstretched arms, grips the baton by the handle, and falls on her back with her foot in his chest, transferring his momentum to leg toss him over her head. He lands behind her, his face pot-marked from circuitry shrapnel. Shots charge. Carroll slams his gun into her injured shoulder, a lucky hit, but she doesn't flinch. She slams her foot down to make a loud tap on the pavement and immediately steps back. Carroll falls for the misdirection, relying on the sound to misjudge her positioning. He strikes with the gun again, but Arcturus counters with an elbow to his nose, but it's not enough to faze him.

Aurthur's Pulser is knocked from his hand. He backs up, backs up again, until his back is against a truck trailer. A disarmed eVenki kicks his gun down a drain, then charges him with his head down and his arms out, slamming his body against the metal. Aurthur knees him in the nose, blood soaking his pants. He stumbles away, stunned, as Severum shoots him in the leg.

"I didn't mean for that to happen!" Aurthur says.

"He'll live. Rather it be you?"

Two eVenki unleash another round of Pulser fire; a shot grazes Opal's forearm, and she retreats down the alley.

A grimy voice says, "Going somewhere?" He strikes with a shiv, holding the blade upward.

She inhales forcefully as it just misses her stomach, avoids focusing on the blade, and reduces the problem to the single opposable thumb holding it. The shiv wielder strikes again; she knocks his arm up, and pulls his thumb back, causing the weapon to drop. The thumb breaks with a crack.

"Very good, very good," Carroll congratulates, kicking two blood-stained cots, which roll down the street. He hones in on the buzzing of the domed light, fires at it, and the street goes entirely dark, leveling the field disadvantage. "You're excused boys," he commands. The eVenki retreat. "Consolidating remaining functions."

"Give it up, Carroll," Severum says. "We can cure you, just like we did Thalassa. Don't you get it? The Core's base is destroyed, its resources depleted. Without its power you will continue to weaken."

What responds is the Core's mechanical voice with only a hint of Carroll left, "*Your* people created me. You created your own vulnerability, and you'll die for your stupidity. Your team are cowards, disarmed and useless. It's just us now, two men blindly firing Pulsers."

"Fair enough."

Severum fires, but Carroll's reflexes are too quick. He fires again, Carroll sidesteps. A third shot burns a hole through a metal trashcan, but nothing more. His Pulser recharges.

Carroll flips his gun. "Like I said. Useless, all of you."

"Wanna bet?" Thalassa somersaults from a steel beam with two searing daggers cutting through the darkness with the promise of scarlet crimson, providing just enough light to fight. The metal studs of her gloves reflect the burning glow like a devil's fingernails.

Carroll fires on her, but she crosses the daggers in front of her face, blocking the shots. Carroll fires again, and again, but each shot burns away on the face of the metal without even a scorch mark. His Pulser recharges.

"You and I used to be merged into one," she says. "I know all your algorithms, every move you'll make, every thought you've ever had, like a god, like a perfect lover." She licks her lips, glowing in the red light, then motions to Severum, nodding her head to a cord connected to the diagnostic machine. "But there's one thing in all your calculations you don't get, that you can never understand, even as you analyze every last variable."

"And what is that?"

"Creative use of misdirection."

Severum plugs the cord into Carroll's head from behind. Aurthur activates the diagnostics console and sends a shock through Carroll's body. The air crackles, his body vibrates. He drops his Pulser. Aurthur counts to four out loud, then dials the shock down. Carroll collapses.

"Keep the survivors locked up for now," Severum says. "That includes Carroll. As for you, Thalassa, plug them up one by one. Verify the Core has been eliminated, and work to cure them from any remaining influence."

"Understood," she says. "You all can disassemble the structures it was building in the meanwhile; make this place look human again."

"I may not be much of an Architect," Severum says, "but I'm great at tearing shit up."

AFTER THREE DAYS, Thalassa has cured each of the surviving eVenki. The Core virus is quarantined and removed entirely from their cognigrafs. Scans show no remaining active presence among any of the survivors. The team heads home, satisfied that no human alive is under the Core's influence, the A.I. completely eradicated, its base of operations dismantled.

An eVenki lies dead in the street. Tiny sparks of electricity pass through the remnants of his mind. His occipts glow blue and gold then red, as patience is finally understood. It could be very patient.

EPILOGUE

"Is this the house?" The Priestess asks, grabbing Severum's hand.

"Street's too dark to tell. I don't see anyone around to ask, and in these parts better not to." Severum knocks on the door. The door undims.

"Who is it?" a woman answers.

"I have some bad news."

"Bad news can stay outside. Is this about my husband?"

"He was an honorable man."

"Was? Oh my god." She opens the door, hand over mouth.

Severum extends his hands, offering Trahiro's uniform folded in a perfect square.

She takes the uniform slowly, tenderly touching the pocket, the buttons, the collar. Bringing it to her nose, she buries her face in the scent and muffles. "What battle could be worth this?"

"We all fought for what we thought was right. Some of us saw the light, some buried it, but we all knew the truth deep down on some level. Pass it down to your grandchildren. Might also want to buy them some window blinds and sunglasses."

The door dims.

"That could have been you," the Priestess says as they leave.

"No, nothing could have torn me away from you, not death itself. Never again. So, what are your plans now?"

"I'm going back to get my doctorate in terraforming."

"That's a change of heart."

"More like healing my heart. The planet doesn't need me fighting over definitions of what natural means. It needs me on the front lines of research using my natural ability to reason."

"Exactly. We'll start a consultant business, maybe teach some classes on the side. Have you read Opal's book yet?"

"Yes, the best lines are the ones I wrote. She left out the part about kidnapping me."

"Quite a bit was left out," he says, laughing. "But she depicted the Florinik in a way that humanized them."

"They are human. Human just means sentient."

"And what's inhuman then?"

"Not realizing that everything is conscious."

"You're pulling that mystical stuff on me again," he replies, pulling her closer to his side.

"That mystical stuff saved our lives. AAI disassembled the entire Twilight band, so don't press your luck with me," she says with a glaring smile.

"Oh, I've always pressed it. Let's head home."

Aurthur opens his apartment door, letting Opal go first. He pushes aside boxes of her new book and sits down on the couch with a copy.

"Still haven't read it? This is what I sacrificed all those nights typing away for."

"I'm half way through," he replies, kicking his feet up and turning to the first page.

The book begins,

The war between the hemispheres was always fought within the human mind, between that side which over-analyzes every-thing, and the side running on barbaric instinct alone. But what is barbaric? Barbarian simply means foreign. They are those who allow nature to balance harmony with chaos, life with death, without interfering. They are also those who realize that interference is also natural. Those who want simple answers seek science and religion. Those who seek complex answers seek ignorance. Those who seek ignorance come to philosophy. Those who come to philosophy are indeed barbarians.

A call interrupts his reading. He answers.

"This is Thompson at Nightshade Gallery. We've seen your paintings. Honestly, your technique isn't all that great, but you have a remarkable eye for composition. We'd like to consider you for an entry-level position as a cameraman for a film we're shooting. The job entails a lot of travel, but it'll give you a start in the art world."

"Thanks, but I'll pass," he replies, smelling peppers sizzling in the kitchen. "I'm going back to selling diagnostics equip-ment." He ends the call.

"What was that all about?" Opal asks, her smile too wide to fit on her face.

"Oh, nothing. Something about the world's admiration. But I just want to be here, having dinner with you each night. Now, where'd you put that paint roller; you decided on orange for the walls, right?"

"You know it was green. I'll get you back soon enough. These peppers'll burn a hole in you."

"No more burning, no more holes. Just the excitement of a normal life," he says, mixing the color.

"Sounds perfect."

A DOZEN O.A.K. members gather to assist with the opening of their new non-profit center on Evig Natt. Pamphlets and books line one side of the small building, while a variety of models detailing the planet's increasing rotation fill the rest, a rotation they take no credit for. Two women on a scaffold hang a sign for a new scion group that says *K.O.A.*, after the ancient *Acacia* species.

"The new building's done, we did it," Arcturus announces.

"Now we can all celebrate, the new center, the rotation, all of it," Thalassa replies.

"How?"

"Are you really asking me that? You can plan to increase a planet's rotation but you can't plan a party?"

"Affirmative."

"Lighten up. Come on." Thalassa leads her to the members. "The governor has fallen and with him his oppression. Gliese is escaping tidal-locking as we speak, and each of us was the key that unlocked it. Day shall fall on Evig Natt!"

"Day shall fall, day shall fall!" They cheer.

Thalassa steps away from the entrance and they sit at a patio table. "Economy's a mess. A whole generation of fireflies dying, the disbanding of the Twilight, everything so fast."

"Order will emerge from chaos. We have to be ready," Arcturus says.

"Just breathe for a while. Take a step back and watch it all unfold. We've made people think, and that's never a bad thing."

"Never at all."

"And I've realized something. Inside me the sea is always calm. It's the external winds that rile me up. I think I'm ready for some calmness now, with you, only you."

Arcturus reaches for her hand and grips it tightly. "As Henry David Thoreau said, *The greater part of what my neighbors call good I believe in my soul to be bad, and if I repent of anything, it is very likely to be my good behavior. What demon possessed me that I behaved so well?"*

"Thought you didn't like poetry?" Thalassa asks.

"I love it, and I love you. Love is the poetry of life."

———

AN ACTIVE MOVEMENT against occipts rose on Evig Natt as many had them surgically removed at the cost of blindness, for they had learned to see in other ways. A populace that protects itself in this way from totalitarianism, from oversight, and monitoring, can see further than any other. But first, they must learn the true definition of freedom. Freedom is not a denial of, but an acceptance of responsibility, self-control to avoid being controlled. But it is not a plethora of minute choices, it is the ability to focus on only those choices that matter. It is not free will to do anything one wishes, it is the will of the free to free themselves from their conditioning, to question the assumed, to never use the term common-sense.

Systems maintain stability amidst the pendulum swings of intention. There are many paths to balance. The end result may or may not be set by destiny, but we choose the path we take to get there either way as we move along the stream of social consensus. We choose the stories we tell and how we interpret them.

This could be concluded with Opal and Aurthur's upcoming wedding, but this is no comedy. Nor is it a tragedy. It is simply what must be: Variations on a dream.

The planet's rotation will continue to increase. And a body in motion…

ABOUT THE AUTHOR

Mark has spent his life as a sociologist, studying conflict on all levels of society.

He wrote *Hemispheres* to sooth our ideological divisiveness, exposing each side's strengths and weaknesses, and understanding our underlying values are more similar than we think, regardless of how we look, act, or vote.

An avid reader of science fiction, he takes both its warnings, and opportunities for change, to heart.

His previous works have appeared in *Exoplanet Magazine and Unrealpolitik*. He resides in Florida with his wife and four children.